FUGITIVE
NIGHTS

BOOKS BY JOSEPH WAMBAUGH

Fiction

The New Centurions
The Blue Knight
The Choirboys
The Black Marble
The Glitter Dome
The Delta Star
The Secrets of Harry Bright
The Golden Orange
Fugitive Nights

Nonfiction

The Onion Field
Lines and Shadows
Echoes in the Darkness
The Blooding

JOSEPH WAMBAUGH

FUGITIVE NIGHTS

A Perigord Press Book

WILLIAM MORROW AND COMPANY, INC.

NEW YORK

Grateful acknowledgment is made for permission to reprint portions of the following:

"Cowboy Logic," by Don Cook and Chick Rains. Copyright © 1987 by Cross Keys Publishing Co., Inc., and Terrace Music. All rights on behalf of Cross Keys Publishing Co., Inc., administered by Sony Music Publishing, 8 Music Square, West, Nashville, TN 37203.

"Brother Jukebox," by Paul Craft. Copyright © 1976 by Screen Gems-EMI Music, Inc./Black Sheep Music. All rights controlled and administered by Screen Gems-EMI Music Inc. All rights reserved. International copyright secured. Used by permission.

"I'm That Kind of Girl," by Ronnie Samoset and Matraca Berg. Copyright © 1990 by WB Music Corp., Samsonian Songs, Warner-Tamerlane Publishing Corp., and Patrick Joseph Music, Inc. All rights reserved on behalf of Samsonian Songs administered by WB Music Corp. All rights on behalf of Patrick Joseph Music, Inc., administered by Warner-Tamerlane Publishing Corp. All rights reserved. Used by permission.

"A Heartbeat Away," by Steve Bogard and Rick Giles. Copyright © 1990 by Chappell & Co. and Dixie Stars Music (ASCAP). All rights reserved on behalf of Steve Bogard administered by Chappell & Co. All rights reserved. Used by permission.

"I Got It Bad," by Matraca Berg and Jim Photoglo. Copyright © 1990 by Warner-Tamerlane Publishing Corp., Patrick Joseph Music, Inc., WB Music Corp., Patrix Janus Music, and After Berger Music. All rights on behalf of Patrick Joseph Music, Inc., administered by Warner-Tamerlane Publishing Corp. All rights on behalf of Patrix Janus Music and After Berger Music administered by WB Music Corp. All rights reserved. Used by permission.

"Never Knew Lonely," words and music by Vince Gill. Copyright © 1989 by Benefit Music. All rights reserved. Used by permission.

"Heartbeat in the Darkness," words and music by Dave Loggins and Howard Russell Smith. Copyright © 1986 by MCA Music Publishing, A Division of MCA, Inc., and Patchwork Music. Rights administered by MCA Music Publishing, A Division of MCA, Inc., New York, NY 10019. All rights reserved. Used by permission.

It is the policy of William Morrow and Company, Inc., and its imprints and affiliates, recognizing the importance of preserving what has been written, to print the books we publish on acid-free paper, and we exert our best efforts to that end.

Library of Congress Cataloging-in-Publication Data

Wambaugh, Joseph.
   Fugitive nights / by Joseph Wambaugh.
   "A Perigord Press book"
     p.   cm.
   ISBN 0-688-11128-9
   I. Title.
PS3573.A475F84   1992
813'.54—dc20   91-17114
                                           CIP

Printed in the United States of America

First Edition

1 2 3 4 5 6 7 8 9 10

BOOK DESIGN BY M & M DESIGNS

To superb editor Jeanne Bernkopf,
with gratitude for urging a return
to the California desert

ACKNOWLEDGMENTS

Special thanks for the cop talk goes to the men and women of Palm Springs Police Department, Cathedral City Police Department, and Riverside County Sheriff's Department, Indio Station, especially to Sgt. D. T. Wright.

Many thanks goes to Dale "Bubba" Johnson and P.I. Bill McMullin for providing Palm Springs local color.

FUGITIVE
NIGHTS

PROLOGUE

It was unbearably thrilling. The police detective who was detailed to provide personal security hoped that the Mayor wouldn't reel in ecstasy onto the tarmac. And it was undeniably historic: the first meeting held on the West Coast between the Japanese and U.S. heads of state in forty-three years. They were calling it the Summit in the Sun.

The cop watched his Mayor very closely. Everyone else—Secret Service, State Department security, FBI, Japanese security—everyone else was watching the gathering crowd and the taxiing aircraft, while Greenpeace demonstrators were handing out Japan-baiting bumper stickers that read, HONK IF YOU LOVE WHALES AND HATE VCRS. When President George Bush finally bounded from the plane the detective was fascinated. The man was all knees and flying elbows, a bouncing collection of angles. He did his usual wing flapping, flailing those elbows first to the right then to the left, trying to hook up with Prime Minister Toshiki Kaifu, who was lost in the clutch of dark-suited Japanese. Finally, the President sprang toward a youngish man in a blue pinstripe, the only one shorter than the Mayor, and did one of his sidearm ball-fisted swings in the Prime Minister's direction, which scared the crap out of the Japanese bodyguards, but was only George Bush's Yalie boola-boola rockem-sockem pantomime, not meant aggressively, only to show he had pep. The Mayor's police escort would recall that George Bush move later in the year when he did it again with Syrian President Hafez al-Assad, and about a hundred cameras got a candid shot of the Syrian grinning like a jackal, saying in Arabic to his aide-de-camp: "Who coaches this dork, anyway?"

When it was the Mayor's turn to greet two of the most powerful men on earth, the little guy was *hovering*. The policeman thought His Honor might come right up out of his loafers. The cop always thought of him as a restaurateur, up to his mustache in spaghetti sauce six nights a week, listening to snow-bird tourists from Minneapolis pretend they knew the difference between cacciatore and calamari, only to ask him questions about his ex! He'd nearly drowned in olive oil back in the sweltering kitchen of that Palm Springs eatery, but he'd emerged pluckier than ever, and defeated the cronies of the old cowboy mayor who'd been in Palm Springs politics a century or so.

Now with Reagan gone where old stars go to watch their orange hair change color, now with Mayor Clint Eastwood sick and tired of debating whether a Tastee-Freez would disrupt the fragile ecostructure of Carmel, now he, the Mayor of Palm Springs, was the only show business legend in American politics. And there was talk about him becoming a U.S. Senator. Today, Palm Springs. Tomorrow . . . ?

The cop figured that the Mayor had rehearsed all he should know about Japan and the U.S., just in case White House Chief of Staff John Sununu engaged him in some heavyweight conversation about the U.S.-Japan trade imbalance.

Suddenly, it was too late for rehearsals! Too late for Japanese GNP and IMF and GATT and all those other confusing goddamn letters that don't mean shit anyway. Because George Bush himself was pinwheeling toward him, those lanky arms lashing out every which way. Someone pointed, and the President *himself* gestured toward the Mayor! Then President Bush flailed back toward the Japanese Prime Minister, almost smacking him across the mouth with a return-of-serve backhand that would've cold-cocked the little Nip.

Then the President careened forward, his right arm whirling toward His Honor, and said: "It's wonderful to be in your beautiful city, Mister Mayor. And to be able to present you to Prime Minister Toshiki Kaifu."

And only the Mayor's police escort was close enough to hear the response. CNN didn't hear it. Nor did any of the panting local newshawks. The only one close enough to hear his response was Detective Lynn Cutter of the Palm Springs Police Department.

The detective later said that the Mayor's eyes glistened, perhaps because he was brimming with thoughts about his bungee-jump career: He, so recently at the nadir of the dive; she, his ex at the apex. Well, let her sit on that Oscar, for he now stood—levitated really—in a place she'd *never* be, facing CNN cameras as a Brother Politician to the leaders of the industrial giants of the planet!

The Mayor said what he *had* to say, the only thing he *could* say given his background, history and experience. The only response that came close to expressing the explosion of emotions as he now soared through the stratosphere on this, the Ultimate Bungee Jump! According to the detective, his boss extended a white-hot palm toward the prime minister of 125 million Japanese and the president of 250 million Americans.

And His Honor, the Mayor of Palm Springs, USA, said: "AWESOME!"

Later that day, when the Mayor was back in his restaurant chopping garlic, the detective was nursing a severely swollen knee. While jogging to keep up with His Honor—who'd gone cosmic from pressing the flesh of world leaders—the detective had stumbled and smashed his one good knee on the curb in front of the Palm Springs Airport.

By year's end he'd failed his police physical exam, had arthroscopic knee surgery twice, and was patiently awaiting an uncontested disability pension allowing him to retire with fifty percent of his salary for the rest of his life. Tax *free*! He figured he owed part of it to George Bush and vowed to vote a straight Republican ticket forever.

And of course, the Mayor would always be his favorite politician. For all those months, while doctors tried in vain to rehabilitate his damaged knees, the detective couldn't stop whistling "I Got You, Babe."

—1—

"What does it make you feel like?" Mrs. Rhonda Devon asked, as the private investigator studied a painting hanging over the mantel: figures in repose by the banks of the Seine, all done in the remarkable brush dots of Georges Seurat's pointillism.

"A cup of coffee."

"Coffee? Why?"

"It makes me think of cafés and truck stops all over this desert."

"Why in the world do you say that?" Rhonda Devon asked. She took the P.I.'s cocktail glass to the bar. Behind her the sun was setting west of Mount San Jacinto, cooling down the un-seasonably hot desert valley very quickly.

"In every single truck stop and café there's a Dot behind the counter. I must've had a thousand cups of coffee served by waitresses named Dot, more dots than you have in this painting."

Rhonda Devon chuckled and brought the P.I. another diet Coke in a cocktail glass. "What else does it make you feel?"

"Poor. I've heard of this artist. The painting's worth more than every house I've ever owned."

"Possibly," Rhonda Devon said, gesturing palm upward toward the sofa by the Seurat.

The P.I. didn't like the sofa's silk floral print, nor the Chinese Chippendale, nor the lacquered nesting tables. The massive old Spanish Colonial house cried out for some masculine bulk.

"I usually ask clients to come to my office for the first interview," the P.I. said, sipping the freshened drink.

"Why did you make an exception for me?"

"You're rich."

"Do you treat rich clients better than poor ones?" Rhonda Devon asked coyly.

"Absolutely. I mean, I would, except poor people don't go to P.I.'s."

"Have you been in business long?"

"Only long enough to get in the yellow pages."

"That's how I chose you, the yellow pages. I liked the name of your firm: Discreet Inquiries. Sounds like a massage parlor."

"How would you know about massage parlors, Mrs. Devon?"

"I used to work in one."

It was best to let that one zing past. The texture of the rosy damask wall covering would absorb the ricochet. The damask was also wrong, the P.I. thought.

Rhonda Devon smiled into her cocktail, then picked up the onion with a plastic toothpick and sucked it provocatively before dropping it back into the gin to bathe a while longer.

Then she chuckled again, and the P.I. wondered how they learn to do that. Regular people guffaw or snicker or giggle.

You even meet a few who chortle, but rich people, they chuckle. Chuckling 1A. They must learn it at boarding school and pass it around.

"We could sit here all evening and you'd never ask, would you? I took a job as a masseuse in order to research a paper in social science when I was an undergraduate. It was fun. I learned a few tricks."

When she said it she sucked on the onion again and smiled. That time there was almost certainly a sexual connotation.

It was easy to see the former undergraduate when Rhonda Devon smiled. The intervening years hadn't been hard on her but why should they be? She probably had a personal trainer to keep the belly hard, and a hairdresser to keep every strand of gray from that honeyed Marilyn Quayle flip, and a weekly visit to a manicurist probably took care of those long graceful fingers, two of which wore diamonds that could bail out Lincoln Savings.

The P.I. was wondering what it would be like to be this rich, when Rhonda Devon said, "Your answering service told me you're an ex-police officer."

"Apparently, they *do* listen to instructions once in a while. I was twenty years with LAPD. Thought it might be impressive for callers to hear about it."

"You *can't* be old enough for that," Rhonda Devon exclaimed.

"I'm old enough." Then, seeing she wasn't satisfied, said, "I'm going on forty-three."

"And you're right back into police work."

"This is nothing like police work Mrs. Devon," the P.I. wanted to say, thinking of the garbage work, such as interviewing witnesses for criminal defense lawyers; that was particularly hateful for an ex-cop. Virtually all defendants brought to trial were about as innocent as Josef Stalin, so most of the defense work consisted of trying to persuade them to cop a plea. This made the local criminal lawyers happier than it made the prosecutors, because the court-appointed lawyer got paid without lifting a finger. The local courthouse, like all others in the U.S., was more cluttered than a dressing room at the Folies-Bergère, so in a sense, it *was* doing what LAPD detectives did: offering tickets to the slam and hoping the defendants would buy.

But all the P.I. said was, "It's sorta like police work. At least sometimes."

"Why didn't you go into another line of work?"

"Well, if I could dance I'd try ballet but crime and crooks are all I know. Depressing, isn't it?"

"Rather."

The vast desert sky was turning ermine black. Rhonda Devon switched on a lamp behind her and the lemony glow highlighted her cheekbones. When she turned in profile there was no telltale glint from contact lenses in her wide-set eyes. The forest-green irises came from DNA, not optometry.

"So, Mrs. Devon," the P.I. said, thinking there'd been enough small talk. "How can I help you?"

"It's about my husband, Clive," Rhonda Devon said. "I'd like you to follow him."

That was a bad start. The P.I. never had any luck with people named Clive or Graham or Montgomery, and once had served at Hollywood detectives under a captain named Clive, hating his guts.

"Is it a woman problem?"

"Yes."

"Mrs. Devon, this is a no-fault divorce state. Most places are, except maybe for Monte Carlo. Prince Rainier and Princess Grace couldn't have afforded to get caught chippying, but it's different here. You don't need a private investigator."

"I'm not trying to catch him in a tryst. I don't care *what* he does."

"Any lawyer would tell you that in a divorce situation in California you don't have to—"

"I don't *want* a divorce. I just have to understand why."

"Why he's fooling around?"

"No . . . yes, that's part of it, but only a small part."

"What's the big part?"

"I think he's preparing to have a child. And I can't understand why."

"You said you don't care if he—"

"I don't care if he has one mistress or ten! But he's having a *child*. I have to understand that."

"Okay, how do you know?"

"I found something quite by accident. Our business manager writes the important checks and handles our portfolio, but we have separate personal checking accounts. It caught my eye, the monthly statement in the pocket of his blazer. It fell out when I hung the jacket in the armoire. I just got a glimpse before he came into the room, but when I returned to the armoire later it was gone. It was a monthly billing from a place called the Beverly Hills Fertility Institute."

"Did you call them?"

"I had my doctor make a few calls. The sperm banks in Los Angeles are administered by a medical director who insists on absolute confidentiality. All they'd say is that the name Clive Devon is unknown to them."

"How old is your husband?"

"Sixty-three."

"And how old're you, if I may ask?"

"Forty-four. I've never had children, and as of last December I won't be having any. I went through the change rather early just like my mother and both my sisters. Clive's obviously planning to have a child by a surrogate! Perhaps he's planning to leave me!"

"Do you care?"

"Yes, very much."

"Maybe he's one of these movers and shakers that can't depart this earth without leaving his genetic code behind. Maybe he's donated his sperm to some study or experiment."

"He's a terribly shy man, an introvert really, with low self-esteem and very few friends. He's never *done* any moving and shaking. He's always lived on trusts. I can't imagine him having a need to leave part of himself behind. Clive being part of an experiment? That's preposterous."

"Did he make you sign a prenuptial?"

"No."

"Then you stand to inherit when he dies?"

"Oh, yes. We've been married for thirteen years. He can't legally leave all his money to a new wife and child."

"Well, did you ever want children?"

"No, nor did he. Neither of us had happy childhoods so we thought we'd keep our neuroses to ourselves and not pass them on."

"Mrs. Devon, why don't you just *ask* him why he made this little bank deposit that's driving you nutty?"

"Oh, I'd never pry. Nor would he if the roles were reversed. We're each very independent. We live apart a good deal of the time. I prefer our main house in Beverly Hills and only come here two weekends a month. He stays here all the time, even in summer. I seldom can get him to spend forty-eight hours at our other home."

"Do you and your husband still . . ."

"He had a cardiac bypass. Arterial insufficiency allows him to ejaculate, but he can't get an erection. We haven't had sex for about five years." Then she added, "At least together."

"Have you discussed this with anyone else? I mean, why he maybe wants a kid?"

"We have the same attorney in Los Angeles, a good friend. He hasn't a clue."

"Of course *he* wouldn't dream of just asking Mister Devon, either?"

"I would never permit it. We do have our private separate lives and we . . ."

"Respect one another."

"Completely."

"Where's your husband today?"

"I have no idea. When I come here we're only together long enough to have dinner or a game of golf. He likes to spend most of his time hiking in the desert. Or so he says."

The P.I. put the cocktail glass on an onyx coffee table that was bigger than a squash court—the only piece with the right scale—and said, "So you want me to conduct a surveillance and find out who, what, where, when and why?"

"Just who and why. I particularly have to know why. If once, in all these years, he'd ever expressed the slightest wish for a child we could have . . . at least talked it over."

"Surveillance is very expensive. It can go on for days and weeks with no satisfaction whatsoever. And by the way, I don't do illegal phone taps."

"All right, just find out who the surrogate is to start with. Who may lead to why."

"Sixty dollars an hour charged against a one-thousand-dollar retainer is what I get for surveillance work," the P.I. lied, half hoping Rhonda Devon would change her mind. This could turn into *real* garbage work. "And when he goes to bed I go to bed. I don't sit outside a client's house running up the meter. If he gets up in the middle of the night for a run to his hired bake-oven I'll never know about it."

"You're very flippant," Rhonda Devon said.

"I don't think I really want the job." The P.I. hesitated for a moment, then said, "I have to ask you, Mrs. Devon, after the cardiac surgery did he *try* with you? Are you sure he has vascular insufficiency?"

"There were a few pathetic attempts. No, I do not believe he's capable of erection."

She looked thinner than ever in the lemony light and shadow. The P.I. was unaccountably sorry for her, and felt odd pitying someone this rich.

"Mrs. Devon"—the P.I. touched an urn on the coffee

table—"are you afraid he's found someone he cares about? Someone he wants to raise a child with? No matter *how* the conception gets accomplished?"

"That's an Etruscan vase," Rhonda Devon said, as though she hadn't heard the question. "Please be careful. I've prepared a file for you with everything you'll need to know about Clive, including a photo. The file's on the table by the door."

Rhonda Devon arose languidly, but staggered a step from too much predinner booze, and swayed across the marble foyer, leading the way to the door.

Before leaving, the P.I. looked at the client, and said, "What'll you do with the information if I'm able to get it? I mean, the name of the surrogate and the reason for your husband doing this? What would you do with the information?"

"You don't have to worry about that," Rhonda Devon said.

"Oh, but I do. In fact, I'm not taking this case if you refuse to tell me."

Rhonda Devon studied the private investigator for a moment, showed perfect orthodontal teeth, and said, "Absolutely nothing. But I have to know." Then she added, "I'd be happy to pay a bonus for results. Say, five thousand dollars? I won't pretend that my husband and I have a close relationship or even a normal one. But I have to know. Surely, as a woman, *you* can understand?"

—2—

On the fourth ring, he picked up the phone, or tried to. He made a swipe at it, but the phone fell off the nightstand. Somebody had squeezed him like a grapefruit. He was all acid and pulp, juiceless. Dry as tumbleweed.

On the seventh ring he found it, a phone in the shape of a boxing glove. The guy whose mansion he was sitting probably had had one intramural match at prep school when he was ten years old, and had gone goofy over prize fighters. The study was full of Leroy Neiman's nervous sports prints, as well as *lots* of boxing photos. Undoubtedly, he was the kind of guy who wouldn't travel without his Water Pik.

"Hello," he croaked into the boxing glove. He heard a muffled reply and turned the phone right side up. "Yeah?"

A woman's voice said, "Detective Cutter?"

"Yeah, who's this?" He felt like somebody had inflated his skull with mustard gas.

"Is it a bad time to call?"

"No, it's a bad *day* to call. What day *is* this?"

"It's Monday, February fourth."

"What *year*?"

"Am I disturbing you?"

"No, I had to get up and puke anyway. Who the hell *is* this?"

"My name's Breda Burrows," she said. "I'm a P.I. here in Palm Springs, retired from LAPD."

"Yeah, so whadda . . . oh, shit!"

Lynn Cutter slouched from bed in his gray silk pajama bottoms (property of the guy who was nutted out over boxers) and scuttled toward the bathroom like somebody trying to run underwater. Because the bathroom was bigger than the Palm Springs police station he didn't quite get to the toilet, but did manage to upchuck in a Jacuzzi tub with gold-plated faucets.

Lynn went down on the cool tile for a minute, examining a crumbled line of grout from a roach's-eye view. He raised up, wiped his mouth on a monogrammed towel, and picked up the extension: a *Sports Illustrated* phone shaped like a sneaker.

Speaking from the supine position, he said, "I'm dying."

"I can call back in thirty minutes."

"They'll be pulling a sheet over me," he moaned. "Look, lady, it ain't easy talking into a tennis shoe. Whaddaya want?"

"Well, Detective Cutter," she began, then thought it sounded stiff and formal. So she said, "Whadda your friends call you?"

"I don't have any." He was feeling more bile bubbling and rising. "But mother calls me Lynn. Kiss her for me. I'm all through."

"Lynn?"

"Yeah, Lynn! I know! Marion Morrison didn't like a girl's name and changed it to John Wayne! I know! Lynn's not a common name but life wasn't easy for a boy named Sue, was it? Now, lady, will you tell me what the hell you want this time a morning?"

"It's one o'clock in the afternoon, Lynn."

"Morning, afternoon! Kee-rist, have a heart!"

"Can I drive over and talk to you? I have something to discuss that might be to our mutual advantage."

He paused, then said, "Save your gas. I ain't about to jeopardize a disability pension by doing favors for private eyes, okay?"

"Hey, I wouldn't jeopardize your pension," she said. "We're in the same society. Society of the badge."

"Used to be. You ain't carrying a badge no more. Far as I'm concerned, you're just fuzz that *was*. Like just about every other P.I. I ever met. Fuzz that *was*."

"But I'll always be a cop at heart," she said. "How about a brief meeting?"

"I gotta go," he said. Then it occurred to him. "How'd you get my number?" He wobbled to his feet, weaved a bit, and considered peeing in the bathtub.

"I'll tell you," she said, "if you'll meet me for lunch."

"Lunch?" He'd only raised his voice to twelve decibels, slightly louder than the sound of human breathing, but it sounded like a concussion grenade. When he turned on the faucet he heard Chinese New Year.

"How about a drink?" she asked. "Let's meet in one hour and have a drink. Whadda you got to lose?"

"The Furnace Room," he said, spotting an empty cognac bottle on the counter beside one of the bathroom sinks. The only thing he remembered clearly was that what's-her-name drank every drop of booze in the house. "You'll love the joint. It's about as bright and cheerful as Gotham City. Can we hang up now? This conversation's going on longer than the Lebanese civil war."

When it was time to shave, Lynn Cutter gave up on trimming his mustache, but held the mansion-owner's electric shaver in both shaking hands and mashed his face up against it. The quiet hum of the shaver sounded like underground nuclear testing. After a hundred mashes or so, he was shaved. Sort of.

Breda Burrows was one of those people who grinned when she was irked. When she was *really* mad the grin widened. Once, when she was working patrol on Hollywood Boulevard she had occasion to grin especially wide after a pimp named Too-Slick Rick, sitting in his Cadillac Eldorado, said to her, "Honest, I don't make these street ladies work for me. I wouldn't lie to you, cross my heart, Officer. On my momma's grave."

And then Too-Slick Rick thought it would be real slick and real cute to cross a heart. Hers. He reached out the window of his pimpmobile, and with a manicured right index finger— longer than a broomstick and fitted with two diamond rings set in a bed of sapphires—he crossed her heart. Right under her LAPD shield. Right on the nipple of her left tit.

She spread out that grin till it stretched from Hollywood and Vine to the Chinese Theater, and said, "On your momma's grave? And does your momma have room down there for one more, chump?"

Suddenly she leapfrogged. She vaulted up and sat down on his extended arm, the way a stuntperson vaults into the saddle over the rump of a horse.

Too-Slick Rick played teeter-totter, with his elbow acting as fulcrum. His head shot up, smashing his mauve fedora flat against the ragtop Cad. Breda's partner said that the elbow made a sound like a steel hull powering through polar ice, only *louder*. Too-Slick Rick didn't beat up any of his girls for a couple of months, not with his left arm anyway.

And the pimp didn't lodge a formal complaint against young Breda Burrows, whose partner told her that if you're going to maim some motherfucker make sure the motherfucker is a motherfucking pimp, because they seldom rat you off to those motherfucking headhunters at Internal Affairs.

When Lynn got to The Furnace Room Bar and Grill, the neighborhood regulars were already on their way to oblivion. It was one of those generic smoky restaurant-saloons with hide-away nooks, walnut paneled walls and red vinyl booths. They mostly served red meat and garlic toast. And brand-new customers felt like they were back home in Indiana the first time they walked through the door.

There were usually three or four ex-actors and actresses in the bar, maybe a dozen other seniors in golfing duds, a cop or two, and a few lawyers, since it wasn't far from the Palm Springs courthouse. The drinks were man-sized and not expensive.

Lawyer and cop jokes were preferred by the ex-actors in The Furnace Room.

Question: "If you were a chef at a banquet for Saddam Hussein, Muammar Qaddafi, and any lawyer of your choice, and you only had *two* cyanide capsules, who would you poison first and second?"

Expected answer to both questions: "The lawyer."

Furnace Room answer: "Nobody. I'd slip the poison in the lawyer's pocket, tell the Arabs it was meant for *them*, and watch while they boiled him in oil and cut off his freaking head."

There was lots of hate in The Furnace Room.

Question: "How many cops does it take to push a hand-cuffed prisoner down a flight of stairs?"

Answer: "None. The asshole tripped and *fell*."

And so forth.

To further amuse the old actors at the expense of cops like Lynn Cutter, the proprietor, a seventy-six-year-old ex-character actor named Wilfred Plimsoll—who claimed he'd doubled for Ronald Reagan in *Hellcats of the Navy*—posted macabre quips on the bar mirror. His latest referred to a newspaper story out of Los Angeles, revealing that in three recent police shootings, cops had claimed that suspects pulled "a shiny object from a pocket," causing the cop to react with deadly force, later to discover that the "shiny object" was only a plastic comb.

One bar sign said: "Use a comb, go to heaven."

Another said: "Combs: O. Cops: 3."

Lynn Cutter didn't so much as glance at bar signs or other customers when he entered. He headed straight for Wilfred Plimsoll and said, "Scotch. Double."

The former actor usually wore a silk ascot and an Out-of-Africa shirt even on sweltering desert days. He poured the booze and watched the cop toss it down, then poured a second, saying, "Better? Need another?"

"Like a goat needs a sidesaddle," Lynn Cutter answered, but drank it anyway.

When Wilfred Plimsoll started to put the bottle away, Lynn said, "One more. Make it Chivas this time. Your well drinks taste like stuff they rub horses with."

Wilfred didn't mind the bitching about his goods or service. He was not a thin-skinned man, not after knocking around movie studios for thirty-nine years.

"Bad night, Lynn?" he asked, speaking toward the clock high on the wall. Wilfred Plimsoll *always* spoke to the wall clock, which displayed bar time, ten minutes fast. He did it to show off his right profile, which photographed best.

Moreover, he always aimed his cigarette holder—held fast in clenched dentures—at that wall clock. This, after he was told at an audition that he, Wilfred Plimsoll, resembled Franklin Delano Roosevelt more than Ralph Bellamy had in *Sunrise at Campobello*. And despite the fact that Wilfred wore a black Burt Reynolds toupee, and had done so long before Burt bought his first rug. Without it he looked more like Benjamin Franklin than Franklin Roosevelt; he was, in fact, a soulmate to the randy inventor in that no woman younger than electricity was safe from his advances. That explained why the more coquettish babes from the Senior Center had their afternoon cocktails at The Furnace Room.

"Yeah, a bad night," Lynn finally responded. "It's amazing what I'll do to take a chance with AIDS. Did I leave here with somebody last night?"

"You're having more blackouts than London in the Blitz," Wilfred said to the wall clock. "Don't you remember?"

"Somebody with tits?"

"Tits? Yeah, I think she had tits."

"Thank God," Lynn said. "I have this vague image in my mind of a blonde mustache."

"She had a mustache too," Wilfred said. "Do they serve testosterone takeout at the health stores these days? She was uglier than all three witches in Macbeth. I'd rather have red ants in my truss. Hope you wore protection."

"Oh, sure," Lynn lied, unable to remember a single thing after the cognac ran out. "I wear camouflaged stitch-on condoms. Don't know they're there and can't take em off. I got more protection than Pinkerton's."

"It's a real mistake, to unmuzzle your snake," Wilfred advised, poetically.

"Yeah yeah, gotta shroud my monkey," Lynn agreed. God, his head hurt!

"She had nice hair though," Wilfred Plimsoll said to the clock. "Like Rita Hayworth in *Gilda*. Did I ever tell you I almost got a speaking role in *Gilda*?"

"Yes," Lynn Cutter said to his booze. "You been telling that one since a peanut grower was president."

"Ah, Rita!" Wilfred Plimsoll mused, and it was too late now. He was losing himself in that golden gossamer mist peculiar to actors, especially failed actors. "Rita was some dish. I heard she could suck-start a leaf blower and the Mexican that ran it!"

"Do you have any aspirin, Wilfred?" Lynn Cutter asked, and now he was talking to the clock. It was contagious.

"I heard you'd have hairline fractures and hickeys on your *knees* after a date with Rita," Wilfred said. "I could tell you something she said to me on location one time, but you wouldn't believe it."

"Sure, I always believe you, Wilfred. Like I believed Saigon Suzie when she swore she loved only me."

Taking the cigarette holder from his mouth, Wilfred Plimsoll said, "It's too bad you're not old enough to remember the great movie palaces, Lynn. The Golden Age it truly was!"

"Yeah, I'm barely potty-trained at forty-five," the cop moaned, "but my liver's eighty-five so maybe my liver remembers. The aspirin, Wilfred!"

Finally, Wilfred Plimsoll seemed to understand that Lynn Cutter had a sick head. He said, "We don't have aspirin. Take another drink and it'll go away." He poured a Chivas for the unprotesting cop.

Another old actor named Reginald Orlando—one of those who never made it trying to impersonate Gilbert Roland—was eavesdropping, and said, "Ah yes, the movie palaces. How I remember Lon Chaney in *Hunchback of Notre Dame*. Ruining his body with a hunchback harness-device for the sake of his art. Nowadays, Warren Beatty couldn't even bring himself to put putty on his beautiful nose to look like Dick Tracy."

Just then a woman's voice behind Lynn Cutter said to Wilfred Plimsoll, "A glass of your best Chardonnay and another of whatever Mister Cutter's having. Over at the corner table, please."

Lynn turned and, headache or not, felt a little rush. His favorite combination: lustrous and abundant earth-brown hair, and eyes so blue the gloom couldn't hide them. Cobalt blue, the kind that go electric when the owner turns them on. She wore a tailored houndstooth jacket and a slim black skirt, a bit wintry for such a hot day. He'd expected her to look matronly. He'd heard about the new P.I. in town who'd retired from LAPD, and he knew that LAPD cops could draw their twenty-year pensions as young as forty-one. She'd been in Palm Springs several months, so she had to be at least forty-two, he figured.

Twenty years of police work in the big city hadn't done much to the outside, but who could tell about the inside with babes like this? "I thought you'd be older," he said.

"I am." When she parted her lips and smiled she looked even younger.

"Somebody musta set your odometer back," Lynn said. Jesus, she had long legs and incredible calves! All buffed up like she played soccer or something. He knew he wouldn't have a chance, so he might as well act as cranky as he felt, *after* he'd gotten his free drink.

They sat at a table in the corner under a series of wall photos of former and present Palm Springs residents: Frank Sinatra, Bob Hope, Ginger Rogers, William Holden, Dinah Shore, Steve McQueen, Lucille Ball, Truman Capote, Kirk Douglas, Ruby Keeler, Red Skelton, Liberace.

What they all had in common is that they wouldn't have set foot in The Furnace Room for the deed to Mount San Jacinto, which loomed two miles high over the city, throwing blue shadow over Palm Springs long before sunset.

"I imagine I'm close to your age, Lynn," she said, as he plopped down in his chair. "I ride a bike at least a hundred miles a week to keep fit."

Lynn said, miserably, "Yeah, well I just had a checkup and I got the stool of a much younger man."

Wilfred Plimsoll, with a fresh cigarette in his holder, put a drink in front of Lynn and jauntily poured a taste of Chardonnay for Breda Burrows. Then, with his best leading man flourish, he adjusted his ascot and said, "Would m'lady wish to let it breathe for a bit?"

"Just *pour* it, Wilfred!" Lynn said testily. "CPR couldn't resuscitate the crap you serve!"

After Wilfred said "Tut tut!" and returned to the bar, Lynn said to Breda, "Well, you got him talking like the Queen Mum so I guess you're accepted in The Furnace Room. He might even buy you a drink for Valentine's Day, but not *this* one."

"How about lunch?" Breda asked. "The food okay?"

"The roaches thrive on it," Lynn said. "That's why they're big enough for choker collars and don't die from a single bullet wound. You might try the chili but I'd rather lick a toad. Now can you tell me what's on your mind and how you got the number of the place I'm house-sitting?"

"Sure," she said. "The number came from your lieutenant. I knew his brother when he worked LAPD. The reason I wanted to meet you is because I'm having trouble getting my business going in Palm Springs."

"Well, you came to the right guy," Lynn said. "I got enough banking acumen to be George Bush's son. Here's what I know: The tourist season goes from New Year's to Memorial Day. That's five months. And some people think May's only a wash, so you're down to four. Yet just because it's so nice in the winter everybody with enough bucks to lease four walls and a roof thinks he can make a living twelve months a year. Restaurants're the worst. Guys keep opening restaurants in the same spot where ten other guys failed. They go over the cliff one after another, dumber than a herd a lemmings. That's it for my knowledge of commerce. So what do I got to do with your business problems?"

Breda Burrows studied Lynn Cutter for a moment, and said, "Feeling better?"

"Yeah, well, I'm not quite ready to do eyelid surgery." Lynn looked at his calendar watch and said, "We only got seven or eight weeks till Easter and I gotta color eggs this year. Do you think you'll get to the point by then?"

For a cynical boozer, he wasn't a bad-looking guy, Breda thought. She didn't like his mustache and he was at least twenty pounds overweight, but he still had most of his hair: sandy gray and curly. He wasn't big but he had good shoulders and big wrists and hands. His brown eyes were intelligent when he bothered to look at her. She suspected he was competent, and she felt like punching him in the mouth.

"Okay, I'll get to the point, Lynn," she said. "I need a consultant."

"Why didn't you say so," he said, finishing his fourth drink, grateful he didn't have to work the next day. Or *ever* again! "There's a gypsy in Cathedral City that does Tarot cards, palms and even tea leaves if you bring the tea. Me, I got a job flocking Christmas trees. It's not real steady work, of course, but I still don't have enough hours to consult even though I gotta admit I'm way ahead a my time in business matters. I went broke two years *before* the recession. My old man was the same way. Went broke in nineteen-twenny-*eight*."

With a grin only half as wide as her pimp-killer grin, she said to this world-class wiseass, "Look, Lynn, I know you don't feel well today and you don't know me and don't have any reason to trust me, but I haven't come here to ask you to compromise your pension and get in trouble. I've learned that Palm Springs and this whole desert valley is a different sorta place, and I'm the new kid on the block. I just need help and guidance from somebody in local law enforcement, and I was told you might be that somebody."

He peered into her eyes then—the electric blue was giving off sparks. Despite his hangover, that irritating grin of hers somehow turned him on a little bit. But he said, "Yeah, I'm full a talent all right. I could probably blow smoke rings if I smoked. I *did* smoke till last May when the doc said the arteries around my heart're like the L.A. interchange at rush hour, so I quit smoking. It was easy to quit, except I got this need to kill six or seven cats a day. I gotta say so long for now and head for the Humane Society to pick up a few. I tried ground squirrels but they don't work."

And to her utter astonishment, Lynn Cutter suddenly stood up, waved bye-bye, and wobbled toward the front door of the saloon! But he was stopped by a large blond woman who was on her way in.

"Lynn," the blonde said, backlit by the brilliant Palm Springs sunlight, which penetrated his skull like hot nails.

"Have we met?" he croaked.

"You *better* remember me. Phyllis!"

"Charmed, I'm sure," he said, vaguely recognizing the mustache. She was wearing what she thought was a drop-dead, midthigh leather skirt that would've turned off Ted Bundy.

"Such a kidder," she giggled. "You said we'd have lunch today."

Lynn was frozen in the doorway, trapped. "I'm sorry," he said. "I forgot about lunch, Phyllis."

"Well I didn't!" she said. "And I don't appreciate being made a fool out of!"

She was taller than Breda Burrows. With heels she was taller than Lynn, and almost as heavy! Her 'stash *was* heavier, in fact. "Phyllis," he said. "That woman over there glaring at me? That's my wife! I can't be seen with you!"

"Goddamnit, you said you were single!" Her voice was like cymbals clashing. "You sang to me: 'I got that lovin feeling!' You sonofabitch!"

God, he *hated* that song! "Well, I'm not exactly married," he whined. "I mean, I'm getting a divorce and we're talking settlement now. And we agreed not to see other people till it's over. Get it?"

Breda Burrows was paying her bill during all this, and was striding indignantly toward the door when Lynn turned a blood-red eye in her direction.

"Breda," he called out. "Breda!" But the P.I. brushed past and was gone.

"She acts like she really cares," Phyllis said, with a hideous smirk.

"Yeah, well, she pretends like she couldn't care less if I

starred in a snuff film or went to Disneyland, but really, she *loves* me. She's a great little mother too."

"You got kids? You asshole! You told me you were single and childless!"

"I gotta go now," he said. "I gotta catch up with my wife. The settlement. The final decree. The property. Our four little ankle-biters!"

Phyllis followed him into the merciless glare and watched as he put on his sunglasses and caught up with Breda, who was unlocking the door of her white Datsun 280ZX. Phyllis gave up when Lynn climbed in beside the P.I.

"Who invited you?" Breda said.

He attempted to smile. "I know I've been a pain in the ass today."

"Any more of a pain and you'd break through my Valium," she said, not asking him to get out, but not starting the car either.

She put on sunglasses with taffy-colored plastic rims, and looked him over. He wore a shabby golf shirt with a frayed collar, tattered cotton trousers, cheap loafers.

"I guess I should at least listen to your offer," he said. "I suppose you heard I got burned for allegedly giving information to a lawyer, and you figured I'm your man, right?" Lynn saw that she wasn't wearing stockings. Her legs were so tan that in The Furnace Room they'd fooled him.

"See, the lawyer was working on a deal for a guy I know, a cop facing prosecution for a bad shooting. He killed a kid."

"How old was the kid?"

"Twelve."

"Twelve years old!"

"Yeah, I know," Lynn said. "Jack Graves is the cop's name. Worked dope down in Orange County. I knew him when he used to work here. Anyway, his department was helping out the DEA with a raid. Supposed to be a dealer's house, wrong house. One a those things where the snitch burned them and everything went wrong. A twelve-year-old that lived there was terrified by all the commotion and picked up a toilet plunger for protection. And he ran right out and into Jack Graves. Jack's eyes saw: Guy-with-Gun. It was dark. Jack reacted, squeezed one off, didn't mean to."

"What happened to him?"

"The D.A. was considering a prosecution for manslaughter. There was a so-called witness, a brother-in-law to the righteous drug dealer that lived next door to the victim. I did the investigation for Jack's lawyer and proved that the dealer's brother-in-law was a lying, cop-hating gob a slime. In the end, Jack got pensioned off on stress. I don't generally go around helping lawyers and P.I.'s, okay?"

"Look, Lynn," Breda said, "I've heard you're just waiting for your disability pension to be approved. And I've heard you might wanna be a P.I. yourself after you get the pension. And I've heard you might need money even though you make it a practice to house-sit for Palm Springs millionaires and exercise their Rolls-Royces when they're not in residence. And I've also heard that these days you don't have enough money to put gas in those cars. That's what I've heard about you, Lynn. Is it wrong?"

"Well, it's true that my last marriage gave me a bigger deficit than Nicaragua, but you don't have it quite right."

"What am I missing?"

"That I do get my paycheck even though I ain't got the disability pension locked up. I mean, I got a pair a knees with all the flexibility of Margaret Thatcher, but the pension ain't official yet, so I don't wanna screw things up by selling myself to some P.I. They call that double-dipping, and I believe it's even against the law, is it not?"

"I got a couple easy jobs where there'd be no written reports of any kind with your name on them. No testifying, nothing illegal or immoral. Just a few little jobs for somebody like you. Somebody *male* as it turns out."

"You were right about the empty tank in the Rolls," he said. "The house I'm sitting has nine bedrooms and eleven bathrooms and *two* Rolls-Royces in the garage with the gas gauges on empty. I'd walk home except I ain't feeling good. Will you drive me? It's still my home for three more weeks, then I hope to house-sit at Tamarisk Country Club for two months."

Breda, deciding it was over, disgustedly started up the 280ZX. After she drove for a few minutes, Lynn said, "How much could I make?"

Breda kept her eyes on the street, saying, "Up until yesterday I couldn't have paid much, but I just got the best client I've ever had. I could pay you as much as a thousand bucks, *if* you can get the results I want. Cash. Nobody'd ever know about it."

"What would I have to do?"

Breda Burrows turned toward Lynn Cutter and said, "I've been thinking about this. One reason I'm going to need a man helping me on this case is because of some special undercover work. The job *might* call for a sperm sample."

Lynn Cutter removed the shades, gawked sideways at Breda Burrows with eyes like bags of plasma, and said, "Lady, you can't be *that* lonely!"

—3—

On the same afternoon that Breda Burrows was learning how easy it would be to hate a world-class cynic like Lynn Cutter, Officer Nelson Hareem was doing what he did best: plotting, scheming and fantasizing about how to secure a lateral transfer from his police department to Palm Springs P.D.

Officer Hareem had worked a total of five years at two police departments, one in San Bernardino County and another in Los Angeles County, before ending up on the wrong end of the Coachella Valley, thirty minutes and millions of bucks away from Glamour. A captain at Palm Springs P.D. told the carrot-top cop he'd consider letting Nelson apply after he "proved himself" for a year or two at one more police department, hinting that it was Nelson's last chance.

The paternal grandfather of Nelson Hareem had been a rug peddler from Beirut, but his three other grandparents were pure Okie from Bakersfield and Barstow. Nevertheless, because of his grandfather and his surname, he bore the brunt of every Arab or Iranian joke in vogue. And of course, because of his reputation, everyone began to call him Dirty Hareem.

Some cops thought that at the root of Nelson Hareem's aggressiveness was a little-man's complex, and because he was only five foot seven, they'd dubbed him Half-Nelson. He'd been given his walking papers by both of his previous police chiefs for being unacceptably "eager." Once, when he'd choked out a San Bernardino County deputy D.A. who'd stopped at a mini-market to buy some nonprescription sleeping pills after a long and arduous trial in which he was prosecuting two outlaw bikers for beating the crap out of a cop.

Young Nelson had been cruising by the minimarket and spotted a bulge under the prosecutor's jacket as the lawyer was leaving the store with his Sominex. And Nelson was sure he was looking at the armed bandit who'd robbed six liquor stores in the area. How was he to know (he later pleaded) that this prosecutor had received a death threat from the biker gang and so carried a concealed firearm even when he went to his daughter's first Cotillion dance, which was where he was headed that evening.

After the prosecutor revived from five minutes of convulsive twitching brought on by Nelson's carotid chokehold—with his wife, daughter and three other little girls in Cotillion chiffon screaming hysterically in his Volvo station wagon—the lawyer became a tad less diligent in prosecuting those bikers for breaking the bones of a cop. In fact, the prosecutor offered to drop the felony charge and let them cop a plea to malicious mischief. That caper put an end to Nelson Hareem's career in San Bernardino County.

In Los Angeles County he was even more eager. While patroling an alley with his car lights out just after midnight, Nelson had spotted a prowler lurking around the side window of a very fancy house in a silk-stocking residential district. Nelson got out of his patrol car and crept quietly into a neighbor's yard, climbed a six-foot wall that divided the properties, and was shocked and outraged to see that the prowler was watching an unsuspecting woman undress in her bathroom. Nelson was even more shocked and outraged when the guy started whacking his willy. When the woman turned and uttered a plaintive little scream at the prowler, Nelson launched himself into space, down on the guy's head, who, it turned out, was the owner of the house, and the biggest commercial real estate developer in town. He also was president of the local Kiwanis, as well as a contributor to the political coffers of a state senator, a U.S. Congressman, and Nelson's boss, the Mayor.

Until that night no one knew that the real estate developer and his wife had an arrangement where once every other week or so, she'd undress very provocatively in front of the window and then scream when she saw him milking the mamba. For which she'd get to overdraw her Neiman Marcus charge card with total impunity. It was a good deal for both of them, until their local policeman, Officer Nelson Hareem, went ballistic and put the hog flogger in a neck brace for three weeks.

Nelson capped it off two weeks later by accidentally firing a shotgun inside his patrol car. When he dashed inside the station to inform his long-suffering lieutenant of an "accidental discharge," the older cop said it was okay, he had them all the time. But when Nelson showed him how he'd put a sunroof in his patrol car, the lieutenant told him to resign at once or face a firing squad.

So, Nelson Hareem was at his last stop in the godforsaken south end of the Coachella Valley. Another massive attack of eagerness would take him to the French Foreign Legion, his new chief had warned when he'd hired Nelson during the previous summer.

Sometimes, Nelson Hareem could convince himself, for a microsecond, that his present job wasn't so bad. Then he'd look around at "downtown," which was terrific if you were into

1952 nostalgia. The way the town looked to twenty-seven-year-old Nelson Hareem, Michael J. Fox should come whizzing by on a skateboard on his way back to the future. Low one-story storefronts a few with corrugated tin roofs, lined the main street where nothing much had changed since the locals helped elect Dwight Eisenhower. There was a hardware store, a bar, a pool hall, a tiny food market, a barber shop run by a cross-eyed barber who scared the crap out of Nelson every time he picked up a straight razor, and of course, a video store. People had to have something to watch on their stolen VCRs.

When Nelson got *real* bored he'd drive over to a neighboring town, population nine hundred, and watch the street melt. He wasn't on the job a week before he'd abandoned the flak vest he'd never gone without in the other two police departments.

"Let them shoot me and put me out of my misery," he said to his sergeant when he hung up the vest. "I'd rather die once than every day from the heat."

From May until October life on patrol was a constant search for shade, and there wasn't much of it. A uniform would turn salt-white after four hours, and he'd be soaked from his armpits to his knees. He'd developed incurable jock itch, and to his astonishment, his leather gear had independent sweat rings. Well, if his leather was still alive and sweating, maybe he could survive too, Nelson thought, but he doubted it. The boredom would kill him if nothing else did.

When he'd first arrived at that south-end police department he'd whiled away the hours cruising out onto the desert trying to spot guys stripping hot cars. That was when he'd found a bleached human skull that prompted a big police search in dune buggies. Nelson had hoped for headlines, except that the FBI spoiled his chance for glory when their lab report said that even though there's no statute of limitations on murder, a three-hundred-year-old skull made the case a tough one to solve.

About seventy thousand acres of the southern Coachella

Valley—the irrigable parts—were used for crops. Palm trees were grown for landscaping the wealthy country clubs at the other end, but big money in the south end came from asparagus, lettuce, oranges, lemons, grapes, and ninety-five percent of America's dates. And from heroin.

Heroin was the drug of choice in the south end. The DEA estimated that seventy percent of California's cocaine came in through Mexico, and *all* of the "tar" heroin came from Mexico, a lot of it right there, only a few hours from Mexicali by car. Nelson Hareem's new backyard was an important distribution point for tar.

The tar, or *goma*, as the Mexicans called it, looked like brown window putty and smelled like vinegar. During recessionary times it cost about two hundred dollars a gram, which resembled a smashed raisin. Twenty dollars would buy one tenth of a gram wrapped in cellophane, covered with aluminum foil. The addict might get four hours of tolerable existence for twenty bucks, but then would need to slam more tar under his "trapdoor" scabs, so called because a convenient place to shoot was *under* the scab. The trapdoor hid the fresh needle marks from the cops.

Mexican brown and China white were almost never seen in the south end, only the tar, but there was lots and lots of tar. Hence, the south end was a dumping ground for dead human beings.

It was estimated that in those local desert towns there lived the highest concentration of parolees in the United States. Some had a need for speed, and did methamphetamine at a hundred bucks a gram, but heroin was king. The addicts were the kind who moved their lips when they read, but not when they talked. You couldn't understand a word they were saying, but outside of science institutes they were the only class of people in the continental U.S. who could think in grams and kilos.

The population always exploded down there during picking season and not just because of undocumented migrant workers from Mexico. Also in those fields were boat people from the Pacific rim, Laotians and Vietnamese mostly. Gambling squabbles were sometimes settled by machete and generally went unreported.

Local humor: Why does a migrant worker have a nose? So he has something to pick, off season.

The residents in Nelson Hareem's part of the world had to get by with swamp-coolers in summer, but one of the local drug dealers had proper air-conditioning. In fact, his house was fenced and gated, and he even had a swimming pool and spa. Nelson fantasized that he'd catch the guy doing a deal, and the young cop often tailed him when the dealer went to the saloon for a game of snooker, mingling with dogs and men who squatted out front by barred windows; their feet were white from the alkali that rose from the earth and produced a layer of crusty powder in that little bit of purgatory.

Nelson was dreaming of Palm Springs on the afternoon that Lynn Cutter was learning about Clive Devon from his new temporary boss, Breda Burrows.

That same afternoon a single-engine Cessna encountered mechanical trouble over the Anza Borrego mountain range, and the pilot of the plane decided to make an unscheduled stop at a small desert airport. It was one of the hottest spots in the nation, over a hundred feet below sea level. The airport had very little traffic, and absolutely nothing resembling a control tower. Pilots had to see and be seen. But the California Highway Patrol and the Riverside County Sheriff's Department kept a chopper and a fixed-wing aircraft at the airport. Often there'd be a cop, wearing an aviation jumpsuit with police insignia, hanging around the pilot's lounge.

The Cessna sputtered once on approach, but landed perfectly and taxied toward the hangar. A mechanic at the airport later told police that the pilot was a nice-looking blond guy in a designer bomber jacket, and that his passenger had spoken a few words of accented English.

The passenger, described as a "bald Latino in a khaki shirt," had looked at a large map on the wall in the hangar while the pilot and mechanic talked briefly. The mechanic later said that the bald man had pointed to some nearby towns on the map, said something to the pilot, and laughed. Then the bald man, clutching a red flight bag, headed toward the airport's public rest room.

Meanwhile, a sheriff's department pilot who was sick of drinking soda pop and reading a three-month-old *Playboy* draped his Sam Browne over his shoulder and headed for the john. He never knew what hit him.

The bald man with the flight bag hadn't locked the rest room door because it was broken. He'd been rooting around in the bag when the uniformed cop barged in on him. The bald man automatically threw a punch that George Bush would've envied. It bounced the cop headfirst off the edge of the door and when he slumped down, the bald guy booted him once in the solar plexus, then jerked the semiautomatic from the cop's Sam Browne.

The bald man, cradling the flight bag to his chest, jumped over the semiconscious cop, ran from the john, looked toward the plane on the tarmac, turned the other way and scooted toward the parking lot. Waving the cop's 9 mm Sig Sauer, he headed straight to a parked truck occupied by a plumber who'd been called to check leaking pipes. The bald guy jerked open the door, pointed the 9 mm at the plumber's bulging eyeballs, snatched the guy out of the seat and careened out of the parking lot in the stolen truck.

While several people scrambled toward the ruckus in the parking lot, the revived deputy hollered for help. The bald guy's pilot must have figured that something very bad had happened because he jumped back in his Cessna and took off, mechanical gremlins and all, causing detectives to later theorize that

46

whatever the deal was, it was worth his risking his life. Naturally, nobody had gotten his plane's number during all that excitement.

Everyone figured it had to have been aborted drug smuggling. There was always a "load plane," carrying pot or Mexican heroin, landing on one of the little desert airstrips, usually at night. In fact, there was one county-owned emergency landing strip that was *only* that, a strip with a wind sock, and nothing more. You could bring in enough Mexican tar on any given night to goon out half the valley, not to mention a cocaine shipment bound for Palm Springs or L.A.

The plumbing truck was eventually found sand-locked up to the axle in a date grove near the Torres Martinez Indian Reservation, a collection of mobile homes, guns, satellite dishes, and clotheslines fluttering in the hot wind. The land belonged to a tribe that had had the misfortune to settle too far south, unlike their luckier cousins, the Agua Calientes, who'd stayed on a chunk of sand now called Palm Springs.

Just as on other Indian reservations, county ordinances were unenforceable on Torrez Martinez land, but beating the crap out of a cop and stealing a truck at gunpoint was more than a county ordinance. So pretty soon dozens of cops from various jurisdictions were swarming all over the reservation searching for the bald guy with a flight bag, who'd been spotted by a curious Indian kid after scuttling the truck.

The Indian kid had watched the bald guy with the flight bag do something strange. Before abandoning the plumbing truck, the guy found a can of grease and smeared it on his mouth and in his nose. Then he took some coins from his pocket and put them in his mouth before walking toward Devil Canyon and the Santa Rosa wilderness on that extremely hot winter afternoon.

An old Indian who'd been whiling away the time by watching the futile search talked to the shy Indian kid after he'd bicycled home. The old Indian explained the grease trick to a few of the cops: The guy had lubricated his mucous membranes, and the coins in the mouth were to diminish thirst. According to the Indian, this proved that the guy with the flight bag had to be a "man of the desert."

Meanwhile, Nelson Hareem, glued to the police radio, was going bonkers because he couldn't get out of town and head for Devil Canyon. He'd been ordered by his sergeant to stay on his beat in his own town.

It was later learned that the bald man had doubled back in the vicinity of Lake Cahuilla, climbed over a grape-stake fence, and kicked in the door of a modest two-bedroom stucco house. The bald guy apparently hid there for a bit, then hot-wired a ten-year-old Ford sedan parked in the open carport. He was long gone while the search for him went on.

Not being a boozer herself, Breda mistakenly thought that coffee would help Lynn. She drove to a coffee shop on Palm Canyon Drive where they sat by a window, and she ordered cherry pie and coffee for two.

He hardly touched his pie, but squinted through the window at aging white-legged tourists, their figures squirming in the waves of heat rising from the pavement. Most of them wore dark socks and stretch pants.

Then he said, "Elastic's done more for Palm Springs tourism than sunshine and movie stars."

When the waitress refilled their cups, Breda Burrows, who'd never been in the eatery in her life, said, "Thanks, Dot."

The waitress said, "My name's Bonnie."

"Really?" Breda said. "Not Dot?"

"Dot works nights," the waitress said.

"That's a relief," said Breda.

After the waitress left, Lynn asked, "What was that all about?"

"Private joke."

"Between you and yourself? I guess you're glad *you're* here, or you'd be bored as hell."

Breda showed him that irritating grin and took another bite of pie. On the drive over, she'd explained everything she'd learned from Rhonda Devon about her husband, Clive. She *didn't* tell Lynn about the five-thousand-dollar bonus. He was already too nosey about fees.

Then he asked, "So how much we charging this Devon woman?"

"We?"

"I've heard P.I.'s say they get maybe forty-five bucks an hour for surveillance. And how much a mile? Forty-five cents?"

"Look, I'm offering you a flat fee of a thousand bucks if you get the results I want. That's pretty generous."

Lynn Cutter liked the way she handled a knife and fork. Too many of the babes he dated talked during dinner with food hanging out their mouths. He hated that more than gum chewing, but when he complained, they always implied that he was awfully prissy for a cop.

He absolutely *loved* the very dark freckle just below Breda's lower lip, near the corner of her mouth. He had a crazy impulse to lick a tiny drop of cherry syrup off that bittersweet chocolate freckle.

Still probing, he said, "I'll bet you demanded a hefty fee up front. If I was doing a garbage domestic case like this I'd ask for two grand."

Breda Burrows quietly ate her cherry pie, chewing with her mouth closed.

Lynn Cutter sipped his coffee, looked into those electric blues, and said, "In this town I bet you can make good bucks for domestic crap. Like when some a these fifty-million-dollar marriages break up they'll fight over a used Maytag washer and hire P.I.'s to tail each other out of spite. *Big* bucks, right?"

"I try to avoid domestic cases. Like you said, they're garbage. And yeah, a P.I. better take a retainer up front and bill against it because you can never make a client happy in a domestic case."

"So how much're we . . . *you* getting an hour for this one?"

She sighed and said, "I asked for sixty an hour. I usually ask for forty-five."

"Beverly Hills broad, Beverly Hills prices," Lynn said, smiling.

"There's a lotta competition," she said, irked by the happy face. "There's at least a dozen P.I.'s in the local phone book. Gotta get it when I can."

"So what're we gonna do about Clive Devon?" he asked. "I hope you don't expect me to hang around in the urologist's alley and go through his trash for *clues*."

"That's not what I had in mind," she said, squinting when the last of the afternoon sun slanted through the window of the coffee shop.

"Why don't you call his doctor's office and tell his receptionist you're from the Beverly Hills Fertility Institute? That you got some problem with the care and storage of his little tadpoles."

"I tried that the moment I left Mrs. Devon's home," she said. "Only I said there was a billing problem at the institute and I needed to verify the client's address."

"What'd the receptionist say?"

"That Mister Clive Devon hadn't seen Doctor Blanchard in over twelve months. That there must be some mistake."

"Maybe he went to some other doctor."

"Mrs. Devon said that Doctor Blanchard's been her husband's urologist for years. Maybe he's lying."

"Hell, most a them lie. My doctor lies every time he sends me a bill for shooting my knee with a needle like a railroad spike. And he tells me he *has* to charge me a hundred 'n fifty bucks for asking, 'Does it hurt?' Far as I'm concerned, my doctor's just a lawyer with a stethoscope."

"She thinks maybe Doctor Blanchard was ordered by Clive Devon to keep mum about the semen sample."

"So whaddaya want me to do?"

"I was thinking you might go there as a patient and say that you and your wife're considering in vitro fertilization and you need to have your sperm checked out. You could consult with him and casually mention that an acquaintance of yours is a patient. You could go with the flow and see where the conversation leads."

"What if he wants the sample?"

"You give it to him. That's one of the reasons I need a man helping me with this one."

"Forget it! I'm not gonna lay there and give up my little pollywogs to some stranger! Besides, it's humiliating!"

"Don't be stupid."

"It wouldn't work anyway. My second and *last-ever* wife insisted I get a vasectomy. My little swimmers're in dry dock. One look under a microscope and he'd wonder what's up."

"Okay, I guess I can still use you on a surveillance. I've got a couple other cases going or I'd do it myself. How are you at surveillance?"

"I can cope."

"Tomorrow morning," she said. "Mrs. Devon said her husband leaves the house at seven A.M. and doesn't come back till four-thirty. He wears hiking boots and takes a canteen. When she goes to L.A. he doesn't seem to go on these hikes. So maybe he can't stand his wife and gets the hell out when she's at the Palm Springs house."

"Seven A.M.!"

"Hey, you don't make a thousand bucks tax-free by staying in bed unless you're working at one of those chicken ranches in Nevada."

"What if he really goes hiking? You don't expect me to tail him out on the open desert without being spotted?"

"Just stay with his car and wait," she said. "I've got some good binoculars I'll let you use. Never let the car get out of sight till he goes home."

"How about after momma goes back to L.A.?"

"Same thing. We'll tail him in the daylight hours and in the evening if he goes out. When he goes nighty-night we go home."

"What if he goes out later in the night?"

"Where?"

"I don't know. Maybe to a hot little sperm receptacle for another donation. How do you *know* he can't get it up? Maybe with his wife he's limp, but with his private squeeze he's Rasputin."

"Why the need for a sperm bank then?"

"Why not? Maybe his friend can't conceive in the normal way. Maybe they decided that test-tubing's the only way to go."

"Let's try it for a few days and see how it goes, okay?"

"If I wasn't totally bankrupt I wouldn't touch this crap," he said. "That'll teach me to let Charles Keating do my income tax."

"Do you go around just pissing off people on purpose? Are you tough enough for that?"

"Yeah, I'm a tough guy," he said. "Except on Tuesdays when I have to get my legs waxed. Is this Tuesday, by the way?"

Breda Burrows' office consisted of a pair of rooms on the second floor of a commercial building just off Indian Avenue. The other tenants included a children's photographer, a C.P.A., an optometrist, and an office for the landlord, who used the digs as a place to clip coupons and get away from his wife, who'd become as touchy as cholla cactus after turning seventy.

The anteroom of Breda's office was really a cubbyhole with a couple of chairs, a small table, and a lamp, all bought at a second-hand store. Her inner office wasn't much more posh. She had an inexpensive computer, a typewriter and a phone with two lines. On the wall behind a desk of oak veneer were several framed law enforcement certificates-of-training from her police days, as well as her B.S. degree in police science from Cal State Los Angeles. It had taken her eight years of part-time study to get the degree.

Lynn slumped on one of the two chairs in front of the desk, and when Breda sat, she put on Yuppie eyeglasses with strawberry frames.

"I been thinking," he said. "Clive Devon oughtta get a splint for his member. I hear they got electronic implants. Only trouble is, if your neighbor hits his garage door-opener you might get a bulge in your shorts."

While Breda was rummaging in her desk drawers for her binoculars and the file on Clive Devon, a shapely young woman entered the outer office and tapped on the open door. She wore jeans and a white cotton turtleneck with a gold Rolex worn over the cuff. She had a raging auburn dye-job.

"May I help you?" Breda asked, and to her astonishment, Lynn Cutter actually stood up. Maybe he wasn't *quite* as crude as a Hell's Angels' picnic.

But then he reassured her by leering at the young woman's tits, saying, "Dazzled to meet you. May I be of service?"

"I'm looking for . . . Ms. Burrows. Is the first name Bretta?" She had a little voice that Lynn Cutter thought went well with big bazooms.

"I'm Breda Burrows. It's pronounced Bree-da. An Irish name."

"I got referred by a friend of a friend. I have . . . a problem I'd like to discuss."

Lynn took his cue and said, "I'll wait in the outer office."

Breda knew he'd scope out the woman's booty before closing the door, and he did. After which, Breda peeked at *his* booty and hated to admit that it wasn't bad.

When they were alone, the woman said, "Before I tell you any names I wanna know how much a certain job'll cost me."

"Let's hear your problem," Breda said.

The young woman said, "I got this boyfriend who's married, see. Met him over at a hotel where I used to do nails. We been going together for three years and he promised he'd divorce his wife and marry me but he keeps making excuses. Now I know he's a cheat and a liar."

"If you know all that what do you want me to do?"

"I want you to take a picture of him having sex with the other woman."

"Another other woman?"

"No," she said, and Lynn Cutter would've been disappointed to see that she chewed gum with her mouth open. "The *only* other woman. Me."

"You want a photo of you two having sex?"

"Yes. A secret photo. *Real* explicit. Without him knowing."

"What for?"

"So I can send it to his wife and show her what a bastard he is."

"You wanna punish him, that it?"

"No. I wanna marry him. I wanna make her dump him. He broke up my engagement to another guy by making me fall in love with him. I'll tell him my old boyfriend musta hired somebody to take the secret picture."

"I'm sorry, I don't do that kind of work."

"Why not?"

"Too complicated."

"Okay, if you did it what would you charge?"

"I wouldn't do it for any amount of money."

Suddenly, the young woman dropped her demure little voice. "Well, no shit! A keyhole-peeper with scruples!"

Lynn could hear Breda raise her voice then, and he heard the shapely young woman raise hers right back.

When the young woman came storming out, she said to

Breda, "I got two words for you, a verb and a noun: Fuck you!"
Then she was gone.

Lynn looked at Breda, who stared at him through her Yuppie strawberry eyeglasses with that irritating grin.

"It's a pronoun," Breda said.

"What is?"

"You. As in . . . fuck . . . *you*."

"Your lenses're fogging," Lynn said. "My musk glands
must be overactive."

Until she was driving home
that afternoon Breda Burrows hadn't realized how stressful the
day had been. It wasn't the Clive Devon case; she'd work that
out or she wouldn't, and either way the money was too good
to pass up. Her stress was caused by having to work with a
man for the first time since she'd retired from police work.

A few of her old police academy classmates had warned
her that after she retired she might spend months remembering
nothing but the good times and then months remembering all
the bad times. Maybe meeting that smart-mouth Lynn Cutter
had started the bad-time memories.

Breda had been one of the female officers chosen to work
uniform patrol when the LAPD first started putting women out
on the street in radio cars. By the time she'd retired in June of
1990 things were a *lot* better for female officers, even though
the younger women complained that not much had changed.

Breda knew better. When she was a young officer on patrol, women *couldn't* complain.

It was considered amusing in those days for male cops to stand around grinning like baboons and watch a female bust her bra trying to wrestle a semiconscious wino from the police car to the drunk tank. And more than once she'd found herself put in a dark and terrifying place, all alone, wondering if they'd left her out there on purpose. Sometimes she'd worried that they wouldn't back her up the way they would a man, until she'd proved she had the moxie of a man.

Proving themselves once was never enough; the women had to prove themselves time and again. If a male recruit made a mistake during his probationary period he was a callow lad who needed seasoning. If a woman made the same mistake she was a useless bimbo who should be fired on the spot. Every woman who went through the rigors of recruit training in those days learned soon after graduation that their troubles had just begun.

Even so, she'd been proud of her badge and had made friends she couldn't seem to duplicate in civilian life. At least when male and female cops were out on the streets—sometimes with personalities as compatible as Gorbachev and Yelstin—each would literally lay it on the line for the other if one's safety depended on it. That kind of experience never happened in civilian life. She missed that bond.

But she didn't miss the male bonding that was an important part of police life, that weenie-welding experience where every practical joke—some of them nasty—was tried on female cops. The women were coffee-talk for the boys who figured that *every* female cop could be had, and it was the duty of each one of the guys to prove it.

And *because* they were women, the females often had to become surrogate mothers or big sisters out there in the patrol units at night to all those blue-suited Rambos who temporarily traded testosterone for teddy bears, whining and whimpering about that bitch they married, or that bastard of a sergeant, or the ungrateful taxpayers. She'd heard every complaint that could be uttered by boys in blue. It seemed that the siege mentality demanded release whenever a woman was riding in a car with a man. *Mommy, make it all better!*

And heaven help the female officer in those days who got pregnant. *Pregnant? Maternity leave? But I didn't make you pregnant, Officer. The department didn't make you pregnant.*

One of the former chiefs had made a public utterance, widely quoted in the L.A. press, to the effect that the females would never measure up to the male cops because, as he put it, "the girls have their monthlies, you see."

Breda had been present one terrible day when a female cop had tried and failed to revive a three-year-old boy who'd fallen in the family swimming pool. The young woman had worked on the tot for fifteen minutes in the back of a police car while Breda drove a screaming code-three run to the receiving hospital. The child was DOA despite the effort, and Breda's partner started to cry and couldn't stop.

Two bluesuits from their own division happened to be in the emergency ward taking an ADW report from a poolshark who'd been beaned with a nine ball tossed by a guy he'd hustled out of fifty bucks.

When the male cops saw the young woman bawling her eyes out, one of them asked Breda, "What's a matter? Did we mace each other by accident and run our mascara?"

The other said, "What's a matter, we having a little P.M.S. attack, are we?"

Breda glared at them with her pimp-killer grin, and said, "As far as I'm concerned, P.M.S. comes from PUKEY MEN'S SHIT, YOU HEMORRHOIDS!"

In the old days, you could just about depend on the guys to call for a female backup every time somebody arrested a fighting-mad dyke who wore leather and spikes and greased-back hair. The guys got off by putting the female officer in the back seat with the dyke and cooing stuff like, "No playing patty-fingers on the way to the station, *girls!*"

And there were citizens who, after calling the police, would gape dumbfounded when a female cop stood on the threshold. They'd usually say, "They sent a *woman?*" And Breda would usually answer, "Yeah. Don't you feel *silly?*"

Rape or sex crimes involving kids usually got kissed off to a female cop. The men would call for them and when they arrived, it was always, "Won't talk to me. Needs a woman's touch. Catch you later. Bye."

And then the male would be off to the donut shop with the other guys while the female might spend the rest of her watch with a woman or child who might've been abused in ways that came back to you in the night. That was one of the reasons Breda had never used alcohol as a sedative. She didn't want the alcoholic wormies at three A.M., because that bed got awfully crowded when you loaded it with little kids. *All* those little kids . . .

She'd worked sex crimes with kiddie victims for such a long time that when she went back to detective duty with grownups, she'd found herself talking like a diaper dick, interrogating forty-year-old burglars and sounding like Mister Rogers: "Now, see, Harry, you have the right to remain silent. Do we under-stannnnnd siii-lent?"

Those sex crimes that were not filed by the D.A. because of insufficient evidence were often memorable. Like the five-year-old girl with new cigarette burns over old ones, who kept repeating, "I'm a bad girl. Daddy did it cause I'm a bad girl." And that child was put *back* in the home!

The wormies at three A.M.: *Boss, I'm outta here! I need a vacation!*

When Mommy or Daddy, or Mommy's boyfriend actually *killed* a child, when she'd attend postmortems with homicide dicks—those from the gag-and-giggle school of corpse-cops—

they'd always make sure she was with a particular pathologist who liked to post a body like he was doing caesar salad for the pathologist's picnic. No tying things off to keep the bile in place, no way. Just mince, dice and *toss*. And all that lettuce and cucumber and bell pepper—which were really tiny bits of a former human child—would stick to her sleeves.

She could deal with the clipping of fingers for hydrating fingerprints, but she *hated* the smell of burning bone when they sawed off the skull cap. The other corpse-cops knew it, and made sure she was up close and personal.

It was hard not to retch when they had a "decomp," one covered with enough "rice" to open a live-bait shop. The pathologist would take a swipe at the "rice" and she might find herself wearing a pair of maggots on her lapel.

How's your tummy? Shall we have enchiladas for lunch or would you like a meatball sandwich?

There were other kinds of guys, good partners. She thought she was in love with one, a training officer at Wilshire Division. They were married in her rookie year and she got immediately pregnant with their only child. He'd been a decent husband, it's just that he should've been somebody else's husband. They'd both sensed it during their first year together, but by then Lizzy was on the way.

Her ex-husband had gone on to become a police commander, later had remarried, and had eventually retired to a job as police chief in a small city in Washington. He'd had two other children and saw Lizzy less and less as the years passed, but he'd always sent the child-support payments, and was generous even after Lizzy was eighteen and his obligation was over.

Breda had never married again and tried not to date cops unless she was absolutely desperately lonely. The last time she was *that* lonely was shortly before she'd decided to pull the pin and take her pension.

That guy had been a gorgeous lieutenant who specialized

in those intense gazes he thought were real spoon-benders. She recalled an evening in the coffee room at Hollywood Station just before her retirement, when he'd shared with her his opinions and philosophy on police discipline.

It seemed that one of the officers had been caught in his patrol car getting serviced supremely by a cop groupie who had balled half the night watch and most of the morning watch during her groupie career. In that the groupie was not a professional prostitute, Breda's lieutenant thought that firing Charlie would be a harsh penalty. After all, in the good old days (cops were big-time reminiscers) even *he'd* committed an indiscretion or two. Wink!

Breda said to the gorgeous lieutenant, "It's okay with me if good old Charlie skates, but tell me something, what if it was one of our *female* officers? How would you feel then?"

And the lieutenant, an otherwise liberated supervisor, made it plain that he'd never entertained such a thought. A female officer? Female officers were *different.* He'd always been pleased with his reputation as a nonsexist police supervisor (pro-choice all the way), but Breda Burrows had just pitched one up there that he couldn't hit. The fact is, it was unthinkable.

"That's *unthinkable!*" he said.

"Why is it?" she asked. "What if it was me out there in uniform listening to Ravel's *Bolero* on a ghetto blaster, getting done by some guy in the front seat of a radio car? Would you think I should be fired?"

He blinked and stroked his handsome jaw and stared at Breda Burrows, this woman he'd dated! as though she'd just offered to jerk off a gerbil. He *had* to come up with an answer, especially after the first words to slide out of his mouth had been the dreaded, sexist: "It's *different.*"

"Why do you think it's different?" Breda persisted, with the little grin that annoyed him.

"Because . . ." He turned pomegranate-pink and sputtered,

"because . . . your trousers would be down! And your Sam Browne! You'd be disarmed! And out of uniform!"

Breda decided to turn it off, all the bad-time memories, when she drove her Z into the driveway. Her house was a three-bedroom stucco with a composite roof, air-conditioning, two and a half bathrooms, and a yard big enough for a pool that she couldn't afford to build. Seven thousand pools around there and she had to cool off with a lawn sprinkler, but at least the house was in Cathedral Canyon, well protected from the winter winds that could blow the paint off a car and the tits off a kangaroo rat, or so the realtor had told her when she sold Breda the house back in the protected cove of the mountain range. There was no big church with spires or Gothic arches in Cathedral City. The town got its name in 1850 when an army engineer—probably drinking fermented cactus juice—saw something in the canyon that resembled a cathedral. But it was an affordable town for cops.

Breda decided she needed a bike ride, and there was enough daylight left. Aside from her Datsun Z, her other luxury in life was a Tour de France–class custom bicycle with a Holland frame. She'd saved up a long time for the bike, and had ridden it in a fifty-mile endurance run down in Baja California, from Rosarito Beach to Ensenada. Every time she'd passed a shabby Mexican kid watching that race she'd wondered if her $2,500 bike was worth more than the shack the kid lived in. Gringo guilt had ridden on her shoulder that day and slowed her down a bit.

Even in a pack of bikers she felt alone, and that was good. Breda's favorite place to ride was in the Indio Hills, where she could gain downhill speeds up to fifty miles per hour. But she never went biking without a seat pack. Her .38 two-inch revolver was in the pack.

Once, while biking on a lonely road near Desert Hot

Springs, two dirtbag rednecks in a raggedy pickup truck had played bumper tag, forcing her off the road. They were the kind that rushed out to shoot a spotted owl as soon as it was designated an endangered species in order to get *theirs* while they had the chance. The kind who hung signs that said "Rattlesnake Farm" on their front gates to ensure privacy, as though anyone wanted to see them in the first place.

One of them had slouched toward her with a beer in his hand, and said, "Hey, pretty baby, you're a long ways from home. Put that bike in the back. We'll take you where you're goin."

Before she could get her bike back onto the asphalt, the other guy, whose only clean flesh was along his upper lip where he'd been licking off the suds, said, "Get in the truck, sweet stuff."

Breda heaved a sigh and opened her seat pack. By the time she'd bicycled away that afternoon, they were both lying face down on the sand behind their pickup, fingers interlocked behind their heads, whining about how they were only kidding. She'd told them she realized it was awfully hot, but their radiator had enough water in it and the antifreeze probably didn't taste as bad as some of the swill they'd consumed in their time, and maybe they should keep their traps shut or she just might forget to keep reminding herself that they were all fellow mammals here.

She'd flattened two tires and took their ignition key with her, tossing it away in the desert. It was actually one of the most enjoyable biking experiences she'd ever had and she'd slept like a baby that night.

Breda Burrows was feeling a lot better about things when, wearing her black Coolmax shirt and black Lycra pants, she bicycled out Ramon Road to Bob Hope Drive, then right, past Dinah Shore Drive to Frank Sinatra Drive, where she made another right and stopped at the oleander-encircled estate of publisher Walter Annenberg, who threw the biggest New Year's bash in the desert, one that Ronald Reagan never missed.

Two private guards were out front, and Breda, covered with a fine layer of sweat and feeling euphoric, yelled to them, "*Again* he didn't invite me on New Year's Eve!"

The guards grinned and waved, and with her earth-brown hair streaming from under the helmet, Breda sprinted past Tamarisk Country Club, the home of Old Blue Eyes himself. Then she was back on Highway 111 pumping toward Cathedral City, no longer feeling all nutted up from her encounter with Lynn Cutter.

Breda overtook a sheriff's unit cruising in the slow lane, and instantly felt a pang of camaraderie. The female deputy was pretty, and as young as Breda had been when she'd started on the job. Breda wondered how long it would be before they put an attractive kid like that into vice duty, the John Squad, make her go out there on the avenue in tight pants and spike heels and listen to all those sweaty guys with wives and kiddies at home, eager to pay twenty dollars for a head job or forty for straight sex or fifty for both.

She wanted to say something to the young woman, but what was there to say? It was not just a job, it was a *way of life*.

Well, she was something else now. What had Lynn Cutter called her? Fuzz that *was*. And she had to earn a decent living to supplement her pension, because a kid at Berkeley was damned expensive, even with her ex-husband helping out.

Since coming to Palm Springs she'd become acutely aware that lots of the poshest dwellings she passed on her bike rides served as second- or third-home getaway destinations for owners who might only visit them a couple of times a year. She wondered what it cost them to keep their house plants alive.

Good things! she told herself, pumping past Date Palm

Drive, sprinting toward a glass of iced tea. Good things! Think of *good* things!

The thing she thought about was that the tropical tan uniform the deputy wore was undramatic, that the sheriff's department and Palm Springs P.D. ought to change color to police blue.

Blue was much more slenderizing.

At the end of the duty tour that day the sergeant of Nelson Hareem thought he recognized something in the eyes of the little redhead as he talked about the hunt for the fugitive who'd cold-cocked the deputy at the airport.

By now, the residents of the house near Lake Cahuilla had come home and discovered that their house had been entered and their Ford sedan was gone. The cops figured that the burglar—car thief had to be the airport guy, and the description of the stolen white Ford was broadcast every thirty minutes or so to all the law enforcement agencies in the valley.

"You *are* gonna beat feet to your little home, aren't you, Nelson?" the sergeant asked with a worried look. Maybe it was the fact that Nelson's haircut looked frizzy and wild. Nelson was giving off an aura you could trip over.

"Sure, Sarge," Nelson told him innocently. "Why wouldn't I?"

"You wouldn't do something *really* goofy, would you? Like trying to get in on the search for the airport guy? I mean, while you're off duty?"

"Of course not, Sarge," the carrot-top cop promised, with a baby-face smile that scared the crap out of every supervisor he'd ever had.

The sergeant was the kind of guy who never did *anything* off duty, except help his wife sell Tupperware. He asked, hopefully, "Isn't there someone at home waiting? Someone to help you chill out when you start getting that Robocop feeling? You look like you could set off smoke alarms."

"I jist live alone with my goldfishes, Sarge," Nelson answered affably.

"You got that certain look in your eye," the sergeant said. "Like you might go out and do something . . . worrisome. You don't own an assault rifle, do you?"

"I learned my lesson, Sarge," Nelson promised. "I don't wanna finish my career in the Legion. Can't speak French."

"Good night then, Nelson," the sergeant said, doubtfully.

And of course, the little cop put on his civvies, jumped in his Jeep Wrangler, and raced straight for the Sheriff's Department in Indio, where he hoped to gather some clues he could work on the next day.

When somebody assaulted a cop like that, it was a *big* deal, a lot worse than a murder of a mere civilian. Everyone got stoked and wanted a piece of the son of a bitch and would be very appreciative of the cop that bagged him. Nelson Hareem had big-time fantasies about *being* that cop.

Sliding the Wrangler into the parking lot he spotted a deputy he knew, a Latino named Morales who was arriving in his black-and-white patrol car.

"Half-Nelson!" Morales yelled, when Nelson jumped out of his Jeep with his tape deck blasting. "What're you doing here?"

"How about the bald guy, Morales?" Nelson asked, leaning in the window. "Any leads?"

"Yeah, he throws a Mike Tyson left hook and kicks like Uncle Bubba's ten-gauge. And he knows how to hot-wire a car."

"Got a better description yet?"

"Naw. The pilot never saw it coming and the mechanic in the hangar, he didn't pay no attention. Didn't even notice the guy's face. Just has the impression of a husky bald Mexican. We're guessing he's middle-aged, but he might be younger. His fringe hair was black. That's all the plumber saw, black sideburns, bald on top, a Zapata mustache and the nine-millimeter. From a muzzle point of view."

"Nothin else?"

"Yeah, an Indian kid from the reservation saw him take a can a grease from the plumber's truck and smear it in his mouth and nose. An old desert trick. There's a lotta desert down in Mexico so he might know about that kinda stuff. I figure he's halfway to L.A. by now. Or maybe heading back home after things went so bad at the airport. I bet he's stole another car by now. He's a savvy smuggler, that guy. Oh, and he left the deputy's gun in the abandoned truck."

"Why would he do that?"

"Maybe because he had his own gun in the bottom of his flight bag. A bigger 'n better one."

"Are the people at the house where he stole the Ford sure there wasn't a car key in the kitchen or somewhere?"

"Positive. He hot-wired it. The guy's resourceful. I bet that flight bag was packed with several keys a heroin. Be pretty neat to take that guy down, wouldn't it?"

"Yeah!" Nelson Hareem said, and it was a good thing his sergeant couldn't see the little cop's bulging blue lamps.

The deputy said, "He did another desert trick. The kid saw him take out some pocket change to stick in his mouth. An old Indian said it diminishes thirst. Called him a man of the desert."

There was a stand of old tamarisk trees twenty minutes by car from the parking lot where Nelson Hareem was speaking with the deputy before going home to his goldfish. The stolen Ford sedan was parked under the shaggy branches of the tamarisks by a bald man who frightened three migrant workers who'd been camping among the trees, sleeping on a bed of needles.

The *campesinos* spoke a few words to the man, who answered in their language, and as soon as they saw he was no threat they returned to their campfire. The bald man urinated in a grape vineyard, climbed into the back seat of the Ford, locked his car doors and went to sleep.

The only reason that detectives would learn about all of this was that one of the migrant workers was spending his last night on earth, and his friends would need to talk to the police.

—5—

His two marriages were part of a rags-to-witches story, Lynn Cutter always said. His first wife, Claudia, had spent him into bankruptcy by finding "little frocks" to wear to Palm Springs restaurants frequented by movie stars, millionaires and swarthy guys with "dapper don" haircuts. But when it came to fancy duds his second wife, Teddi, could spend California out of a recession in a day and a half.

His marriage to Claudia had lasted eighteen months. She was a good-looking flight attendant based in L.A. who liked to visit the desert every chance she got. Claudia always stayed at a cozy hotel near the Tennis Club in the days when tennis was tops, when developers there wouldn't dream of doing a hotel, condo or country club without top-drawer tennis facilities. Even Cathedral City—at that time a community of blue-collar folks who serviced the resorts—was pouring a lot of concrete for the sport of strings.

Claudia's favorite hotel was one of the hideaways snuggled up against the mountains. The first time Lynn saw her she was wearing tennis whites, lounging by a pool that reflected a sparkle of sunbeams, framed by a backdrop of mocha desert hillside laced with purple verbeña. *Enchantment.*

He'd decided he had to learn to play tennis for Claudia, so he'd signed up for five lessons a week. Those flat-bellied young pros used to run him down like process servers. He'd go out to the playground as soon as he got off duty and smack balls against a concrete wall until his elbow got so sore he couldn't lift his arm higher than his shoulder. He'd later admitted to his pals that Claudia had him busting more balls than the Gabors, who also lived in Palm Springs, where they got a fleet discount on face-lifts.

Lynn and Claudia had decided against having kids in that her paycheck was urgently needed if they were to live like deposed Iranians. In those days a relative of the shah had visited Palm Springs with her pet peacock and lost it. Lynn was one of the cops assigned to the peacock posse and he'd tracked the bird by listening to its Roseanne Barr screams. Peacock wrangling, that summarized Palm Springs for you, Lynn always said.

But one day Claudia had returned from a flight and informed Lynn that she'd met somebody in Denver who'd "opened up new vistas" for her.

He asked, "Is it okay for you to ball someone out of state? I mean, if it's a different time zone is it still considered cheating? I'm just wondering."

Claudia answered by saying, "I hope you'll be *man* enough to deal with this maturely."

Lynn said, "I'll try to pinch off my tear ducts. Goodbye, Claudia."

He'd gone out and gotten hammered that night, relieved that he'd never again have to feed her Doberman, which she called her "DNA dog." The little charmer had trained it to eat anyone with a nonwhite genetic code.

His second ex-wife, Teddi: Now there was a woman *nobody* could figure out. She was about as understandable as acupuncture. On some days, her idea of a profound decision in life was whether or not to have her lug nuts chromed, but a day later, she'd drag him to a poetry reading at the University of California, Riverside, where some hairball who could make a rap group throw up would scream "poems" at them. As far as Lynn could discern, they were all about excrement, necrophilia, incest, rape, mayhem and vomit.

Teddi had gotten positively moist at their last reading, when they were allowed to shake hands with a poet and buy an inscribed copy of his work, published by some vanity press in San Francisco. As the poet took Lynn's bucks for the book, he asked whether Lynn had enjoyed the reading.

Lynn said to him in front of thirty people, "Oh yeah, very tasteful. I never once heard you mention pus or vaginal discharge."

On the drive home to Palm Springs that night, Teddi told Lynn that she thought they lived in two different worlds, and that his was without "texture, subtlety or nuance."

"You're not ready to change for me," she informed him that night.

"I got *cut* for you," he reminded her. "Your Siamese tomcat now has the only fully operating pair a balls in the house."

"You only see things in black and white," Teddi told him.

"You want Technicolor, you better hook up with Ted Turner," he responded, long before the mogul's merger with Jane Fonda.

A highway patrol officer-cum-lawyer had handled that divorce, giving him a police discount. The lawyer told Lynn that he knew a doctor who would reverse the vasectomy if Lynn ever got married again.

But Lynn had informed the lawyer that women were about as impenetrable as the Dead Sea Scrolls, and that as a single man he was happy as a rutting rabbit, intending to stay that way forever.

His "dates" in recent years usually began at The Furnace Room, but all relationships withered after a few weeks or months. Wilfred Plimsoll announced that Lynn had the staying power of a cherry popsicle.

Lynn had forced himself not to have more than half a dozen drinks the night before, but hadn't gotten to bed early enough. Still, he'd set the alarm and managed to arrive at the home of Clive Devon in Las Palmas at 6:30 A.M.

The desert sky was breathtaking at that hour. Cloud shadow made the Indio Hills shimmer in dappled silver light. All of the pastels in the desert landscape had deepened. The sky was dove gray, with burgundy smears behind pink cotton cumulus, as he sat in his car and drank coffee from a thermos.

At 7:00 A.M. Clive Devon drove out of his driveway in a black Range Rover. He was wearing a floppy hat, a knit shirt, chinos and hiking boots, dressed very much like Lynn except for the hat. He meandered slowly through the narrow streets of Las Palmas, traditional home of Palm Springs' old money. It wasn't an ideal place to hang a tail on somebody. The streets twisted too much, and there were too many huge homes with whitewashed adobe walls and ten-foot oleander hedges for privacy. There was no place to hide on streets like that, and there were no cars to get behind at such an early hour. Mostly there were just gardeners coming to work in pickup trucks, with mowers and gardening tools stacked in the truck beds. Clive Devon turned on Via Lola because it flowed into Palm Canyon Drive, and you could go either way on that main artery.

Fortunately, Lynn Cutter's old Nash Rambler looked like it could belong to a Mexican gardener, or to a black maid from north Palm Springs. Lynn had gotten a good buy on the car from a used-car dealer in Cat City whom he'd once stopped for drunk driving on Christmas Eve. Instead of booking the guy he'd driven him home, mostly because the lawyer for Lynn's second wife had opened Lynn's veins and he figured it might be prudent to make pals with a guy that dealt with rent-a-wrecks and second-hand wheels, the kind of cars he could afford. And at least the Rambler had a new engine and retreads.

They drove past Gene Autry Trail and the Desert Princess Country Club, finally heading to the south end on Highway 10. Lynn began to wonder if this guy was one of those eccentrics who drove several hundred miles on a whim, maybe to see the Phoenix Suns play the L.A. Lakers? Lynn figured he had enough gas money in his pocket to get back if Clive Devon didn't travel more than sixty minutes from home. He was glad when the Range Rover turned off the freeway, heading back to Highway 111, passing by the little airport that had made a lot of cops breathe hard the night before, during the long and fruitless search for a fugitive.

Obviously Clive Devon wasn't a man who worried about somebody following him. Lynn soon realized that he could bumper-lock the Range Rover and never be noticed. The sixty-three-year-old man was moseying toward the Salton Sea, a thirty-five-mile lake near the foot of the Chocolate Mountains. What the guy intended to do by the north shore of the desert lake, where only a few hundred people lived in mobile homes, Lynn Cutter couldn't imagine.

The Salton Sea was a mistake of man and perhaps of nature. Just after the turn of the century, some railroad builders made a horrible error with the Colorado River, and a levee burst, allowing millions of cubic feet of water per day to rage into a huge salt marsh left over from an ancient inland sea. The new Salton Sea submerged everything under water fifty percent saltier than the ocean. It was said that pumice rock could float in this saltiest of water, 235 feet below sea level.

Many of the migrant workers, particularly Asian boat people, liked to fish the salt water for local corvina, using illegal ıl nets. The cops figured that anybody hungry enough to eat the mutant fish from that selenium-loaded water—polluted by sewage and agricultural waste—should be welcome to it.

Lynn Cutter was astonished when the Range Rover parked at a café that advertised itself as a bait shop, near the north shore marina. There were several gulls lurking around the parking lot but not much else. The desert wind ruffled across the green-yellow water, making it very chancy for two fishermen trying to launch a small dinghy.

Clive Devon strolled inside the café. There was one old pickup in front and Lynn didn't dare get too close. The only convenient place to park and observe was five hundred yards down the highway, so he decided to use Breda's fancy binoculars.

He was watching the café when a man ran across the highway from the direction of the All-American Canal, a twenty-foot wide artery of fresh water from the Colorado River. Lynn didn't pay much attention to the guy, who wore a baseball cap and a dark windbreaker. He was wondering why a rich guy like Clive Devon would hang around this dying place. Even the lowliest desert denizens had just about given up on the Salton Sea. That morning the wind was blowing a foul algae-sewage smell his way.

Clive Devon came out of the café with a six-pack of something, beer or soda pop, and what looked like a bag of potato chips, and stood by his Range Rover. The man in the baseball cap also walked out, with a newspaper, and ran across the road, disappearing from sight.

Early that morning the migrant workers who'd camped in the stand of tamarisk trees had awakened to find the bald man driving away. He was gone for perhaps thirty minutes. When he returned he took off his jacket, parked under the trees once again and began reading a newspaper. After a little while he started the car as though to back out from under the trees, but just then a police car cruised down Box Canyon Road. When the police car had gone, the bald man jumped out of the Ford with his red canvas bag.

Before he left them he warned the three *campesinos* in Spanish that the car was stolen and that they must not drive it. He asked which way it was to Palm Springs and if he could get there by going the opposite way from where the police car had gone. They pointed him toward Highway 10 assuming he would hitchhike.

The Ford was a big temptation for three migrant workers, the oldest of whom, though he looked thirty, was only twenty years old. He had lived by his wits for five years, and had made many illegal crossings from Mexicali to work in the fields of the Imperial and Coachella valleys. He knew how to start a hot-wired car. Skillful driving was another matter.

Through binoculars, Lynn watched Clive Devon drink two soda pops during the half hour that he remained in the parking lot. Lynn saw only three other cars coming and going from the café during that time. Then a rusty old Plymouth rattled down the highway from the direction of Mecca and Thermal, and pulled into the parking area. A short slender woman got out. Even from his distant vantage point Lynn could see that she was young. Her shiny black hair hung down to her waist and she wore a blue T-shirt and jeans.

The young woman and Clive Devon greeted each other, but they stood on the far side of the Range Rover. Lynn's view was completely blocked and he could only get glimpses of Clive Devon through the side windows. He thought they stood close enough to be kissing but he couldn't be sure.

A large brown dog leaped out from the backseat of the rusty Plymouth and bounded toward Clive Devon; then he too was blocked by the Range Rover. After a moment Clive Devon

75

opened the door of the Range Rover and the dog jumped up onto the backseat. Then the young woman got into the front next to Clive Devon, who started the Range Rover and drove back toward Mecca and Thermal.

By the time Lynn had allowed them some lead time he had to floor the Rambler because the Range Rover was accelerating. Lynn tried to see the license number when he passed the rusty Plymouth in the parking lot, but couldn't. He figured he'd get it on the way back. He was very surprised when the Range Rover turned right on Box Canyon Road and headed toward a county park.

The three migrant workers had pooled their money at the north shore café to buy a bag of tortilla chips and two cokes to be split three ways. Then they got back into the hot-wired Ford and cruised out Highway 111. They'd decided to drive to Thermal, hoping to impress some girls.

The driver had learned to operate a car in Calexico, where he had a job cleaning restaurant grease traps, so filthy that cats wouldn't even touch them, but that brief driving experience wasn't enough. He zigged across the double line as a big rig was roaring toward him, and the eighteen-wheeler clipped the Ford.

The car went airborne and came to earth upside down with an explosive crunch. The two lucky ones were blown out and suffered broken bones and a few internal injuries. The passenger in the death-seat was decapitated.

Like too many police agencies, the sheriff's department hired few Hispanics, and neither of the two deputies who arrived before the paramedics could speak Spanish. Nor could Nelson Hareem, who sped down the highway and skidded to a stop across the highway from the overturned Ford. But the next unit to arrive was driven by a CHP officer who at least spoke Border Patrol Spanish and was able to ask a few questions.

The headless corpse and the crash itself no longer interested anybody. What the cops were all excited about was that the crunched Ford bore the license number of the one stolen by the smuggler the day before. For the least injured of the migrant farm workers, a slow and painful interrogation continued until the ambulance arrived.

The Chippie, frequently interrupted by Nelson's "Whadhesay?," learned that the husky bald man had stashed the stolen car in a stand of tamarisk trees the night before, and ditched the car that morning.

As the paramedics arrived and began loading the more seriously injured farm worker first, the one doing the talking kept telling the cops that he wouldn't have kept or sold the stolen car, that they only wanted to use it for a day or so, because of the girls in Thermal. And just before being lifted into the ambulance, the young farm worker volunteered that the husky bald man was about thirty-five years old and *muy intelligente*. He was certainly not a farm worker, the young man informed them.

The cops immediately called in a chopper, which thudded over the canyons all the way from Highway 10 to the Salton Sea before giving up. Everyone figured that the bald smuggler had probably hitched a ride moments after he'd started out on foot.

Lynn followed the Range Rover to the county park, where to his surprise, Clive Devon got out with a shopping bag, spread a blanket and laid out a little picnic on the desert floor for man, woman and dog. Lynn made an approach on foot and lay flat on his belly, watching from behind a clump of sage. He used his elbows as a tripod to steady the binoculars and was able to see that the woman was a young Latina, probably in her early twenties, and the brown dog knew Clive Devon *very* well. The animal was jumping all over him and cuddling up to him, being fed by hand from the picnic bag. Lynn Cutter had gotten a cramp in his neck and had mighty sore knees by the time the happy picnickers picked up their litter and got back inside the Range Rover.

Nelson Hareem returned to the station to have a chat with his sergeant.

"Sarge," he said, "have you heard that the hot car from yesterday, the one the smuggler was driving, got wiped out near the Salton Sea?"

"Yes, Nelson," the sergeant sighed. "Calexico's only eighty miles from there, and you can spit on Mexicali from Calexico, so I'd say the guy's home free by now. South of the border planning to hire another load-plane."

"But Sarge," Nelson said, "he stayed in the area last night cause he didn't know where he was for sure. He didn't take a chance and drive out on the highway where he might get spotted. He holed up and waited out the night. This guy might do the same thing again. He might *still* be burrowed, waitin for an absolutely safe way to Palm Springs."

"How do you know he's going to Palm Springs?"

Nelson didn't want the boss to know he'd been out of town interrogating the injured *campesino*, so he said, "Well, I'm jist guessin. He's not some lettuce picker. And he's prob'ly packin a bag full a dope and waitin out the daylight so he can take his drugs to Palm Springs."

"That's pure speculation, Nelson," his sergeant said.

"Sarge, I been thinkin, maybe if it's quiet this afternoon you might let me go back down around Box Canyon and . . ."

"Stay in your own backyard, Nelson," the sergeant said warily. "You could fuck up a one-car funeral. Several years ago a guy like you brought down a president. It was called Watergate. The guy was a hotdog of a loose cannon named G. Gordon Liddy, ever heard of him?"

"Sure!" Nelson said. "My hero. He went to the joint but still he didn't rat off nobody. I named one a my goldfish Liddy. The other one I named Ollie after Colonel Oliver North."

"Why doesn't his choice of role models surprise me?" the sergeant said to nobody.

After a pause, Nelson said, "I guess you're right. He's back in Mexico by now. I'll forget all about it and go back out on patrol."

The sergeant made a note to check up on the carrot-top cop who the lieutenant said was more dangerous than body fluid in a whorehouse, and about as controllable as a feral cat. But the sergeant got totally distracted when his wife called to announce that her Tupperware hostess had gotten the flu and the shindig was being moved to their own house.

The sergeant had to run to the store and buy some onion dip and Fritos while Nelson Hareem went rocketing down the highway toward the vicinity of Painted Canyon.

Lynn Cutter had left all the fancy stuff in the trunk of his car: Breda Burrows' commercial-grade video camera with the twelve-to-one zoom and her 35 mm for still photos. It was all useless on this caper. He'd draped the binocular strap around his neck because it was about all he could manage if he was going to tail Clive Devon and a woman and a dog into the desert.

The Range Rover had kicked up dust on the road leading into Painted Canyon, helping to obscure Lynn's Rambler, but he thought he was going to have to abandon the tail when they got close to the canyon itself. He was lucky. There happened to be a van full of kids also driving into the canyon, so he was able to drop in behind them. Also, there were some nature lovers in a big Winnebago RV, setting up day camp farther down on the road that penetrated the twisting canyon walls.

A few other nature lovers had found a few early specimens

of dune primrose and were photographing the delicate white blossoms. Three kids of college age were hiking alongside the mouth of the canyon, gingerly examining the joints of a jumping cholla cactus whose nearly invisible barbs can penetrate flesh like sewing needles, and yet provide a nesting place for cactus wrens. The Range Rover stopped two hundred yards ahead, and Lynn parked beside the larger group of ecos who'd fanned out near the canyon mouth. His car didn't look particularly conspicuous next to theirs.

The Painted Canyon cliff face looked as though a huge can of watercolor paint had spilled over it. Burgundy hill formations abutted persimmon hills, next to chocolate hills, next to sandalwood hills. There were clumps of puffy blue-gray smoke trees on the desert floor, and the clean dry desert was in his nostrils and in his mouth as he panted to keep up with the hikers. His goddamn knees were killing him! He stopped, unlaced his shoes, and dumped sand.

Lynn was startled by a roadrunner scampering past with topknot trailing. The bird seemed to be slowed by a full tummy, perhaps from attacking and consuming a sidewinder. Lynn could never make much of a case for the rattlers.

Once when he'd been part of a team of cops looking for the remains of a dope dealer who'd welshed on a deal with the wrong buyer, he had occasion to roam the canyons of south Palm Springs where he'd encountered a gunnysack hanging from a green-barked paloverde tree. Lynn had been about to open the sack when an old desert rat appeared from nowhere yelling at Lynn to keep his damn hands off his goods. The sack, Lynn later discovered, contained a dozen speckled rattlers! The desert rat told him that he expected to get pretty nice bucks when he sold the snakes to makers of antivenin.

In twenty minutes, Clive Devon, along with the young woman and the dog, hiked into a narrow canyon where ancient earthquakes, followed by centuries of erosion, had honeycombed the Cenozoic cliffs into tormented ghostly shapes. Furrows and chiseled gashes in the rock added ominous shade. Even the early spring flora contributed to the spookiness of that shadow-shrouded canyon. The crooked fingers of the ocotillo plant writhed spidery in the wind that moaned ceaselessly, echoing off the canyon walls.

Lynn crouched behind a dune, next to a beaver tail cactus that would soon have a lovely magenta blossom guarded by punishing spines. The sand was blowing in Lynn's face and his sunglasses weren't keeping all of it out of his eyes. He wiped his face on his shoulder.

When he looked up through the binoculars, he saw that the picnickers were standing beside an ironwood tree. The dog wagged its tail but didn't approach a man who stood on the other side of the tree. The girl stayed a few steps back with the dog, but Clive Devon advanced and spoke to the man for several minutes. They all turned then and began moseying back the way they'd come, back in the direction of Lynn Cutter.

And the man came *with* them, back to the Range Rover, while Lynn had to retreat to his Rambler. The man wore a baseball cap and a dark windbreaker, so Lynn thought he might be the same man he'd seen at the café buying a newspaper. The man was now carrying a red bag.

—6—

By the time the Range Rover was returning to the café by the Salton Sea, the wrecked Ford was long gone, and the half-hearted search for a bald hitchhiker had petered out. Because the bald man had asked directions to Palm Springs the detectives had alerted the other police agencies in the valley, even though they figured the guy was headed home to Mexico.

Detectives at the sheriff's department had little or nothing to go on as far as the bald man was concerned, except for a bit supplied by the injured *campesinos*, who said that the man did indeed have a drooping Zapata moustache and was younger than the cops had first assumed from his hairless pate.

Both injured farm workers said that the man had only spoken a few words in Spanish and could've been from any-where. But the words he had spoken were "well said," by which they meant articulate and authoritative. And that he'd looked like a man who, unlike themselves, was used to *giving* orders.

At the café by the Salton Sea was the rusty Plymouth belonging to the young woman with long hair. Lynn Cutter was afraid to try driving past to get her license number. He decided to park his Rambler on the Mecca end of the highway, and watch them through binoculars. The smell of red tide was blowing in his direction, and from a distance the polluted water looked like it had a crust you could walk on.

He couldn't understand about the guy with the baseball cap. Lynn had assumed that he must have a disabled car on the canyon road and had simply needed a lift to a telephone, yet he hadn't left the Range Rover.

Before saying goodbye to the woman, Clive Devon knelt down beside the rusty Plymouth and hugged the brown dog. Then he said something to the young woman and she put the reluctant dog into the backseat of her Plymouth. Lynn wondered if Clive Devon and the young woman would've shown more affection if they'd been alone. And he wished he could've gotten the young woman's license number.

Then, to his surprise, the guy with the baseball cap climbed into the passenger seat of the Range Rover. In a moment, they'd be coming his way on the open road, and Lynn found himself in the position that every one-car surveillance driver hates: He was being followed by his quarry. The Rambler groaned when he stepped on the gas and made a fast U-turn.

Lynn stayed a hundred yards in front, driving by rearview mirror. He didn't get to drop behind Clive Devon until he was in the town of Thermal, finding a safe place to make a turn and parallel the Range Rover. Once the Range Rover had passed through the city of Coachella and was entering Indio, there was plenty of traffic and the surveillance got easy again.

Lynn kept expecting Clive Devon to pull over and drop off his passenger, but he did not. He drove at a leisurely speed out of Indio, past Indian Wells Country Club, where part of the Bob Hope Classic was being played, and through Rancho Mirage, which called itself the "home of presidents." That meant home of Gerald Ford, who was a member of every country club in the desert for free, because of a freak accident of history, without which he'd be beaning folks at the Grand Rapids muni-course. They never called the place "home of vice-presidents," though Spiro Agnew lived in exile there.

Then the Range Rover was out of Rancho Mirage, cruising through Cathedral City, finally entering Palm Springs, and Lynn still couldn't figure out what the hell was going on. Why hadn't he dropped his passenger long before now? Clive Devon didn't unload the guy until he neared downtown.

Lynn saw the guy with the red bag go to a GTE phone stand at a gas station across from the Alan Ladd hardware store, and Lynn figured maybe he was just a tourist hoping to buy an old movie poster from *Shane* or *The Great Gatsby* at the Alan Ladd store. But what the hell had he been doing on foot out there in the canyon?

For a second or two, Lynn was almost curious enough to turn around and tail *that* guy. But he stayed with Clive Devon, per instructions of his temporary boss, Breda Burrows.

His heart was crashing against his breastbone. He was suddenly *very* frightened, now that he was standing alone on a busy street in Palm Springs, California. He was dripping sweat, and was about to remove his baseball cap to wipe it off when he caught himself just in time. They were looking for a bald man, so he had to wear a hat for the rest of his time in this city.

He ran across Indian Avenue, realizing halfway that he should have gone to the intersection, to a crosswalk. He wasn't at home now. He'd have to be very much aware of traffic laws.

Having come this far it would be a tragedy to be caught because he'd failed to cross a street at the right spot.

He went to the phone stand, keeping his red flight bag pressed against his chest, wanting to get rid of it as soon as possible. He wished he had any color other than high-visibility red, but he couldn't have anticipated the policeman bursting into the rest room like that.

He'd read the morning news account, in which the policeman said he'd only entered the rest room to relieve himself, that he probably wouldn't have paid any attention to the other man inside. Easy to say now, but what does a policeman in the States do when he sees a man of the Third World get off a private plane and carry a bag to a rest room? Except that the policeman claimed he wasn't even aware of the private plane having landed with engine trouble on its way to who-knew-where.

He leafed through the yellow pages at the telephone stand while the unplanned events of the previous day blazed through his mind. It was almost impossible to read in English and think in his own language, so he put the phone book on the tray, telling himself to be calm. He'd simply panicked yesterday, and now he had to deal with the unexpected turn. He was a fugitive and that was a fact.

The fugitive found what he wanted on page 571 of the Palm Springs yellow pages. He tore the page from the phone book, folded it, and put it into his jacket pocket. Then he leafed through more pages until he found the listing for used car sales. He took change from his pocket, then cursed. They were the coins he'd been given in the cantina in Mexicali, after he'd received his forged documents. Useless. He had to get some U.S. coins to make calls.

The fugitive left the coins on the tray and walked toward the gas station just as a Palm Springs police car cruised by. The fugitive ducked behind the gas station until the car had passed, then thought he'd better get into a shop immediately and buy some clothes. He removed a package of one thousand U.S. dollars from the red flight bag. He wished he'd brought a change of clothes for an emergency such as this, but it had been decided by the others that he'd buy his clothing in Palm Springs. They had wanted him to look as much as possible like a tourist.

He chose to head toward the mountain, and walked north on Belardo Road in the direction of downtown, avoiding both Indian Avenue and Palm Canyon Drive, which he knew from his map and briefing to be busy thoroughfares. He was ready to leap from the pavement at the first sign of a police car.

Thinking of the police made him regret kicking the policeman so hard. As to the blow that put the man down, reflexes did that. Danger was there, the adversary was identified, and he had put down the adversary just the way he'd been taught. The only deliberate thing was the stomach kick to keep him down long enough to escape. The fugitive was glad that the policeman had not been badly hurt. There was no point in hurting anyone, except for the one he had come here to find.

When he saw Clive Devon turn into his street in Las Palmas, Lynn Cutter broke off the surveillance and sped back toward the Alan Ladd building, his curiosity killing him. But the guy with the baseball cap was no longer at the phone stand. Lynn got out of his car and went to the phone, looking for what, he didn't know, perhaps a phone number scribbled on the writing tray.

There were no numbers and no scraps of paper on the tray, but there were four coins that somebody had left. Three were Mexican, the fourth a ten-peseta Spanish coin. Lynn examined that one just to be sure it was Spanish.

Not knowing why, Lynn put the coins into his pocket and walked toward the Alan Ladd hardware store. He looked inside but the man was not among the customers wandering around. He couldn't afford to waste any more time, so he returned to his Rambler, sped to Clive Devon's house in Las Palmas and parked on the next block. Then he strolled past the Devon house, stopping to peer through the oleander. He was relieved to see that the Range Rover was in the driveway next to Rhonda Devon's silver Mercedes 560SEC.

When Lynn was finally back in his own car, massaging his aching knees, he began truly regretting that he hadn't broken off the surveillance at the Salton Sea and followed the young woman. He was even sorrier he hadn't indulged his whim and stayed with the guy in the baseball cap.

The sun was still high, white as bone, and hot, but the sky was streaked with a pearly hint of sunset. Lynn leaned back and closed his eyes. At six o'clock he was startled by a familiar voice. It was Breda Burrows, who had parked behind and walked up on him.

"Damn!" he said, disoriented. "You scared me!"

"Next time I'll wear a cowbell," she said with that mean little smile. "What happened today? And don't bother with a description of your wet dream."

She got in his car on the passenger side.

"I wasn't asleep."

"Okay, you always snore on stakeouts. So what happened today?"

God, the woman had *such* an irritating grin! Lynn said, "This guy Devon's gonna be harder to trace than the Basque language. How much did you say you were making for this job?"

"Never mind that," Breda said. "What happened today?"

Lynn was stalling while he pulled himself together, trying to sneak a peek at his watch, stunned to see it was nearly 6:00 P.M.! All that running and skulking like a goddamn coyote had obviously drained him, except that coyotes had sense enough to hole up in the daytime.

"The guy has a friend," Lynn finally began.

"What kind of friend?"

"A young woman."

"I'll be damned. Who is she?"

"I don't know," Lynn said. Then, "Can we drive some-where and talk? Clive Devon's not going anywhere." He couldn't admit to Breda that he'd been so out cold he didn't know if Clive Devon was at home or surfing in Malibu.

"We better hang around here this evening," Breda said. "Mrs. Devon said she might go home to L.A. today. If she's gone he might not stay home."

"Wait here," Lynn said.

He jumped out of the car and did a very painful jog on water-filled knees to the Devon property. Peeking through the oleander he saw both the silver Mercedes and the black Range Rover. Pausing a moment, he also saw a slender woman in lounging pajamas walk past a window with a drink in her hand. Then he jogged even more slowly back to his Rambler.

"She's there having a drink," he told Breda. "And she's wearing her Frederick's of Hollywood silkies for beddy-bye. With that drink in her hand she ain't going to L.A. till to-morrow."

"Okay," Breda said. "Let's go back to the office. I want to hear *all* about today."

"The Furnace Room?" he said hopefully. "You can buy me a drink."

"Not The Furnace Room," she said. "I sat in chicken gravy last time. Do they ever clean that dump?"

"Couldn't a been chicken," Lynn said. "Wilfred doesn't serve it. Was it sorta sweatsocks gray? I think I know what Wilfred calls it but I dunno what's in it."

In ten minutes they were seated in the bar of a French restaurant with huge tapestries on the walls, where sauces were identifiable by name and ingredients, not by color. It was a very expensive, quite lovely restaurant that Lynn had never entered in the twelve years he'd lived in Palm Springs. When the valet had taken their cars Breda had to assure Lynn that she'd take care of the tips.

They sat at the bar and were served by a Belgian in formal attire. One wall of the barroom was lined with low plush banquettes, and the place was bustling with well-heeled drinkers. Lynn doubted that the management needed to reduce prices at happy hour. He figured that when people drank from crystal tumblers and goblets they weren't worrying about price.

Most of the chic older women were drinking white wine, of course, and Lynn was surprised when, after he ordered Chivas, Breda said, "Two."

"I'm trying to learn to drink like a P.I.," she explained. "I never did learn to drink like a cop, and all my male partners were *so* disappointed in me."

Lynn took a couple of big hits of Scotch, showed her a yum-yum smile, then said, "Okay, here's how *my* day went. First I followed him down to the Salton Sea. Ever been there?"

"Not on business," she said. "I've done a few bike rides around there. What was he up to?"

"Met his squeeze," Lynn said. "They went for a picnic out near Painted Canyon. It was touching. She even brought her doggie along."

"Did they do anything besides picnic?"

"He didn't spread anything on the blanket except maybe peanut butter," Lynn said. "And he fed her doggie from his very own sandwich. It was a domestic scene if ever I saw one. After they were through they went for a hike in Painted Canyon."

Lynn hesitated, finished the drink, and nodded to the bartender for another. Breda noted that the nervy bastard didn't bother to ask if she'd pop for one more.

After he got his fresh drink, Lynn said, "Only thing is, I wasn't able to get the babe's license number."

"Shit!" she said. "Why not?"

"Hey, I was lucky he didn't make me! It's open country

out there. I got enough sand in my shoes to toilet train a thousand cats!"

"Okay, but do you know where she lives?"

"I didn't follow her. You said to stay with his car. He drove her back to the café and then went home. But there was a weird part."

"What?"

"He wasn't alone. He picked up a guy in Painted Canyon. Devon and the guy drove back to Palm Springs together. He dropped him down by Indian and Ramon Road. Weird."

"What'd the guy look like?"

"Dark, maybe Mexican. Husky. Wore a baseball cap and a windbreaker."

"I wish you'd followed the woman."

"You told me to stay with Devon."

"I know."

"I wish I'da followed the guy with the baseball cap."

"Why?"

"It bugs me. Who *was* he?"

"Some guy that needed a lift."

"But all the way to Palm Springs?"

"Maybe he lives in Palm Springs."

"Then how'd he get to Painted Canyon?"

"Does the Sun Bus run down there? What difference does it make?"

"I don't like third parties barging in on a nice clean soap opera is all."

"I just wish you'd followed the woman."

"You said that. How about buying me another drink?"

Breda pushed her tumbler of Chivas toward him. "Here, drink mine," she said with a barely concealed sneer.

And then her jaw muscles tightened because the son of a bitch turned the lipstick mark the other way before he drank!

"Okay," he said, "next time I'm using my own judgment.

If Clive Devon starts picking up mysterious people and I think they oughtta be followed then I'll follow em."

"I assumed you'd use your own judgment. You've been a cop long enough. By the way, how long *have* you been on the job?"

"Thirteen years in this town. Six years before that with San Diego P.D. I came to the desert when I hurt my knee and started getting problems from the dampness down there. Now both my knees're so wrecked I could live in Greenland, it wouldn't make no difference."

"When's your pension coming through?"

"Hopefully this month," he said. "That's why I don't want anybody at the department or anywhere else to know I'm running around the desert in places a bighorn wouldn't go. The great giver-of-pensions might have second thoughts about my disability."

"Going to get a P.I. license after the pension's in the bag?"

"Why not?" he said. "Anybody can from what I see."

"How sensitive you are."

"I wasn't referring to you."

"Of course you weren't."

"I don't insult people when they're buying the drinks. Not on purpose."

"I've gotta make a call," she said, getting up, and he watched her walk toward the restroom, admiring those cyclist's calves. He *loved* babes who wore tailored jackets and skirts, with buffed-up calves!

After rooting inside her purse, she found her phone file jammed under her holstered two-inch revolver. Everyone said that after she'd been retired a few months she'd stop carrying a gun. Most P.I.'s wouldn't carry one even if, like Breda, they were retired from police work on a service pension and could do so anywhere in the state. P.I.'s who weren't retired from police work seldom even bothered to try for a gun permit. But

Breda was used to having a gun handy, and hadn't broken the habit as yet.

Rhonda Devon had assured her that her private line was safe and that Clive Devon seldom answered it. If he did he wouldn't think anything of a woman asking for his wife. It was Rhonda Devon who picked it up on the second ring.

"Mrs. Devon?"

"Yes."

"It's Breda Burrows."

"Yes."

"Can you talk?"

"Not really. We're having early dinner."

"I want you to ask your husband where he went today. Don't press him, but try to get a few details about how his day went and if he was alone."

"Why?"

"He went on a picnic with a young woman, a woman with long black hair, maybe Mexican. She has a big brown dog and drives a rusty old Plymouth. Do you know anyone fitting that description?"

"No."

"Does it surprise you?"

"Very much."

"Can you talk to him and phone me?"

"We can get together."

"Soon?"

"Yes."

When Breda told Rhonda Devon where she was, her client said, "I can be over in fifteen minutes, Margie. But don't show me *too* many vacation pictures, okay?"

By the time Breda had returned to the bar, Lynn Cutter was leaning on the baby grand, talking to an attractive female piano player who had just come to work and was warming up with a Cole Porter medley.

The piano player was blond like Rhonda Devon, but not

a real blonde. She wore slinky black, and the way she smiled at Lynn made Breda take a closer look at him. He really wasn't a bad-looking guy if only he could get that smart-mouthing under control, and damn it, he *did* have nice buns. Suddenly Breda realized that she hadn't been to bed with a man since she'd left L.A.!

Lynn returned to the bar after Breda sat down. He held his empty glass in his hand with a wistful look.

"*One* more," Breda said. "We're meeting Rhonda Devon."

"Yeah? Where?"

"Here."

"All right! That glimpse through the oleander was interesting."

"Try to maintain," Breda said. "We don't fraternize with clients."

As the bartender set the Chivas in front of Lynn, Breda decided she ought to deduct his drinks from any fee she owed him. Then he'd owe *her* money before the week was out.

Rhonda Devon was thirty minutes and two drinks late, as far as Lynn was concerned. The reason was understandable. She looked like Rodeo Drive, before going shopping at Chanel Boutique, or after lunch at The Bistro Garden. Breda recognized the Liz Claiborne persimmon leather handbag, the cheapest item on her person. Breda could only wonder where she'd bought the persimmon and black velvet jacket with all those pleats. And her black suede pumps probably cost more than Breda's entire outfit.

And yet, the soft dim bar light had an effect not intended. Rhonda Devon looked sleeker but *older* than she had when Breda Burrows had seen her in her living room in the late afternoon twilight. Breda was certain that Rhonda Devon was several years older than she'd admitted.

It was easy to see that Lynn wasn't thinking about calendars. He was looking at money. Ogling, actually. Breda couldn't wait to be rid of this guy.

She said, "Mrs. Devon, this is Lynn Cutter. He's helping me with your problem."

"I thought you worked alone," Rhonda Devon said, not offering her hand to Lynn. She wore an eighteen-karat canary diamond on her left hand. It looked like a popcorn kernel.

"Shall we sit over here?" Breda indicated a banquette in the corner, far enough from the piano.

"Vodka martini," Rhonda Devon said to Lynn, the way she'd say it to a waiter. "Dry, a twist, no olive."

While Breda and Rhonda Devon got settled at the low banquette Lynn ordered the martini, and another Scotch for himself. Then he sat opposite the two women, across a low enameled cocktail table. Rhonda Devon was smoking and looked not at him but at the martini he'd fetched.

Breda noticed. *Another* rummy, she thought.

Speaking deliberately, having poured too much down on an empty stomach, Lynn described in detail the events of his first day of surveillance. When he'd finished, Rhonda Devon was not quite as contained as when she'd walked into the bar.

Breda detected a perceptible quiver when Rhonda Devon said, "This is unbelievable. I can't imagine it. A young Mexican woman?"

"Probably Mexican," Lynn said. "She was dark."

"Why would he want to have a baby with a *Mexican* woman?" she asked her martini.

"Why not?" Lynn said. "I wouldn't mind. For starters there's Vikki Carr and Linda Ronstadt. Then there's Millie Valdez, she owns half of a Toyota dealership down in Indio. And there's . . ."

Vowing to cut off his booze, Breda interrupted him. "How about the rusty old Plymouth, Mrs. Devon? Is it familiar?"

"The car, the woman, the dog—none of it means anything to me."

"How about the guy your husband picked up in Painted

Canyon?" Lynn asked. "Baseball cap. Husky. Late thirties maybe. Probably another Latino. How about him?"

"I can't understand that either," Rhonda Devon said, and now Breda thought that both her voice and her chin quivered. "The man must've needed a ride. My husband would pick up *any* stray. He's always been that way. When we're in Los Angeles he gives money to every beggar on the street." Then she said angrily: "He's a child, really. He never had to work for anything in his whole life. He doesn't understand how . . . vile people are. I don't understand what he's doing!"

"He's a man of a certain age," Breda said. "This sort of thing happens, Mrs. Devon."

"But to want a baby when he can't have sex. And with a . . ." Rhonda Devon realized that she'd raised her voice, and covered her discomfort by taking a sip of the martini. Then another. Her hand trembled when she smoked.

"How far do you want us to go, Mrs. Devon?" Breda asked, with more compassion in her voice than Lynn thought she owned.

"I have to know it all now," Rhonda Devon said.

"You're still not ready to confront him and just *ask*?"

"No. This is his affair . . . I guess that's an apt word, isn't it? And . . . he's never questioned me about anything in all our years of marriage."

"Were you married before?" Lynn asked.

"Yes," she said. "Twice."

"And was he?"

"No," she said. "I was his first and only love. He always *said*."

Lynn glanced at Breda and said, "When Breda phoned you a little while ago and asked you to talk to your husband, did you?"

"Yes, I asked him very casually about his day, after I'd told him all about my rotten day on the golf course."

"And did he tell you he went hiking?"

"Yes," she said, "but not in Painted Canyon. He said he'd driven down to the Indian reservation and hiked in Andreas Canyon. He said it was wonderful because there were no tourists. He said it was spectacular looking at cottonwoods and sycamore and wild tamarack. He said the water in the creek was especially cold . . . and sweet."

—7—

$\mathbf{B}$efore Rhonda Devon left the French restaurant, Breda asked her a few more questions about the household and got a list of all service people from the maid to the pool cleaner. After finishing her drink Rhonda Devon said good night, adding that she now wanted progress in a hurry.

Breda's plan for the next day was simply for Lynn to do a reprise. She had a detailed report she had to write for a defense attorney, and had already decided to advise the lawyer to plead the guilty bastard guilty. Breda hated to admit how much she needed Lynn's assistance.

She tipped the valet parking boy for both her car and Lynn's, and her parting shot to him was, "Go straight home for a change. Get a good night's sleep and maybe you can stay awake on a stakeout."

After giving her one of the most insincere smiles Palm Springs had seen since Tammy Faye Bakker sold her house, Lynn

Cutter did what she figured he'd do: He drove straight to The Furnace Room.

By the time Lynn entered the saloon it looked like someone had tossed a smoke grenade. Everybody was always bitching about the lousy air conditioning, but this night was the worst. Lynn took a few gulps of outside oxygen and practiced shallow breathing.

Wilfred Plimsoll, wearing a peacock-blue Ascot, spotted Lynn when he bellied up to the bar. The old actor poured him a double Scotch, then went back to a thespian argument with a pair of drunks who had "conventioneer" written all over them.

Wilfred bellowed, "De Niro! Pacino! Only the *serious* artists work on the boards!"

One of the locals, a retired dentist with a mouse-gray hairpiece going green around the sideburns, said, "Like Magic Johnson, Wilfred?"

Wilfred moaned painfully. "Not *those* boards! I'm not talking slam dunks! The boards! The stage! Where the bard speaks!"

"Movies're where it's at today," one of the conventioneers insisted.

"You oughtta simmer down, Wilfred," the dentist advised. "I've seen blood clots with better color."

"The age of enlightenment this isn't!" Wilfred cried. "Don't you people understand? The first cousin of today's cinema is the comic book!"

Lynn noticed that Wilfred had done some work on lawyers that day. A new sign over the cash register was headed, "Nature Guide to the Desert."

And below that, "Endangered species: Fringe-toed Lizard, Bighorn Sheep, Honest Lawyer (If the latter is ever spotted, do not attempt to feed ordinary lawyer bait: i.e., greenbacks, cocaine, hookers, deep-pocket defendants, adolescent boys.)"

Wilfred Plimsoll had assumed his stubborn Franklin Roosevelt pose. The cigarette holder danced as his jaw jutted presidentially.

The booziest conventioneer turned to Lynn Cutter. "Did he really have a part in *Mildred Pierce*? I just *loved* Joan Crawford."

"Yeah, but he's a real Shakespearean," Lynn said. "Only guy west a Buckingham Palace that can blow out a candle saying why or when or whoopee cushion."

The dentist, who had sonar like a bat when a free drink was in the offing, sidled up and said, "Wilfred's been in lots of movies. I saw him standing behind Cyd Charisse in that picture with Fred Astaire. Cyd and Tony Martin come to town a lot. I did a root canal on her maid's sister. Wanna hear about it?"

Another drunken tourist turned to Lynn and said, "Hey, buddy, where's the action in this town? And I don't mean these old actresses. Best-looking actress I seen so far coulda played the lizard in *Night of the Iguana*. Any broads around here young enough their vaginal walls ain't collapsed?"

"Hey, don't sell The Furnace Room short," Lynn said. "It's a hotbed of intrigue. Only reason it's so tame tonight is the temperature dropped five degrees. When it's cool outside these pensioners get sorta quiet. When it heats up this whole joint goes on a rampage. Sorta like a yeast infection."

Wilfred Plimsoll, who'd won fifty bucks betting on the L.A. Kings that evening, aimed his cigarette holder at the wall clock, and with a sidelong glance at Lynn's glass poured half a refill saying, "On the house, my boy."

"Armageddon comes to Palm Springs!" Lynn said. "Must be the end a the world!"

"Not so loud!" Wilfred said in a stage whisper.

"Are you Detective Lynn Cutter," asked a boyish tenor behind him. The speaker was obscured by cigar smoke and by two pensioners, one of them so loaded his hearing aid was in backwards. The deaf guy kept saying, "Speak up! Speak up!" to everybody.

"Who wants to know?" Lynn asked the boy tenor, trying to nudge the deaf pensioner aside.

The old guy yelled, "Can't ya say excuse me?"

"Excuse me," Lynn said.

"Speak up, goddamnit!" the pensioner hollered at him.

Lynn leaned toward the old guy's ear and said, "Either turn your hearing aid around or lemme hang on to it and you do the lindy hop or the hokey pokey. One spin'll set it right, okay?"

"What? Can't you speak up?" the old geezer yelled.

Lynn finally got a good look at the owner of the tenor voice. He was a short kid with red hair, big blue eyes and a Bugs Bunny grin. He wore jeans, red lizard cowboy boots and an L.A. Raiders sweatshirt. "Are you Detective Lynn Cutter?" the young man repeated.

"Yeah, who're you?"

"My name's Nelson Hareem," he said, showing Lynn his police I.D. card "I work at . . ."

"You the one they call Dirty Hareem?"

Nelson sighed, hung his head a bit and nodded. "Uh huh."

"AKA Half-Nelson?"

"Uh huh."

"You're famous!" Lynn said. "I heard about you from some cops in San Berdoo. I didn't know you were working out here in the desert."

"One more famous episode and I'll be workin a beat in a *different* desert, that's what they told me."

"Sahara?"

"Uh huh. Everybody jist wants me to handle NRC calls and go home at shift change."

"What're NRC calls?"

"Nobody really cares."

"Try Somalia. They kill their whole police force every Friday or so. Lots a openings for an ambitious lad."

After shaking hands with the police celebrity, Lynn said, "My favorite Dirty Hareem story was when you accidentally turned your Holstein into a convertible with your gauge. I never actually met anyone that cranked one off through his own roof."

"Can I talk to you for a minute?" Nelson asked.

"Sure," Lynn said, noticing that the kid's beer glass was empty. "Wilfred, a flagon on my tab."

When Nelson got his fresh beer they weaved through the crowded barroom to the same corner table where Lynn and Breda had sat. There was an old woman from the Seniors Center sitting there who hadn't left since happy hour. She was bombed, and had returned to 1944, singing "We'll Meet Again," like Vera Lynn.

Ignoring the old doll, who didn't even know they'd joined her private party, Lynn said, "What's up, Nelson? How'd you find me?"

"I called Palm Springs P.D. after I couldn't find you at your DMV address in Cathedral City."

"Yeah, I had to move from Cathedral City after my second divorce. Everybody thinks a single guy in Cat City *has* to be gay, and I can never remember which ear to wear my gold stud in. Is it left for gay and right for straight, or vice versa?"

Nelson Hareem actually squinted through the smoke to see if Lynn had a pierced ear, making Lynn realize that all the things they said about this goofy kid were probably true.

"Anyways," Nelson said, "the new owner at your old house is the one told me you're a Palm Springs police detective."

"So you went to the P.D.?"

"Yeah, and a detective told me you're on medical leave and nobody knows where you live cause you house-sit for rich people, but everyone knows where to find you after nine o'clock."

"Morning or night?"

"Huh?"

"Never mind. So you found me, Nelson. Why're you running my license plate. Did I get a parking ticket, or what?"

"Well, sir, I'm sorta workin on somethin . . . unofficially."

"Call me Lynn. I'm younger'n I look. Everybody around here is."

"Well, Lynn, I wouldn't like you to tell nobody about this,

but I'm workin on a deal on my own time, you might say. It's about the ADW where the smuggler beat up the deputy down at the airport and stole two vehicles?"

"Haven't heard about any smuggler," Lynn said, wondering how the hell his own glass got so empty so fast. He looked suspiciously at the nearly comatose old babe.

"You ain't heard? It was all over the local TV news last night."

"Tell you the truth, I only watch TV when George Bush is giving a speech. I stood real close to the guy once at Palm Springs Airport, and I came to love the suspense of whether he can utter two sentences with the grammar and syntax right."

"It was in the paper this mornin. Even the *L.A. Times.*"

"Got up too early to read the paper. So tell me why you ran me to ground."

"Cause you were down in Painted Canyon today. Unless you sold or loaned somebody your Nash Rambler."

"You're right, I *was* down there. How'd you know?"

"I was there too. See, the guy I'm . . . the guy the sheriff's department's lookin for was hangin around there, so I was cruisin the canyons most a the day. I wrote down every license number of every parked car I saw, includin yours. Then I had to go back to my beat to handle a couple calls. When I went to Painted Canyon again your car was gone. A bunch a people in a Winnebago said they saw a guy park the Rambler and go for a hike. Musta been you, right? I ran your license number and got your old address in Cathedral City."

"You sure went to a lotta trouble, Nelson," Lynn said.

"Cause the people in the Winnebago told me they also saw a man and woman in a Range Rover go into Painted Canyon and drive back out with a *second* man! When they told me that, I drove all around the canyon but there's no abandoned car in there. So to me it meant the Range Rover picked somebody up. Unless it was you he picked up?"

Lynn Cutter gawked at the carrot-top cop like he'd just

found Jimmy Hoffa's pinkie ring in Ivana Trump's hair, while the old babe at their table segued into "Embraceable You," like Helen O'Connell.

"Nah, couldn't be," Lynn said, shaking his head. "Couldn't be."

"What?"

"What's the guy look like? The smuggler from the airport?"

"Mexican. Medium height, husky build, bald. Maybe thirty-five to forty."

"Husky build?"

And then the young cop started getting *very* excited. "You saw him, sir! I mean Lynn! You saw him!"

"Chill out, Nelson. I saw a husky Latino, yeah. He wore a blue baseball cap so I don't know if he was bald. It coulda been a Dodgers cap, so maybe it was just Fernando Valenzuela out there prospecting for gold."

"It *was* him!" Nelson cried. "I know it was him!"

Suddenly, the old doll emerged from her stupor and yelled, "Garçon!" at Wilfred Plimsoll, after which she lapsed into a chorus of "I'll Be Seeing You."

"We don't know that, Nelson," Lynn said. "There could be lots a reasons why the guy I saw was out there on foot."

"The Range Rover," Nelson said. "Do you have any idea who was drivin the Range Rover?"

"None," Lynn Cutter said, avoiding eye contact.

Nelson Hareem was quiet for a moment, then he said, "Lynn, what were *you* doin out there?"

"You're gonna have to read me my rights before you take that approach," Lynn said.

"I'm sorry, Lynn," said Nelson. "It's jist that I got somethin here, I know it. And it's my *chance*."

"Chance for what?"

"To get outta town. I don't wanna work down there where nothin ever happens. I wanna work where there's some lights and action."

"Talk to Wilfred, the owner a this joint. You're describing the movie business except you left out camera between lights and action."

"I wanna work for Palm Springs P.D., Lynn."

"And here I been celebrating for months because I'm leaving Palm Springs P.D."

"Yeah, but I'm still young."

"Go up there and get us a couple drinks, Nelson. Scotch for me. Let this old man gum on this smuggler business for a while."

After the kid had gone, Lynn thought, It couldn't be. Ridiculous. Just a coincidence. Damn, he wished his guy had taken off that baseball cap! By the time Nelson returned with the drinks, Lynn had convinced himself that it absolutely positively couldn't be.

"It *couldn't* be, Nelson," he said. But then, "Was the smuggler wearing a dark windbreaker?"

"Had on a short-sleeved khaki shirt when he kicked the deputy's dick in the dirt."

"Well, my guy had on a dark windbreaker."

"Maybe he had a change a clothes in his flight bag," Nelson said, taking a sip of beer, the foam lying on his fuzzy upper lip.

"Flight bag?"

"Yeah, the smuggler carried a flight bag. We figured it was full a heroin, but maybe he had some clothes in it."

"What color flight bag?" Lynn asked.

"Red," said Nelson Hareem.

During the next thirty-five minutes, Lynn told most of his Clive Devon story and got a complete rundown on the bald smuggler, followed by a sketch of Nelson Hareem's police history, which had brought him to a place where his shoeshine turned viscous by eleven A.M. on summer days. They continued to talk even as they walked out of the saloon while the old doll at their table was singing "It Had To Be You," like Helen Forrest.

"So you see, I'm helping out this retired cop till she gets her business in shape," Lynn said to Nelson while they stood under a desert sky so clear the dipper looked like it might fall on them and shatter into topaz.

"I understand, Lynn," Nelson said.

"I don't want you to say a word about this to anyone. I don't want nobody at Palm Springs P.D. to know I been goat-footing it around the canyons for a P.I. named Breda Burrows. Understand?"

"The guy's a wanted felon. What if he kills somebody or somethin? We'd have to tell the detectives that you traced him to Palm Springs."

"If he surfaces again we can reconsider. For now, what difference does it make if the sheriff's department knows he got this far? He's *gone*."

"What happened when he went to the phone stand down by the Alan Ladd hardware store, Lynn? Think he mighta jotted down a number there?"

In that too many of Lynn's neurons were swimming for their lives in Wilfred's booze, Lynn blurted, "No, I already checked that. Left his pocket change on the phone tray, is all."

That got the young cop stoked. "You found pocket change?"

"Yeah."

"Where is it?"

"I don't know. In my other pants, I guess. Just a few coins, Mexican coins. And one Spanish coin."

"Spanish? You sure?"

"I didn't have my jeweler's loupe handy but it sure looked like a Spanish ten-peseta coin."

"That's really weird. Think he's from Spain?"

"No, I think he's a drug smuggler, same as you think. He

probably flew up from around Mexicali or Tijuana. I went to Tijuana with my first wife one time. It was the world's most expensive weekend in a place that's supposed to be cheap. In one a the saloons a bartender gave me pocket change from three countries. In those border towns you got people coming from everywhere with different kinds a money."

"If only you'd seen the TV news last night!" Nelson said. "You *had* the guy!"

"If it was him."

"The red flight bag, Lynn!"

"Yeah, I know. It *mighta* been him, I admit. He probably went to Palm Springs Airport and booked a flight home."

"Can you forget about it that easy?"

"I already did. I'm going home and I'm going to bed. You do the same, Nelson."

"Good night," said Nelson Hareem. "I'll keep your secret so long as the guy don't surface again and hurt somebody."

"Me, I'm going to bed," Lynn said. "I'm not a real cop anymore."

Lynn Cutter watched Nelson jump in his topless Jeep Wrangler and squeal out into the heavy tourist-season traffic. Then Lynn got into his Rambler, turned south, drove three minutes and parked at a gas station across from the Alan Ladd hardware store. Lynn was staggering just a tad when he walked to the phone stand with his flashlight.

And because the whole world was sneaking up behind him lately he wasn't even surprised when a tenor voice said, "You're *still* a cop, Lynn. You can't fool me."

Then, while Lynn Cutter surrendered to his fate, Nelson Hareem borrowed Lynn's flashlight and started searching for clues.

"People write down numbers anywhere at public phones," Nelson said.

"Please chill out, Nelson," Lynn said. "It's embarrassing enough being out here like this. Only guy that'd hang around a public phone this time a night is either a candidate for AIDS or somebody from the planet Krypton."

"Can I see the coins tomorrow?"

"You ain't gonna lift prints from coins, for chrissake!"

"The guy was seen puttin coins in his mouth."

"What was he doing with coins in his mouth?"

"Diminishes thirst, we were told. He's a desert rat, this guy."

"And what difference would it make, pray tell, if I found those particular coins?"

"They might have old saliva on them. I read where DNA technology can sometimes match up somebody from saliva. See, our eyeball witnesses're really lousy; they'll never ID the guy even if we bring him down."

"That's space-age stuff, Nelson. Match up somebody from degraded saliva on a coin? Jesus! How do we know they were his coins? Anybody coulda left some foreign coins here. You could have all ten fingerprints, it wouldn't mean a thing. He's probably got no record here in the States. He's a foreigner!"

But undeterred, Nelson Hareem put the butt end of the flashlight under his chin and started whipping through the Palm Springs yellow pages with both hands.

Suddenly he cried, "Tits!"

"What?"

"This is absolutely tits! We *got* him!"

"What're you talking about?"

"Look at this!" Nelson said, pointing to the yellow pages.

"I don't see . . ."

"He tore out a motel page! A through C! All we gotta do is find another phone book and check all the motels that begin with A, B and C! There's only thirty or so, I bet."

"How do you know *he* did it?"

"Same way I know he left those coins! I got his scent!"

"Nelson, unless you lift your leg to pee you don't have his scent. And you *don't* know if he left those coins. The fact that he may have left a Spanish coin is irrelevant."

"He's ours!"

"Nelson, when you gaze up at the stars do you get lonely for home?" Lynn wanted to know.

"You can't bail out on me, Lynn!"

"Whaddaya mean?"

"I never worked detectives. You got the experience."

"I'm going home."

"Well, I guess I got no choice. I guess I jist gotta turn all this information over to . . ."

"Nelson, I told you . . . warned you I don't want anybody finding out I'm working for a P.I. Understand?"

"But Lynn, I gotta *do* somethin about this! If I can't tell the sheriff's department then we gotta work it ourselves."

"We gotta . . . Nelson, you're a madman!"

"Get a good night's sleep, Lynn, but first gimme the number at your house-sittin gig. I'll call you tomorrow. And gimme Breda's number."

Lynn Cutter had to go to bed. He had to think. He gave Nelson the phone numbers because he had no choice.

Before Lynn could get into his Rambler, Nelson showed him that daffy grin and said, "If we get him I hope you'll put in a good word for me with your ex-captain. I jist gotta get a lateral transfer to Palm Springs P.D. They got eighty-four officers so there's always somebody retirin or leavin. They *gotta* take me!"

Lynn couldn't remember if his gun was in the trunk, but what good would it do? The Dirty Hareems of this world couldn't be stopped with silver bullets. They just keep going and going and going, with more lives than that Energizer battery and Richard Nixon.

"I gotta go home and mull this over, Nelson," Lynn said wearily. "The guy's a foreigner: husky, bald, resourceful. I wonder if he has a big pink birthmark on his forehead?"

—8—

One slice wheat toast no butter, a small grapefruit juice, a multivitamin, two cups of coffee. Breda hadn't altered that breakfast since she'd moved to the desert. That, coupled with all the bike riding, and measuring red meat portions by their atomic weight, had gotten her back into a size six where she intended to stay.

But she had to remain longer at the breakfast table since moving from Los Angeles. Now she had to read the local paper for potential business information, as well as the L.A. *Times*. The local obituaries were grim. The desert valley had one of the state's highest per capita incidences of AIDS victims. The obituaries would usually begin: "After a long illness . . . And survived by longtime friend . . ."

Being a single woman she often thought about AIDS, but in the months she'd been in the desert it wouldn't have mattered to her personal safety if the whole male population had hepatitis.

Working to get her house and her business established had left Breda little time for men. She'd had drinks with a few, and dinner with a Palm Springs lawyer whom she'd met through another attorney client, though it wasn't actually a date. They just went to the same place after a meeting, and had sat at the same table, and he'd paid. He'd called her several times, but she learned he was married. Breda didn't have time in her life for complications like that.

She finished writing a letter to her daughter, Lizzy, stacked the breakfast dishes in the sink, checked the time and hurried to the bathroom to brush her teeth. A silk jumpsuit, blue to match her eyes, and white flats seemed okay for this day's work. She had a "shopping" job she had to do in the afternoon, if she could find the time.

Shopping to a P.I. meant loss-prevention work. Breda had been hired by a downtown department store to investigate the sales clerks. The store had been having some unexplained losses in the sportswear department, and three clerks were suspected. For over a week Breda had been trying to give two hours a day to the shopping job but hadn't spotted anything unusual.

She hated shopping jobs but hated another job even more, and one of those too was on her calendar. She'd been retained to investigate the bartenders at The Unicorn, a restaurant recently opened on south Palm Canyon Drive. The owner of The Unicorn had hired a new bartender who wore a Rolex and a diamond ring, and this alone had worried the boss, who was sure that one of his bartenders was ripping him off.

Breda told her client that he should be glad that the new bartender had the Rolex and ring because it meant that he'd already stolen the money to buy them from somebody *else*. She told him that if he wanted an absolutely honest deal from a bartender he'd have to make the guy work in a Speedo swimsuit, follow him every time he went to the john, and hire someone from Chicago to search his body cavities at closing time.

Breda decided that she'd give the saloon job to Lynn Cutter and take over the Clive Devon surveillance that morning. She couldn't bear the thought of sitting in a gin mill like a daytime barfly, avoiding the moves of local lotharios so old Clive were moldering.

She drove to Clive Devon's Las Palmas home and found Lynn in his car half a block away drinking coffee. He'd parked in the opposite direction this time so as not to alarm gardeners, maids or other servants who might get curious. This time he spotted her in his rearview mirror before she opened his car door.

Without so much as a good morning, Lynn said, "It's too bad I'm not an Augua Caliente Indian. Just think about it. I could get drunk and raise hell anywhere I want, and keep the law out by claiming I live on *sacred* ground. I could plug the cracks in my walls with five-dollar bills. I could use my spa to barbecue cows in. I could have Kevin Costner speak up for me if anybody tried to throw me in jail, and no one would dare say I was a drunk, or even dumb. They'd say I'm an Indian. I wish I was a Palm Springs Indian. I'd never have to worry about money again."

"What brought all this on?" Breda asked.

"This job you gave me," Lynn said. "I met a guy last night, a little policeman from the south end, they call him Dirty Ha- reem. And he informed me we're in the middle of some kind a smuggling conspiracy. Or at least, Clive Devon might be. And I don't need a thousand scoots bad enough to jeopardize my pension by getting involved in whatever it is."

"Explain, please."

"Have you heard or read anything in the past couple days about some smuggler jumping out of a private plane long enough to do a soccer demonstration on some deputy?"

"Sure. It was on all the local news programs."

"I just gotta start watching something besides *The Simpsons* and *Tag Team Wrestling*. Guess what? The guy Clive Devon

111

picked up in Painted Canyon yesterday? He's the fugitive smuggler they're looking for! I think. Why don't I look for a safer job? Maybe the President of Haiti needs a food taster."

"Are you hung over again, or just nuts?"

"Both, but I'm coming around. I'm gonna go talk to one a those ex-FBI agents that run security for Thrifty Drug Stores. I'd rather be a drug store dick than a P.I.'s helper, cause I'm not as nuts as I was when you found me."

"Are you ready to explain in full?" she asked, with that irritating smirk.

Funny how the little freckle on her lip looked darker today. How come that freckle aroused him, he wondered. "First you'd have to meet Nelson Hareem," he began. "His paternal grandfather came from Beirut, but Nelson's not really a Muslim terrorist or anything. They'd never have him cause he's too fanatical. Here's what he told me. . . ."

Breda Burrows hardly blinked while Lynn Cutter told her the whole story, and why Nelson Hareem was, in effect, forcing him to dick around at motels and hotels from the A to C yellow pages.

When Lynn was finished, Breda sat back and stared toward Clive Devon's house for a few minutes. Then she said, "This is truly nuts."

"Sure it is," Lynn said. "So's Nelson. But he's still capable of turning over all his hot little clues to the sheriff's department. After which somebody would no doubt contact me. After which somebody else would no doubt contact my department. After which . . ."

"Okay, okay, I get it. You're worried about your disability pension, I *get* it!"

"Not at all," he said. "Who needs a pension? I got enough money to last till one o'clock this afternoon if I don't buy that bag a potato chips I been craving."

Breda reached in her purse, removed her wallet, and took

out three twenties. "Here," she said. "For expenses. Doesn't the guy whose house you're sitting have a pantry?"

"Yeah, and I ate everything in it except the cat food, which ain't my brand. How about another couple a these?"

Breda gave him another two twenties and said, "This is an advance against your fee. If you earn the fee."

"If I . . . hey! I already earned something! I'm risking my pension with all this smuggler bullshit!"

"That's *your* problem."

"*My* problem. Yeah, because I took on this job!"

"We had a deal. I didn't plan on some drug dealer entering the picture. I don't think he *did* enter the picture. I think Clive Devon is just a nice man who gave a ride to a guy, and he doesn't know zip about drug smuggling or any other felony or misdemeanor."

"Well I'll stop worrying then. One a these days an earthquake's gonna hit the San Andreas Fault so hard Palm Spring'll just liquefy and turn into quicksand anyway. We'll be all gone like Sodom and Gomorrah. And here I am worrying about starving to death! I *must* be crazy!"

"I'm taking over the surveillance today," Breda said. "Why don't you go talk sense to this cop, Nelson Hareem. Explain to him that this smuggler business can't go anywhere. Make him see."

"He couldn't see with the Hubble Space Telescope. He's got an obsessive-compulsive personality. He's gonna call you today, and if I know Nelson he'll be flying in your airspace and mine till we start doing legwork at motels that begin with A, B and C."

"You can do another job for me since you've got money now," Breda said. "Go to The Unicorn restaurant on south Palm Canyon and watch the two bartenders. Someone's stealing a hundred bucks a shift, or so the owner thinks."

"Do I get extra pay for another job?"

Breda showed him her world-champ sneer and said, "All right, *another* hundred. Meet me at seven o'clock tonight. Clive Devon's always back home before seven in the evening, girl-friend or not."

"Let's meet at The Furnace Room."

"Okay, I'll see you there at seven. Remember, Nelson Ha-reem's your problem. Deal with it."

"My first wife always said that to me," Lynn informed her. "*Deal* with it. You're a lot alike."

Knowing it was probably a mistake, Breda said, "And what was she like? A bossy bitch, I suppose."

"More self-indulgent than a spaghetti western. She liked to make me sweat for hours while she'd decide whether or not to pump a few *more* slugs into my fun zone."

"Do you think I overreacted, sir?" Nelson Hareem asked his police chief when he was called before him at nine o'clock that morning.

"No, I wouldn't think so," the chief told him. "No more than the Chinese in Tiananmen Square, or the Russians in Lith-uania, or the U.S. Cavalry at Wounded Knee."

The chief was sweating Nelson Hareem because of a threat-ened lawsuit from a mortgage banker who'd passed through their little town two weeks earlier in a Porsche 928 while driving from a seminar in Scottsdale to his home in Encino. The mort-gage banker had turned off Highway 10 intending to get one of those tasty date-shakes he'd heard so much about. He'd care-lessly blown past a stop sign without making a complete stop, and quickly found himself lighted up by the whirling gumballs of Nelson Hareem, who happened to be dawdling down the street at a poky seventy miles per hour, the speed limit he or-dinarily reserved for parking lots and residential driveways.

After that, the story was open to interpretation. The mort-gage banker, having contributed heavily to the reelection of one of Southern California's most prominent sheriffs, possessed one of those courtesy badges that the sheriff handed out as a thank you. The mortgage banker had pinned the badge inside his alligator wallet next to his driver's license for just such eventualities as this.

First, the banker had handed his driver's license to Nelson and then he flipped open the wallet. With one of those "You got the loan at *prime!*" banker grins, he'd said, "How far will this go, pal?" referring to the badge.

But Nelson thought that the banker was referring to a fifty-dollar bill, whose corner was clearly protruding from the alligator wallet, thus signifying a bribery attempt. Nelson became totally indignant, incensed, offended and finally *outraged* by the insult.

Nelson said, "I don't know how far it'll go. Let's see!" And he impulsively ripped the wallet from the fat guy's hand and sailed it like an alligator Frisbee over his shoulder into the passing traffic, where it happened to land on the bed of a flatbed truck bound for Phoenix.

Then there was a semidesperate wrestling match out there, with outraged little Nelson Hareem rolling around on the ground with an equally outraged mortgage banker before Nelson managed to get the fat guy hooked up with his hands cuffed behind him and proned out on the ground, and only a few bumps and bruises that had to be treated.

But that wallet was never seen again, and the mortgage banker claimed he had over a thousand bucks in it. The banker got cited for running the stop sign, but was booked into jail for battery on a police officer. The deputy district attorney said that Nelson Hareem might use a tad more patience and better judgment next time he *thinks* he's being offered a bribe.

The morning after Nelson had met Lynn Cutter, his chief said to him, "The guy's lawyer's offered to drop the five-million-dollar lawsuit if we drop the charge of battery on a police officer, along with the vehicle code violation. And the city manager wonders if this might be a bargain for all of us. He also wonders if a daily dose of one thousand milligrams of Thorazine might make you a nondangerous citizen of our community."

Nelson gulped, and his baby blues rolled, and he said, "Chief, if I could get a lateral transfer to another department, say, Palm Springs P.D., would you be willin to recommend me favorably?"

The chief said, "I would tell them you're the finest police officer since Eliot Ness! Since Wyatt Earp, even! Do you think it's possible they might take you?"

"I think I'll have a good chance real soon, sir," Nelson said. "Meantime, could I take about a week off from my compensatory overtime? Startin right now?"

"Are you sure a week of your comp time is enough?" the chief asked, hopefully. "They really want you at Palm Springs? Honest?"

By eleven o'clock that morning, Nelson Hareem was visiting various motels and hotels in and around Palm Springs, beginning with the letter A.

Clive Devon was apparently waiting for his wife to leave for Los Angeles before going out. Breda watched the electric gates roll open at 10:10 that morning as Rhonda Devon's silver Mercedes swung out and drove away between the walls of oleander, plaster and brick that lined both sides of the winding palm-studded street.

Five minutes later, Clive Devon pulled out in the Range Rover and drove to a grocery market five minutes from his house, the kind of market where shallots and saffron are available year round, not to mention truffles so expensive you could bribe a judge with three of them.

Breda waited outside the market for a few minutes then moseyed inside, got a shopping cart and strolled through the aisles. She picked up a few brand-name sundries she could have bought for half the price at her local Sav-On Drug Store. Then she stood in one of the two checkout lines where she could watch Clive Devon from behind.

His groceries were checked by a pretty young Latina with long black hair. Breda watched very closely, but nothing more than a few smiles and pleasantries were passed. Still, she *did* fit the description given by Lynn Cutter. Breda decided to send him in as soon as possible to have a look at this grocery checker.

Clive Devon, with the help of a box boy, loaded his grocery purchases into the Range Rover and headed back home. Breda parked in the usual place until he was inside, then she got out and took a walk down the curbless residential street, pausing behind a palm tree across from the Devon property. She watched as the maid helped her employer unload the groceries.

Rhonda Devon had said that the live-in maid's name was Blanca. Like all Mexican maids she had no family name until Breda asked for one. It was Blanca Soltero. She was middle-aged and spoke only passable English, according to Rhonda Devon. She had been in their employ for eight years. On Monday, her one day off, she was always driven by Clive Devon to her daughter's home in the barrio of Indio. Rhonda Devon said that Blanca Soltero was extremely loyal to Clive Devon, for whom she cleaned and cooked, and that Blanca might very well keep any female dalliance a secret. Clive Devon paid her in cash, and Rhonda Devon wondered if he might offer bonuses to keep her mouth shut.

When the sturdy woman lifted the last grocery bag from the Range Rover, she brushed back a wisp of gray hair and happened to glance out through the driveway gates, spotting Breda, who quickly pretended to be removing a pebble from her shoe. Then Blanca Soltero closed the door of the Range Rover and went back inside the house.

Breda returned to her Z, settled back and started thinking about Lynn Cutter. He was *not* going to be the police connection she needed in her business, not even a connection *to* a connection. She could get most civil information she needed from a computer data-base company, and she'd made friends at title companies and banks, so when she wanted a real estate title search or a credit check she could usually manage to get it without the subject being notified that it was being done.

But criminal background checks were a problem. Convictions are public record, but like any cop—and Breda still thought and worked like a cop—she wanted a real rap sheet with all arrests listed, not just convictions. Rap sheets were available only to people actively working in law enforcement, but she'd already learned a trick or two as a P.I. When a subject was convicted of a crime and the probation department was doing a report to help the judge with a sentencing decision, the report and a rap sheet became public record for about ten days. That was one way to get it. But there were too many occasions when Breda wanted a rap sheet on someone who wasn't facing any sort of prosecution. At those times she felt impotent. She felt like a *civilian*. That's when she needed a discreet police contact.

Breda had promised herself never to ask one of her old pals at LAPD to run somebody's criminal record. Technically, it was a crime for her to solicit it, and the cop could get in trouble. What she'd been looking for was a local police officer, somebody she *hadn't* worked with for twenty years, somebody who was willing to take small risks for money. Somebody she needn't worry about, someone like Lynn Cutter, but more sane and sober.

While Breda was thinking of who she might develop as a proper law enforcement contact, a rusty old Plymouth turned into the Las Palmas area from Palm Canyon Drive.

Meanwhile, Lynn Cutter was wondering why, with all his years of experience at sitting in saloons, he hadn't been able to spot any of the typical bartender scams. The noonday crowd was big and noisy, lots of business people were coming in The Unicorn for lunch or a drink in lieu of lunch. It was one of those "California cuisine" minimalist restaurants where you'd be served by young people who'd say, "We got real *rad* black squid risotto today!" There were plenty of gawking tourists looking for Palm Springs celebrities who weren't there.

The bartenders weren't pouring from any suspicious bottles, not that Lynn was able to spot. The oldest bartender trick was the one where they'd bring their *own* bottle of hooch and pour from that one until it was empty, keeping all of the proceeds from that bottle for themselves.

Neither bartender had brought in a suspicious thermos that could be full of booze, a variation of the same gag. Both were working furiously to serve customers, as well as the waitresses at the service bar, and neither was making any funny moves such as dime-stacking, one for every drink they didn't ring up in the register. A stack of dimes or paper clips was a bartender's abacus, so they'd know how much they could safely pocket at the end of the shift. *One for the boss. One for me. Two for the boss . . .*

Lynn didn't see any of that, but what he did see was the unveiled hatred that all the employees had for the restaurant proprietor, a smarmy guy in a double-breasted Ralph Lauren, named Mr. Riegel, who came from Las Vegas and wasn't the kind of guy that cried at bar mitzvahs.

Lynn heard Mr. Riegel's voice booming from the kitchen, screaming at a Mexican dishwasher. He'd seen Mr. Riegel walk behind the bar to count and examine the bottles, and check the register when a round of drinks was rung up by the older bartender, a guy with a bad henna job and nicotine-stained teeth, who flashed a malevolent grin whenever the boss turned his back.

I wouldn't want *that* bartender as an enemy, Lynn thought,

then he said to the younger bartender, "Gimme another, will ya? This time not from the well. I can't drink too much pre-pubescent Scotch."

"What's that?" the bartender asked.

"Under twelve years old," Lynn answered, and the bartender shrugged and poured one that cost an extra six bits, but had pubic hair.

There was only one bit of irregular behavior going on that Lynn had spotted. The bartender with the henna rinse made trips to an alcove that was between the service bar and the kitchen. During the forty-five minutes that Lynn had sat there the guy had made three trips. But there was absolutely no way he could be carrying a container of his own liquor from the alcove to the bar, booze that he could pour instead of the house liquor. The guy would simply go to the alcove, disappear from sight for a minute, then he'd head back to the bar and wash glasses.

At last Lynn got up, pretending to be uncertain where the men's room was. He walked into the alcove "by mistake," discovering that it was a place for waitresses to take a quick break. There were folding chairs, a tiny table, an ashtray and nothing more. Lynn decided that the bartender was making those trips so he could do a few lines of blow, which he probably kept stashed in his sock.

When he got back to the barstool, Breda was sitting there ordering a Perrier, allowing Mr. Riegel to see that she was on duty.

Lynn said loudly, "Hi! What're you doing here today? Business slow?"

Breda said, "Yeah, we only moved a few units. Two Hondas and a Mazda. How about you?"

When both bartenders were at the service bar, Breda said to Lynn, *sotto voce*, "Baby longhair showed up at Devon's house in the old Plymouth."

"Yeah? What happened?"

"She's been there over an hour. They're swimming. I prowled along the wall and I could hear them splashing and barking in the pool."

"They bark?"

She smirked and said, "She brought her dog. And I'm positive the maid is in on the whole affair. I could hear her yelling stuff in Spanish to the girl."

"Now what?"

"We still haven't answered Mrs. Devon's big question. Why's he doing business with a sperm bank?"

"Simple," Lynn said. "He's made a deal with some white Anglo-Saxon surrogate, and when his WASP baby's born he's gonna kiss off Rhonda Devon and live happily ever after with his little Mexican hardbelly. She's gonna be an instant mommy. Then, Daddy, Mommy, Daddy's pink WASP baby and Mommy's big brown dog are all gonna live happily ever after."

"That doesn't sound right."

"Okay, let's do it this way. His little pepper pot with the long black hair is gonna *be* the carrier of his baby, but . . . naw, that doesn't work. He wouldn't need a storage locker. My first scenario's the right one. He wants her and a WASP baby. He's just gotta find the right WASP carrier."

She handed him a piece of notebook paper. "Can you make a call and have somebody at the P.D. run her license number real quick?"

"They sometimes do audit tracks on clerks that run license numbers. Everyone has an operator code so they can find out who ran it."

"Come on, you must have somebody that owes you a favor. We need the information right now and I don't want her or Clive Devon to find out we're running her license number."

He hesitated, but got up to go to the public phone. Before leaving he whispered, "I'm positive neither bartender's so much as pocketed a wrong tip. Your client may be giving these bartenders a bum rap."

121

"He says he's sure he's being jobbed," Breda said.

"Well, your client's not exactly a blithe spirit loved by all. He gets off on browbeating all these young kids named Heather and Chad. Look at his eyes. They're shiftier'n Iran."

"Run the number," Breda said. "I'll take Mr. Riegel outside and have a chat."

Breda found her client directing traffic in the foyer. She caught his eye and motioned toward the door. When he met her outside Breda said to him, "I've had a man at the bar for an hour. There's nothing going on."

A hurried conversation turned into an ultimatum from Mr. Riegel. He wanted somebody watching the bartenders that evening. He was having a private party in the banquet room, and was expecting a very large group from the convention center plus the regular in-season crowd.

"I'll try to be here for a few hours, Mister Riegel," Breda assured him.

"I want you or one of your people here from seven till eleven," he said, "or you're fired."

It was only after thinking of Lizzy's tuition, books and board that Breda showed him her pimp-killer smile and said, "Sure, Mister Riegel. I'll have somebody here all evening."

She caught up with Lynn before he'd returned from making the call, took him to the foyer and said, "You're right, he's slime. Can you come back here this evening for a couple hours?"

"Tell him to shove it."

"I *need* this sleazy job!" she said. "I'm trying to get some nice clean insurance frauds to work on, but right now I need this client."

"It gets expensive sitting at a bar," he said.

"I'll pay for the drinks."

"Do they go against my fee?"

"No," she sighed. "You'll actually get paid to slosh down the booze."

"I think I can handle that." Then he looked at the notepaper and said, "The car's registered to Blanca Soltero. Lives in Indio."

"That's Clive Devon's maid," Breda said. "The girl must be her daughter. Shit!"

"He might have something going with the maid's daughter."

"No, that doesn't work," Breda said. "Not with the sperm bank business."

"Look, he lied to his wife about meeting the girl, didn't he? There's something happening between them."

"No wonder nobody wants these crappy domestic cases," Breda said. "Meet me at my office in thirty minutes. I'm gonna see if the Plymouth's still at the Devon house."

Twenty minutes later, Breda was on foot again, peeking over the wall at Clive Devon's pool. She had to retreat to her car when the dog started barking. The girl and her car were gone, but she'd have to return for her dog, Breda surmised.

When she got back to her office she was surprised to see someone in the waiting room with Lynn Cutter, who was slumped in a chair, looking gloomier than usual.

Lynn opened one eye and said to her, "Help's arrived, and he's very helpful. Actually, he's the kind a cop that'd do a Heimlich maneuver on your pet, even if the pet was a parakeet. He always means well, this young man."

"Hi, Miss Burrows!" Nelson Hareem said, sticking out his hand and grinning like Bugs Bunny. "I think we're getting a little closer to the drug smuggler!"

—9—

 $\mathbf{B}$ y four o'clock that afternoon
they'd been presented with a Nelson Hareem scenario that made
Breda's neck hair do the lambada. Not because she thought it
was remotely plausible, but because it proved that Lynn Cutter
was right: The kid was a banana.

"You think the guy's what?" Lynn asked, after Nelson had
announced his hypothesis.

"An Arab terrorist," Nelson repeated calmly, with that
agreeable smile. "It's very possible."

"It's very possible," Lynn said to her.

"I hear him," Breda said. "You mean the guy's not a drug
smuggler? The kind that comes into this valley in a private plane
because his flight bag's full of dope and panics when he's taking
a pee and suddenly sees a cop in uniform? He just couldn't be
that kind of ordinary scumbag crook?"

"No."

"Why, Nelson?" Breda asked. "Not that it makes any real difference in my life. But why? I'm curious."

"The coins in the mouth were the first tipoff," Nelson said. "The old Indian at the reservation said it proves he's a man a the desert."

"I see. He couldn't be a man of the Mexican desert?"

"At first I thought so, till Lynn found this." Nelson handed a dime-sized coin to Breda. "It's Spanish. *Diez pesetas.* See the profile of King Juan Carlos? I figure the guy flew to Mexico on Iberia Airlines by way of Spain. I figure he's from Algeria, maybe Morocco. That's right near Spain."

"I know. I saw *Casablanca*," Breda said.

"But that's only part of it. There was the thing he said to the pilot when they talked to the mechanic at the hangar."

"I thought he only spoke Spanish."

"But he pointed to the map on the wall, and he said something the mechanic thought was in Spanish. And he laughed. Well, jist look at your map a this valley. Know what's one of the closest places to that airport?"

"What?"

"Mecca! He saw *Mecca* and made a joke about bein near a holy place. I mean, it fits!"

Lynn and Breda looked at one another, and Breda slipped into a little grin of derision, saying, "Then it wasn't Spanish he spoke?"

"Mighta been," said Nelson. "Or it mighta been *Arabic*. He probably speaks two or three languages."

"Nelson," Lynn said, "they got a Coke machine downstairs. I'll buy if you go get em. My left knee's so swollen it's grotesque. The other's even worse. You wouldn't know it from Marlon Brando."

"Sure, regular Coke?"

"Regular," Lynn said.

"Diet," Breda said.

"My treat," said Nelson, and dashed out the door.

"See?" Lynn said when they were alone. "He has cosmic reasons for doing what he does."

"He's real cute," Breda said. "I feel like taking him to the zoo or maybe buying him some Gummi Bears, but he's a nutter, all right. Wacko. No telling what's bubbling in his brain."

"Unfortunately, I have to work with him for the next two days or he turns over all his information to the sheriffs. That means they find out about Clive Devon, et cetera."

"They'd interview Devon!"

"Of course they would."

"He'd find out about the surveillance! That'd screw me out of five thous . . ."

Too late! Lynn put on a happy face you couldn't remove with a chisel. "You little dickens!" he said. "Aren't you the one? *Five* grand? And here I am risking my entire pension for a measly thousand bucks?"

"If we get to the bottom of the Devon affair, I'll give you another five hundred," Breda said, regretting the day she'd set eyes on this grinning dipso. "But I need help."

Nelson Hareem came bursting back into the office with the cold drinks, beaming with anticipation. "Can we start real soon, Lynn? I got a need to proceed. Big time!"

Lynn took his Coke and said to Breda, "Remember that guy Jack Graves? The one that got a stress pension after shooting the kid? Jack needs something to do, something to take his mind off the accident. Let's see if he'll take on your bartender case. He used to do lotsa undercover assignments in bars when he worked dope. You could watch Devon's house tonight. Me, I could check out motels that begin with A, B or C for a bald-headed smuggler." Then he turned to Nelson and said, "Excuse me, I meant terrorist. By the way, who's he terrorizing?"

"Could be anybody," Nelson said. "How about an ex-president? Gerald Ford lives here."

"Why would *any* self-respecting terrorist bother with Gerald Ford?" Lynn wanted to know.

"How can I get hold of this Jack Graves?" Breda asked.

"I'll take you to see him now," Lynn said. "Lives in a motor home up in Windy Point. I try to visit every couple weeks."

"Lynn, I've only had a chance to check out five motels," Nelson said. "Don't you think . . ."

"Go get yourself a hamburger," Lynn said. "Meet me right here at six o'clock and we'll spend the whole evening working on the A's, okay?"

"Okay," Nelson said agreeably. "I know a good orthopedist who could look at those knees."

"Too late," Lynn said. "I already had two surgeries by a goon that's destroyed more knees than the IRA."

Windy Point was aptly named: Breda held on to her purse with both hands and hoped she wouldn't be wind-stripped of her jumpsuit. There was a little grocery store and gas station in Windy Point, but that was about it for commerce in the working-class enclave just north of Palm Springs. Both she and Lynn had to lean into the whistling gale as they walked across Jack Graves' little cactus garden toward his mobile home.

"After slogging through this hurricane I hope he's home," Breda shouted, feeling the sand peppering her sunglasses.

"Jack's always home," Lynn shouted back above the blast. "That's the trouble. He needs to get out more."

Lynn banged on the metal door of the mobile home and yelled, "Jack, put your pants on. Brought a visitor."

Jack Graves was wearing a T-shirt and jeans, and was barefoot. He was much taller than Lynn, very thin and gaunt. He had a kindly face and was gray around the sideburns, but the hair on top was as dark as Breda's and his chin stubble was black.

Breda could've picked him out of a lineup from hearing his story. There was a lot of torment in the eyes of Jack Graves.

127

"Meet Breda Burrows," Lynn said. "She's a new P.I. in town, retired from LAPD. I'm helping her on something."

When Breda shook his hand it felt clammy, and she could see droplets by his hairline and above his lip. It wasn't *that* hot in the mobile home. He must be sick, she thought.

The living room was small and exceptionally neat; everything was in perfect order. Breda sat on a daybed sofa next to Lynn.

"Can I get you something?" Jack Graves asked. "How about a beer or a soft drink?"

"Nothing, thanks," Breda said.

"Just had a soda pop," Lynn said. "How you been?"

"Fine." Jack Graves smiled. He had heavy dark eyebrows and thick lashes which made his eyes even more sunken.

Lynn said, "Jack, you get any skinnier you'll fit through a mail slot. I gotta take you out for some burritos."

"Just getting over the flu," Jack Graves said.

Lynn Cutter noticed the perspiration, and said, "You're gonna have to back-comb your pubic hair to hold your pants up!"

"Flu's all better now," Jack Graves said. "I'll gain some weight."

"How's your ankle?" Lynn turned to Breda. "Jack sprained it chasing a gopher outta his garden. Can you imagine? Living out here, anybody else woulda shot the . . ."

Then Lynn caught himself, and Breda saw the expression change on Jack Graves' face. You didn't talk about shooting *anything* with this man.

Breda covered for Lynn by saying, "So the ankle's fine?"

"Yeah, I must be getting old," Jack Graves said. "And I tripped coming out of the market the other day and landed on my hip." Then to Lynn, "Remember when I told you about that hip pointer I got in the car wreck where I went in pursuit?"

"Yeah, same hip?"

"Uh huh. It's bothering me a little bit."

"Can you walk around okay, and maybe sit at a bar for a few hours tonight?"

"A bar?"

"We got a job for you," Lynn said. "Not big money, but something to do."

"Well, I don't know," Jack Graves said. "I really oughtta take care of my washing and ironing tonight."

"Please, Jack," Lynn Cutter said, in a gentle voice that Breda hadn't heard him use before. "It's a little job that has to be done and I don't have anyone else to do it for me."

"Okay, Lynn," Jack Graves said. "I guess clean underwear can wait."

Lynn took five minutes to explain The Unicorn bartender-watch to Jack Graves, and Breda realized that this was a Lynn Cutter scheme to help the man.

Breda saw six photos of a child on the wall, from when the boy was a chubby two-year-old to a lad of twelve or thirteen. She figured that Jack Graves was a divorced man with a son, perhaps a boy close to the age of the one he'd killed when they'd raided the wrong house.

When Breda and Lynn were driving back to her office, Breda said, "That was a nice thing to do for him. And I can use the help."

"Jack's gotta get out," Lynn said. "He's dwelling on that shooting. I been with him when we drive past Mexican kids and he gets a look on his face. Jack's in trouble."

"Whadda you make of all his accidents?"

"Same as you," Lynn said. "You didn't hear the half of it. He also *accidentally* cut his hand while slicing onions. That one took about thirty stitches. He broke two toes when he dropped a five-pound sledge trying to put up a fence. All this in a period of a couple months. That guy's carrying so much guilt the next *accident* might be fatal. If you could maybe come up with any other little job he might do for you, I'd appreciate it."

"He needs psychiatric counseling."

"He needs body armor. Unless he can get busy and take his mind off it. You can't be *alone* like that, not all the time."

"I could use some help with the surveillance on Clive Devon. Could he take your place while you go sleuthing with Nelson?"

"Sure," Lynn said. "Nelson promised he'll give up and forget the whole thing in two days if we don't get a lead on his smuggler. I mean his terrorist."

"Of course his fee would come out of your share."

"Yeah, I figured." Lynn surprised Breda when he added, "It's worth it if it gets him away from *himself*. You can't be *alone* all the time."

"If Clive Devon hooks up with that Mexican girl again I'm risking a dog bite," Breda said. "I'm gonna sneak and peek and find out what they're doing."

"Be careful," he said. "That dog's goofier'n a blind date."

"I think he's just a big puppy."

Lynn looked at his watch and said, "Time to face up to an evening with Nelson Hareem. You're right, Nelson's adorable, but why is it every time I look at that kid I hear the shower music from *Psycho*?"

Out-of-towners equated Palm Springs with glamour and money, and there was still a lot of it around. But the big money was relentlessly moving south in the valley, to Rancho Mirage, Palm Desert, Indian Wells, and even La Quinta now that PGA West was there. One didn't find the Forbes Four Hundred bucks around the Las Palmas neighborhood anymore, but there was still old quiet money, like Clive Devon's. It was in the downtown commercial section of Palm Springs that the big change showed, more than in the residential areas. Many of the shops were vacant now, even in season. There were signs in too many windows saying, "Moved to Palm Desert," to El Paseo, a shopping area with pretensions of becoming another Rodeo Drive.

Most desert residents are blue collar, or live on fixed incomes, in places like north Palm Springs, or Desert Hot Springs or Cathedral City. It was in such off-the-avenue districts, whose motels were both low profile and low-priced, that Lynn Cutter and Nelson Hareem were searching.

"We'll max out with the fifty-buck-a-nighters," Lynn suggested. "In fact, thirty-five-a-nighters would be a better bet if there *are* any that cheap in season."

The first few were easy enough. The employees on night duty showed Lynn and Nelson the motel registers with hardly a glance at the badge Lynn presented, and despite the fact that Nelson—in a Los Angeles Lakers blue and yellow T-shirt with Magic Johnson's number 32 on the back—looked more like one of the weekend, student hell-raisers than a cop.

Lynn noticed the bulge under the arm of Nelson's T-shirt and wasn't surprised. He'd figured Nelson to be a leg holster type as well. And he probably carries a dagger, and maybe a derringer in his shorts, Lynn figured. The Nelson Hareems of this world were as predictable as August heat rash.

It was dark when they got to the fourth one, Bessie's Apartment Motel, north of Desert Hospital, just a few miles and a few million dollars from the *other* Palm Springs. It looked promising, a run-down stucco one-story, with a white rock-composition roof.

Bessie herself was working at the reception desk, and wasn't overwhelmed by a Palm Springs police badge being waved under her nose. She'd been watching *Wheel of Fortune* and dreaming of winning a Beverly Hills shopping trip. She didn't look quite as masculine as George Burns, whom she resembled, but her voice was more gravelly.

Bessie glanced at Lynn and said, "What is it, another run-away from L.A. get in trouble?"

"Need to talk to a guy who mighta checked in yesterday afternoon. He's a Mexican . . ." Then Lynn looked at Nelson and said, "Or maybe he's from the Middle East."

"Like Kansas?"

"That's Middle West."

"Like the guys that're behind the counter in a Seven-Eleven store," Nelson offered.

"Oh, Eye-ranians?"

"Yeah, like that," said Lynn. "But maybe he's a Mexican."

"Mexican, Eye-ranian, gimme a break!" Bessie said. "Think anybody can tell the difference?"

"He's bald but might be wearing a blue baseball cap or some other hat," Lynn said.

"Then I wouldn't know he was bald, would I?"

"No," Lynn said.

"He's maybe in his late thirties, early forties. About my height but huskier. Strong-looking guy. With a big droopy black mustache. Might not have a car."

"He sounds like every gardener I ever seen around here," Bessie said. "Gimme a break!"

"Right," Lynn Cutter said, and indicated to Nelson that it was time to let Bessie return to her *Wheel of Fortune* fantasies.

"But," she said, "it maybe sounds like a guy named Vega in bungalow four."

"What?" Lynn and Nelson said in unison.

As they headed for the two rows of semidetached cottages making up Bessie's Apartment Motel, Lynn Cutter got a load of what a few others before him had seen and would never forget—Lynn got to see the carrot-top cop when he put on his *game* face!

The first thing Nelson did was reach up under his Lakers T-shirt and grab hold of the .38 in the upside-down holster.

"Puh-leeeeze!" Lynn cried. "This is prob'ly just a snowbird from Walla Walla. Let's not kill him right away!"

"Ain't you carryin a piece?"

"No."

"I got an extra one!"

"I figured."

"Want it?"

"No."

"Then stay behind me."

"With pleasure. But puh-leeeeze don't Schwarzenegger the door. Let *me* handle it."

"I'll whistle when I'm in position!" Nelson whispered. "Like a whippoorwill!"

Nelson squatted down so he could pass under the front window of bungalow four and not be spotted. He duck-walked toward the rear of the building, and when he was in position to watch the back door, he whistled from the darkness.

It dawned on Lynn. There's no whippoorwills in the frigging desert. Not even one scraggly-assed whippoorwill!

Lynn knocked. No answer. He knocked again and said, "Mister Vega! Bessie sent me to tell you the gas meter shows a leak in one a the bungalows! Mister Vega, you there?"

Lynn put his ear to the door. He walked to the corner of the bungalow, peered toward the darkness out back and saw Nelson crouching with his gun extended in both hands just like on television. When Lynn Cutter had first become a cop nobody extended *two* arms to hold *one* little gun!

"Nelson!"

"Yeah?"

"Nobody home. We'll come back later."

Bessie had turned off *Wheel of Fortune* by the time they got back, and was busy registering a nervous middle-aged guy who had a babe outside in his car.

When the cops reentered the motel office the nervous guy

was writing "Mr. and Mrs. Johnson" in a counterfeit scrawl, and had given a wrong license number. As though anybody gave a shit about him and a teenage hooker from Indian Avenue.

Lynn said to the motel proprietor, "Bessie, we might come back later. Don't say anything to the guy in bungalow four, okay?"

"Think I'm gonna nail a notice on his door?" Bessie snorted. "Gimme a break!"

"Okay, Bessie," Lynn said, and the cops left her to tend to the nervous guest who kept watching the street for cops.

But before Lynn and Nelson could get out the door, Bessie said, "Hey! Here comes Mister Vega now."

Lynn grabbed Nelson's arm to anchor him and took a good look through the motel window at the burly man walking their way. He was carrying a bag of take-out food and he *did* look like the guy with the baseball cap, right down to his Zapata mustache, except that he was wearing a straw cowboy hat.

Before Nelson could start blasting out windows, Lynn opened the glass door and dashed out, as though hurrying toward the parked car containing the Lolita.

Suddenly, Lynn stopped in his tracks, turned to the dark burly man, and said, "Sir! You have a wasp on your hat!"

And the burly guy dropped his bag of ribs and whipped the hat off all in one motion. And his hair fell out. He had more than Milli Vanilli, all done up in double braids, Injun style.

"Where is it?" the guy yelled.

"It's gone," Lynn said. "I oughtta get a job with Terminix Pest Control. Boy, I can spot a nasty wasp faster'n the Anti-Defamation League."

Even in Nelson's topless Jeep Wrangler, cruising along Palm Canyon Drive at night was beautiful. Rows of light washed high up on the towering palms that lined both sides of the avenue.

There were throngs of in-season tourists strolling about, and college kids scoping out the hardbodies.

Of course, during Easter week there'd be hell to pay when Palm Springs tried to keep forty thousand vacationing students under control after they got drunk and turned Palm Canyon Drive into a honking blaring screaming parking lot.

A television crew would be on hand then, which would encourage lots of on-camera miniriots. There'd always be a few coeds hanging on the back of a bike, or sitting up on the trunk of a convertible, flashing the crowd. One would probably start it off by removing her bikini top. Then another might stand up in a pickup and show everyone that her bikini bottom was on backwards. Then somebody would take it *all* off.

Then a macho sophomore would no doubt run out into the street to cop a feel, or steal the bikini, or otherwise prove to the coed that she shouldn't have had that last six-pack. And she'd scream for help, and a fight would start and lots of students and maybe a few cops would all end up with contusions and abrasions. It happened every Easter week: traffic jam, gridlock, flashing, fighting, riot.

And every year, a coed would have to flash at least one cop by lifting her T-shirt to reveal her address written across her tits. After which, she'd utter some variation of, "Officer, I'm lost. Here's my address. Can you take me home?"

The last one to do that to Lynn Cutter—when he was in uniform with a squad of cops from five different jurisdictions —was a nymphet with creamy shoulders and a pouty candy-apple mouth. While her pals snickered and guffawed at the cop-flashing, Lynn had said to her, "I can tell by your nipple development that you're under the age of eighteen. There's a curfew law. Go home."

She'd covered her boobs very quickly, wiped off her smirk, and said, "I'm seventeen and ten months! I consider myself eighteen!"

135

"So do I," Lynn said, "but that doesn't change reality for *either* of us. Go home!"

As Nelson Hareem revved the Jeep Wrangler, it jerked Lynn Cutter out of his reverie.

"Wanna try Desert Hot Springs or Cathedral City, Lynn?" Nelson asked.

"Why don't we finish up here in town first?"

"Okay," Nelson said, agreeably. "There's one on Chaparral that looks likely. Thirty-five a night isn't too much for a terrorist, is it?"

"I don't know, Nelson," Lynn said. "I haven't called the terrorist hot line lately."

"Wanna hear some Dwight Yoakam?" Nelson started thumbing through his country cassettes.

"Never heard of him."

"How about George Strait?"

"Is George Strait the one that wears a Gene Autry hat?"

"Damn, Lynn!" Nelson was incredulous. "What kinda music do ya like? Waltzes or somethin?"

"As a matter a fact 'Tennessee Waltz' is a big-hit single in The Furnace Room. Has been for thirty-five years or so. The only cowboy song I can identify with is 'She Got the Goldmine (I Got the Shaft).' "

Nelson said, "My favorite lately is 'Chasin' That Neon Rainbow.' I guess maybe that's what I'm doin, but damn it, I need some bright lights! I wanna get outta the desert and come to town!"

When Nelson changed lanes to lunge past some cruising kids in a van, Lynn almost got whiplashed. "Puh-leeeeze, Nelson! I'm getting seasick. Do I have to buy a patch to wear behind my ear?"

They checked out two more Palm Springs motels, but got no report of a single man fitting the smuggler's description. Nelson said, "We oughtta drive up to Desert Hot Springs now."

"Gimme a break, Nelson!" Lynn moaned. "Jesus, I'm starting to sound like Bessie."

"Okay, let's see, how about the Cactus and Sand Motel? Know anything about it?"

"Yeah, it's fifty-five a night. No terrorist has that big an expense account."

"How do ya know it's fifty-five?"

"I got picked up one night by some babe at The Furnace Room. She complained about how much it cost her. That was when Washington was talking about cutting Social Security checks and she didn't know if she could afford me."

"You went to a motel with a woman that's on Social Security?"

"I'm the hottest number The Furnace Room's ever seen," Lynn said. "I've put more a those old babes in bed than broken hips ever did. In fact, I sorta promised myself to the one that sings "The Little Old Lady from Pasadena" every Thursday night. Remember that one, Nelson?"

"That's sick, Lynn!"

"I know. I don't understand how you can stand me. Why don't you drop me at The Furnace Room where I can indulge my perverse desires and buy myself Wilfred's easily chewable supper, if there's any left over from the early-bird special."

"Okay, let's make a pit stop," Nelson said. "I could use a beer."

"I could use a pension," Lynn said. "And Doctor Ruth for counseling. I wouldn't be in this mess if I had any kind a sex life. It's that damn freckle."

"*What* freckle?" Nelson wanted to know.

-10-

The dog started barking the second she stepped onto the driveway that night, frustrating her plan to force open the electric gate far enough to squeeze inside. The barking came from upstairs-front, in what Breda assumed was the master bedroom suite. Then someone, perhaps the maid, opened a downstairs door and flooded the entire property in light. Breda had to hurry back to her Datsun Z, fire it up and drive away. That goddamn slobbery brown dog!

Rhonda Devon had left a message with Breda's service that she'd expect a progress report by the weekend, but Breda knew that her client would really expect a satisfactory answer, not just a report. Breda wondered what Lynn Cutter and Nelson Hareem were up to, checked the time, saw that it was 8:30 P.M., and even though she was exhausted, decided to see if Jack Graves had been having any luck at The Unicorn. Her flagging morale required some sort of resolution to at least one of her cases.

When she got to The Unicorn, there were no less than 150 diners being served, the foyer was packed with people waiting, and they were two deep at the bar. One of those at the bar was Jack Graves.

He was sitting quietly near the service area, sipping beer from a bottle. He wore an old Pendleton shirt, a soft tan corduroy jacket, khaki trousers and well-worn moccasins. He smiled from time to time at a guy next to him who was half bagged and loud. Breda walked up behind Jack and put her hand on his shoulder.

"Hello, Breda," he said. "Wanna drink?"

"I can use one," she said. "Chardonnay."

Jack Graves gave his stool to Breda and stood behind her. The suspect-bartender wiped the bartop and bared his tobacco-stained teeth in what passed for cordiality.

"Chardonnay, please," Jack Graves said to him.

When the bartender was gone, Breda asked, "Any luck?"

"Oh yeah," Jack Graves said quietly. "Mister Riegel was right. The bartender's supplementing his income at Riegel's expense. My guess is he makes an extra thirty or forty bucks a night, not worth firing him for. He's a very good bartender."

"Maybe he'll just warn the bartender."

"He'll put the guy in the hospital."

"What makes you say that?"

"I know your Mister Riegel from when our guys worked a deal with the Palm Springs Special Enforcement Unit," Jack Graves said. "That's when I became friends with Lynn. Riegel pals around with an Arizona crime family. See, Palm Springs is a neutral town. Mob people from Chicago or wherever, they can come here with no worries. And they *do* come. Palm Springs even gets some bad guys from as far away as London."

"As in England?"

"The British accent's a great advantage for con men around these parts, particularly with bankers, it seems. And cocaine sells for at least a seventy percent profit in London over what it sells for here."

"In this little city there's all that going on?"

"At your old department, at LAPD, they got fifty people doing intelligence work that *one* guy does in this town."

"And my Mister Riegel is active?"

"He's never gone to tea dances, I bet, but he's semilegit now. Look around. This restaurant's doing bust-out business."

"I won't be taking any more jobs from him," Breda said, "but I'll finish this one. So tell me, how's the bartender scamming his boss?"

"It's a variation of the old BYOB gag, but in this case he didn't bring his own bottle and put it behind the bar. He has some kind of container stashed back in that alcove area. He's pouring his own booze and pocketing the proceeds."

"How's he get it from back there to here? Lynn watched him and said he's positive the guy doesn't carry *anything* when he goes back and forth."

"He doesn't, not in his hands."

"How's he do it then?"

"Enjoy your wine and watch him," Jack Graves said, smiling. "It's good to have somebody to talk to."

Breda looked into Jack's brown eyes. They were nice eyes, but sad. She said, "Okay, Jack, I'll enjoy my wine."

A group of six at the bar were called to their table by a bosomy hostess in an off-the-shoulder beaded dress. When they'd gone the bartender glanced down the bar, peeked out toward the front, then headed for the alcove.

When the bartender came back, Jack Graves whispered to Breda, "Watch him wash the glasses."

Breda raised up a few inches on the barstool for a better look. The bartender nodded to a customer who called for a

Tanqueray on the rocks, and then bent over the sink to rinse out a few glasses, just as Jack Graves had predicted.

"Did you see it?"

"No," Breda said. "What?"

"He's carrying it in his *mouth*. That guy can probably carry six ounces of Scotch without changing expression. When he bends over to wash glasses, he's spitting it into a bowl next to the sink on his end of the bar. His partner may or may not know what he's up to."

"Ree-volting!" Breda shuddered. "Dis-gusting."

Jack Graves grinned. "It really is. I've never seen it before."

"I guess I should tell Riegel right away. Jesus, what if the guy has AIDS or something? Gross!"

"I wish you wouldn't," said Jack Graves.

"Why?"

"Your Mister Riegel's pals back in that banquet room have been ordering a lotta Scotch. He might think they got some from his bowl."

"All the more reason!"

"They aren't the kind a guys that have cucumber sandwiches every afternoon. They'll hurt this bartender."

"I can't let my client serve second-hand Scotch!"

"Lemme have a talk with the guy. Gimme a few minutes."

He signaled to the bartender and when the guy came over saying, "Another beer?" Jack Graves simply said, "If you take one step toward that bowl of booze behind the dirty glasses I'll stop you from dumping it. Then my partner here'll call your boss."

"Who *are* you?" The bartender jerked his face toward the front door at the mention of Riegel.

Jack Graves said, "Someone who doesn't wanna see your legs broken. Just go straight back to that alcove, retrieve whatever you have stashed there, and grab your coat at the same time. On the way out tell the hostess you're getting severe chest pains and a numbness in your arm. Tomorrow you can call Riegel and say you had a mild heart attack and you're quitting your job. And if you ever work in any other bar in this valley I'll tell Riegel what you did to him."

"Who *are* you?" the bartender demanded.

"I'm the timer," Jack Graves said, looking at his watch. "You got exactly three minutes to get it all done and be outta here. If you don't, whatever happens to you tonight isn't my fault."

The bartender looked at Breda, then back to Jack Graves. Then he looked at the boisterous crowd of cigar smokers in Armani suits with Mr. Riegel in the banquet room.

The bartender turned and headed for the alcove. Less than a minute later he came out wearing a cardigan sweater and said something to the hostess on his way out the door.

"Tell Riegel you spotted the guy serving lots of free drinks," Jack Graves suggested to Breda. "Tell him you're sure he was just giving away booze for big tips and he must've figured out who you are and panicked."

"Riegel'll probably try to withhold some of my fee for letting the guy spot me."

"He'll be glad you got rid of him. People with egos like Riegel's can't stand to be had. He knew the bartender was having him, he just couldn't spot it."

"What if the guy *does* have AIDS?"

"I don't think he's an AIDS candidate," Jack Graves said.

"That'd add new meaning to the term, 'dying for a drink,' " Breda said.

"Everybody dies," Jack Graves said, light glancing off his bony cheekbone. "Why not for a drink? How about another Chardonnay?"

By the time Lynn Cutter and Nelson Hareem had consumed their first drink at The Furnace Room, another failed actor and longtime friend of Wilfred Plimsoll was ranting about how television had destroyed his profession and, parenthetically, been the cause of the fact that in the past thirty years he'd been gainfully employed for about twenty-two days, all told.

The actor, Walter Davenport, had blue-white hair, wore a plaid double-breasted sport jacket, white cotton trousers, white leather loafers and a school tie from a private academy he'd never attended.

"TV?" he bellowed. "They do TV shows about pimply kid-doctors named Boobie or Doobie or something! When I die I want my ashes mixed with toxic waste and dropped on Burbank Studios!"

"Let's go find a table, Nelson," Lynn suggested. "I can't bear too much sound and fury tonight."

This time they avoided the old warbler who was at her favorite table, joining in when the piano player played a few bars of "Sentimental Journey." They spotted an empty table for two beside the used-brick fireplace that hadn't been lit for a decade.

"Let's grab that deuce," Lynn said, pointing to the table. "My aching knees could end the California drought."

When they were safely seated, Nelson asked, "Do you actually like this place?"

"It's all these old actors," Lynn Cutter said. "I don't feel like such a failure when I'm around them. Far as all the other old geezers, I don't feel so old when I'm around them. Far as lawyers, I *definitely* feel morally superior when I'm around them. So I guess The Furnace Room satisfies a lotta needs."

"Pretty strange crowd," Nelson said.

"We got lotsa power lines out by Highway Ten that could produce mutants, which might explain this joint. But it's kinda strange to hear *you* call people strange."

Changing the subject, Nelson Hareem asked, "Where ya gonna live, Lynn, when your house-sittin jobs run out?"

"I honestly don't know, Nelson."

143

"Gonna be a private eye like Breda after your pension starts?"

"She's not making enough money to keep her in Kibbles, which is what I been eating lately. And the work's sleazier than the state legislature."

"You and Breda'll each have a pension. Half your salary each adds up to one full salary."

"What're you saying, Nelson?"

"You could work together and maybe be housemates. I saw the way you looked at her, Lynn," Nelson said, wrinkling his nose. "And the way she looked at you."

"Why, Nelson, ain't you the little matchmaker!" Lynn said, draining the last of his Scotch. But then, "How *did* she look at me?"

"Same way you looked at her."

"I don't have a freckle on my lip."

"What?"

"Nothing. Breda and me'll be housemates when Salman Rushdie opens a laundromat in Tehran."

"I think she likes you more'n you think," Nelson said. "I could read it in her eyes."

"I could read the Rosetta Stone easier," Lynn said. "Think we should have another drink?"

"I'll buy," Nelson said.

"Oh please don't, well all right," Lynn said, just as Breda Burrows and Jack Graves entered the smoky saloon looking for them.

"Over here!" Lynn called out. "Next week, Wilfred's receiving his first order of used Israeli gas masks!"

After they sat down, Nelson shook hands with Jack Graves, who described the successful resolution of The Unicorn job, saying, "If Riegel found out how the bartender was doing him, the guy'd be discovered out on the desert next week. Or part of him would, the rest having passed through some coyote's bowels."

"That's a complete gag-me-to-the-max trick," Lynn said. "No wonder I didn't spot it."

"I've decided Jack might be able to help us on the Clive Devon case too," Breda said to Lynn. And then, seeing concern in Lynn Cutter's eyes, she added, "Of course, you and I still have our original arrangement."

Lynn was satisfied that she'd decided to pay Jack, but there was a little something else going on in his own head that Lynn didn't like. Breda was saying in effect that Jack Graves was a better cop! Lynn felt another stab when she smiled at the gaunt man. She'd never looked at him like that.

Son of a bitch! Lynn thought. I'm jealous!

Breda said to Lynn, "Jack's gonna watch Clive Devon tomorrow from the moment he gets up till he goes to bed. I presume Nelson's going to give you back to me soon?"

"Day after tomorrow," Nelson said, nodding agreeably, and Lynn had a sudden urge to reach over and grab the little cop by the throat, except he was certain that Nelson would just look at him with disappointment and never understand. You hated to strangle somebody unless they knew *why*.

"I been thinking, Nelson," Lynn said. "Maybe the guy really is a Spaniard. Is Seve Ballesteros playing in the Bob Hope Classic? Your guy may be a super Seve fan."

"If I can offer an opinion," Jack Graves said quietly, "Breda's told me what you're doing and I been wondering if the guy's a Colombian. You know, with all the heat in Miami, they been running all the cocaine from Peru, Bolivia and Colombia through Mexico to southern California. Why not a Mexican load-plane full of Colombian cocaine?"

"There's no desert in Colombia," Nelson Hareem said. "Our guy's a man of the desert."

"*That* again." Lynn Cutter sighed.

"Some tar heroin from Pakistan and Iran also comes through Mexico," Jack Graves said. "They got some very dry terrain in those countries, I believe."

"Here I thought I was coming into semiretirement in a nice quiet resort," Breda said.

Jack Graves said, "This little metropolis has more Secret Service assigned on a per capita basis than anywhere in the world including Washington, D.C., because of who lives here and who plays here. The FBI has three resident agents in and out of Palm Springs because of all the interstate major frauds, and a lotta presidential nominees get interviewed right out on these golf courses. The air traffic controllers in this town direct squadrons of executive jets."

"Sounds great to me!" Nelson said. "I can't wait to get a lateral transfer. I'm sick a taking theft reports on stolen dates. And I hope I never see another date beetle! Ugh!"

"I gotta admit, Nelson, I'm a little intrigued with your terrorist idea," said Jack Graves.

"At last!" Nelson beamed.

"I don't find it totally convincing," Jack Graves said, "but we're getting a few people in for the golf tournament who could be targets."

"Not Dan Quayle, for chrissake!" Lynn said. "When Reagan came to town they'd have to close all airspace over the city for fifteen minutes to deal with the huge crowds. When Prince Charles came to play polo they had a traffic jam five miles long. When Dan Quayle came to play golf at PGA West, we detailed two reserve officers and three detectives to help Secret Service protect him from the adoring throngs . . . which ended being a guy and his wife, both Young Republicans. Who the hell is gonna terrorize anybody by going after Dan Quayle?"

"You sure hate Republicans," Nelson said.

"I am a Republican!" Lynn informed him. "A *poor* Republican. It's unnatural, like a vegetarian vampire."

"I wouldn't completely rule out heroin smuggling," Jack Graves said to Nelson, "even if your man of the desert's from the Middle East. I remember the time when some Algerians came to Palm Springs with a load of heroin sewed inside the Spandex waistbands of their pants. They beat all airport security with that one."

"Algerian?" Nelson said thoughtfully. "Maybe! Who else is comin for the golf tournament that's terrorizable?"

"According to the papers, there's a Saudi billionaire coming to play tennis in a pro-am," Breda said. "He might qualify. And Benazir Bhutto from Pakistan is here, now that she's out of work."

"Aw-right!" Nelson said. "Now we're gettin somewheres!"

"A Saudi sheik?" Lynn said. "Maybe I can meet him and learn a few tricks. I married two women and my life's wrecked. Sheiks get married a hundred and four times and fly to Palm Springs for a weekend a tennis. There's a moral somewhere."

"Lynn knows Palm Springs a lot better than I do," Jack Graves said to Nelson. "I'd trust Lynn's instincts."

Lynn said, "If it's Middle East types you're after, an Iranian recently bought a bar in Cathedral City that caters to a gay clientele."

"Maybe it wouldn't hurt to ask a few questions around there tomorrow," Nelson suggested.

"Why not?" Lynn said. "But if we have to do lunch, you might end up being the catch of the day."

When Nelson went to the bar to fetch more drinks, Lynn said, "Jack, I know how cute he is and all, but I wish you wouldn't encourage him with all these crime stories. He already thinks everyone he meets in Palm Springs is Mafia if their name ends with a vowel."

Lynn didn't fail to notice that Breda was getting a glow. He figured her for a three-drink woman, and she'd already downed two.

She said, "If you don't get away from Nelson after tomorrow, we'll have to make a new arrangement. How's he keep his job, all the trouble he gets in?"

"He must have a witness pool that'll swear to anything he says," Lynn answered. "One thing I know, he's fearless. And me, I'm afraid a guys that ain't afraid. Guys like Nelson're a greater danger to society than MTV. I like him, but he wouldn't know the difference between dandruff and date rape. How about another Chardonnay, Breda? *I'll* buy a round."

That shocked her so much that she accepted, even though she'd had enough. Then to her dismay, when Nelson returned to the table, he said, "Y'know, Breda, I think I can help you with your Devon case."

"Can't afford any more employees," Breda said. "Eastern Airlines went under because of too big a payroll."

"Oh, I wouldn't charge you nothin," Nelson said. "It's jist that I think your Clive Devon has a definite connection with my . . ."

"Smuggler-terrorist-mafioso," Lynn said. "Actually, your guy's a double hyphenate."

"Whatever," Nelson said. "Anyways, some streets out there, there's so many motels he could use a different one every night. Maybe Clive Devon's the key to it. Maybe our smuggler phoned Clive Devon."

"About what?" Breda challenged, and Lynn definitely liked her better with booze in her. She didn't show that odd little grin so often. He couldn't take his eyes off the bittersweet chocolate freckle next to her lip.

"I don't know, but for starters, what if he told Devon about what went down at the airport? And that he couldn't go to their . . ."

"Rendezvous is the word you want," Lynn said. The freckle glistened now when a drop of wine bathed it. And she *licked* the freckle!

"Yeah, rendezvous. Maybe the guy told Devon he couldn't risk drivin to Palm Springs in a hot car, and that Devon should come pick him up."

"In Painted Canyon?" Breda asked, incredulously.

"Well, it worked, didn't it?" Nelson said. "Nobody spotted him."

"What the hell could he have that Clive Devon wants or needs?" Breda asked.

"Everybody needs somethin," Nelson said.

"What do *you* need, Nelson?" Breda asked.

"Shade."

"Shade?"

"Yeah, I can't do another summer down the other end a the valley. You can tell how many days a guy's worked by countin the sweat rings on his shirt. There's *no* shade. At least up here in Palm Springs you got the big mountain for afternoon shade. I gotta have shade. I need number seventy-five sunscreen and it don't go that high."

"Shade," Breda repeated. It was so simple. Nelson Hareem just wanted a little shade!

"I'm itchy all the time down there," Nelson explained. "Athlete's foot, jock itch. By September it'll feel like I'm wearin barbed-wire Jockey shorts. It got so dry last summer, all my elastic died and my shorts kept fallin down."

Jack Graves put his hand on the young cop's arm, saying, "I'll do my best tomorrow, Nelson. If I can tail Clive Devon, and he teams up with your dark bald smuggler, I'll get a hold of you. I'd like you to get your shade."

Breda was looking at Jack Graves, and Lynn could plainly see that she liked him. But he was no longer jealous. Jack was too troubled to even notice that exquisite freckle near the lip of Breda Burrows.

Nelson finished his beer and said, "Well, maybe we should go home and get a fresh start tomorrow, Lynn."

"I know it's time for *me* to go," Breda said.

"You okay to drive?" Lynn asked, hopefully.

"Of course!" she said, indignantly.

"I'll be on stakeout in front of Clive Devon's house by six," Jack Graves promised Breda.

"Six-thirty's early enough, Jack," she said.

As Lynn Cutter was getting to his feet, wincing from pain

in his right knee, Nelson said, "I'd like to suggest somethin and let you all think about it tonight. It might sound crazy."

"Nothing crazy about you," Lynn said. "Fourteen percent of adult Americans say they've seen UFO's."

"I want you to consider that maybe he had somethin in that flight bag that none of us thought about."

"I'm afraid to ask," said Breda.

"Maybe he had a detonator and a nice big blob of Semtex," Nelson said.

"Semtex?"

"Same stuff that brought down the Pan Am flight over Scotland," said Nelson. "Maybe the Dan Quayle idea isn't so far off. Or maybe there's another big politician here for the Bob Hope Classic. There usually is."

Breda and Lynn gaped at one another, while Nelson silently showed them his agreeable expectant grin.

Lynn said, "Well, Nelson, I'll have to sleep on that one. Semtex, huh? I gotta admit one thing: that stuff'd kill a politician faster 'n an endorsement from Jesse Jackson."

-11-

She owed herself a bath like this one, Breda thought. She'd been soaking in bubbles and bath oil for more than an hour, refilling the tub every time the water got tepid, and to hell with California's water shortage. The desert valley had underground water.

There was no getting around it, she *needed* Rhonda Devon's five thousand dollars, less what she'd have to pay Lynn Cutter and Jack Graves. But Breda was beginning to doubt that tailing Clive Devon to picnics and swim parties with Blanca Soltero's daughter was going to resolve anything. Maybe they were just friends.

Breda had been toying again with the idea of having Lynn pose as a patient in need of Clive Devon's urologist. Even if he didn't actually give a semen sample for a fertility check, he was smart enough to interrogate a receptionist, and might learn something about Clive Devon's link to a Beverly Hills sperm bank.

Lizzy needed six hundred dollars next week to cover room and board for a month, and at least another two hundred for her birthday present. Breda thought it best to send money on all holidays and birthdays, because Lizzy needed too many things for her mother to risk buying unnecessary gifts.

Another twelve hundred was due for the home mortgage, and a thousand dollars in office rent was due. Her landlord was the kind of guy who would tip a parking attendant fifty cents and expect to be thanked for it. When she'd complained about her rent the old geek had rolled his watery eyes, leaned over his desk until she was breathing his ghastly cologne and said, "Breda, we could work out something, you and me."

Breda cooled him down by saying, "Melvyn, I'm going to have to trim your nose hair if this conversation is to continue. I've painted my kitchen table with smaller brushes than that."

The crap a woman alone had to put up with to stay in business!

Breda's wildest hope was that Jack Graves would tail Clive Devon to a tryst and videotape it with the camera she was going to provide. She felt certain that if she had absolute proof of a lover, Rhonda Devon would be satisfied enough to confront her husband and deal with the sperm bank question on her own. By now, Breda was certain that the sperm bank *must* have something to do with an heir and money.

She was also sure that, in her own strange way, Rhonda Devon wanted to keep her husband even though she probably had more affairs than the Rolling Stones, and probably with both sexes. Breda hadn't forgotten the way her client had looked at her while drinking that martini. Maybe it wasn't exactly love that Rhonda Devon had for him, but a need for something more than his money.

Well, it was silly to try to understand people who were that rich. They *were* different, Breda was sure of it. So she'd be there in the morning with the video camera and hope that Jack Graves might get the chance to use it. She had faith in him.

Jack Graves. Breda wondered if he and his wife had split up before or after the shooting of the child. She hoped it was before, that a wife wouldn't abandon a man after something like that. He wasn't the first cop to get involved in that kind of a shooting. She could've done it herself once.

Breda and two male detectives had been attempting to serve a felony warrant for murder on a gangbanger at a housing project in Watts. They believed he was at home, but nobody answered their knock at 1:10 A.M. One of the detectives slipped the lock with a credit card and all three entered, guns drawn. Breda took the back bedroom. She heard footsteps. She wheeled and aimed! It was a rabbit.

A white, pink-eyed rabbit was hopping around a bedroom in the ghetto of Los Angeles. There was rabbit shit everywhere, but no suspect. She'd come within an ounce of trigger pull of blowing that bunny's ears off and a lot more. The rabbit stood in front of an infant lying on the floor in a nest of blankets, where she'd been left by her addict mother.

According to Lynn, Jack Graves had killed a twelve-year-old Mexican kid. His bunny had been a human child. Maybe Lynn was right, that getting out of the mobile home and back into something that at least approximated police work would help him. But Breda didn't think it would.

She'd worked with a cop who had the same look as Jack Graves. Stan McAffee, her old partner, used to complain of migraines for which they could find no physiological source. She'd liked Stan, everyone did. They'd go to ball games, movies, even out to dinner. She'd allowed herself to have a belated romance with him, but it was too late. The headaches had grown unbearable, or so he claimed. Three weeks after retiring from LAPD, he'd swallowed The Big .38 Caliber Aspirin.

She'd cried her eyes out at his funeral when the solitary police bagpiper played a somber march while they lowered the casket. Stan had eyes like Jack Graves.

When he got back to his mobile home in Windy Point, Jack Graves carefully watered all his indoor plants. Today was the day to do it, but he hadn't because he'd been busy helping Breda Burrows. He'd have to set the alarm for 5:30 A.M. to allow himself enough time for a bowl of cereal and two cups of coffee. He wouldn't have time to read the paper but he could take that with him. While sitting in his car on Clive Devon's street he'd probably have lots of time to read the paper. He did everything carefully, meticulously. He'd developed an overriding need for order.

The yip yip yip of coyotes. Then a keening, almost lost in the wind. Then more coyote voices, a pack of twelve sounding like a hundred. Jack Graves opened the door and stepped out into the desert night to listen. The wind was howling down the pass and the moon flooded the foothills with white light. And there was a white glaze across the sky but beyond it he could see the dipper. Perhaps the brooding wind or the eerie light was stirring the wild hearts of the little desert wolves. They sounded deliriously happy.

The coyotes were full of themselves all right, singing their songs, wild *young* songs. Jack Graves felt old, and cold to the bone. His teeth clicked together when he walked shivering back inside the mobile home.

The alarm clock was set. He was prepared for tomorrow. Before going to bed he scooped coffee into the automatic coffee maker and poured water from a plastic bottle into the tank, setting the timer for 5:20 A.M. When he put the plastic bottle back into the cupboard he slammed the cupboard door on his fingers.

He cried out, ran to the sink and held his throbbing fingers under cold water. The blood surfaced black, and spread to the size of a bullet wound. He thought he'd probably lose the fingernail. Jack Graves hoped he could sleep with the pain. He was becoming so clumsy that he wondered if, at age forty-six, he was developing a neurological disorder of some kind. So many accidents.

But he slept less fitfully than usual that night. Somehow, the pain was comforting.

The ten o'clock news hadn't ended by the time Nelson Hareem got home to his bachelor apartment in Indio. Nelson went into the bedroom and took off his T-shirt, then went into his kitchen, the size of a large bathtub, and fixed himself a peanut butter sandwich and a glass of milk. Then he switched channels to CMT, since country music was his only passion outside of police work. While Travis Tritt sang "Put Some Drive in Your Country," Nelson dunked the sandwich into the milk, then watched a commercial for mail-order toothpaste that claimed to give you a smile that movie stars paid thousands of dollars to get. He dunked the peanut butter sandwich again. His ex-girlfriend, Billie, had said it was uncouth to dunk, but he'd grown up dunking and couldn't quit.

Restless, he switched back to the TV news, which was still about the war. The Middle East had always depressed him. He didn't feel a shred of kinship with the people of the region, even those in Lebanon. In fact, Nelson had never known his Lebanese grandfather, who'd died when Nelson's father was still a boy. Nelson felt sort of Bakersfield-Okie like everyone else in his family, though he and his sisters had been mostly raised in San Bernardino after his mother had remarried.

Then Nelson got up to switch off the TV, wishing he could remember to buy batteries for the remote control. That Sony was his other real luxury, next to the Jeep Wrangler that he couldn't afford but had to have.

The aquarium looked okay, but he'd have to change the water soon. He sprinkled some food into it and said, "Hello Ollie, hello Liddy" to his two mongrel goldfish, which he liked better than all the fancy ones they'd tried to sell him.

Nelson thought about reading the issue of *Soldier of Fortune* he'd bought in the hope of learning something about terrorists now that he might be on the trail of one, but it seemed to be all about people who'd gone fruity over anything cylindrical that belched flame.

It was discouraging to think of trying to drag Lynn Cutter up to Desert Hot Springs the next day, but really, some of the motels up there would be even better bets for a fugitive seeking a remote base of operations. But Desert Hot Springs was several miles from Palm Springs so the guy would need a car, a cold car. Nelson was turning over in his mind the thought of checking car rental offices. The more he thought about it, the better he liked the idea.

By eleven o'clock he was in bed enjoying a fantasy of being interviewed by *The Desert Sun* after catching the bad guy. In this particular fantasy, the terrorist was trying to plant a plastique explosive on the eighteenth hole of Indian Wells Country Club, where the trophies and checks would be handed out by Bob Hope. Thus, Nelson Hareem was going to single-handedly stop a foreign power from blowing the living shit out of the guy who'd entertained the troops in Saudi Arabia.

The former renter of Nelson's bachelor apartment had tried scratching out a living as a telephone solicitor for anybody that'd pay her a minimum wage, and there was a stack of telephone books in the apartment with listings for most of Riverside and San Bernardino counties, two of the largest counties on earth.

Nelson jumped out of bed, grabbed the bathrobe his ex-girlfriend had given him for his twenty-sixth birthday, and rummaged through the pile until he found the Palm Springs directory. He turned to the yellow pages but was discouraged to see how many listings were devoted to automobile renting and leasing. He should've expected as much in a city that hosts hundreds of thousands of tourists during the season. He tore out the sheaf of pages and put them with page 572—the single page of motel listings A through C that corresponded to the page ripped out of another book by the terrorist.

Nelson spread page 572 flat on the coffee table beside the car rental pages. He had no interest in its other side. Page 571 listed some M's preceding the motel listings. There were modeling agencies, money order services and monument designers.

The fugitive was drinking coffee and studying page 571 of the Palm Springs yellow pages. There were only four listings that concerned him on the page, and he'd decided to memorize those listings and dispose of that page he'd torn from the phone book, just as he'd disposed of the red flight bag. Now he had a beautiful blue leather bag that would fit under an airplane seat, and yet was large enough to carry everything he'd need.

The fugitive read the business names, addresses and phone numbers aloud as he paced back and forth in his motel room.

"Desert Trail Monuments," he said aloud in slightly accented English.

Then he read aloud for practice: "Depend on us to provide the perfect memorial in granite, bronze or marble."

He went into the bathroom and splashed a little more shaving lotion on his face. His upper lip was still pinpointed with a raw and tender telltale rash, where he'd shaved off his mustache. He'd had that mustache since he was twenty-three years old and hated losing it.

He wondered what his wife would say when he got home. He had to admit that he looked a few years younger. Most people said he looked older than thirty-nine years, but it was only the premature baldness. His mother's father had been bald, and three of her brothers. But without the mustache he *did* look younger, he was sure of it.

He resumed his pacing. The second company under monuments was Johnson and Son Memorials. The company was in Desert Hot Springs.

He said it aloud, "Johnson . . . J-J-Johnson." It was hard to say J's.

He'd worked many years at perfecting what everyone said was excellent English, and he'd tried to convince his children that they could not hope to succeed in the future without a solid knowledge of the English language. He was very much aware that one of the reasons he'd been chosen for this mission was because he spoke English better than any of his comrades.

The fugitive began to pace with more determination while he committed the address and telephone number of Palm and Sand Markers. When he was finished with that one, there was one more in Cathedral City, Serenity Markers and Memorials. He liked the name of that one: Serenity. He understood the word very well.

He paced and said quietly: "Serenity, Serenity, Serenity . . ."

-12-

No sneaking up on a guy like Jack Graves, Breda thought. He must've been a pretty good dope-cop. They had an awful lot of dope down there in Orange County where he'd done his work. Breda would've used a man like that in intelligence gathering rather than in drug raids, then he never would've shot that boy. Or was it written somewhere?

He stuck his hand out the car window and waved when she was still thirty feet from the right rear fender of his Mazda. Breda opened the passenger door and got in just as the first low rays were washing over the valley from above the Santa Rosa Mountains.

It wasn't like getting into Lynn Cutter's messy Rambler. Jack Graves' Mazda was disturbingly clean and tidy. He had a thermos of coffee waiting, and two mugs inside a vinyl gym bag. Along with a plastic container of real cream and another of sugar, there were two plastic spoons in a folded paper napkin; everything ready for her, including three pieces of Danish to choose from.

"I thought you might not have time for breakfast," he said, as Breda put the binoculars, video camera and the Clive Devon file folder on the rear seat.

"What, no espresso?" She tore off a piece of Danish to be polite, poured herself some coffee and added a few drops of cream, no sugar. "What time did you get up?"

"I always get up at five-thirty," Jack Graves said, and Breda was sure that it would be at 5:30 A.M. *exactly*. Not 5:20, not 5:40.

"When this case is wrapped up I'm gonna sleep till noon," Breda said.

"Then you'd miss the sunrise. Sunrise and sunset are a part of it. That's when the desert tells you that no matter what, everything's gonna be burned up and blown clean. That's a big part of it, living in the desert, I mean."

Breda sipped her coffee and studied the gaunt, sorrowful face. Then she said, "Know how to work the video camera?"

"Sure. We used them all the time when we worked the Peruvian smugglers. That a Panasonic?"

"Uh huh," Breda said, taking another nibble of Danish though she knew she shouldn't.

"I doubt that I'll be able to tape anything you'd recognize, even with the zoom. The open desert doesn't let any hunter get very close."

"Do the best you can," she said. "Who knows, he might go straight to the Soltero house down in Indio. Far as I'm concerned, if he's swimming and picnicking and visiting that young woman at her house, his wife can start to draw a few conclusions."

"I'd sure hate to tape any hanky-panky through somebody's bedroom window, but I said I'd do the job and I will."

"I don't think it'll come to that," Breda said. "I don't know why, but I don't." She noticed that he couldn't use the word *shoot*. It was *tape* any hanky-panky, not *shoot*.

"I considered getting in the P.I. business," he said, "but I didn't think I'd like it."

"I don't think I like it, but my only skill and training involves dealing with the worst of people, and ordinary people at their worst."

"A lotta the police in this town work the security jobs at the big hotels when they're suspended or on medical leave. I thought about trying to get a security job like that. Trouble is, after you do real police work for a long time you feel over-qualified for the other stuff. I wish I could work with my hands, but I'm not so good with my hands."

Breda looked at the long bony hands of Jack Graves. The first three fingers of his right hand were bruised and swollen. She was almost certain that last night his hands were okay.

She was afraid to ask what happened. "You make good coffee," was all she said.

"That I do," Jack Graves said, smiling. "I guess I could get a job as a short-order cook, couldn't I?"

Breda finished the coffee and the last bite of Danish, and said, "You're set then? You can read the profile I've done on him. It's not very helpful, but if he heads into the barrio down in Indio and loses you, you can figure he'll go to the Soltero house. How about meeting me at The Furnace Room at seven o'clock if he's safely tucked in at home."

"The Furnace Room?"

"Yeah, it's Lynn's home, office and refuge. I've learned to go with the flow, far as he's concerned."

"Okay, see you at seven unless I'm involved with something worthwhile. If I am you won't see me, but I'll call when I can."

"I hope these goodies weren't made with saturated fat," said Breda, enjoying the last crumb.

He liked the blue Buick very much indeed. He would love to have a car like this at home. He believed they wouldn't look for him in a car like this. Besides, he liked big American cars.

The used car had been far easier to buy than his comrades told him it would be. He had a forged California driver's license, obtained in Mexicali. And he had a Mexican license, also counterfeit, in case he needed it. He was simply a Mexican national, in California to do a bit of business with a Los Angeles firm that was trying to set up a *maquiladora* factory south of the international border, using cheap Mexican labor for the assembly of circuit boards.

The Palm Springs men's shop had been expensive beyond belief. His shoes alone—white loafers with little tassels—had cost him $185 U.S. He'd never even bought a suit of clothes that cost that much, not in his whole life. But the clothes made him feel more confident.

The salesman in the shop had chosen a maroon blazer for him, cream-colored trousers and three casual shirts. He'd told the salesman he wanted to be well dressed for Palm Springs evenings. He decided that when he returned home he'd give the coat and trousers to his brother-in-law, who would be only too happy to wear a wine-red coat with gold buttons. He would keep the shirts though; they were cotton, the finest cotton he'd ever seen. The pink one lay softly against his skin. He looked in the rearview mirror as he drove and was relieved to see that his upper lip was healing nicely. The shaving rash was all but gone, and the only evidence of absent facial hair was that his upper lip was not as tan as the rest of his face.

He'd bought two hats, one a Panama, which the salesman in the shop had insisted was "your type of hat." And he'd bought a gray straw snap-brim like the ones he'd seen some of the Palm Springs tourists wearing. There were many bald men in this city, what with so many older people walking about; still he thought he should keep a hat on his head at all times.

He had refined his cover story for two weeks and had no fear in that regard; the only real fear he had was that somehow he'd left a trail after he'd panicked at the airport. He just had to continue reminding himself what he knew to be true, that they were not superdetectives, the U.S. police. It was so easy to feel inferior. In fact, that's what most people in his country did best: feel inferior to Americans.

Real life wasn't like the television shows where the U.S. police could solve any crime with the most sophisticated technology imaginable. The one thing his comrades kept telling him in preparation for this mission was that the U.S. police were no better than he. They were just ordinary police who failed to detect the vast majority of their serious crimes. And he spoke English probably better than any one of them could speak his language. So who was inferior to whom?

He made a right turn on a street in Desert Hot Springs, a street whose name he'd committed to memory. He was in a commercial district with a great deal of light industry, but even in an industrial area there were beautiful trees and plants. On each side of the building there were fan palms, nearly thirty meters high. A heavy thatch of dead palm fronds hung down around their trunks like a young girl's petticoat. It was reassuring to see the fan palms. They were very prevalent in his country. Perhaps it was a good omen. He put on the jacket with the gold buttons and entered the office.

One woman was working at a desk and another was answering a telephone by a filing cabinet. There was a half-door with the top open leading into a small warehouse where he could hear people talking.

"Can I help you, sir?" the woman asked.

She was about his wife's age, but blonde and fair, not half as pretty as his wife, and she wore makeup like the Mexicali whores who'd kept propositioning him when he was trying to secure the forged documents.

"I would like to see about a gravestone, please," he said, in his slightly accented, singsong cadence.

"Would you like something in imperial black?" She opened some brochures stacked on the desk. "You can have a plaque sixteen by twenty-eight for a little over four hundred dollars. I think you'll find our prices competitive. But if you'd like the best, I'd suggest blue pearl granite. It's from Norway, and it's about one thousand dollars. Two hundred more for a custom job."

He leafed through a few pages and said, "You see, I was talking to a man who buried his mother in the Palm Springs area last year in September. He described her monument to me. It was so very lovely, he said. The monument may have been made here. I must have one just like it."

"We don't make our plaques here. We order them. What was the name of the client?"

"That is the problem. I do not know."

"What was the name of the deceased?"

"I am afraid I do not know that either."

"How can I tell you then?" She was one of those American women who had chewing gum in her mouth when she talked. She didn't chew it, but it was there, and she had to move it from side to side in order to speak. He had never found women in the U.S. to be particularly attractive.

"I know the exact date when he called to arrange for the monument," he said. "It was on day thirteen of September."

"Was the deceased buried at the memorial park in Cathedral City?"

"I do not know. I am sorry. I know very little, except that he ordered a tombstone for an old woman on that date. With orchids carved on it."

"Orchids? It was a custom job then."

"Yes, I believe that is so."

"We can do an orchid or any other flower for you. We can order red stone, or green. Green can be quite lovely."

"No, no, please," he said. "I need a monument precisely the same as the one that was arranged on day thirteen of September of last year."

"Just a minute," she said, and picked up the telephone.

It frightened him, the sudden move to a telephone, but this time he didn't panic. He said to himself: What could she be doing? Only calling her boss, nothing more.

"Sam, come in here a minute, will ya?" she said into the telephone.

He pretended to be perusing the brochures until a man in coveralls entered through the Dutch door and said, "Yeah?"

He was a hard-working man. The fugitive had already learned that it was more comfortable to be around working people here than the other kind. This man had hands like those boys he'd met in the stand of tamarisk trees, those boys who had disobeyed him when he told them not to drive the stolen car. He'd read in the newspaper what had happened to them, but it was not his fault, they should have obeyed him. This man had hands like those hard-working boys.

"Sam," the young woman said, "did you deliver a custom order last September for a . . ." She turned to the fugitive and said, "Was it imperial black or what?"

"I am sorry," he said, with an apologetic shrug.

"Okay, coulda been marble, granite, bronze. Did you take any sort of custom job where the client wanted orchids on the plaque?"

"For an old woman," the fugitive said.

"Lots of roses," the man said.

"Orchids," the fugitive said. "For an old woman."

"What was her name?"

"We already been through that," the young woman sighed. "He doesn't know."

"Orchids? No, we didn't deliver no orchids." Then he said, "A daisy. We delivered a daisy plaque for a little girl's funeral."

The mansion was an elephantine dead-white stack of rectangles—a Frank Lloyd Wright ripoff that didn't work—but it was a short walk to downtown so the location was okay.

"You don't look so good," Nelson said, when he arrived and Lynn answered the door in pajamas.

"I was gonna go home early but I ran into a manicurist I met once before in Breda's office. This time she didn't look at me like I was something that'd go tits-up if you found it in your underwear and covered it with blue ointment."

"Did you do her?" Nelson asked, and the leer looked particularly silly on him.

"I hope not," Lynn said. "Cause anyone that'd ball me'd ball *anybody*, and that's scary. But I'm prob'ly safe. In Zimbabwe when a chameleon crosses your path you become impotent. I think it's also true of Palm Springs lizards."

"Come on, Lynn, take a cold shower and let's jam," Nelson said. "I got some new ideas."

When Lynn lurched past a huge gold-leafed mirror in the foyer of the massive house, he looked at his reflection and said, "I'm puffing up like a pigeon. I got MFB."

"What's that?" Nelson asked.

"Massive fluid buildup. I'm horny enough to do the tailpipe of a Studebaker, but it's no use. My sex life's history!"

When they were out on the road in Nelson's Wrangler, with the desert wind in their faces and Lynn nursing a sick head, Nelson put in a tape. "I know you don't like country, but wait'll you hear *this* guy. It's Clint Black. Listen for the cryin harmonica."

Lynn groaned and said, "Got any Furnace Room music? You know, Snookie Lanson's greatest hits?"

"That house you're livin in is the most fantastic place I ever seen," Nelson said as he downshifted, causing Lynn to lurch forward painfully.

"Yeah, it's cozy, like the Kremlin, except the owner has the taste of a Manila pimp. I gotta line up another house-sitting job real soon or I'll be begging a bed from a rich Indian I did a favor for one time. He might take me in. He lets his horse sleep on the patio. I could maybe do his gardening, trade in my gun for a weed-eater. Except his goats do it better. They live on his tennis court."

"How do ya get house-sittin jobs, anyways?"

"Used to be, it was easy. There was always some millionaire looking for a Palm Springs cop to sit his house for a few weeks or a few months. We provided very cheap security for rich guys. But like always, some cop screwed up the deal. One a the house-sitting gigs turned into Animal House Revisited—a party for about twenty cops and two thousand and twelve beauticians, cocktail waitresses and masseuses. The rich guy's dune buggy ended up in the swimming pool. When he got back from Aspen he had to be real careful with his swan dives and back flips. The word got out that cops're unreliable house-sitters."

"You're right," Nelson said with disgust, "there's always a cop that'll screw up the good things for all the others. Some stupid selfish *moron*."

"That's what everybody called me all right," Lynn said. "For the longest time."

Breda opened her office very early and used the quiet time to write checks, both personal and business. She looked through the local paper to see if there was any appropriate office space for rent that she hadn't already called. There wasn't. She started to make coffee but decided she'd had her morning limit. The fact was, it was too damn early to be in the lonely office. Early birds and worms had nothing to do with her business. She was wondering if there were enough clients in Palm Springs for the number of P.I.'s.

Breda looked at her watch. Most physicians opened up at 9:00 A.M. In that Clive Devon's urologist was either stone-walling or knew nothing, she decided to take a shot at his G.P.

The medical building wasn't far from Desert Hospital. In the days of Gable, Tracy, the Marx brothers, Garbo—in Palm Springs' golden age—the hospital had been the city's finest resort hotel, El Mirador.

The receptionist in the G.P.'s office wore a nameplate with only a first name, much like those worn by cocktail waitresses. And indeed she looked like a drink-wrangler. The nameplate read "Candy."

"Good morning." Breda was pleased that there was only one patient in the waiting area, an elderly man who had more than urinary problems; his face was alive with skin cancer.

"Yes?"

"I'd like to talk to Doctor Gladden. It's about my husband."

"He's not with you?"

"No, he's not willing to come in yet," Breda said quietly, glancing at the old man, who was busy reading *Palm Springs Life.*

"Do you wanna make an appointment for him?"

"No . . . yes. I mean, I'd like to talk to the doctor. You see, I'd like him to take a semen sample."

"A fertility check?"

"We're pretty sure he's okay in that regard," Breda said. "Actually, we're considering in vitro fertilization with a surrogate. For now, we'd like to have my husband's sperm stored at whatever sperm bank you use."

"Doctor Gladden's seventy-three years old," Candy said. "He's semiretired and almost never takes a new patient. He's never done anything involving sperm banks in the two years that I been here."

"Really? We have a friend, Clive Devon, who's a patient

of Doctor Gladden. I thought he had it done here, the taking of the sample, the storage, all of it."

"We haven't seen Mister Devon in over a year," Candy said. "Doctor has very few patients these days. If Mister Devon's done something like that it musta been with another physician." Then the young woman said doubtfully, "Are we talking about the same Mister Devon? He's getting on in years, the one we know. A sperm bank?"

The Range Rover cruised south on Palm Canyon Drive and just kept going, to the Indian canyons. Clive Devon was going into the reservation, he and the young woman's big brown dog.

Jack Graves wondered what he was doing with the woman's animal. She'd have to come back to get it, or maybe Clive Devon and she were going to meet up for a desert picnic like the one Lynn had described. Jack Graves hoped there'd be other cars by the Indians' toll booth, but there was only one vehicle on that narrow road. He decided to hang back and allow the Pace Arrow RV to pass, separating him from the black Range Rover. He paid $3.25 admission fee to a huge Indian woman sitting inside a wooden shack.

When the Range Rover got to the fork and turned right into Murray Canyon, Jack Graves stopped his Mazda and waited, letting a station wagon pass him. Then he too made the turn, staying behind the wagon. There were mostly four-wheel drives and station wagons in Murray Canyon that day, and Jack Graves counted at least fifteen hikers already up on the rocks and trails, so he felt safe when he pulled into the unpaved parking area with the other cars.

Jack Graves was wearing his hiking boots and a floppy hat. He'd brought a small canteen and a day-pack. He was ready to cover some ground but he didn't believe that Clive Devon would attempt a strenuous hike. Certainly not to Upper Palm Canyon Falls.

Jack hadn't seen those falls in several years, not since the drought. White water used to drop straight down in a serpentine, between gashes in the granite, and when the light hit the falls just right, the chunky rock glinted like quartz. Cactus and wild-flowers shot out wherever the gashes were wide enough to trap sand and seed. Clumps of leaning yucca lined the granite rock face, lending the oasis effect that made it one of the most pho-tographed sites in the valley. But that was before the five-year drought.

Upper Palm Canyon Falls had always been Jack Graves' favorite spot in all the world. He could stay forever, there by the falls, if such a thing were possible. That's what he'd always thought.

As soon as Clive Devon and the dog began walking, the animal started to bark and romped into a tiny patch of desert sunflowers, Indian yellow, interspersed with the violet-rose of the verbeña. Jack Graves watched through binoculars as Clive Devon whistled for the dog, obviously not wanting him to paw the ground like a young bull and destroy the lovely wildflowers. The flowers were very early, believing spring had arrived.

As soon as he'd offered the minor correction, Clive Devon knelt and roughed up the dog's ears and hugged him. Then they were off again, the man hiking briskly, the brown dog frolicking like a pup, bounding into the cold water of Andreas Creek, which meandered down from the mountains and passed through the palm-shrouded canyon oasis where the rocky cliffs jutted out at 45-degree angles. In past years, Jack Graves had spent hours picking out the profiles of people or the heads of animals in them, nature-carved.

He hiked into Andreas Canyon alongside a group of a dozen riders on horseback, men and women in western garb, two of them on the most beautiful Appaloosas he'd ever seen. There were many places of concealment within the tunnels of palm and rock that sheltered those canyons.

In the afternoon Clive Devon removed his day-pack and

shared a picnic lunch with the dog. Using the pack as a pillow, the man reclined on the hillside with the dog's head on his chest and fed the dog tidbits from his hand. Jack Graves watched from the crest of a terra cotta hill of rock and sand, a hundred yards above them.

Then Jack Graves dug out a nest for himself behind a shelf of rock the color of iron ore, near some Neowashingtonia Filifera palms, seventy feet in height and up to two centuries old. The fan palms were native to the valley, and their presence assured that there was sufficient water either on the ground or close underneath.

He smelled sage, and saw bluebirds overhead, and several waxwings carrying palm fruit. As he watched, a falcon hovered high, then dropped like a rock, swooping up just before crashing into the face of the cliff, snatching something from the crevices that no man could see.

Sometimes he'd been lucky enough to spot some of the endangered bighorn sheep, most of them wearing transmitter collars attached by state conservationists who were trying to guarantee the sheep's comeback. They were majestic beasts, the rams in particular, with their curled, furrowed horns and snowy haunches.

The elusive cougar was probably gone forever except for an occasional cat who'd roamed hundreds of miles from home. Years ago he'd seen one, hiding under the branches of a smoke tree.

He knew there were more than three hundred species of birds in the desert that went unnoticed by the golfing and tennis hordes in the valley below. Jack Graves was glad that the Agua Caliente band of Cahuilla Indians were still the proprietors of these canyons as they'd been for centuries. There would be no resorts in this 32,000-acre reservation.

He looked through the binoculars again and was positive that man and dog were sound asleep now, alone out there by the canyon oasis, shielded from sun and wind by rock and palm, just as the Indians had been shielded since ancient times. He felt very sleepy too. Jack Graves put his floppy hat over his face and laid his head on his own day-pack.

He wasn't close enough to the stream to hear trickling water, but the birds were trilling, and the wind whistled softly. The whine of bees sounded like a plane in the distance. Beyond that was silence, desert silence.

Five minutes later, he was jerked upright by a dream. He was trembling, and droplets of sweat ran from under his hat. He knew that the recurring dream must've started, but it shouldn't come in the daytime! His mind had a new trick: Stop the dream before it gains momentum!

There he was in the darkness, outside the modest little house, the wrong house. He'd been detailed to watch the back door . . .

Nelson Hareem wasn't fooling around anymore. This was his last day with Lynn Cutter so he was going to go for it. He'd even dressed better. He wore a shirt with a collar and long sleeves. And he wore Levi Dockers instead of jeans. But he still wore his red snakeskin cowboy boots.

The sun was high and the desert was warming fast, but Lynn in a short-sleeved knit shirt was chilled from riding in the topless Jeep Wrangler. Hanging on to the roll bar didn't help his sick head. Nelson's jerky driving made him nauseous. Lynn rubbed his arms with both hands trying to help circulation.

Nelson noticed and said, "You still cold, Lynn?"

"Not at all," Lynn said. "Of course I don't expect to find my shriveled balls till April or May, but what the hell, they're useless anyhow."

"How many motels we got left?" Nelson wanted to know, punching his cassette until he got "Miles Across the Bedroom."

Hearing those lyrics, Lynn said, "Please, Nelson, that's the story a my life. Haven't you got something old and appropriate? How about "The Wayward Wind" by Gogi Grant, since you insist on keeping your top down in hurricanes, with snakes and raccoons soaring across the desert like turkey buzzards."

"How many motels, Lynn?"

"Four. We've visited every motel in Palm Springs and Desert Hot Springs that begins with A, B or C. Four more and that's it. I've earned my freedom. Lord a'mighty, free at last!"

"I'm coming back tomorrow alone," Nelson said. "I'm personally gonna check every car rental in this part a the valley. I don't care how long it takes me."

"I believe you," Lynn said, as Nelson made a sharp turn, tossing Lynn against the door of the Wrangler. Without a seat belt he'd have been gone in the first quarter mile. "You march to a different drummer, and a restraining order couldn't stop the beat in your little head."

"I can't help it," Nelson said. "My sergeant says he thinks I'm full a naked aggression."

"Can't we put clothes on your aggression and go home?"

"Only four more motels, Lynn," Nelson reminded him. "There's the next one: The Cactus View."

This one was on the mountain side of Highway 111, in the old residential section of Cathedral City, zoned for single-family residences, apartment buildings and motels. In past years it had been very cheap to live in this part of town, the high-density portion of the working-class community that was sandwiched between big-bucks resorts in Palm Springs and Rancho Mirage. Lately, with the population of the Coachella Valley booming, some very posh homes were sprouting up in Cat City, in the cove near the mountains.

The Cactus View Motel was ripe for redevelopment. It was a one-story, room-and-a-bath accommodation, tucked behind the commercial buildings on the highway. Old bougainvillea had overgrown all of the walls on the sunny side, and was creeping across the cracked and shattered Spanish tile roof. The whitewashed walls on the shady side were blistered, and streaks of rust from the rain gutters stained the stucco.

"This looks like the kinda place a terrorist'd hide," Nelson observed, as Lynn yawned and looked at his watch. It was 2:25 P.M. Just a few more hours.

The manager's office was wide open. Like rattlesnakes, the desert flies laid low during the winter. A pale, watery-eyed guy, bonier than Jack Graves, sat behind a formica counter on a low stool doing a crossword from *The Desert Sun*. He had a sparse tattered fluff of hair like a windblown dandelion. His arms were utterly hairless, and Nelson was astonished to see that he had hardly any eyelashes and eyebrows on one side!

Lynn recognized the motel manager immediately.

"Carlton!" Lynn Cutter cried. "It's you!"

"It's me," Carlton the Confessor agreed. "Yeah, it's me it's me."

He dropped the crossword and slunk from behind the counter like a bag-of-bones coyote. If he'd had a tail it would've been tucked.

"It's me it's me," he repeated. "Ya got me again."

Lynn turned to Nelson and said, "This is Carlton. Everybody knows Carlton."

"Yeah I done it," Carlton the Confessor said. "I done it. I'm ready to go back. I'm ready to go. They never shoulda let me out. I warned em I warned em."

Nelson Hareem stared slack-jawed as Carlton the Confessor began nervously and compulsively pulling at his right eyebrow and eyelashes, where there weren't any left!

"I was tryin to go straight, that's why I took this job, but it ain't no use, is it?"

"Wait a minute, Carlton," Lynn Cutter said. "We just wanna ask a few questions."

"You a captain, sergeant, lieutenant, what? I forget."

"Detective," Lynn said.

"Robbery, burglary, auto theft, what?"

"I used to work CAPS. Crimes against persons."

"What department, I forget."

"Palm Springs," Lynn said.

"Oh yeah, I can clear a lotta old DR's for ya. Oh yeah, I can," said Carlton the Confessor. "Strong-arms, I did lotsa strong-arms nobody knows about."

Nelson Hareem could see that Carlton the Confessor couldn't strong-arm a sand flea, so he thought he better let Lynn handle this guy.

"We'll talk about clearing up our DR's later, Carlton," Lynn said. "First I wanna know if you checked in a guy on Tuesday. A husky dark guy, maybe Mexican or maybe even an Arab. Bald, maybe wore a baseball cap. Coulda carried a red bag."

"What'd he do, burglaries? I done burglaries too. I can tell ya about lotsa burglaries. You show me the reports, gimme the addresses, I'll tell ya if I done em. Prob'ly I done em."

"Wait a minute, Carlton, you can confess later," Lynn said. "First, the dark bald guy. Did you see him?"

"Ain't seen him," Carlton the Confessor said. "Bald? Naw, I checked in six people during the last few days. Four women, two men. Everybody had hair and was very well groomed. No nubs under their arms. I think all a them was gay. I ain't gay. God created Adam 'n Eve, not Adam 'n Steve."

"Scratch this one from your list," Lynn said to Nelson, who sighed and took out page 572 of the motel listings from the pocket of his jeans. Nelson spread the page on the formica counter, but it was face down. He'd left his ballpoint pen in the Jeep so he couldn't draw a line through the listing.

"What else can I tell ya?" Carlton the Confessor wanted to know. "Auto thefts? I done em. Hundreds."

"Yeah, well, I'll come back when I got a whole burglary series I'd like to clear up," Lynn said. "You got a nice job here."

"Yeah I know I know. Lucky to have it, recession and all,"

Carlton the Confessor said. Then he looked down at page 571 of the Palm Springs yellow pages, and said, "What's this? Ya checking out modeling agencies or money order services or monuments and memorials? I done em all. Burglaries were they?"

"Sure," Lynn said. "I hope the monuments and memorials weren't too heavy to carry."

When they were leaving, Carlton the Confessor yelled, "Don't forget to come back when ya need me!" Then he found one eyelash left and plucked it out.

After they were back in the Wrangler heading for the last three motels, Lynn said, "In the old days of questionable statistics I've been told that detectives'd come from miles around to clear up their stats. Carlton'd confess to anything for a ride in a police car and some Famous Amos cookies. Mighta been all that sugar wrecked his brain, I dunno."

–13–

The penultimate motel on their list was several cuts above The Cactus View Motel. It was just off Date Palm Drive, in a more recently developed part of Cathedral City. On the way there, Nelson Hareem finally found a country song with which Lynn Cutter could identify. It was Patty Loveless singing "The Night's Too Long."

Nelson said to him, "This one's about a waitress in Beaumont, Lynn."

"I used to date a waitress from Beaumont!" Lynn said. "I've dated a waitress from every town around here, come to think of it. That might be what killed my sex life, all that greasy food and caffeine."

Nelson was disappointed when he saw the Blue Moon Motel. It had a sign done in pencil-thin pink neon, and the building was peach, pseudo Southwest, with faux-adobe walls, a flat roof, and even two imported saguaro cactus sentinels on each side of the driveway. It was too trendy for a terrorist, Nelson thought.

This time there was a pair of young men at reception. One of them, a big guy with a small head and a fifties flattop, looked at Lynn Cutter's I.D. and said, "How can I help?"

And before Lynn had completed two sentences, the young guy said, "I think that man *was* here. I remember the hat and mustache and the red flight bag. He was in room D, Tuesday night.

"What's his name?" Nelson blurted, and Lynn said, "Easy, Nelson."

The clerk looked through his register. "Mister Ibañez, Francisco V. Residence address is . . . let's see . . . Las Palmas . . . de . . . Gran Canaria, wherever that is."

"I know *exactly* where that is!" Nelson said to Lynn. "I been studying the atlas! The Canary Islands! A Spanish possession across from the Sahara!"

Nelson was so excited he barely listened when Lynn wrote down the scanty register information, complaining to the young man that the guest had failed to fill in the automobile data.

The young guy apologized saying, "The man was in a big hurry and said he'd fill it in later. We always try to get that information."

"Yeah, yeah, okay," Lynn said. "Why'd he only stay one night? Any problem?"

"*That* I can help you with. Said he was attending some kind of seminar or conference. Only staying one night with us because there was a problem with the hotel he'd booked. His room wasn't available till Wednesday."

"Which hotel?"

"He didn't say."

Lynn said, "There's dozens a seminars and conventions this time a year. Did he look like a businessman, a professional man? What?"

"Tell the truth, I didn't pay much attention. The phone

was ringing like mad and I was trying to train my assistant. I just remember the mustache and the red bag. He blew his horn for service when he first drove up, like he thought we did curb service. Never took off his hat so I don't know if he was bald or not."

"And it was a baseball cap, right?"

The young man paused, thought about it, and said, "I can't say for sure if it was a baseball cap."

"Was he pretty scruffy?" Lynn asked. "Like he coulda slept in a car all night? Something like that?"

"Yeah, he was grungy all right. Said he'd been on an airplane eighteen hours."

"Did he speak good English?"

"Real good."

"Could his accent a been, like an Arab accent instead a Spanish?" Nelson asked.

"Gosh, I don't know," the young man said. "He spoke real good though, with a slight accent."

"Did he have any other bags, like maybe in the car?"

"I don't know. Becky took him a feather pillow later. She might know."

"Where can I find Becky?"

"She's back in room D changing linens. That's where he stayed. She didn't get to it yesterday like she shoulda. We're kinda slow right now."

They found a young black woman in room D, watching a soap and having a smoke. She jumped up when they entered.

"We're police officers, Becky," Lynn said, showing his badge. "What can you tell us about the Spanish gentleman that checked into this room on Tuesday? He had a mustache and carried a red bag. You took him a feather pillow, remember?"

"Spanish?" she said. "I thought he was Eye-ranian."

"Whatever," Lynn Cutter said. "Did you see his car?"

"No."

"What kinda hat did he have on?"

"I don't remember," she said. "Did he have a hat on?"

"Was he bald maybe?"

"He was old enough to be bald, but I dunno if he was bald."

"How old *was* he?"

"As old as you almost."

"Anything else you can tell us? Did you see him later when he came or went?"

"No. When I came by with the feather pilla he was crawlin on the floor when I opened the door."

"Crawlin on the floor?" Nelson said.

"Yeah, I figured he lost a contact lens," Becky said. "That's all I seen. He said thanks for the pilla."

When they got out to the Jeep, Nelson was practically hyperventilating. His blue eyes pulsated when he cried, "You know as well as I do! He was praying to Mecca!"

"Calm yourself, Nelson," Lynn said, "or I'll have to give you mouth-to-mouth. And with the women I been seeing lately, you *don't* wanna kiss me."

He'd been saving Serenity Markers and Memorials till last. He was discouraged, but he was also superstitious. The word *serenity* had a pretty sound, and few English words sounded pretty to his ear. If this was not the correct place he was finished, and might as well begin his trip home.

This one was in a Cathedral City industrial park on Perez Road. On both sides of the street there were dozens of shoebox buildings with overhead metal doors. Some had the business names stenciled or painted on the office window. This one had a large wooden sign up near the roof on the face of the building: SERENITY.

He was wearing the Panama. It was too hot to put on the gaudy blazer. He was hungry and wanted a beer, but wouldn't have a drink while he was working. When he entered the office, he found a workman dressed in denim, using the phone in the office. The workman's black hair was covered with pale dust, and a pair of goggles hung on a strap around his neck. This company obviously made their own memorials rather than stocking mass-produced plaques like the others he'd visited.

When the workman hung up the phone the fugitive smiled and said, "Can you help me, please? I am looking for a gravestone just like the one that was made for a woman who died last September. It was a beautiful stone. I must have one like it."

"Did we do it?"

"I am not sure. I think yes, but I do not know the name of the dead woman. It was ordered on day thirteen of September."

"Who was the customer?"

"I do not know, but he showed me a photograph of the stone. It was so lovely. I must have one for my aunt who died last Friday."

"Last September you say? What'd it look like?"

"From the photo I cannot be sure if it was marble or granite. But there were orchids carved on it."

"One on each side a the woman's name," the workman said. "Single grave, sixteen by twenty-eight, right?"

"You did the work?" the fugitive cried.

"Sure," the workman said. "Only time I ever got a call for custom orchids."

"Please! I *must* see the stone with my eyes to be sure it is exactly what I want for my aunt! Please to tell me the name of the person who ordered the stone?"

"Well, I only do the engraving and sandblasting," the man said. "Martha's the one you should talk to. She's gone to the bank to make a deposit. Can you come back later?"

"When?"

"Twenty minutes maybe?"

"Do you remember the name on the stone?"

181

"No, I can't remember. I do so many."

The fugitive needed all his self-control to remain calm and businesslike when he said, "I have a problem at the moment. I need very much to order the stone at once. I must go to Los Angeles on business. If you can look in your files for last September it might be possible to find the name. Then I could contact the customer and discover where the stone is placed so that I can see it with my eyes."

The man smiled, shook his head, and said, "Not me, Mister. Martha'd kill anybody that went into her files. Besides, I don't have no idea how to work a computer."

"Oh. Your transaction is on a computer?"

"I don't know nothing about that part of it. I can do a design and tape it off and I can sandblast it till you have the prettiest orchids you ever seen. But I can't go into Martha's files."

"I understand," the fugitive said. "I may wait here until the lady returns?"

"Help yourself," the workman said. "I gotta get back to work."

When he was alone, the fugitive sat and picked up a magazine, thinking about Martha and what he would say to her. What if she was one of those officious Americans who would only give him enough information to select his gravestone and nothing more? Then he'd have to take the information by force, or risk burglarizing this place. He was sure that the building had an alarm system.

The fugitive could hear the hiss of sandblasting outside the office. He got up, went to the front door and looked outside. There was no car parked immediately in front, not even his own. He made a quick decision, and walked around the reception counter to the file drawers. The first one contained nothing but brochures for memorials of all kinds.

He opened another and discovered what looked like order

forms. The company had a computer, but they also had an invoice system. He found some orders that were placed by those other companies he'd visited. Serenity appeared to be the only manufacturer in the area. He worked from front to back and discovered that they were in chronological order.

Locating September, he found a large number of invoices. He grabbed the entire batch including some from August and October, just to be sure.

He was shoving them inside his pink cotton shirt when a woman said, "What're you doing?"

He would've recognized Martha. She was taller than he, and almost as heavy. She was a woman of about sixty years, and was so angry there was no point in talking. What could he say, in any case?

The fugitive simply smiled in embarrassment and walked deliberately toward the door, holding out his hand as though to say, "Please, Martha, step back." But he said nothing.

"Who *are* you?" Martha demanded. "And where do you think you're going with those?"

He kept advancing, meaning only to fend her off so he could get to the door, but she grabbed his arm and said, "Here, you! Drop those files! Then she screamed: "MIKE! COME QUICK!"

The fugitive shoved the woman hard and heard her grunt when she thudded into the wall and fell to the floor.

She screamed, "MIKE! HELP! HELP!"

The fugitive was glad he'd done one thing right, at least. He'd parked out on Perez Road, just in case. He hadn't wanted anybody writing down his license number if something went wrong. He certainly didn't want to steal any more cars.

He ran through the parking lot with no one chasing him. When he got to his car and started it, he made a U-turn to avoid being seen by anyone running out the front door, and as he drove, he was careful not to exceed thirty-five miles per hour.

He was approaching Date Palm Drive when he saw a Cathedral City police car about to turn west on Perez Road. He wheeled into another industrial park. He believed that the response time to Martha's call would be fast, so he only had a few minutes.

He waited a moment, then eased his car back onto Perez Road, but he saw that the police car had pulled over to the side of the street. The officer was writing something. The fugitive couldn't wait any longer. He drove out and turned west on Perez Road away from the police car, but as he neared Cathedral Canyon Drive he saw yet another police car! He was about to be sandwiched!

The fugitive made himself turn left into *another* business park, hoping both police cars would go by. He drove to the rear of the building, but slammed on his brakes when he found himself confronting four more Cathedral City police cars!

The fugitive wheeled around and was retreating out the driveway when the first policeman he'd seen came right at him! The fugitive stopped.

When he did, the policeman pulled his car alongside, facing the other direction, and said, "Looking for the post office?"

Too frightened to speak, the fugitive nodded and tried to smile.

"Around the front," the policeman said. "To your right."

The fugitive was afraid to say thank you. He merely waved, and did as the policeman said. He wanted to speed away on Perez Road, but he did not. He pulled into the front parking lot with all the other cars.

It appeared to be a little shopping center like so many he'd seen. The Cathedral City police station was just a series of storefronts, tied together. In a bizarre way, it was reassuring. It was the way it would be in his own country: a police station crammed between a post office and an Armenian chiropractor.

When the fugitive finally did begin to drive back out onto

Perez Road, a police car squealed from behind the police station, heading east on Perez, no doubt on its way to take a report from Martha. The fugitive turned west, back to Palm Springs, and only then did he relax enough to pull the wad of invoices from inside his shirt. They were slimy from his sweat. His beautiful new pink shirt was drenched. He couldn't wait to get back to the hotel and order a beer. *Two* beers.

He wondered what the policeman would make of it, someone stealing work invoices. Probably that he was a madman. That's what a reasonable person would make of it. He suddenly felt weak, and the tension started to dissipate. He smiled when he thought of all those police cars, Chevrolets, each with a wide blue stripe and a stylized decal on the door: a mountain, a palm tree and a red fireball of sun.

They even have beautiful police cars in this country, the fugitive thought, admiringly.

When Nelson was driving south on Date Palm Drive intending to take Lynn back to The Furnace Room, he was still pumped. "Lynn, you gotta admit we done a good job even if we sorta ran outta leads temporarily."

"Nelson, we still don't know for sure if Francisco V. Ibañez from the Canary Islands is your drug smuggler, pardon me, your terrorist."

"We know in our hearts, Lynn. Anyways, I'm gonna keep diggin. I'm gonna call or go to every single car rental company in Palm Springs tomorrow. I got a hunch he's after somebody big, somebody that's here for the Bob Hope Classic."

"Good luck, Nelson," Lynn said. "You might see if Donald Trump's playing. If he is, don't try to stop the bad guy. There's such a thing as *good* terrorism, you know."

"By the way," Nelson said, "Francisco V. Ibañez blew his horn when he wanted service at the motel, didn't he?"

"So?"

"That's real uncool, honkin your horn in California. Only tourists do it."

"So? He's a tourist, ain't he?"

"In *Arab* countries they use their car horns for everything. They play sonatas with em. I read it somewheres."

Then Nelson noticed the local TV news car driving on Perez Road, and Lynn almost got thrown into Nelson's lap when the little cop whipped the Wrangler to the right.

"What're you doing, Nelson?" Lynn demanded.

"Might be a two-eleven in progress or somethin! Let's check it out!"

"Get me outta here!" Lynn said, but Nelson stomped down and sped toward the TV news car as it was about to turn into the industrial park. While the news car waited for the oncoming traffic to clear, Nelson pulled up beside them and flipped out his badge.

"What's up?" Nelson asked them.

"Offbeat story," a camera guy said. "Somebody roughed up an old lady at a tombstone company and stole her work invoices. We're gonna do an interview under the 'Some-guys'll-steal-anything' sort of story."

"I'll watch for it tonight," Nelson said, as the news car turned into the parking lot and stopped in front of Serenity Markers and Memorials.

"That's not a bad lead," Nelson said to Lynn, and kept driving west. "Some guys'll steal anything."

"We had a patrol officer, tried to put together a video on offbeat crime," Lynn said. "Spent a fortune on video equipment, but all he ended up with was a boring two hours that showed what everybody already knows: people're thieves. The *Heaven's Gate* of home movies is what he ended up with."

All of a sudden, Nelson screamed: "TOMBSTONE COMPANY!"

And this time he jumped on the brakes, wrenched the wheel, and spun a U-ee at the same time.

Lynn had to grab the roll bar with both hands and hang on while Nelson roared back to Serenity Markers and Memorials code three, but without a siren.

When Nelson slid the Jeep to a stop, Lynn said, in the monotone of a psychopathic killer, "You better have an explanation for this, cause now my neck hurts so much I don't even know I *got* knees anymore. You have maybe two minutes to live."

But Nelson already had page 571 of the Palm Springs yellow pages unfolded and was waving it before the bloodshot eyes of Lynn Cutter, saying, "Remember Carlton the Confessor? What he said about markers and memorials? This is it, Lynn! This is why Francisco V. Ibañez tore out the page!"

Nelson's stubby little finger was pointing to a list on the page, at the same name that was painted on a sign high on the face of the building.

"We shouldn't get too excited about this!" Nelson warned, spraying the older man's face with saliva. "We gotta stay cool till the reporter gets outta there! THIS IS OUR DEAL, LYNN, NOBODY ELSE'S!"

"Well, that's it," Lynn said, in resignation. "I don't know how it's gonna end, but I'm being dragged to destruction. I'll be tits up on a slab, either a victim of Francisco V. Ibañez or Nelson Hareem."

"Y'know somethin I noticed back at the motel?" Nelson said, as they waited in the Jeep.

"I don't wanna know."

"There was *wire* outside the room where Francisco V. Ibañez stayed at. A few pieces a colored wire were in the maid's trash bin."

"I'm afraid to ask for the significance."

"Coulda been from his timing device. For a Semtex bomb!"

"I won't bother to point out it also coulda been from the electricians working on the air conditioning," Lynn said, in his new monotone-of-the-doomed.

After the TV people drove off, Lynn and Nelson found Martha, with a bruised elbow, torn pantyhose and a big, big smile. She was going to be on the eleven o'clock news!

Martha didn't mind talking to two more cops. She hadn't had so much attention since she'd taken down the license number of a drunk delivery man who'd destroyed four parked cars and the entire corner of Duncan's Discount Golf before a cop blew out the drunk's tire during a freeway pursuit. She'd gotten thirty seconds on screen that time.

"Like I told the uniformed policemen and the reporters, he was a maniac!" Martha told them. "Wanted a grave plaque for his aunt. Mike is the one talked to him, but when Mike left him alone he helped himself to our files. A maniac!"

"What'd he look like?" Nelson asked.

"A Mexican, about forty, stocky build."

"Bald?" Nelson asked.

"Can't say. Wore a straw hat, like a Panama hat."

"Did he have a mustache?"

"No."

"What kinda gravestone did he want?" Nelson asked.

"He wanted orchids. A custom job with orchids engraved on it. Said we did one like he wanted for somebody last September thirteenth."

"Did you?"

"Yeah, but I don't know who. He stole all the September invoices."

Nelson said, "Whyn't ya jist pull it outta the computer?"

"Sorry, hon," Martha said. "I'm just learning about computers. Taking a course over at College of the Desert, and soon as I learn how, we're gonna computerize our files."

"Nothin's on the computer yet?"

"Nothing to do with our business."

Lynn, who was coming out of the mental state in which all of this had placed him, said, "How about the guy he talked to? What can he tell us?"

"Mike? Nothing more than he told the other policeman. The guy wanted a plaque with two orchids, like the one Mike did last September. Didn't know the customer's name. Didn't know the name of the deceased woman. Orchids. That's about all he knew, orchids. A custom job."

Lynn said, "Give Mike a call and ask him to come in here, will you?"

A few moments later, Mike entered the office, less dusty than when he'd talked to the fugitive.

Martha said, "These guys're policemen, Mike. They wanna hear again about the guy that wanted orchids."

"I told the other cop everything I know," Mike said. "If I can ever think a the woman's name I'll call and let ya know. But I can't right now."

"If you ask me he was just some lunatic," Martha said.

"But he was right about the stone," Mike said. "I *did* a plaque with a woman's name on it, and two orchids beside the name. And it mighta been last September, like he said. I never done orchids before. It was a beautiful custom stone, I remember that much."

Lynn said, "Mike, when you do a beautiful custom job you're proud of, don't you ever take a picture of it? You know, to show other customers?"

That caused both Mike and Martha to look at each other and smile. Then Martha said, "The *boss* does!"

Mike was interested enough to hang around while Martha went through the boss's desk, explaining that he'd gone skiing for a few days. She found a manila folder in a drawer and waved the cops inside his office.

Then she handed a batch of photos to each of them and said, "Look for orchids."

They were only looking for a few minutes when Mike said, "I *thought* it began with an L. There it is: Lugo."

Lynn, with Nelson draped over his shoulder, looked at a photo of a large flat grave plaque engraved with:

María Magdalena Lugo
Born 23 May 1901
Died 12 Sept 1990

"What information is on your invoice?" Lynn asked.

"It'll have the deceased's name and what the customer wanted on the plaque. It'll say how much we quoted and who ordered it. With a phone number, *maybe*. With an address, *maybe*. We had some temporary help working here last summer." Then Martha said, "You can keep the picture if you want it."

"Give it to whoever does a follow-up investigation," Lynn told her.

"Isn't that what *you're* doing?"

"No, we're not from Cathedral City P.D.," Lynn said. "We have another matter, possibly involving the same guy."

"Yeah?" Mike said. "Is this guy Mafia or what?"

"Why do you say that?" Nelson asked.

"The Italian name there, Lugo. Could be Spanish, I guess."

Lynn decided it was time to get out of there before they started asking too many questions. He pushed Nelson toward the door before Martha asked something he didn't want to answer, like, "What's *your* name, officer?"

As she was about to speak, Lynn quickly said, "Hey, Mike. On that subject, know what FBI stands for?"

"What?"

"Forever bothering Italians," Lynn said. "Or, famous but incompetent."

Mike let out a hoot and said, "That's good! Hear that, Martha?"

When Mike turned back toward the door, Lynn and Nelson were gone.

The fugitive was disappointed at what little information was on the invoice. He'd decided to telephone every funeral director in the Coachella Valley. On the sixth call he reached the correct one.

The fugitive said, "Please, can you help me? I am trying to be in touch with an old friend. I think perhaps you assisted him with the funeral of his mother. Her name was María Magdalena Lugo. She died in September of last year. It is *urgent*."

The woman who'd answered the phone said to him, "That was our funeral, but Mister Lieberman isn't here at present. He'll be here for a service this evening at six. If you'd care to come by, he can help you."

When he thanked her and hung up, he looked at his watch and resisted the temptation to have the beer he longed for. This was definitely duty time. He took a shower and shaved, the second shave that day, and he put on his eggshell-white cotton shirt. Since he had not worn the gaudy blazer into Serenity Markers and Memorials, he thought it was perfectly safe to wear that evening.

He put on the blazer and looked in the mirror. He wished he'd been able to have the sleeves shortened a bit, but of course there'd been no time. Now time had new meaning.

When they were once again rocketing down Perez Road in the Jeep Wrangler, Lynn grabbed the roll bar and said, "Nelson, where in the hell're you going?"

"I dunno!" Nelson said.

"Then why're we in such a hurry to get there, goddamnit? Anyway, the guy didn't have a mustache!"

Nelson slowed down and said, "He shaved, is all. Where we going, Lynn?"

"To a phone. Drive to a phone and get me a couple dimes."

They parked at a gas station on Cathedral Canyon Drive, and Lynn looked up the phone number of the cemetery while Nelson went to get change.

When Lynn placed the call, he said, "Hello, my name's William Lugo. I'm trying to get in touch with a family member I haven't seen in several years. This relative arranged for our aunt to be interred at your cemetery last September. Her name was María Magdalena Lugo. Can you help me?"

Nelson paced, then Lynn said into the phone, "Yes? Yes, I do understand. Thanks."

He hung up as Nelson said, "So tell me!"

"They won't say anything over the phone about their clients. All she'd tell me was that Mrs. Lugo's funeral was handled by Lieberman Brothers Mortuary in Palm Springs."

"Let's go!" Nelson said.

"I think it's time to call the cops," Lynn said, "even though I'm sure *you* think *we* qualify."

-14-

The fugitive tried to look as different as he could, given his limited wardrobe. He would not wear the Panama again, not after the episode with Martha, so he wore the snap-brim hat. He'd considered buying a wig after he saw them advertised in the window of a shop in downtown Palm Springs, but he was certain that a bald man with a wig would look like a bald man with a wig. He might call *more* attention to himself if the police were intensifying their search for a bald man.

He realized that most of his fears were groundless. They'd probably given up on finding the drug smuggler from the airport. They must still think he was a drug smuggler, what else would they think? As far as the episode at the gravestone company, well, that would just seem like the behavior of a crazy man, that's what the fugitive believed.

He found the mortuary on a street near Gene Autry Trail.

In the magazine at the hotel, the fugitive had read that Gene Autry was a famous old movie star, but he'd never heard of him.

It was only six P.M. but it was very dark. The desert always seemed dark even on nights when the moon and stars were especially brilliant. He thought it was the way the clouds scudded across the moon, hurling patches of shadow down onto the desert floor. He thought of all the predators hunting and being hunted amongst those desert shadows.

When his father used to take his family out to their own desert to visit his grandmother's village it always made for a great holiday. He'd always felt good in the desert, but frightened too, and that made him more alert.

The fugitive parked the Buick, as always, half a block from his destination. Better to run half a block during an emergency than to have his license number written down. While he was walking along the pavement toward the funeral home, still thinking about deserts and old times, a Jeep Wrangler without a top sped past him and squealed into the parking lot.

That's how young people drove in his country too, the fugitive thought. Soon his son would want to drive the family car. He dreaded that day, but what could he do? Suddenly, he couldn't wait to get his terrible assignment finished and return home to his wife and children.

There were several people getting out of cars to go inside the mortuary. He decided to wait until the parking lot was quiet before entering.

The argument had begun at the telephone stand, continued all the way up Cathedral Canyon Drive, intensified when they crossed the bone-dry wash of Whitewater River, subsided when Nelson turned south from Ramon Road onto Gene Autry Trail and parked in front of the mortuary.

Lynn Cutter said, "This . . . is . . . freaking . . . it, Nelson!

I'm gonna go along and see what this Lugo thing might or might not have to do with Francisco V. Ibañez, who might or might not be the guy from the airport. But then, if any a this crap makes any sense whatsoever, I'm calling the Indio sheriffs and turning this garbage over to them! Whether you like it or not!"

"One more day, Lynn! Jeez!" Nelson's hair had been blown into tangles and he was glowing with frustration. "*One* more day! I'm close to this guy!"

"Tell you what," Lynn said. "I won't call the sheriffs. I'll let *you* either call em or not call em. After we talk to this mortician, *I'm* outta this mess, hear me?"

Nelson stalked out of the Jeep, managing to keep his mouth shut, and followed Lynn to the door of the funeral home where they could hear an organ playing softly.

It was a sprawling T-shaped building with add-on construction. On the left was the embalming room and private offices. To the right was the foyer and a viewing room—chapel where about forty people sat while a priest said a few words about a deceased parishioner, prior to saying the rosary.

The priest said, "Many's the time we heard Denny O'Doul's lovely tenor leading the choir during the years he lived in happy retirement in our parish."

A man in a shiny gray suit said to Lynn and Nelson, "Would you care to sign the guest book?"

"We're not here for the service," Lynn said, showing the man his badge. "Are you Mister Lieberman?"

"No, he's in his office," the man said. "Down the hall."

Lynn and Nelson walked along the tiled corridor and heard a man in a small office beside the embalming room, talking on the phone. Holding his badge aloft, Lynn stood in the open doorway and knocked softly after the man hung up.

The mortician was barely able to squeeze out of his high-backed executive chair. He was a three-hundred pounder, without a neck, but with a wheeze that sounded like worn-out brake shoes.

"I know this is a bad time," Lynn said, "but it's urgent. We need to find the next of kin of María Magdalena Lugo who died last September."

"Is something wrong?" the mortician asked, wheezing as he lit another cigarette.

"It's important for him that we have a talk. If it was a him, the next of kin, I mean."

"Mister John Lugo," the mortician said. "Couldn't forget him. Wanted the best of everything for his dear mother."

"And where does Mister Lugo live?" Lynn asked, as Nelson advanced expectantly.

The mortician opened his desk drawer, removed a Rolodex, then wheezed again. He thumbed through the Rolodex and said, "I don't know his permanent address, but he gave a local address and local phone number, as well as an L.A. phone number." He pushed the Rolodex across the desk to Lynn, who took his half-glasses from his shirt pocket, wrote down the information on a note pad, tore out the page and handed it to Nelson.

"Hope there's no trouble," the mortician said. "He was really a fine gentleman. Small funeral, but so elegant. And orchids. I never saw so many. His mother had raised orchids."

"We'll give him your regards," Lynn said. "By the way, do you know what business he's in?"

"No," the mortician said, "but he must do very well. He had his own limo and driver, not leased, he owned it."

"Is he a Spanish gentleman?" Nelson asked.

"I don't know," the mortician said. "Lugo's one of those names, isn't it? He seemed more Italian-American than Hispanic, if you know what I mean. But he could've been a Latino, I just can't say."

Never one to give up gracefully, Nelson asked, "Could he've been an Arab?"

"Oh, I wouldn't think so," the mortician said. "But these days, who knows? If I were an Arab-American I'd change my name to something like Lugo, wouldn't you?"

"Maybe I would," said Nelson Hareem.

"Thanks for your trouble," Lynn said.

When they were at the door, a man in a maroon blazer, wearing a snap-brim hat, stepped back politely to allow them to leave.

They didn't pay any attention except that Nelson said, "Thanks."

When they got to the car, Lynn said, "Damn, I left my reading glasses on the desk. Be right back."

Lynn walked inside just as the rosary was starting in the viewing room. A few of the more robust among the faithful were kneeling on the floor, but most were seated while they prayed.

"Hail Mary full of grace, the Lord is with thee, blessed art thou . . ."

Lynn was thinking about the first drink of the evening while he walked toward the little office and saw the back of the bald man in the maroon blazer, who was holding his hat in his hands.

Mr. Lieberman looked up and said, "Oh, you've returned! I was just telling this gentleman that the police were *also* trying to find . . ."

The fugitive suddenly lunged at the card, ripping it from the Rolodex. Then he mashed his hat against the face of Lynn Cutter, hooking a short right to his solar plexus that made Lynn double up and out-wheeze the mortician, who yelled, "Hey!"

The fat man got up and lumbered forward in time to grab the collar of the maroon blazer, but the fugitive ducked, spun, and hooked the mortician with the same shot. The mortician was encased in so much blubber he only wobbled, so the fugitive popped him again with a straight left that caught him on the temple, and the mortician skittered like he was dancing on marshmallows, then teetered and collapsed on Lynn Cutter, who was trying to *breathe* with the mortician on top of him, flopping like a gigantic trout.

The fugitive scurried into the corridor but his new white

leather shoes slid from under him. He went down, bounced up and, trying to get traction, smacked into the gangling guy in the gray suit who'd come running down the hall toward the ruckus.

The fugitive didn't have to hit him, and had almost made it back to the foyer when Lynn Cutter leaped on his back and they knocked over the guest-book table, sending a huge floral arrangement spinning into the wall in an explosion of gladioli.

The fugitive, who was in better shape, bulled Lynn off his back and muscled under him now that he was standing on carpet, but Lynn grabbed on, whirled, and spun the fugitive through the open double doors. And suddenly the fugitive was smack in the middle of kneeling mourners. Then: pandemonium!

Everybody started hollering and screaming and trying to stream out, including two Irish nuns, and Lynn Cutter plowed through the panicked crowd, walking over a pile of old Micks who couldn't get off their knees fast enough. The fugitive shoved two guys into the priest, who knocked over two candelabras and another floral spray, and water flooded everywhere!

The fugitive, leaking blood from his nose, crouched and waited, while old folks hollered and hissed and stacked up at the door like heaps of brittle sticks.

Lynn warily advanced toward the fugitive until he had the guy backed up against the bier of Denny O'Doul, who looked like a painted mummy.

And then, still gasping and bug-eyed, Lynn charged! The fugitive feinted and threw a short punch that didn't land. But he grabbed Lynn by the curly hair, jerking him forward until his forward motion plunged Lynn's head and shoulders *inside* the casket. Then the fugitive slammed the lid on Lynn's neck, and those poor old mourners who had the courage to look started wailing and keening, like at a real old-fashioned Irish wake!

Denny O'Doul's rosary beads got looped around Lynn's ear, and the old tenor's hands had come unclasped, dead cold and papery against Lynn's face, and Lynn couldn't breathe again! But when he turned his head sideways to inhale, he smelled corn flakes!

The fugitive put his weight on the casket lid and kept hooking Lynn, once, twice, three times in the ribs and kidneys, bashing more air out of him while Denny O'Doul's eighty-five-year-old widow passed out cold, and nutty notions roared through Lynn's skull, like: Why the fuck does Denny O'Doul smell like *corn flakes?*

Then the horrible pressure was released, and Lynn shoved backward as hard as he could, popping out of the casket like a cork, falling and tumbling over backward.

By the time Lynn's world had straightened out, the fugitive had crashed through the fire exit opposite the foyer and was gone.

Nelson Hareem was sprawled in his Jeep with his earphones on, listening to Reba McEntire singing "Rumor Has It." But Nelson pulled off the ears when he saw a bunch of people running out the front door of the mortuary and *screaming*. Then he saw Lynn Cutter sort of running out after them!

When Lynn got under the palm tree lights Nelson saw that he was limping and had blood on his face!

Nelson jumped from the Jeep when Lynn was thirty feet away, but Lynn screamed: "GET US OUTTA HERE!"

Lynn groaned in pain when he jumped into the Jeep, snatching at the bar with one hand, holding his ribs with the other, as Nelson backed up the Jeep and painted two rubber stripes on the parking lot.

"Did you see a car?" Lynn hollered.

"What car?"

"Any car! Did you see one?"

"There were some headlights a minute ago!"

"Catch that fucking car! And gimme your gun!"

They *didn't* catch the fucking car. In fact, they didn't even see taillights when they got out onto Gene Autry Trail. Nelson didn't know whether to go north or south.

"What'll I do, Lynn?" Nelson wanted to know.

"I'm outta ideas," Lynn moaned.

"What happened in there?"

"He beat the crap outta me! He put me in a coffin!"

"Who?"

"Francisco V. Ibañez, that's who!"

"What?"

"Don't gimme *what*! Drive!"

Nelson was so baffled, confused, excited, that for once he wasn't even speeding. "How could he be in there? How could he put you in a coffin?"

"Not very gently! Will you step on it?"

"Where?"

"The Furnace Room. Where else can I escape this miserable insane lunatic case?"

"You're bleeding, and you're nuts!" Nelson said, stomping on the accelerator, swerving around a white Caddy.

"That's *his* blood! *I'm* bleeding internally! The sonofabitch tried to bust my spleen!"

"How could somebody put you in a coffin, Lynn? Tell me what happened!"

"We fought! He won!" Lynn yelled. "I did a whoop-de-do into the coffin! Then he slammed the goddamn lid on me!"

"Good Lord!" Nelson cried. "That's the scariest thing I ever heard of!"

Suddenly, Lynn looked bleakly at Nelson Hareem and said, "Now I know what poor old Bela Lugosi and Christopher Lee went through all those years! My sphincter's slammed shut!"

"I know how you feel!" Nelson cried. "It feels like some-body's Krazy-Glued *my* asshole too!"

This was the first time the fugitive regretted not choosing a cheap motel for more privacy. The layout of this elegant hotel almost guaranteed that guests would be seen entering and leaving by way of the expansive lobby.

When he parked the Buick in the guest parking lot he took off the maroon blazer, and was glad of the color. He used it to wipe the blood from his face.

The fugitive wasn't badly hurt, just a nosebleed. He'd had a tendency toward nosebleeds since childhood. When he was a boy playing soccer, his jersey was always blood-soaked by the end of a game, and his mother would weep at the sight of him.

He was hatless and his face was slightly swollen, so he kept his head down and walked briskly across the lobby to the elevators, the blazer over his shoulder, hiding his shirt. A woman standing by the elevator looked at him curiously and he realized that his right nostril had started leaking. He patted his pocket reassuringly, touching the Rolodex card, and pushed the elevator button for the third floor.

When he got to his room, he removed the card from his pocket and switched on the lamp beside the king-sized bed. He read the name John Lugo, and the Palm Springs address, and the phone number, which he realized was local. He saw another phone number which he thought was probably somewhere in Los Angeles. He would memorize all of it, but later.

His beautiful new shirt had three buttons missing, and the breast pocket was torn and hanging loose. He stripped off the shirt and crammed it into the wastebasket. The fugitive sat on the bed, pulled off the white loafers and lay back on the pillow, sniffling gently, waiting for the blood to stop.

His confidence had been very badly damaged. He couldn't begin to imagine how they'd found him. Of course, he would've recognized the one with curly hair as a policeman the second he saw him standing there, even if the mortician hadn't verified it. The man just *looked* like a policeman. But how had he been traced? Maybe they *were* as efficient as on the TV shows!

Yet it made no sense. Why would they devote such diligence to tracking a man who'd simply pushed an old lady down and stolen some files? Was it conceivable that they'd begun hunting him after he'd attacked the policeman at the airport? That was a more serious crime, of course. But how could they have connected him to that incident? Impossible!

Then he remembered reading a news story in his country about a California man who'd raped a teenager and hacked off her arms, leaving her to die in the desert, but miraculously, she'd survived. That man had served only eight years in prison and was now free on parole! The story had been given prominent coverage to show his people what it's like in the United States. The implied question was: Do you really want to live in a country where someone can commit such a horrible crime and be a free man after only eight years?

And yet . . . and *yet*, for a minor crime like pushing an old woman and taking some worthless files, he was pursued and hunted down with unbelievable speed. And almost caught!

If he got home alive, and now he'd begun thinking *if*, he would never set foot in this crazy country again, not as long as he lived. *If* he got home alive . . .

Lynn had wiped the fugitive's blood off his face, but he looked grim as he entered The Furnace Room. He gimped along, passed Wilfred Plimsoll without so much as a wave, and headed straight for the table in the back, near the yawning fireplace. He was as happy as he could be under the circumstances to see that Breda was already there, waiting.

Nelson said, "I'll get the drinks, Lynn."

When Lynn plopped down across the table from Breda, he was hanging on to his ribs like his guts were falling out. His right eye was slightly swollen and his knuckles were scuffed and raw.

"Did you get in a fight, or what?" Breda asked. "You look awful!"

"As a matter a fact I've been in bed. Dracula's bed."

"Whadda you mean?"

"I was in a coffin."

"You mean, like a small room?"

"Well, it was pretty small," Lynn said. "And there were two of us in there."

"Care to explain?"

"Can I have a drink first? I got a taste of formaldehyde I gotta get rid of. And the smell of corn flakes!"

Lynn didn't really begin explaining until he'd had his second dose of eighty proof anesthetic. When Lynn finally got into it, Breda listened in disbelief to the day's antics. And Lynn lost his train of thought once or twice, because he found himself paying too much attention to the freckle on her lip.

After he was through, Breda handed her glass to Nelson and said, "I think I need another one, Nelson, do you mind?"

When Nelson was at the bar fetching another round, Breda said, "Did you give your name to any of those people today?"

Lynn shook his head slowly and said, "At least I had that much sense. I flashed my buzzer, is all. There's gonna be a lotta speculation about a middle-aged fat guy and a red-headed munchkin in red snakeskin cowboy boots impersonating officers of the law."

"What're you gonna do about all this?"

"Eat. Wanna go to dinner? I'll even buy, as long as it's not one a those yuppie joints where they serve radicchio and tofu. The way they *don't* decorate those hard-surface joints, the decibel level gets so high I wanna stuff my ears with their angel hair pasta. Which generally ain't edible anyway."

203

"That's one of the more unusual dinner invitations I ever got," Breda said, as Nelson returned.

"Hope I didn't miss anything," Nelson said.

"I wouldn't think you oughtta be wrecking funeral homes and stuff till you get a lock on that pension," Breda suggested to Lynn.

"I been sorta thinkin the same thing," Nelson said. "And it prob'ly wouldn't help me to get a transfer to Palm Springs P.D., would it?"

"I think we're all in agreement that we gotta keep our little project mum," Lynn said.

"I sure wouldn't blame ya if ya never wanted to see me again," Nelson said. "But I ain't quittin. I'm checkin out the car rentals tomorrow till I come up with where Francisco V. Ibañez is stayin."

"What happened to Jack?" Lynn wanted to know.

"Said he wouldn't be here if he got on to something," said Breda. "That might mean he tailed Clive Devon to a love nest. I'll call him in the morning unless I get a beeper message."

"I guess I might as well break it to you now, Breda," Nelson said. "I intend to talk to Clive Devon tomorrow."

"You what?" Breda and Lynn said in unison.

"You can't screw up my case!" Breda said.

"That ain't your business!" Lynn said.

"Look," Nelson said, *trying* to be agreeable. "Francisco V. Ibañez and the guy at the airport and the guy at the tombstone company and the guy that Clive Devon picked up in Painted Canyon and the guy that slam-dunked Lynn in a coffin are all the same guy! A detective's gotta consider every angle. Everybody's a suspect to a homicide detective, that's what it says in the books."

"This ain't a homicide," Lynn said, glaring at Nelson. "Yet!"

"Well, it's gotta be somethin serious," Nelson said, "and Clive Devon's in this till we . . . till I eliminate him."

Seeing his thousand bucks vanishing, Lynn shot Nelson a dangerous glare and said, "Nelson, somebody might eliminate *you*. This is blackmail!"

"Wait a minute," Breda said. "Let's all be reasonable."

"Okay," Nelson said, reasonably.

"You could check out the car rentals and talk to John Lugo for the next day or so, couldn't you? Give us a chance to wrap up our business with Clive Devon. After we're through and I get my fee, I don't care if you swing through Clive Devon's bedroom window on a vine!"

"Tit for tat," Nelson said. "What'll ya do to help me with my case?"

"Okay, you'll find a guy over there at the far end a the bar," Lynn said. "He's one a the younger customers, maybe seventy or so. They call him Ten-till-six. Tell him Lynn wants to see him. But first, buy him a whiskey."

"Why do they call him Ten-till-six?" asked Nelson.

"You'll see," Lynn said.

"What's that all about?" asked Breda when Nelson was off again.

"I don't like to get Nelson too excited, but I *have* developed a passing interest in his case as of an hour ago. I guess I just don't like guys using my head for stuff-shots." Lynn reached up and gingerly touched a swelling near his crown.

"How's it feel?" Breda asked.

"I won't be break-dancing for a while. My head spins're wrecked."

Breda glanced up at an old dipso shuffling their way, wearing a Kmart jogging suit and brown leather dress shoes, and she said, "I see why they call him Ten-till-six."

It was obvious. He leaned to starboard from the waist up.

"A few more drinks, he'll lean the other way," Lynn said. "Then they'll call him Ten-*after*-six."

"Hi, Lynn!" he said, when he got to the table.

"Hi," Lynn said. "You already met Nelson. Breda, this is Ten-till-six."

"Hey, good-lookin," said Ten-till-six. His nose was bulbous, wrapped in a pink hairnet of veins. Like many of the other

Furnace Room Romeos, Ten-till-six wore a thatch of man-made hair on top. It was slightly askew because of his starboard lean, and his lower dentures were in his shirt pocket.

Lynn said, "You know everybody in this town. How bout John Lugo? Lives up on Southridge. Only eight or ten houses up there, that should be an easy one."

"Easy, breezy!" said Ten-till-six, winking at Breda. Then he said, "Ya know, Breda, Bob Hope lives up there in that big airplane hangar with the swoopy roof? Looks like the hats women wore in nineteen thirty-two? Know the one? Has a swimming pool shaped like his profile."

"Well, who's John Lugo?" Nelson demanded.

"Everybody knows John Lugo," said Ten-till-six. "Used to own the Barrel Cactus Lodge. Or at least he fronted it. Coulda been Vegas money behind it, I dunno."

"Sure!" Lynn said. "John Lugo. I *knew* that name was familiar."

"Who is he?" Breda asked.

"Came to town, oh, twenny years ago," said Ten-till-six. "Bought the Barrel Cactus and turned it into a first-class hotel. Lotta Vegas guys use it when they come to town. And he bought a vending machine company and some other stuff. I think he lives mostly in Beverly Hills or somewheres."

"But he still has a house up on Southridge?" Nelson asked.

"Far as I know," said Ten-till-six. Then to Breda he said, "William Holden lived up there too. Nice man. Drank too much for his own good though." Ten-till-six shook his head sadly and drained his whiskey.

"Lemme buy you one," Breda said. "How do you take your whiskey?"

"Naked and in bed is the way I like it best," said Ten-till-six, winking at Breda again, and smacking his lips toothlessly.

When he staggered back to the bar they noticed that he'd tilted to ten-*after*-six.

–15–

The day had been far from uneventful for Jack Graves. After he'd tailed Clive Devon out of the Indian canyons he'd followed the Range Rover north on Palm Drive, and out of Palm Springs. At twilight, they'd crossed the freeway and continued on into the community of Desert Hot Springs, home of hot mineral baths and wind. It was a great place to spend the winter, locals said, as long as you didn't develop a fondness for paint. The gales through Desert Hot Springs could sandblast a car's paint-job to the metal in two hours, or so the inhabitants claimed.

But then, the locals told a lot of tales about the legendary wind, as well as other folklore. One such yarn was being spun when Jack Graves took his biggest risk of the day by following Clive Devon and the big brown dog into the Snakeweed Bar & Grill. He quickly saw that Clive Devon was so well known in the Snakeweed that he could've brought in a litter of coyotes and nobody would've complained.

Jack Graves heard at least five of the locals say, "Howdy, Clive!" when they shambled in for a pitcher of beer at happy hour.

Almost everyone knew even the dog's name. One trucker sitting at the bar sliced off a four-ounce chunk of steak from his T-bone and yelled, "Hey Clive! Okay to give Malcolm a bite?"

"If it's okay with Malcolm!" Clive Devon yelled back, grinning.

Of course, the big mongrel dog bounded across the saloon like George Bush, jumped up, forefeet on the bar, and gobbled the steak right off the guy's fork.

The bartender, who looked to be about one-half Morongo Indian, hollered, "Clive, if the health inspector ever comes in here, be sure to act blind and tell him Malcolm's a seeing-eye dog!"

Three people yelled variations of: "Your booze'd blind *any-body*, Otis!"

One knotty pine–paneled wall was devoted to cowboy hats, another to a wagon wheel draped with an American flag. There was a U.S. marine pennant over the bar with a homemade sign saying DESERT WORM under a caricature of Saddam Hussein being kicked in the ass by a marine. And naturally, there was a "Die, Yuppie Scum!" bumper sticker plastered to the bar mirror.

Country music was blasting from a fair-to-middling sound system and, perhaps due to the Gulf War, "Heroes" was getting a very big play. It was loud enough to've made Malcolm howl, if he hadn't been so preoccupied with steak.

The dozen tables were covered with checked tablecloths, topped by a sheet of plastic so they didn't have to be washed very often. It was a country version of The Furnace Room, but also featured shuffleboard and snooker tables, both of which were seeing action by the younger patrons, those under the age of fifty. It was one of those places where the barstools are screwed to the floor so you can't throw them, and you half expected to see sticky curls of paper, studded with fly carcasses, dangling from the ceiling.

Clive Devon sat with his back to the wall, a mug of beer in his hand, beaming at all the desert locals who spoke to him and Malcolm while Jack Graves nursed his beer, thinking that he might return for supper sometime. The steaks were big, the aroma from a greasy kitchen grill was terrific, and the prices were as cheap as he'd seen anywhere in the desert.

At the table by the end of the bar where Jack Graves stood sipping his beer was a trio of eco-freaks with designer cowboy hats and kneeless jeans that looked like hand-me-downs from Devil's Island.

One of the Snakeweed's clientele, an old desert rat named Luther, with the biggest lip-load of snuff Jack Graves had ever seen, was regaling the eco-freaks with lore, and they were buying it all, as well as an endless supply of whiskey for the geezer.

"It's all these city people that cause our problems," Luther complained to the city people, who nodded somberly. "They come out here towing their ATC's and run em all over the desert like Patton did with his tanks when he trained out here. You think the bighorn's the only animal in trouble?"

After the eco-freaks shook their heads, Luther said, "How bout the poor old stick lizards?"

Which got some of the other desert rats at the bar snickering and poking each other.

"The most amazing creature in the entire desert is the stick lizard," he told them. "Carries a lil stick in his mouth whenever the temperature rises above a hunnerd 'n fifteen degrees. On'y desert creature ta forage for food at high noon. Know how he does it?"

The punch line was worth a dramatic pause, and another shot of bar whiskey which the eco-freaks were only too glad to pay for.

Then Luther said, "When the sand starts burnin his feet, he'll dig a hole for that stick, 'n he'll push it vertical in the sand, 'n he'll climb up it. He'll jist hang there a few minutes till his feet cool off." Luther finished his whiskey and said, "Ain't too many stick lizards left. Definitely endangered."

Just then a dazzling old gent in olive-green and chrome-yellow golfing duds entered and headed for the bar.

"Hi, Doc," said the trucker, who was still feeding Malcolm from his plate.

Doc gave Malcolm a scratch, then grabbed his muzzle and opened the dog's mouth. "That lip healed right up, didn't it, Malcolm?" he said to the dog. Then he turned to the saloon keeper and said, "Otis, how about a sloe gin fizz?"

"You're the only guy this side a black 'n white movies that still drinks those things," Otis said.

"That's why the world's gone to hell," Doc said. He spotted Malcolm's companion and yelled, "Howdy, Clive!"

Clive Devon smiled and raised his beer mug. After Doc got his drink he walked over to Clive Devon's table, shook hands and sat down.

Jack Graves moseyed down the bar toward Malcolm. He nodded a howdy to the guys on each side of him and said to the trucker, "Nice big dog you got."

"Ain't mine. Belongs to Clive over there."

"Who's the other guy?" Jack Graves asked. "I think I played golf with him one time, but I can't remember his name."

"That's Doc Morton. You mighta played with him. He plays every day, now he's retired."

The Snakeweed began filling up with Canadian snowbirds, and the Mexican cook in the tiny kitchen couldn't turn out the steaks fast enough. Pretty soon the cooking smoke was too much for the air-conditioner and things got more obscure than in The Furnace Room on Saturday night. It was the kind of joint where supper was over by eight o'clock, and then there'd be a night of hard drinking for the hangers-on, Jack Graves guessed.

At six-thirty Clive Devon looked at his watch and ordered three steaks with fries, two salads, two orders of garlic toast. Jack Graves ordered a steak sandwich rare and another beer.

When the food arrived at Clive Devon's table, he cut one of the steaks into bite-size chunks and moved a chair out of the way so Malcolm could dine with him and Doc. The regulars had seen it before. The big brown mongrel put his face in the plate and devoured a twelve-dollar steak. Clive Devon watched Malcolm like a proud daddy, and even Doc offered Malcolm some bites of garlic toast soaked in steak juice.

Jack Graves made an impulsive decision. He carried his plate over to their table and said to both men, "Looks like there's no place else to sit. Mind if I join you?"

A deal was struck with Nelson Hareem when the three of them walked out of The Furnace Room that evening.

Breda surprised Nelson when she asked him, "What'd you get for Christmas?"

"From who?"

"Whoever buys you Christmas presents."

"Well, I got a cowboy hat and a burglar alarm," Nelson said. "The Stetson came from my folks and the burglar alarm from my sister. It's one a those do-it-yourself alarm deals. I don't have nothin worth stealin but my sister worries about me."

"How much do cowboy boots cost?" Breda asked.

"There's lotsa kinds. Why?"

"Is there a pair you've got your little heart set on?"

"I admire the Dan Post peanut-brittle lizard boots," Nelson said. "But I can't afford em."

"How much are they?"

"Three hunnerd 'n fifty bucks."

"If you promise not to screw up my deal with Clive Devon till I get my fee, I'll buy you a pair of Dan Post peanut-brittle lizard cowboy boots. Deal?"

"You don't have to buy me nothin," Nelson said. "I already decided to do it your way."

"I *want* to do it," Breda said. "Just lay off Clive Devon till I say it's okay. Okay?"

"Okay," Nelson said.

"Nelson," Lynn said, "I been thinking, I gotta tag along for one more day. I kinda got personally involved tonight. I don't like guys doing slam-jams with my head. Pick me up at nine o'clock tomorrow."

"Awwwrriiiiiight!" Nelson cried, and before any of them could change their minds he took off, jogging to his Wrangler in his red snakeskin cowboy boots, dreaming of peanut-brittle lizard. "Nine o'clock!" he yelled to Lynn.

When he was gone, Lynn said, "You never said if you wanna have dinner."

"In The Furnace Room?"

"I'm feeling better but not well enough for that. Someplace nice?"

"I'm really not hungry," she said.

"How bout a drink then? You ever been to the top a the tram?"

"Never had time."

"Lemme take you to the top a the tram for a drink," Lynn said.

"I've already had two drinks. That's my limit when I'm driving."

"One more won't hurt," Lynn said. "And I'll drive your car. I got a tolerance built up to Furnace Room booze. They could soak me in it and light a match, I'd never burn."

"Okay, just one drink," she said.

Lynn Cutter was getting the guilts for what he was trying

212

to do. Of course, he doubted if it would work, but he *was* getting the guilts. She wasn't a drinker, and even if she had been, she didn't know what could happen when you put down a few ounces of booze at the top of the tram. He'd had half a dozen drinks up there one time when a bunch of cops were celebrating a retirement, and they had to carry him to his car. At that altitude he'd felt like he had the bends.

While he was driving her Z on north Palm Canyon Drive toward Tram Way, Lynn said, "You know, the upper tram station is in the sheriff's jurisdiction, and the lower station belongs to Palm Springs P.D."

"That's interesting," Breda said drowsily, and Lynn could see that she *was* feeling The Furnace Room booze.

"One time there was a safe job done up there," Lynn said. "Somebody burned and pried a safe and hauled it all the way down. First thing the dicks did was check the emergency rooms for hernias."

"Interesting," Breda said, slurring slightly, and Lynn thought he might not even need the goddamn altitude!

He thought it was time to get personal, so he said, "Guess you date a lotta guys around town, huh?"

"Actually, just about none. I've been too busy setting up a business since I moved here."

"Divorced, right?"

"Yeah."

"I'm oh-for-two," he said.

"Got a steady?" Breda asked.

"Every woman I know's either old enough to get a discount at the movies or so young they only go for these naked-savage nail-pounders in the hard hats."

"No in-between ages available?"

"I haven't found many," Lynn said, shooting her a tentative look. "Got any kids?"

"One, she's in college." Then after a pause, "You?"

"My first wife was a kid, emotionally. Wore braces till she

was thirty-two. Had to hide ol' tinsel-teeth under a table in a lightning storm. My second wife was about as trustworthy as Iraq. You don't wanna hear about Precious. Lots a women throw their husband's clothes out in the front yard, right? She cut pieces outta mine before she tossed em. Only woman I ever knew with real imagination like that. Lucky for me neither of them wanted to have my child."

"Lucky for the child," Breda said.

"I always thought I coulda done a decent job raising a kid. I ain't the judgmental type. Life's knocked that outta me."

"Guess you won't be trying marriage a third time?"

"The best laid plan of mouse and man takes a dog-leg left the second you get that license."

"Then they decide they don't like you, is that it?"

"Why wouldn't they like me? They never even knew me," he said. "Neither one a them."

The valley station of the Palm Springs Aerial Tramway was located three miles from Highway 111 at 2,643 feet above sea level. They arrived just in time to take the last tram car at 8:00 P.M.

There was a gift shop for Palm Springs souvenirs, and a bar at the valley station. Lynn had to use a credit card to pay for the tram tickets, which were $13.95 each. Breda definitely decided she didn't want dinner up there when she learned that you could buy a ride 'n dine ticket for only four bucks more. She told Lynn that after she'd retired from police work she'd vowed not to have any more four-buck dining experiences.

There were two dozen other passengers taking the last car, and most of them looked like they'd been drinking at least as much as Breda. Lynn remembered the old days when if you wanted an easy drunk-driving arrest you just had to hang around on Highway 111 and catch them coming down.

The tram ride was more impressive in daylight, but plenty thrilling at night. At Lynn's insistence Breda had taken her windbreaker from the trunk and draped it over her shoulders. It was possible for the temperature to vary 40 degrees Fahrenheit from the valley floor to the top of the aerial tram.

"I had no idea it was so steep," Breda said when the car started climbing on the two-inch cable. "It's straight up."

"Almost," Lynn said. "Over a mile vertically."

Most of the passengers in the enclosed tram car were at the rear of the car hanging on to the handrails, gazing down on the Coachella Valley. The clusters of lights showed that more people lived and played in the desert valley than most people supposed.

The tram car glided with hardly a ripple over the cable that was stretched over five towers, erected by helicopters in the early 1960's. As they climbed, Lynn could sense that Breda was maybe a bit uneasy. Her body pressed against his, perhaps to steady herself.

"God, look at the stars from here!" she said, and his body felt disturbingly good to her.

"The desert sky," Lynn agreed.

He looked up at bushels of diamonds scattered on black satin. And the moonlight flooded down behind them from over the mountains onto the snow-patched limestone and granite through which they soared. As they ascended through the crags, Breda could see swirls and marbling in the cliffs, and clumps of palm, yucca and cactus swaying in the whistling freezing wind.

In fourteen minutes they were at the mountain station, at 8,516 feet but still 2300 feet from the peak of Mount San Jacinto, overlooking 13,000 acres of state park wilderness. When they stepped from the car a blast of wind made her glad she'd brought her windbreaker. They scurried inside the mountain station with other giggling passengers, none of whom were properly dressed for the ride.

Just climbing the steps to the observation area made Lynn a little dizzy, and he could guess how Breda felt even though she was in better shape, a lot better shape. They stepped out onto the observation deck, and the moonlight took her breath away. Thousands of sugar pines—bearers of the world's longest cones—filled the air with pine scent. There was sycamore up there, and cottonwood, alder, black maple. Even wild grapevine grew on the mountaintop. The cloud shadow on the snow seemed fluorescent.

"One a the reasons we live out here," Lynn observed.

"Magic!" Breda said.

And then she *did* lean against him. She might just be giddy from the altitude, he thought.

She was fighting an impulse to be held in his arms. It might just be the cold and the altitude, she thought.

"They got hot butter rum inside," Lynn said. "Ever tried it?"

"How about Irish coffee?"

"Let's go," he said, guiding her to the glass doors.

When they got to the cocktail lounge there were a dozen tables of drinkers and one cocktail waitress serving. Lynn considered sitting at the bar, but thought better of it when he envisioned what a few drinks might do to her. She could fall off.

"I gotta go to the john," Breda said. "Grab us a table with a view."

The drinking area of the mountain station didn't lend itself to viewing, it lent itself to drinking. The decor was faux-alpine, with peg-and-groove flooring, and there were flags from Alpine countries attached to poles extending horizontally from the walls. There were posters from Lucerne, Innsbruck, Grindewald, Zermatt. The chunky cocktail tables and ersatz captain's chairs were like those you see all over California in medium-priced restaurants where booze is a big item.

When the waitress came to the table, Lynn said, "Irish coffee and Scotch on the rocks."

"Baileys or Jameson's for the Irish coffee?"

"Jameson's," Lynn said. "Double, okay?"

"Okay," the waitress said.

When Breda got back from the restroom, Lynn actually made a feeble attempt to stand up, causing Breda to say, "Don't overdo it. Too much gallantry makes me flutter my eyelashes and I'm not wearing them tonight."

"You don't need em," Lynn said, gazing for a moment at her electric blues. "Your eyelashes're almost as thick as Jack Graves'."

"Wonder what he's up to," Breda pondered.

When the waitress brought the drinks, Lynn said to her, "Run a tab."

Breda sipped the hot Irish coffee. "Wow! By EPA standards this oughtta blow up!"

"The altitude makes the alcohol jump out and seem strong," Lynn lied. "There's a reason for it but I forget what it is."

"So," Breda said, "Nelson's not gonna run out and buy a terrorist-killing rocket launcher or anything, right?"

"I think he'll have to let loose of that one," said Lynn. "Arab terrorists don't usually terrorize tombstone companies and mortuaries. This deal's about something else."

"Any idea?"

"*Nada.* Zip. Zero. I think we gotta talk to John Lugo to see what he knows about Francisco V. Ibañez. I doubt the car rental angle's gonna work. If Ibañez rented a car I bet he wouldn't put the right hotel on the rental agreement."

"His I.D.'d have to be good," Breda said. "And he'd need a good credit card to rent a car."

"There's no question in my mind, this guy's gonna have whatever he needs. He knows how to hot-wire a car. He knows how to get information and he'll do anything he has to do to get it. He sure as hell knows how to fight. So far he hasn't wanted to kill anybody but I'll bet he can do that real good too."

"You're positive he's the same guy you saw through the binoculars down in Painted Canyon?"

"Without the stash," Lynn said, nodding. "It was him."

Lynn noticed that after her Irish coffee cooled, Breda drank it easily.

"This stuff isn't bad," she said.

"Warms you right up," Lynn agreed. "Think I'll have one if you'll go for another."

"*One* more," she said, and he saw that her eyes weren't quite focusing. The high-altitude drinks on an empty stomach were even causing him a few problems. Her freckle was a bit fuzzy.

While Lynn and Breda were busy getting bombed almost two miles above sea level, Jack Graves was still on his second beer and cold sober, watching a young cowboy and a middle-aged woman slow-dancing between the shuffleboard and the snooker tables to "Heroes and Friends" by Randy Travis.

By then, Jack Graves was well acquainted with Malcolm the dog, Doc the vet, and Clive Devon, in that order. The steak was pretty good, and he'd already heard about thirty-three golf jokes from the retired veterinarian.

All of a sudden Clive Devon looked at his watch. "Well, gentlemen, it's time for Malcolm and me to cut trail."

"Good to've seen ya, Clive," Doc said, reaching over the table to shake hands.

"Nice to meet you, Jack," said Clive Devon, shaking hands with the man who'd dogged him unobserved for thirteen hours.

"It was my pleasure," Jack Graves said, and he meant it. He liked Clive Devon. "So long, Malcolm," he said to the big mongrel dog.

Jack Graves didn't get up even though he'd paid his bill. He stayed with Doc and watched the action now that two other couples had gotten up to dance to "Cowboy Logic." The lyrics held Jack Graves in place.

> *Cowboy logic . . . ev'ry cowboy's got it*
> *He's got a simple solution for jist about*
> *Anythaaaaaang.*

That's when it came to him! Jack Graves had always done police work grounded in the belief that there's a simple solution for just about anything. With notable exceptions. He knew all about exceptions and insoluble dilemmas.

He turned to the old vet and said, "How about another drink, Doc? I'd like to hear a little more about your golf course up here. I'm thinking about joining it."

Breda had switched to Scotch at Lynn's suggestion. She spilled some when she made the second unsteady pass at her own mouth, and didn't say a word when he ordered her another "to replace spillage."

He decided to put a stop to it after this one. Her freckle was swimming all over her lower lip! They were both tanked, and into cop-talk, which is inevitable when cops get that smashed.

"I used to work with . . ." She lost the thread, then picked it up after another sip of Scotch. "Oh yeah! I was saying, I used to work with this alky detec . . . detec . . ."

"Detective," Lynn said, helping her.

"Yeah. Anyhow, he went through treatment programs three times. Last time he fooled his wife for six months. He's the one that told me a twenty-five-foot garden hose holds a pint. A fifty-footer holds a quart."

"That's sad," Lynn said sadly, putting down a big gulp, watching that freckle bounce and dive, pitch and roll. "I worked with a lieutenant who made four trips to the hospital. They had him make moccasins for therapy. All those trips, he coulda made a hand-tooled saddle."

"Real sad," Breda said, and this time she splashed booze all over the front of her silk blouse, but didn't notice.

"You miss it, Breda?" he asked. "The job?" He was concentrating as hard as he could to make the freckle stop dancing.

"I miss *some* stuff," she said. "Like when I worked at Hollywood station there was a toilet stall in the women's john. Called it the Hollywood Times. Everybody wrote stuff in there. When you got back from vacation you had to run to the john to find out the latest dirt. If it was in the Hollywood Times, it had to be true, Virginia."

"That reminds me," Lynn said, giggling. "I heard you had a female lieutenant in your department that was always on a diet. And the guys that worked for her'd always put a note with her uniforms when they went to the cleaners, telling them to take the uniform *in* a quarter of an inch!"

"Huh?"

"Don't you get it? Her clothes were forever tight no matter how much weight she lost!"

Lynn got the screaming giggles until Breda glared at him and leaned over the table saying, "That's the kinda juvenile crap the female officers've been putting up with since the goddamn world began!"

Lynn stopped abruptly, and said, "Oh. Well, I also heard they jacked up her car a few inches and when it wouldn't go she couldn't figure it out!"

Those cobalt blue eyes froze his giggle in place, so he said, "That ain't funny either, is it?"

"It's asinine!"

"That's just what I was thinking," Lynn said, slurring. "I feel the same way about the time they taped a hard-core porn poster to the top of her police unit and when she was directing a field operation every helicopter in the city was doing a flyover."

All of a sudden Breda screamed, "*That's* funny!" And the

waitress shook her head at the bartender. It was, "Cork all bottles as far as those two're concerned."

Lynn gave up then. He couldn't tell anymore what was revolting and disgusting and what was funny. He hadn't meant to get this hammered!

He called for the waitress and paid the bill. The next move was going to be very interesting. Breda was going to try to stand up.

Lynn tried it first and was astonished by the movement under his feet, like maybe a 6.2 earthquake had jolted the San Andreas Fault. Jesus, this was a dumb idea!

There was no point coaxing and coddling. He just put his arm around her waist and said, "Let's go, boss," and she didn't argue.

"What's in that goddamn c-c . . ."

"Coffee," he said, guiding her toward the departure lobby and the last tram car, which was leaving at 9:45 P.M.

"I shouldn't a . . ." she said, but trailed off.

"Caffeine'll kill ya!" he said. "Next time we'll have decaf Irish coffee. It's the caffeine causing your problem."

She almost fell asleep standing up on the ride down the mountain. There were only seven others on that last car and they were all subdued: three amorous couples and a single guy who looked lonely standing among the others.

Lynn kept his arm around Breda's waist to steady her, and she didn't resist. That bike riding paid off, he thought. Her muscles were a lot harder than his.

"What's your size?" he asked.

"Six," she said. "And . . . I'm . . . staying a six."

"You are a *buff* size six!" he said, looking down at her cyclist's calves. Then he said, "Do you like mustaches?"

"I hate mustaches!" she said. "Half a the LAPD has em!"

"Even the females?"

"Macho crap!" she said gruffly. "All those blue-suited stashes strutting around!"

221

"I been thinking of getting rid a mine," he said.

Descending the steps of the valley station was a matter that took some planning. Finally, he hung on to the handrail with his right hand, and kept her pressed against him with the left. She was too tanked to know how tanked she was. Lynn knew she'd be dying in the morning.

He half lifted her into her car, and when he got into the driver's seat and started the engine, he turned the radio from soft hits to the country station.

"This is Nelson's influence," he said. "I never listened to country till he came along, but I've discovered that country music's all about *me!*"

And as though to prove him right, Mark Chesnutt sang:

> *Brother Jukebox, Sister Wine,*
> *Mother Freedom, Father Time,*
> *Since she left me by myself*
> *You're the only family I got left.*

"See what I mean?" Lynn said. "All about a guy that hangs around in bars. A lonely guy."

"Huh?"

"Never mind, go back to sleep."

He drove straight to his mansion. The automatic security lights were on, illuminating the acre of cactus garden as though it were daylight. Neighbors couldn't complain because Lynn's patron had surrounded his property with a high wall and oleander, to block the glare.

Lynn had to get out of the car to open the electric gate. It would stay open automatically at 6:00 A.M. for the gardener, pool cleaner and other service people.

"How do ya like my digs?" he asked, and she opened her eyes lazily and said, "Uh huh."

As he was pulling into the garage, Patty Loveless sang:

There's a man in a Stetson hat
Howling like an alley cat
Outside my winda tonight.

"My God!" Lynn said. They knew! They knew every move he made! He *was* an alley cat!

A little sensitivity
Always seems to get to me . . .
I'm getting tired of these one night stands,
But if you're looking for a real romance
I'm that kind of giiiiiirrrrl.

Suddenly, he felt awful! Talk about the guilt monkey! An orangutan had him in a headlock. He looked at poor helpless Breda. This was pathetic. This revolted and humiliated him. He despised himself. He was a sorry excuse for a man. He was slimier than a lung-cookie hacked from the death-cough out of the putrid blackened lungs of the most low-down crack-smoking degenerate in the county.

He was all of that. But he was also the guy who continued to lead the nearly comatose P.I. up the carpeted stairway to the master suite where there was a round waterbed bigger than Sinatra's helicopter pad.

When they got into the bedroom, he left her sitting on the water-filled mattress at the five o'clock position. He went around to eleven o'clock and turned on the radio with some difficulty, and found the country station.

Breda clearly didn't know where she was and was too drunk to care. She stared unbuttoning her blouse and kicking off her shoes. The effort made her fall back on the waterbed, sending a wave under Lynn Cutter and a powerful thrill through his loins!

Breda rolled off onto the carpet and unzipped her skirt

while sitting on the floor. Lynn got up, and with his back turned started undressing.

He said aloud, "This is *not* my fault." But there was nobody there to hear him. Breda certainly was past understanding.

"I'm *not* gonna do this!" he cried hoarsely to the ceiling, but then Michelle Wright began singing with one of those low sexy country voices.

> *You'll know that it's true*
> *'Cause I'll be there for you*
> *Just a heartbeat awaaaaay.*

It wasn't his fault! There was Breda, just a heartbeat away, sitting on the waterbed at six o'clock, glassy-eyed and struggling to get out of her bra and panties. Her underwear was sort of violet, like verbeña! What was he supposed to do? He didn't know what was the right thing to do in a situation like this! He didn't know she'd have nipples like ripe swollen berries!

When she was completely naked, she just crawled across the round waterbed toward twelve o'clock. She probably didn't even know where she was. The poor kid. She had *such* buff calves!

Trying hard to say something nice, he finally said, "I guess I seen tighter skin in my time, but only on a plum!"

All of a sudden she looked up at him and said, "Lynn?" As in, "Lynn, what the hell're *you* doing here?"

He crawled toward her under the sheet. Like a sidewinder. Like a scorpion. Like a goddamn tarantula!

She looked so pathetic and helpless. Her lustrous earth-brown hair cascaded. Her eyes, like wet turquoise, were at half mast. Her lips were wet and partially open. That frigging freckle was just sort of trembling there beside the corner of her lower lip!

If only Michelle Wright didn't have that low sexy voice.

You'll know that it's true
'Cause I'll be there for you
Just a heartbeat awaaaaaaaay.

Okay, I'm just gonna kiss that freckle once or twice, he swore to himself. Maybe touch it with my tongue, that's all. He just had to do *that*. It wasn't his fault! It wasn't! It was that goddamn bittersweet chocolate freckle!

–16–

The fugitive is cramming Lynn's head into the coffin! The fugitive is gnashing and growling and *jumping* on the coffin, cracking Lynn's vertebrae with the lid! The fugitive is smacking Lynn across the face because suddenly the fugitive is *inside* the coffin with him and Denny O'Doul, the poor Irish son of a bitch! And a sloppy undertaker has gone and spilled corn flakes in the coffin! And somebody on a ghetto-blaster is yodeling country music while Denny O'Doul's widow keels over in a faint!

Lynn woke up when she slugged him the *third* time. "Ooooooooooo!" he moaned.

She was wearing her skirt, and strangely enough her shoes! But she was still bare-breasted, sitting astride him, smacking him across the face!

The bedside radio had never been turned off. Rob Crosby

was singing "Love Will Bring Her Around" while she beat the living shit out of him!

"You dirty sneaky depraved sonofabitch!" she shrieked.

"Oooooooooooo!" he wailed, without being awake enough to stop her!

His face was on fire and he was being whacked from one side of the pillow to the other! Finally, he came to enough to raise up and dump her off backwards where the ebb and flow of the waterbed easily sloshed her onto the floor because she wasn't all that sober yet!

"I'll *kill* you, you rotten sleazy bastard!" she screamed and the first thing he thought was: *The gun*! He'd seen it in her purse! The gun!

He looked around desperately, but the purse was nowhere to be found! Then he realized it must still be in the car, thank God!

Then she got up and whacked him again across the right ear and his whole head started ringing!

"Stop hitting me!" he screamed, trying to hold her off.

But she was literally *leaking* venom! He saw a trickle of saliva on that goddamn freckle! Her electric blues had short circuited! She was looking for something to brain him with! She grabbed for the lamp, but he wrestled it away and toppled her onto the bed again and fell on her and they both wobbled and bounced on what seemed like a vat of Jell-O! Her raspberry nipples were bobbing at eye level!

"Stop it!" he yelled, finally able to crawl onto the floor and scuttle like a naked scorpion toward that humongous ugly bathroom. When he got inside he slammed the door and locked it.

There was silence in the bedroom, and he thought: *She's getting the fucking gun*! He looked behind him, but the only bathroom window was one of those shitty little openings high on the wall that slid open for ventilation. He couldn't have squeezed out of that even when he was still thin. He was doomed!

Then he heard something. It sounded like she'd fallen down. He called out, "Breda! Whatever's troubling you, I'm sure we can talk about it!"

No answer.

"Breda!" he yelled, picking up the tennis shoe telephone. "Don't make me call nine-one-one!"

No answer.

He wrapped a towel around his waist and unlocked the door. He had a crazy idea that he didn't want to be found naked and dead, like a fucking book title.

"Breda!"

She was sitting rigid as stone on a straight-backed chair by the window, staring outside with her back to him. She was fully clothed now, but panting from the pounding she'd given him.

"Breda," he said softly. "I think I can understand why you're mad at me, but honest, I had too much to drink! I didn't know what I was doing!"

She never turned around when she said, "You're the most vile evil horrible person I've ever known."

"I ain't *that* bad," he said.

"You raped me," she said quietly.

"What?"

"Date rape," she said. "And I'm going to sue you, you filthy perverted creep!"

"Date rape! I didn't rape nobody! I just put you to bed cause you were drunk! Hell, I was drunk too! If I hadn't a been drunk I woulda noticed that I put you in the *wrong* bed is all. Date rape? Gimme a break!"

She still hadn't turned around when she said, "I'll pay you what I promised, but then I never want to see your slimy rotten self ever again."

He looked at his watch. Three A.M. The Drinker's Hour. All the grief and agony of mankind happened at three A.M., after booze made the blood sugar drop.

"Breda," he said, "we're both still a little bit lubricated. We shouldn't try to communicate right now."

Finally, she turned around and he saw that her face was white as china and tear-stained, and all of a sudden he *did* feel like a rapist!

Choking back a sob: "How could you do that to another human being?"

"Know what I did? I kissed your freckle. That's all I did. That's all I *could* do. I admit I had some other ideas, but I was too drunk. I just kissed your freckle maybe three times. Then I passed out."

"You kissed what?"

"The freckle there by your mouth," he said. "I had this uncontrollable desire to kiss your freckle since the first time I laid eyes on you." Then he staggered sideways and had to sit down on the bed. It went GLUP!

"Christ, I *hate* this freaking bed!" he said. "It makes me nauseous." He *was* nauseous, and his head was pounding. "Breda, I'm still hammered," he whined. "You must be at least as drunk as me?"

"You got me that way so you could rape me," she said. And that caused him to look frantically around the room again. Was that fucking purse still in the car or not?

"Look, we're grownup people," he pleaded. "You got your forty-third birthday coming up, for chrissake!"

"How do *you* know when my birthday is?"

"I had you run through DMV. The second of April. You're almost as old as me."

"You ran my name through DMV? You swine, how *dare* you!"

"I did it right after we met. I only do stuff like that when I *like* a woman!"

"When you'd like to *rape* them, you mean! You had your way with me!"

229

"Had my . . . Jesus! That kinda line went out with the zoot suit! Had my *way*? This ain't *Forever Amber*! Look, we're just two lonely middle-aged people is all we are! This can't be such a big deal!"

"I'm *not* lonely, you bastard! And if I was, that doesn't give you the right to . . . to . . ."

"To kiss your freckle? I told you, that's all I *did*. I passed out. You wanna give me a sobriety check? I'll prove I'm still tanked. I couldn't walk a line you painted with a push-broom. Honest!"

Now she seemed uncertain, but even angrier. "So you just take off a woman's clothes and slobber on her and . . . and *degrade* her! You think *that's* okay, you foul slithering vermin!"

"You're mad if I *did* it! You're madder if I *didn't* do it! And in the second place I didn't take off your clothes. But you ain't gonna listen to reason. Why'nt you just shoot me and get it over with."

All of a sudden she jumped unsteadily to her feet and said, "I *will*, you asshole!"

"WAIT A MINUTE!" he screamed. "WHERE'S YOUR PURSE? WHERE'S THAT GODDAMN PURSE?"

Then she sat down again and he could see that she was sick, very sick. He crept a little closer.

"You're whiter'n Gramma's undies," he said. "I think you oughtta get in the bathroom real quick."

She did. He heard her throwing up two seconds after the door slammed. Then he weaved his way down the hall to the guest bath. Christ, his head! He got a glass of water and a clean towel and returned to the master suite, standing outside the door.

It was quiet inside. He took the opportunity to put his pants on, but he looked awful with his belly hanging out. He put on a pajama top, and said, "Breda! Would you like a little drink a water? And an aspirin?"

Then the door opened and she came out, paler than Denny

230

O'Doul, but seeming more sober than before. She stormed by him and headed for the staircase.

He followed behind and said, "Breda, you ain't being reasonable. This is *not* such a terrible thing, anybody would tell you that!"

"If you mention this night to a living soul I *will* sue you!" she said, pausing on the staircase.

"Sue me?" he croaked. "You don't need to. All I own is a tennis racquet with busted strings that I haven't used since my first wife boogied and my knee blew out! You can *have* it! And my new shock absorbers I got at the swap meet!"

Even shaky and white as salt, with her hair messed up and her eyes all swollen, he thought she still looked great. "I wouldn't tell nobody," he said. "Look, we're real close on the Ibañez thing, and I think we gotta see that one through. Nelson, me *and* you."

"And why would you think that matters to me?"

"Why? Because we're cops. Sort of. I mean we used to be cops and we're on to something and it's important and we all know it. And we're gonna wrap up the Clive Devon thing too, I promise."

"I said I'd pay you."

"You don't have to," he said, unconvincingly. Christ, he was down to his last twenty bucks!

"All right," she said. "I'll see it through, and then I don't want you to ever cross my path again."

"Breda, I ain't all that weird!" he cried. "I mean, I don't go around putting rattlers in mailboxes! My entertainment consists of hanging around with coupon-clippers at The Furnace Room, most of em on walkers! I say stuff to women like, 'Gee, you look swell today, Agatha!' So how depraved can I be?"

As she descended the staircase again and was clicking across the marble foyer, it was *his* turn to feel a bit angry and indignant. Now that he wasn't going to be shot dead *his* feelings were hurt too, goddamnit!

Besides, back there in the bedroom, somebody was singing: "Talk Back Tremblin' Lips."

Deciding to do *just* that, he yelled, "I didn't do anything so awful! Whaddaya want from a guy before he brings you home? His old handcuff key on a gold chain, or what?"

She slammed the door so hard a painting fell off the wall and cartwheeled down the staircase. It was one of those crappy prize-fight scenes that the owner of the house was so proud of. But it was an original, not a litho, so Lynn hoped he could reglue the ugly frame together.

As he staggered back to bed he thought of how they were, all of them! Their goofy heads full of female litter! There was more mess and litter in her head than you could shovel off the floor of a sorority house! She was squirrely, wacko, batty!

He fell onto the waterbed and had to endure a nauseating rock and roll for a few seconds. When the bed quieted down he knew he wouldn't be going back to sleep for hours. Lynn stared at the ceiling, furious at the world. Matraca Berg was singing country blues.

I been snagged, I been hoooooked . . .

How many years did Breda think they had left, the two of them? You'd think somebody her age would behave like a sensitive compassionate grownup!

Oh, my God, what's my world coming toooooo?
I got it baaaaaaad, for you.

His head hurt and he was trying not to vomit. His ears were still ringing where she'd slugged him. He had to get up in the morning and face Nelson Hareem. And the country blues made him want to cry! His heart ached!

Oh, my God, what's my world coming tooooo?
I got it baaaaaad, for you.

How did they know? How did those goddamn redneck country hicks always know just what the fuck he was *feeling*?

Jack Graves was awake at 3:00 A.M., but it had nothing to do with drinking. He'd stayed at the Snakeweed Bar & Grill talking to the veterinarian for two hours, but never even finished the second glass of beer. Doc, however, drank *lots* of beer and three more sloe gin fizzes, which Jack Graves had been glad to buy.

The old vet was thrilled to be regaling such a willing listener with every golf story he knew. Doc promised to sponsor Jack Graves at his country club if he was serious about joining, but he warned Jack Graves about the frustrations associated with golf, and that golf spelled backwards is flog.

And through all the drinking and the golf lore, Doc had never noticed the dozens of subtle questions that Jack Graves would slide into the middle of a golf tale, questions about Clive Devon, most of which Doc answered freely, anxious to get to the next golf anecdote.

After Jack Graves was certain that Doc had had more than enough, he'd asked his questions more directly. Doc was by then a fast friend to this neophyte golfer, and only too happy to answer after a boozy admonition not to tell anyone else about Clive Devon's little secret, even though Doc had told all of it before to half the customers in the Snakeweed.

At midnight, Jack Graves was back home in Windy Point, standing out behind his motor home listening for the coyote pack, disappointed that they weren't hunting in his range that night. He did hear an owl and even thought he heard the sound of a rattler in the brush. It was extremely unlikely in winter, but he walked toward the brush and obeyed an irrational impulse. He kicked at it, and there was a sound of scurrying. There were desert creatures that could imitate rattlers to frighten away predators, and it was probably one of them. Despite the dangers in the desert, Jack Graves was without fear, without *that* kind of fear.

He knew that he should feel happy about what he'd accomplished. Breda and Lynn would be thrilled when he told them what he knew about Clive Devon. It pleased him to think of helping them, but he still didn't feel happy. On the contrary, he felt very uneasy, and he noticed that his palms were clammy. He wiped them on his jacket as he listened for the coyotes who never came.

He was lying awake at the same time Lynn Cutter was lying awake, but Jack Graves was not listening to country blues. He was indulging a very unhealthy compulsion. Before they'd given him his stress pension he'd been warned by a psychiatrist that if unsummoned images swept over him, that was *one* thing, but he must not probe the wound. A person could cause a deadly infection, the psychiatrist had warned him, picking at wounds.

Yet he was doing it, summoning ghosts. He listened for coyotes, anything to distract him, but there was only wind out there, desert wind gusting across the sand, sighing high up in the mountain pass. The wind did that sometimes, sighing. If only the little desert wolves would come . . .

He'd been detailed to guard the back of the house. If his partner had not hurt his back they'd have been swinging a battering ram, and they'd never have been back there when the boy ran out . . .

The fugitive was doing something that he'd never done before, something that he should have done before leaving home: He was writing out his last will and testament. He would have done it at home if he'd ever dreamed that this assignment could be so dangerous, if he'd even thought for one moment how it could all go so wrong.

It was after 3:00 A.M., and he hadn't slept at all. How could he? After the terror in the mortuary, and the horror that still awaited him? He wondered if that policeman with curly hair had found John Lugo already and had asked the man questions. The fugitive still had one thing in his favor: John Lugo would not have the faintest notion what the policeman was talking about. Why would the man know about someone trying to trace him by way of his mother's funeral?

The policeman had done an amazing thing in finding him, but neither he nor John Lugo would have any idea of the significance of María Magdalena Lugo's tombstone. At least he *hoped* that was the case. It would take a great deal of thinking and questioning of others for anybody to figure it out. By then it would be too late. The fugitive would have his work completed, that's what he prayed for.

Then he put down the pad upon which he was writing his will. He would post the letter tomorrow. The will was an easy thing to write. He left everything he owned to his wife and children: the car and furniture, and the little four-room house that was not paid for, a house that would still be too small for his family even if he did not come home to them. He was thirty-nine years old and had accumulated pitifully little in a lifetime of hard work.

He had to sleep for the sake of his mission. He wished he had some powders to make him sleep. If he was at home he could walk into a pharmacy and buy whatever he needed. In this country they made you go through a physician for everything.

Then the fugitive picked up the writing pad again, turned to a fresh page and wrote:

My dearest wife,
    When you receive this letter I shall either be at home by your side or God shall have taken me. If I am gone to God you must be very strong for the sake of the

But the fugitive couldn't go on. He got up and went to the bathroom. He drank some water and looked at himself in the mirror, determined not to weep.

Breda Burrows had slept in her clothes, the only time in her life. She had an all-world hangover, the first since she was twenty years old. She felt like maggots were eating her brain. And *still* the phone wouldn't stop.

Without attempting to raise up, she scooted on her back and groped around to where the phone should be, finally finding it on the floor. When had she put the damn phone on the floor?

" 'Lo," she whispered into the mouthpiece.

"Sorry to call so early," Jack Graves said, "but I might be able to wrap up your case by this evening."

"Really?" she said, too loud. A sharp knife stabbed across her forehead and settled behind her right ear up to the hilt.

"I'll be tailing him again today," Jack Graves said, "and I *think* I know where he'll be going. What I'd like you to do is, I'd like you to call Rhonda Devon and ask her to call her husband and say she's coming to the desert at six o'clock this evening."

"I doubt if she'll come," Breda said, painfully forcing herself to endure the agony of sitting up. "She only comes once every couple weeks or so."

"I don't care if she actually shows up," Jack Graves said. "Just so he thinks she's coming. And the other thing I need for you to do is, I need for you and Lynn to go to Clive Devon's house at six o'clock this evening and have a talk with him."

"About what?"

"About the drug smuggler he picked up in the canyon."

"How can we do that without blowing the whole thing?"

"First, have Lynn badge him. Then tell him half the truth, that a policeman from the south end took license numbers of every car he saw in Painted Canyon including the Range Rover, hoping he could find a witness to the airport incident. Describe the smuggler to him."

There was a pause and then Breda said, "I . . . uh . . . I can't use Lynn on this job anymore, Jack."

"Why not?"

"It's too complicated."

"You can't go there and represent yourself as a police officer, Breda," Jack Graves said. "You have your P.I. license to think about."

"I don't think Lynn's much use to me on this one," she said. "And he's gonna be busy with Nelson."

"But he's still a police officer. He can show his badge and ask questions. I need Clive Devon to believe that you're investigating a serious crime that involves a righteous bad guy that he picked up in the canyon. Okay?"

"Okay," she said. "I'll take him with me. Six o'clock, you say?"

"Six o'clock. After that, I'd like both of you to meet me, and maybe I'll have your answer."

"Where?"

"My place, okay?"

"See you in Windy Point after we talk to Clive Devon."

When she hung up, she felt bilious. She could still smell the booze. She lurched unsteadily into the bathroom and ran a bath, then she changed her mind and took a hot shower followed by a cold one. It was pure agony, but she reveled in the suffering, knowing that the sniveling debauched lowlife villainous bucket of dog vomit was hurting just as much as she was.

He was hurting, but not quite as much as Breda Burrows. In the first place he hadn't drunk as much in relation to his capacity and tolerance. In the second place, every time a wave of agony would sweep over him he'd think of how she'd looked lying naked under the sheet, with her eyes narrowed to slits of cornflower blue, and that freckle quivering!

He showered, shaved and even trimmed his mustache, no mean feat when he was that shaky. He forced himself to eat a scrambled egg, and drank a glass of orange juice to replenish vitamins. He had coffee, the last of it. There wasn't another goddamn thing to eat or drink in the house.

Lynn had exactly ten more days of existing there before the owner took over, and he didn't hold out much hope for the house-sitting gig at Tamarisk Country Club. He figured he was about to join the ranks of the homeless.

The only chance he had was if the pension came through. It should've been granted a month ago. Every time he called about it he'd get some spineless double-talking bureaucrat too incompetent to flip burgers at Jack in the Box.

He was standing out on the street reading his press notices when Nelson roared up the street at 8:55 A.M. grinning like he'd learned how to make shade.

"You're up and ready!" Nelson said, as he slid the Wrangler to a risky stop three inches from Lynn's body.

"The game's afoot," Lynn said. "I couldn't wait. Like I can't wait to wear support hose and live for fiber. You see this?"

He handed Nelson the third page of the local paper. A small headline, BRAWL AT FUNERAL HOME, was followed by: *Police are baffled by a violent fight between two men that took place in the early evening hours during a rosary service at Lieberman Brothers Mortuary. Both men were seeking information on an undisclosed client of Lieberman Brothers. One man claimed to be a police officer, but police spokesmen believe that his badge was bogus. The case is being investigated.*

Nelson said, "Yeah, I'm gonna get a scrapbook." Then, "Did you and Breda go out for supper last night?" And he winked!

"What makes you ask that?"

"The way you were lookin at her, all googly-eyed."

"Yeah, well you won't be seeing no more googles. That babe's a nut case."

"Somethin happen?"

"Nothin a person your age'd understand."

"Wanna hear my new country tape?"

"Not if it's about a guy whose girlfriend beats the living shit outta him and threatens to call a lawyer. Is *that* what it's about?"

"No."

"Okay, play it. Maybe they don't know every freaking move I make, after all."

"Who?"

"Nashville or wherever it is they spy into people's heads and turn out those goddamn songs."

Nelson said, "I don't think I wanna know what happened to you last night."

He punched in a Garth Brooks song, "If Tomorrow Never Comes."

"JESUS CHRIST!" Lynn yelled, and his voice exploded in his ears like a magnum round.

"What's wrong?"

"Whaddaya think you're doing, playing *that* song? Do you realize we're going after a guy that tried to stick me in a brass-handled sedan before my time? And might try it again with more success?"

If tomorrow never comes, Garth Brooks sang. The song was an omen.

Nelson didn't say a word. He ejected that mother, pronto.

When they knocked on the door of the pink Mediterranean house up on Southridge, they were met by a handsome guy in his mid-thirties. He wore matching flowered shirt and shorts, and leather sandals. He was dark and had a streak of white running through his black power ponytail. He stood blocking the entry, but smiling.

Lynn showed his badge, but this guy was different. This guy said, "Got an I.D. card to go with that?" Lynn reluctantly showed his police I.D. and the guy read it and said, "Yes, Mister Cutter, what can I do for you?"

"Are you John Lugo?" Lynn asked.

"No, this is his home, but he's not here. Can I help you, sir?"

"Is he at his L.A. home?"

"No, he's in Hawaii for a few days playing golf. Why don't you tell me what it's about, sir."

It was going to be like that, Lynn thought. This guy wasn't going to let anybody get close.

"Can I have *your* name?" Lynn asked.

"Sure, Mister Cutter. Bino Sierra."

"Bino."

He touched the snowy streak in his hair and said, "Short for Albino. I was born with this."

The guy hadn't stopped smiling since he'd opened the door. He had brilliantly white teeth and you could see all thirty-two of them. It was *that* kind of smile. He wore rings on both hands, and a gold chain with a cross on it hung from his neck, all but vanishing in a thatch of chest hair. Bino Sierra wasn't a typical butler, and he didn't cut the grass, that was certain.

"When will he be back from Hawaii?"

Shrugging, Bino Sierra said, "Mister Lugo comes and goes in his own good time. But you can talk to his lawyer."

The smile got even wider when Lynn said, "Does his lawyer sleep here or does he have an office?"

"An office in Palm Desert. Name's Leo Grishman."

"Where's the office?"

"The new building across from the college," Bino Sierra said, again touching the white streak. Then he said, "Funny, a detective from Palm Springs P.D. phoned this morning to see if Mister Lugo could shed any light on a brawl that happened in a funeral home last night. Involved a couple a guys looking for Mister Lugo. He didn't say he was sending detectives to the house. But it's okay, we're anxious to help."

Bino Sierra was still smiling as he closed the door.

When they were back in the Wrangler, Nelson Hareem said, "*This* ain't gonna be so easy."

"That smile was about as genuine as an agent's kiss," Lynn said. "That's what the old actors at The Furnace Room would say."

-17-

The law office was in a fairly
new professional building on Fred Waring Drive in Palm Desert.

After they'd gotten the Wrangler parked and were walking
toward the flat-roofed, brick-and-glass building, Nelson said
nervously, "Guy's gonna be a mob lawyer, ain't he?"

"Oh, *sure*," Lynn said. "When we come outta here you'll
have to start your Jeep with a long stick or suddenly we'll be
residing in three states."

"Know what I was thinkin? If the Palm Springs cops got
the guy's hat after he mashed it in your moosh they could get
his genetic fingerprint from the sweat on the hatband. I was
readin where the technology's gettin that refined!"

"I just know you were the roomie of Doctor John Watson
in another life," Lynn said.

When they were ascending the stairs to the second floor,

three workmen carrying a huge roll of carpet were staggering down the staircase.

"Comin through!" the guy in front said.

"Leo Grishman law offices up there?" Lynn asked.

"I'll say it is," the guy in back said, panting. "And I wish it was on the first floor, I can tell ya."

The double doors of the law firm were wide open, and a huge carpet pad was being trimmed and stapled to the floor.

A little man about Wilfred Plimsoll's age, wearing shapeless ancient tweed, was yelling at a natty young guy in a butterscotch three-piece Italian suit. The young guy had his hands full of carpet and fabric samples.

"Do I complain, Roger?" the old guy complained to the young one.

"No, Mister Grishman," Roger replied.

"Then why can't you give me texture? You give a woman color, you give a man texture, that's how it should be. That's all a man needs, along with an easy chair and a used-brick fireplace. Is *that* asking too much?"

"No, Mister Grishman," Roger said, looking down at the old lawyer. "Except for the used brick. You don't have a fireplace here."

"Do my clients want to be walking around for two weeks on carpet pad because *you* couldn't bring me the carpet I ordered? I'll tell you the answer. The answer is no. Is that too difficult to understand, Roger?"

"No, Mister Grishman," Roger said.

"Go find me some texture, Roger, please. They have to sell it somewhere. You people must learn where to buy it in your interior decorator school. It's got to be for sale! Texture!"

"I'll get right on it, Mister Grishman," the interior designer said. "I think I know what you want."

Roger's butterscotch coattails were flying past Lynn and Nelson before the little attorney even noticed the visitors. Then

243

he saw them and said, "He thinks he knows what I want. I've only been working with him for six months and he *thinks* he knows what I want. I asked for subtlety. Graceland is more understated. Come in, gentlemen. Whom did you wish to see?"

Lynn displayed his badge and said, "It's about the matter at the funeral home last night, Mister Grishman. I suppose Mister Lugo's man has contacted you?"

"Matter of fact I just hung up from talking to Bino Sierra, and to Bob Lieberman at the mortuary. Bino said you'd be dropping by. Come on in. It's all unbelievable."

Lynn and Nelson stepped over the carpet layer and around the secretary, who was trying to work at a desk that had been pushed into the closet. Her lanky body warranted a second glance from Nelson before they entered Leo Grishman's office and closed the door.

Roger had doubtless done *this* interior under the strict supervision of Leo Grishman. It said Old Lawyer all the way. The walls of law books were interrupted only by an occasional display of awards that the attorney had been given over a career spanning fifty years. Most were from service work he'd done in Los Angeles and Beverly Hills.

His writing table was traditional walnut with brass drawer pulls. His executive chair was a leather wingback with mahogany legs. There was a regency japaned chair next to the bookshelf, and plenty of texture everywhere.

"Only been in these offices nine months," Leo Grishman said, "ever since I moved my practice out here to the desert. My wife has a touch of emphysema, feels better in desert air. What can I say about that incident last night, except that I'm mystified."

"So are we," Lynn said. "I'd like to speak to you in complete confidence, Mister Grishman."

"That's what lawyers're for," the old man said. "Want a coffee or something?"

"None for me," Lynn said.

"I'll have a cup," Nelson said, thinking that Slim with the long legs would be bringing it in.

Leo Grishman pushed a button on his phone and said, "Sally, one coffee, and a tea for me, please."

Lynn said, "The thing I'd like you to keep confidential is that we're working on this matter *sub rosa*, for a private investigator named Breda Burrows."

"But the badge? You *are* a Palm Springs policeman, right?"

"Soon to be retired," Lynn said. "I was doing a job that happened to bring me in contact with the dark bald man who started the brawl at the mortuary."

Leo Grishman peeked over his glasses at Lynn's still slightly swollen eye, and said, "You were the brawlee, I take it."

Lynn nodded and said, "The bald guy got the name of the mortuary from the tombstone makers who . . ."

"I know, I know," Leo Grishman said. "Bob Lieberman at the mortuary backtracked it that far and filled me in. Have you talked to your detective colleagues?"

Lynn shook his head and said, "They know far less than we do and I'd rather not involve them for a while, unless it's really necessary. Can I rely on you to keep mum?"

"Son, I got no reason to call the cops," Leo Grishman said. "Besides, I got a soft spot for P.I.'s I musta paid out half a million bucks in fees to P.I.'s over the past fifty years. Mostly back in the days when domestic cases were our bread and butter. But you understand, I have to protect my client, John Lugo."

"Sure," Lynn said.

"Has he been your client long?" Nelson asked.

"I didn't catch your name, son," Leo Grishman said.

"Nelson Hareem. I'm a policeman, but not with Palm Springs P.D. Not yet."

"Both of you're doing a little moonlighting for a P.I., eh?" the lawyer said, with a knowing grin. "That's admirable, boys. I know it's tough to make it on a cop's salary. To answer your question, I was John Lugo's lawyer for twenty-five years in L.A.,

245

ever since he started making serious money in the development business."

"What's he develop?" Lynn asked.

"What's he develop?"

"Yeah."

"Anything that needs developing," Leo Grishman said.

"I see," Lynn said.

"Now don't get the wrong idea, son. As far as I know, he's a legit businessman, and all I do is advise him on contracts and liability problems."

"Such as?" Lynn asked.

"I don't talk about 'such as,' " Leo Grishman said, just as the door was opened.

Nelson was disappointed to see that it wasn't the long lanky one. The young woman who brought the hot beverages and cookies was so big he'd have to adjust his headlights if she got in the back of his Jeep.

After she'd gone, Lynn said, "When's your client coming back from Hawaii?"

The old lawyer laughed and said, "He's not in Hawaii. He's playing in the Bob Hope Classic."

"But Bino Sierra said . . ."

"Bino automatically says that to everybody. Then he sends any unusual inquiries to me. That's Bino's way, I don't argue with it. And to save you the trouble, Bino has a minor rap sheet, but from what I hear it was stuff from his youth in East L.A. A little bit of gang stuff. He's been straight since he went to work for John Lugo five or six years ago."

"What's he do?"

"He's a driver and looks after the home. Kind of a personal assistant."

"Uh huh," Lynn said.

Nelson sipped his coffee and was pleased to see that Leo Grishman dunked his cookie in the tea before taking a bite. And him a lawyer.

"I suppose you and Bino and Mister Lugo tried hard to figure out the mortuary connection?"

"Bino swore he hasn't a clue, and neither does John. Bino called John this morning over at Bermuda Dunes soon as he heard about it, that's the course John's playing today. John was all excited about getting to meet Arnold Palmer. Said he didn't know diddly about any dark bald guy trying to find him. Only bald guy he cared about was Gerald Ford. Might get to meet him tomorrow when he plays at Indian Wells."

"Has he ever had a guy of that description in his past?" Lynn asked. "Maybe one he owes, or who owes *him*?"

Leo Grishman sighed and said, "Look, son, a guy like John Lugo probably has a thousand dark guys in his past, with and without hair, who feel that somebody owes somebody. John's sixty-seven years old now and he's living in retirement. He plays golf five times a week. He doesn't cross the wrong people anymore. Besides, anyone could find John Lugo without asking questions about his mother's funeral, for God's sake! Everyone knows he's got a big house up there in Bob Hope's neighborhood."

Lynn studied the lawyer, and said, "The real brain buster is, the guy didn't even know John Lugo's name. All he knew about was a tombstone, a tombstone with orchids on it. A tombstone that John Lugo ordered for his mother's funeral last September. *That's* how he arrived at the mortuary. Can you explain it?"

"Son, you got me. I couldn't explain that one with a Ouija board. I *can* tell you that I'm the guy who handled some of the arrangements for his mother's funeral. The stone with orchids on it was her last request. Believe me, I'm way too old to be lying to a cop. If I had something I didn't want you to know I'd just refuse to talk to you."

Nelson put down his half-drunk cup of coffee and said, "Mister Grishman, is there any connection between your client and somebody from Spain?"

The old lawyer thought it over and said, "Spain? No, I don't think so. Puerto Rico maybe. He was involved with a group that did a resort near San Juan some years back. Spain? No."

"How about the Middle East?" Nelson asked.

"I don't know anybody from the Middle East, believe me," Leo Grishman said. "John's done some vending machine business with a local guy that's Syrian, if that helps."

"Might," Nelson said. "What's his name?"

"Look, not everybody appreciates getting visits from the cops," the lawyer said.

"I took a bad thumping last night," Lynn Cutter said. "I feel like I got spit on and run over by a herd a camels, but I'm willing to stay on this if I get cooperation. Your client might be in danger, and I can promise you this bald guy ain't the kind that's gonna swoon over Bino's campy version of Sicilian opera."

"Bino's not Sicilian, of course. He's a chicano from L.A.," the lawyer said. "And so is John. They both came up the hard way in Boyle Heights. And so did I, I might add, back when Boyle Heights was still a Jewish neighborhood with only a few Mexicans."

"The point is, we're trying to catch a guy who's risking *his* life to reach John Lugo. Why shouldn't you do everything you can to help us?"

The lawyer thought it over and said, "There's a new bellydancing restaurant in Cat City called The Fez. The Syrian's name is George Tibbash. He's a good friend of John's. I'll call him and tell him you're on the way, and I'll explain what's going on and recommend that he talk to you. Maybe *he* can think of a Middle East connection, or even a Spanish one. I can't." Then the lawyer wrote a phone number on a business card and said, "This is my home number. Keep me posted if you learn anything we should know. I don't want anything happening to John Lugo."

"How about the name Francisco V. Ibañez," Nelson said. "What's it mean to you?"

"Diddly," said the lawyer. "That name doesn't mean diddly."

"We'll let you know what we come up with, if it concerns your client," Lynn said.

"Glad to help," the old lawyer said as they were leaving his office. "If we don't meet again, I hope you have good luck in retirement, and may all your polyps be benign."

When they were back in the Jeep, Lynn said, "I thought you'd given up on your terrorist obsession."

"We're going to visit a *Syrian* in a couple minutes!"

"That doesn't make this a CIA case. I'm now inclined to think that our bald guy was coming to Palm Springs in a private plane from . . . I don't know from where. To play catch-up with John Lugo for some deal they did together in . . ."

"Puerto Rico."

"Yeah, Puerto Rico."

"They don't use Spanish pesetas in Puerto Rico."

"I thought I explained that. You can get *any* foreign coins handed to you at any airport in Mexico, or even in any border town. Christ, the border's only a few hours from here, Nelson!"

"You're saying the guy came from Puerto Rico to Mexico where he picked up the coins somehow, then he hired a plane to fly to Palm Springs, got engine trouble, and landed before they got to the right airport? Right?"

"Yeah," Lynn said, "something like that."

"There's no desert in Puerto Rico," Nelson said.

"Why oh why do I keep forgetting about the man of the desert?" Lynn said, eyes rolling up at cloudless blue. "You keep saying it but I don't hear you. Both my wives always told me I had a great ear for anything except their voices. Must be the same with you, huh?"

"About *your* theory, explain one thing."

"Okay."

"If one a John Lugo's old business associates was tryin to plant a bomb in his golf cart or somethin, why would they have to go to a mortician that buried his mother even to find out his name? Explain that."

Lynn Cutter stared through the windshield for a moment and said, "It's amazing how confused I've allowed myself to get since I met you. You're right. My theory's about as accurate as a Scud missile."

"I ain't doin no better. My imagination's taxed to the max. The only thing we know is, if Francisco V. Ibañez gets within a hundred yards a John Lugo, Lugo's life ain't gonna be worth ten pesetas."

"If that bald-headed sonofabitch hadn't shoved me in the box last night, I wouldn't much care," Lynn said, "especially after meeting Lugo's man, Bino. I'd say let the bald guy do the world a favor."

"So maybe we'll bring the guy down *after* he dusts off Lugo. Long as we get him, I don't care if it's before or after."

Nelson showed Lynn his bunny grin. If he had a carrot he'd look just like the Warner Brothers rabbit.

The Fez was one of those ersatz-Moroccan restaurants with Moorish arches and blue tiles and huge coffee tables where everyone sits on enormous floor pillows and eats without utensils unless they demand some, in which case they're begrudgingly given a tablespoon so they can look like infants while they dribble their couscous. A huge banner announcing its grand opening hung across the facade of what had been a Mexican restaurant that had folded. A posted menu offered a half-price luncheon as a promotional gimmick.

The place was so dark it took a moment for their pupils to dilate as they went from harsh desert sunlight to Moroccan gloom. There were about twenty other customers, and a belly dancer was shaking it all around for some Japanese tourists who were only too happy to shove dollar bills inside her costume. Nelson counted seven ones and three fives folded and protruding from her sequined bra.

Each of the waiters wore a hooded djellaba and most looked Arab, though there probably wasn't a genuine Moroccan in the place. The busboys were Mexicans and obviously uncomfortable in the strange getups. The bartender wore a tarboosh and the tassel kept falling in his face.

The only guy in the place in a business suit approached them and said, "A table, gentlemen?"

He was tall and erect, with a curved nose as thin as a blade. He had large penetrating eyes, doeskin complexion, and his silver hair was combed straight back from a widow's peak.

"Mister Tibbash?" Lynn asked.

"Ah, you must be the two policemen," George Tibbash said. "Of course I'm happy to cooperate. Mister Grishman told me all about it." His accent was so slight that for a moment Lynn thought he was American-born.

"Where can we talk?" Lynn asked.

"Because I've just opened I'm needed every moment for emergencies," George Tibbash said. "Would you mind if I left you for now? I'll return promptly."

"Okay with us," Lynn said.

"Of course, you are my guests for luncheon," he said, leading them to a low table near the dance floor where the belly dancer was scooping up all the dollar bills that had dropped out of her costume during her last shimmy.

She dashed offstage as the taped music dropped a few decibels and several degrees in heat. A baritone started wailing something that sounded like an Arabic version of "I Love Paris."

After Lynn and Nelson sat down on the floor pillows, George Tibbash said, "If you'll permit me, I'll order for you. Unless you're familiar with the cuisine?"

251

"Not me," Lynn said. "I survive on Dunkin' Donuts and Fritos. You know, all that nighttime crime-fighting fuel."

"Me too," said Nelson. "I can't jist say no to McDonald's. A major grease abuser is what I am."

"We'll start you with harira, a Moroccan soup, and a bastella appetizer," George Tibbash said. "That's a pie of minced chicken, almonds and eggs. Then I think chicken tagine. It's flavored with saffron, pickled lemons and ginger. And couscous, naturally. That's steamed semolina topped with a lamb stew. How about drinks?"

"Scotch rocks, tall," Lynn said.

"Bottle a beer," Nelson said. "Any kind."

"Coming up, gentlemen," George Tibbash said. "And I'll be joining you as soon as I can. Our purveyor hasn't shown up with tonight's order, so it's crisis time. Meanwhile, enjoy yourselves."

Nelson looked around with a big grin and said, "See? See why I wanna work Palm Springs P.D.?"

"This ain't Palm Springs, it's Cathedral City," Lynn reminded him.

"I know, but it ain't the back a the bus with all the diesel fumes neither."

A black man wearing a djellaba brought the drinks on a copper tray. Nelson figured he was probably just some local guy from north Palm Springs until he said with a Middle East accent, "Who gets the Scotch, please?"

After he was gone, Lynn took a gulp of the Scotch and said, "I can't see how I let that guy get away last night. I mean, I had him backed up like bad plumbing, and all of a sudden I was bunking with Denny O'Doul."

"You're not that young anymore."

"How charming of you to remind me."

"Maybe you lost a step or two since you were a young guy patrolin a beat. It happens."

"The guy knows what he's doing, that's all I'm thinking."

"Then why didn't he jist blow you away? That's what a self-respectin terrorist shoulda done in that situation."

Lynn said, "He's been up against two cops already, and he only did as much as he *had* to do."

"You tryin to say he's not a killer? What's he gonna do to John Lugo, cure his duck hook?"

"Permanently," Lynn said, "but maybe he's not anxious to do fatal damage to anybody else."

"Unless he has to."

"Unless he has to.

"You'll recognize him if you see him again, won't ya?"

"If he was in a scuba suit and snorkel I'd know him," Lynn said. "How bout you?"

"I didn't really look at his face when we walked past him at the mortuary," Nelson said.

A different waiter brought mint tea along with a brass basin and ewer for hand washing, as well as another round of drinks.

When the food arrived the waiter said, "The harissa is for the couscous. It is sauce of red chili."

Nelson looked around for utensils and said, "Don't we get chopsticks or somethin?"

When they were in the middle of lunch, and their hands were gooey with cinnamon and powdered sugar, the belly dancer returned. In age, she was somewhere between Nelson and Lynn, that is to say, experienced but not over the hill, with the kind of belly muscles that could roll a quarter from below her navel to her breasts, a trick she saved for the Japanese.

She did a bit of bumping and grinding and swaying in front of Nelson, who grinned and blushed. The delighted Japanese kept shoving currency inside her costume, while the zils, tied to her writhing fingers, rang like chimes in their overheated ears.

George Tibbash did not return until Lynn and Nelson had dipped their fingers in bowls of lemon water and dried them on towels supplied by the waiter. When he did return, he was carrying a demitasse cup of tea. Nelson admired the way he held the cup when he sat down. His little finger was curled slightly and he kept his elbow down. Nelson never trusted guys who drank with their elbows up. The little cop wondered if George Tibbash was a dunker.

Lynn squirmed into a more comfortable position with his legs straight out. His knees were aching from having sat cross-legged.

"You get used to it," George Tibbash said, indicating the floor pillow. "Tourists love it."

"I guess Leo Grishman explained the whole deal?"

"That's one of the reasons I've left you alone," George Tibbash said, his eyebrows peaking. "I've been searching my memory for something, anything. Leo said you suspect some sort of connection between John Lugo and a man from either Spain or the Middle East?"

"Maybe," Lynn said, with a glance at Nelson.

"I really can't think of anyone who'd want to hunt down John Lugo. In the first place—"

"Everybody in town knows who he is and how to find him," Lynn said.

"That's right. And not just this town. He's done business in Los Angeles and many other places. I was only involved in the Puerto Rican resort project, and for a time I was a limited partner in the vending machine business. As far as I know, I'm the only person from the Middle East that was ever associated with those projects."

"How bout the Canary Islands?" Nelson asked.

George Tibbash paused and said, "Now that you mention the Canary Islands, I think there was a man who headed up a rival consortium on the Puerto Rican project. . . . Yes, I'm *sure* of it. We outbid them and got it. Yes, the Canary Islands."

"Was his name Francisco V. Ibañez?" Nelson asked quickly.

"Ibañez," George Tibbash said. "Perhaps. Of course, he

had a Spanish name, but I don't speak the language. John Lugo did all of the Spanish-speaking when we were down in San Juan. He might remember the man's name. It *could* have been Ibañez."

"Did you have any more dealings with the man?" Lynn asked.

"No, John may have, but I did not. I returned to L.A. and John stayed for about a month, as I recall."

"I think we'll have to talk to John Lugo right away," Lynn said to Nelson.

"You'll have trouble this week," George Tibbash said. "John's a fanatical golfer and he's playing in the Bob Hope Classic."

"He's gotta stop after eighteen holes," Lynn said.

"But he doesn't," George Tibbash said, finishing his tea. "John will be with the golfing crowd from the moment he arises until he goes to bed at night, and he may even have a famous golf professional staying at his house. If you want to see him you'll have to go to whichever golf course he happens to be playing. On Saturday, the last day for amateurs, he'll be at Indian Wells, I believe. Then on Saturday evening he'll have a huge party in his home on Southridge for all the professionals that care to come, along with hundreds of friends from his country club, as well as some of the amateur players from the tournament. He does the same thing every year without fail."

"Can you think of anybody from your past association with John Lugo, anyone from any foreign country, who'd want to hunt him down? Does he have enemies?"

George Tibbash smiled and said, "A man like John Lugo would have to have enemies. He rose from the barrios of Los Angeles to Southridge, to the top of the mountain overlooking all of Palm Springs. But I would think he's outlived most of his enemies. Now, if you'll excuse me, I must get back to my kitchen. And I *do* hope you've enjoyed our food and that you'll tell your friends about us and come again."

After they'd thanked George Tibbash and were walking toward the door, Nelson said to Lynn, "Wait a minute. Got a couple bucks I can stick inside that dancer's bra?"

Lynn reached in his pocket reflexively, but then shook his head, saying, "I got a roll a dimes, but they're at the house. I got a credit card, but it's more overextended than Poland."

The dancer's entire body glistened with an oily sheen when she did a sweaty, groin-throbbing shimmy right in the face of the oldest Japanese.

Nelson stopped to gawk, but Lynn grabbed his sleeve, saying, "C'mon, kid. They're all alike. They make you beg for admission to that thing, but the truth is, Jacques Cousteau could use it for a shark cage."

-18-

"Whats our next move?" Nelson wanted to know, during the drive back to Palm Springs.

"I'd say we phone car rentals and hotels for Francisco V. Ibañez," Lynn said. "There's nothing else to do till we get a chance to connect up with John Lugo."

"Wish we had an office," Nelson said.

"We do," Lynn said with some hesitation. "Breda's."

"Let's get started on those calls."

"On second thought, it might not be a good idea to bother Breda."

"She's a nice lady," Nelson said. "She wouldn't even mind long distance calls."

"I gotta admit, she's worth a couple grand over blue book in a tight market," Lynn said. "Okay, I'll risk it."

Nelson said, "Ain't police work funny? We got the power to deprive people of their freedom. We got the power to take a human life. But we gotta get permission from our sergeant to make a long distance phone call!"

Breda was wearing a blazer the color of a smoke tree, a blouse just a shade more smokey, and cuffed rayon and linen trousers with a check pattern. It was the kind of thing she could mix and match, and had bought after laborious searching at department store sales. The entire outfit had cost $115, but looked plenty expensive.

She was also wearing her strawberry eyeglasses, and was busy at the computer when Lynn sheepishly followed Nelson into her office.

Before Lynn could say anything to her she said, "I've been trying to reach you at your house. Jack Graves wants us to interview Clive Devon at six o'clock tonight."

Lynn was delighted that she was behaving in a seminormal fashion toward him. He gave her the happiest smile he had with him that day, and asked, "What's it about?"

"Jack says he might be able to clear the case. He wants us to question Clive Devon about the guy from Painted Canyon. I'll pick you up at your house at quarter to six. Any problem with that?"

"No problem," Lynn said, still beaming. "I'm glad to be of help."

"It's because you're gonna have to flash a badge. Otherwise I'd be doing it myself," she said with a look that could deflect .38 hollow-points.

Flashing the badge again! When he'd started this job, she'd promised that he'd never have to use his official position in any way. Yet in the last forty-eight hours he'd shown his badge to half the registered voters in Riverside County. That pension had better come fast.

After Nelson told Breda about their interviews with Bino Sierra, Leo Grishman and George Tibbash, he said, "We're down to calling car rentals and hotels for our guy from the Canary Islands. So can we use your phones?"

"Help yourself," she said, and went back to the computer, without so much as another glance at Lynn.

"I'll take the car rentals," Nelson said, handing Lynn a phone book.

"How come I always get screwed like a June bride," Lynn grumbled. "There's probably a couple hundred hotel listings."

"I'll help you if I don't make a score with the car rentals," Nelson said.

It was going to be a very long afternoon but Nelson never lost enthusiasm for a moment. He'd pick up the phone and say, "Hello, this is Officer Pacino from the police department calling. We think we might have a car a yours that was impounded. The tow driver failed to give us the license number and make, but it was rented to Francisco V. Ibañez. Is he a recent customer? No Francisco V. Ibañez? Must be some mistake. Thanks anyway."

Lynn's calls were delivered with far less vivacity: "Hello, this is Sergeant DeNiro from the police department. We've found a wallet belonging to a tourist we think is staying at your hotel. Francisco V. Ibañez from the Canary Islands? No? Wrong hotel. Thanks."

And so it went for an hour.

Lynn made a try at conversation *once*. He said to Breda, "In a state with a hundred and forty thousand lawyers, a state that leads the universe in bodily injury claims, in the insurance-fraud capital of the galaxy, I'd think you'd be able to get more insurance company clients. I'm gonna talk up your name to every lawyer I know."

Breda didn't even look up.

Then, while Lynn tried to get up the guts to ask her if she'd like a diet Coke, Nelson leaped from his chair and snapped his fingers to get Lynn's attention while he talked into the phone and wrote down a hotel's name: "Yes! Yes! No, there's no real problem with the car! We just have to talk to him about a found wallet in the car! Yes! Thanks!"

That got Breda out of the computer. She said, "A score?"

"We *got* him!" Nelson cried, hanging up and showing Lynn the name of the resort hotel.

"We got him, *maybe*," Lynn said. "If he gave the correct local address when he rented the car. That's a huge hotel. I wouldn't've expected him to stay at a place like that."

"Has the guy did *anything* you'd expect so far?" Nelson wanted to know.

"You wanna call first or just go?"

"Let's go. This is about our last shot till we see Lugo."

"Okay," Lynn said, standing up and massaging his right knee.

Breda surprised him by taking off her yuppie glasses and looking directly at him. "Do you have a gun with you?"

"No," he said, "but Nelson carries more firepower than Israel."

"I'll watch over him, don't worry," Nelson said to Breda.

Encouraged by her concern, Lynn said to her, "I know I pleaded poverty but I been holding out. If anything happens to me I want you to take my bank card to the beg-a-buck machine and take it all: thirty-three bucks. You can even have the coupons I been saving for a carpet-cleaning discount. Nelson, he gets my steering wheel cover and my bowling ball. If *he* survives."

Breda didn't answer. She put her strawberry glasses on and went back to the computer, not even bothering with a mean little grin.

There was a one-hundred-foot drop from ceiling to lobby floor. And the lobby, the size of a small town, looked like it had been designed by a mathematician. Geometry dominated.

There were tiers of half-hexagon stone planters overflowing with flowers, ferns and exotic plants, as well as octagon reflecting pools.

Above the ground were half a dozen floors offering rooms whose doors opened out onto a view of the colossal lobby on one side and the desert panorama on the other. More descending tiers, these full of water, spilled down into a canal upon which guests could ride to their rooms in an electric boat with a surrey top, captained by a girl in sailor whites. The only real drawback to the concept was that all of the indoor water emitted a dank odor.

Lynn had only been inside the resort hotel twice, but Nelson never had. They moseyed around before Nelson spoke to a young woman at the reception area. "I'd like to leave a message for Mister Ibañez. Francisco V. Ibañez. Unless he's already checked out?"

She went to a computer, punched a few keys, and said, "No, we have him until Monday. You might try the house phone around the corridor to your right."

When they got to the phone, Lynn said, "If he's in, you'll be somebody from the car rental. He's gotta bring the car back because there's been a mistake. It was promised to somebody else."

"Yeah, I'll tell him we'll give him three days for free because a the mixup."

"Don't overplay your role," Lynn said. "One free day's enough."

Nelson picked up the house phone and said, "Mister Ibañez, please."

He let it ring ten times, but shook his head at Lynn and hung up.

"Okay, let's cruise," Lynn suggested. "If I spot him, I'll give you a signal and turn my back so he doesn't recognize me."

"Then what?" Nelson wanted to know.

"Then while you keep an eye on him I'll go straight to the phone, call the sheriffs and tell them to come pick up their smuggler."

Lynn had expected anything but reason and common sense from Nelson Hareem at this point, yet Nelson said, "I agree."

"I could kiss you, kid," Lynn said.

"You already warned me against that," Nelson reminded him.

With the thirty-second annual Bob Hope Chrysler Classic going on, the hotel was like just about every other hotel in the desert: fully booked. Lynn and Nelson went out to the pool area and studied all dark bald men, as well as all dark men wearing hats. There were a lot of both, what with so many tans.

Their progress was temporarily halted by a champagne blonde at poolside modeling a passion-pink floral bikini, and a golden cotton-weave sun hat. First she'd pose with, then without a matching cover-up, while a fashion photographer clicked away.

Nelson ogled, then resumed his stroll, splitting off from Lynn, looking for "possibles" worth a second look. He saw a lot of young women his age with old men Lynn's age.

There was a breeze blowing, but the pool decking trapped and intensified the heat and the water reflected a blistering glare. Lynn was hot, but resisted the temptation of buying a drink from one of the strolling cocktail waitresses in sarongs. The smell of coconut oil reminded him of many failed poolside romances during the years in Palm Springs when he'd still believed a deep tan would bring him love, not just skin cancer.

Now, resigning himself to lonely middle age, he just stayed out of the scalding sunlight as much as possible. Wilfred Plimsoll said that his saloon was the safest place in town. Not a single case of basal cell carcinoma had been triggered by the gloom in The Furnace Room.

There were several dark husky men wearing hats who made

Lynn's heart pump for a few seconds, but when he'd get close to them it was always a no-go. *His* guy had small, very dark eyes and slightly flared nostrils, at least they'd been flaring when he'd waited, hands held low, for the charge of Lynn Cutter.

"Whaddaya think, Lynn?" Nelson asked, after they'd lingered for nearly thirty minutes.

"Another phone call?"

They went back to the house phones and tried again. Nelson let it ring even longer before shaking his head and hanging up.

"Lemme try something," Lynn said, and Nelson followed him back to reception.

This time there was a young man behind the reception desk. Lynn said to him, "I've been trying to reach Mister Francisco Ibañez all day. Did he leave a message in his box for me? My name's Costner, from Desert Car Rentals."

The young guy disappeared for a moment, then returned and said, "Mister Ibañez has gone to L.A. till tomorrow, but there's a note from the concierge that a clubhouse badge will be delivered for Mister Ibañez this afternoon. Are you delivering it?"

"Do you mean for the Bob Hope tournament?"

"Yes," the young man said. "Are you the person with the badge?"

"No," Lynn said. "Not that badge. Thanks anyway."

When he and Nelson were leaving the monster lobby, Lynn said, "Guess you and me're going to a golf tournament tomorrow. Wear your plus fours."

"What're plus fours?" Nelson asked.

"Knickers."

"What're knickers?"

Lynn said, "I think our generation gap is insurmountable. I'll bet you've never tasted a stewed prune. Plus fours? Like Payne Stewart wears?"

"Wanna stop by John Lugo's house on Southridge before we go back to Breda's?" Nelson asked.

"He'll still be out on the course."

"Okay, wanna go get a pick-me-up at The Furnace Room, and then come back here and stake out Ibañez?"

"I gotta do the other thing with Breda, remember?"

"How bout afterwards?"

"I'm not coming back here tonight," Lynn said. "I'm getting a good night's sleep. We're gonna wrap this up tomorrow by catching Ibañez here in the morning, or by staying closer to John Lugo than his caddy."

"How do ya wanna do it?"

Lynn said, "Here's what I propose: Tomorrow morning I'm coming back to the hotel bright and early, ready to spot him if he returns from L.A. to pick up his clubhouse badge. If by chance he decides to go straight to the tournament without stopping here, *you'll* be there."

"But how'll I know him? I didn't get a good look."

"You'll know him," Lynn said. "After all this, you'll know him, won't you?"

Nelson looked at Lynn for a second and said, "Yeah, I think I would, if he gets near John Lugo."

"Okay, the obvious thing to do is, find Lugo and stick with him. If our guy shows up wearing a wig, or a Batman suit, or cross-dressed to look like Bette Midler, you'll be there."

"Don't worry, I'll recognize him. I *think*."

"When you drop me off, go straight to a phone, call Lugo's lawyer at home and tell him you're gonna hang around his client tomorrow. Grishman'll tell Lugo you're around. He doesn't want anything to happen to his old-age-annuity client."

"How bout Breda?"

"I'm gonna ask Breda to shuttle back and forth from the golf tournament to the hotel if necessary, or to relay phone messages between you and me."

"Sounds okay," Nelson said.

"Try to look like a golf fan tomorrow."

"Do golf fans wear cowboy boots?"
"Only one. Glen Campbell."

After Nelson dropped him at the mansion, Lynn went directly to the ice maker in the pantry and scooped some cubes into a Ziploc bag to put on his throbbing knee. As he sat there in the "gourmet kitchen," thinking that a thousand Chilean miners must've died for *half* the unused copper pans in the butler's pantry, he plunged into a lightweight bout of depression. He realized that when he finally lost this house-sitting job he'd probably end up in a couple of rooms that were smaller than this kitchen that had never even served more than four people at one time, according to the homeowner.

Lynn wouldn't be sorry to see the last of the place. The scale of the house was making him feel more alone than he'd ever felt in his life. And feeling alone made him think of Breda.

He took his ice pack with him and climbed the staircase to the master suite. He wanted to lie in a warm bath with the ice on his knee until it was time for their six o'clock date with Clive Devon. He turned on the country station, and by the time he'd gotten into the Jacuzzi tub, Vince Gill was singing for him.

Never knew lonely could be so blue
Never loved someone like I love you
Never knew lonely till you.

Well, there wasn't any sense feeling spooky about it anymore. The rednecks had his number, that's all there was to it. But, whatever the hell they sang about always applied to losers, so maybe that was the logical explanation.

He should've known the relationship couldn't go anywhere. What'd he have to offer? But wait a minute! He did have some connections in this town just by virtue of having been a cop for a long time. And he'd have a fifty percent pension tax-free, which, even allowing for the greater salary she'd earned at LAPD, would be worth more than *her* retirement checks. So maybe the sugar-coated fantasy he'd nibbled at for the past several days wasn't so farfetched, the fantasy of working part-time with her in her business. Maybe it could've worked out if her head wasn't more twisted around than the kid in *The Exorcist*.

And all the while, Vince Gill never let up, not for a minute.

Never knew lonely could be so blue
Never knew lonely till youuuuuuu.

She picked him up in front of the house at twilight: low, blue and purple twilight. Breda didn't say anything at all when he got into the Z, so he said, "Nelson and me struck out today."

"I know. Nelson called me."

"I figured he'd fill you in, that's why I didn't call you," Lynn said, causing her to show him that smirky little grin of hers that said: I don't give a ferret's fuck whether you ever call me, scumbag!

"I'll do the talking with Clive Devon if you don't mind," she said, with a voice pretty far up on her irritation scale.

"It's *your* case," he said. "I'm along to flash my buzzer at the only guy in this hemisphere that I ain't shown it to since I met you."

"Look, I know things haven't turned out the way I said they would."

"Not quite. I almost got killed. I probably *will* get killed sometime tomorrow when our bald guy goes after John Lugo or me, whichever one he spots first."

"So explain," she said, not looking at him as she roared away from a red light, all of a sudden as macho a driver as Nelson Hareem. "Why're you risking your ass like this?"

"Tell you the truth," he said, "I'd call the sheriffs tonight and lay it all out for them if we really had anything to lay out. Believe me, if I spot the bald guy tomorrow morning I'm picking up the phone and calling nine-one-one. I'll point out their smuggler to the first deputy that arrives, and let their detectives work out what all that tombstone stuff is about."

"Call the sheriffs now," she said. "Let them in on it now."

"I would if . . ."

"If *what*?"

"If I was more sure that all a the work we've done means anything at all. We're not positive Francisco Ibañez is the guy we're after. I don't wanna look stupid if we got nothing."

Breda switched on the headlights and rolled her eyes the way he'd done so often with Nelson Hareem.

"Men!" she said. "Typical male-pattern bullshit! He put some hurt on you last time, yet you'd let him hurt you a lot, even to the *max*, rather than risk looking stupid in front of the other boys!"

"We all have our idiosyncrasies," he said. "You ain't exactly a mental-health poster girl."

"At least I stay sober, *most* of the time! At least I have a job!"

"I'm gonna have one soon as my pension comes."

"What, bartending at The Furnace Room, when you're sober enough?"

That did it! He was really steamed! "Maybe!" he said. "But at least I won't have somebody at The Furnace Room calling me a sick degenerate when about the most decadent thing we ever do in there is sit around watching 1950's black-and-white movies with edgy background music about girls that look for love in all the wrong places with oily guys named Nick!"

When he finished that speech he wondered if it made any sense whatsoever.

The argument stopped when she made a screeching left turn from Palm Canyon Drive into Clive Devon's Las Palmas neighborhood.

The sky was darkening fast as Breda parked on the street. They walked to the gate of the Devon house and rang.

The maid, Blanca Soltero, answered the intercom. "Who ees there, please?"

"Police," Lynn said. "We'd like to talk to Mister Devon."

"Moment, please," she said.

Then Clive Devon's voice came on the intercom and said, "Hello, can I help you?"

"Police Department, Mister Devon," Lynn said. "We have to talk to you for a few minutes."

"Can you tell me what it's about?"

"We're investigating an assault on an officer. It involves the man you picked up three days ago in Painted Canyon."

There was silence for a few seconds, then Clive Devon said, "Come in, please."

An electronic beep opened the swinging double gates, and Breda led Lynn up the driveway.

Clive Devon stood in the doorway, apparently relieved to see a woman. He barely glanced at Lynn's badge before he stepped back to allow them to enter. Lynn saw that it was one of those Spanish colonial houses he'd always liked, with shuttered windows deeply inset, Mexican tile roof, and stucco walls a foot thick. But it didn't have the massive masculine furniture usually found in this style of house. The place was full of lighted paintings on rose-colored wall covering. The drapes were meant to imply natural desert pastel, but it was all too feminine, an obvious attempt to please Rhonda Devon, Lynn decided.

Clive Devon was as tall as Jack Graves, but not nearly as thin. His hair was sparse and white, and he had regular sun-burned features and a prominent chin. He wore a knit shirt, chinos, and bedroom slippers. He shook hands with both of them but Lynn didn't volunteer their names.

"How did you know I'd picked up a man in Painted Canyon?" he asked, as they sat down in the same living room where Breda had first met Rhonda Devon.

"Your license number was taken down by a policeman patroling the canyon that day."

"But why would he do that?" His eyes were pale blue and nervous. He instinctively dropped them whenever he started to speak, and then, as though by force of will, he'd raise them and look uncomfortably into the eyes of Lynn or Breda, and speak so softly they had to listen attentively.

"Did you see the news story about the sheriff's deputy who was assaulted down at the airport the day before you went to Painted Canyon?" Breda asked.

"I might've," he said. "I think I may've heard a news report."

"We believe the man you picked up was the man who assaulted the deputy," Lynn said.

"I can't believe it!" Clive Devon said, sitting back on the sofa. His genuine amazement actually caused him to relax slightly.

"What were *you* doing down there?" Lynn asked.

Clive Devon didn't answer that. He said, "But how? How could the policeman have seen me pick up the man and not question us right then, if that was the man he was after?"

"He, uh, wasn't sure," Lynn said, "and then he got an emergency call at that moment. A fatal traffic accident. He had to leave."

"I see," Clive Devon said, drumming his fingers on the arm of the sofa.

Breda repeated the question. "How *did* you happen to be down there?"

"I went with a friend," Clive Devon said. "Hiking."

"We may need to question the friend," Lynn said.

Clive Devon dropped his eyes again and didn't raise them when he said, "I wouldn't want to frighten her. Esther's a very shy young woman. She's the daughter of our housekeeper. I'm sure I can tell you whatever you need to know."

When he looked up, Breda said, "How did you happen to be with the man?"

"It was very strange," Clive Devon said. "He just appeared

269

out of nowhere and said his car had broken down farther up in the canyon. And that he needed a ride."

"To a phone?"

"Yes," Clive Devon said. "To a phone."

"And did you take him to a phone?" Lynn asked.

"No, that was more peculiar. I dropped Esther back where her car was parked, and the man changed his mind. He asked where I was heading, and when I said Palm Springs he said that's where *he* lived and would I please take him with me."

"What about his car?" Lynn asked.

"I asked about that too," Clive Devon said, "but he told me he preferred to wait till his brother got off work, that they could go back down and haul it out themselves to save a tow charge."

"*Did* you take him home?" Lynn asked.

"No, when I asked him his address he said just to drop him downtown, that his brother worked nearby in a restaurant. So I did."

"Where?" Breda asked.

"Near Indian and Palm Canyon Drive."

"By the Alan Ladd hardware store?"

"Yes."

"And that was it?"

"Yes. I didn't see him again."

Lynn said, "The policeman who took down your license number said there was a dog with you."

"Yes," Clive Devon said.

"At first he thought the dog might've belonged to the man you picked up."

"No," Clive Devon said.

"What did the man look like?" Lynn asked.

"He was a Mexican. Young. Well, young to *me*. In his forties, I should say. A burly man about your height."

"Bald?"

"He wore a baseball cap, as I recall," Clive Devon said, "and he carried a red canvas bag."

"Did he say what was in it?"

"Yes. Lunch and clothing. But he never opened the bag. He said he'd camped out in his car and couldn't get it started when he was ready to leave."

"Was he Mexican or Mexican-American?" Breda asked.

"I'd say he was from Mexico. But he spoke beautiful English with a pleasant accent. More grammatical than most Americans."

"Do you have anything else to add that might help us?" Breda asked.

"No, except that I can't believe he's a criminal."

Lynn said, "I'll bet even the dog liked him."

"Yes, and Malcolm's a good judge of character," Clive Devon said softly.

Recalling all the barking when she'd tried to prowl the property for a sneak-and-peek, Breda asked, "Where's Malcolm now?"

"With Esther at her house," Clive Devon said.

"Does she ever bring him here?" Breda remembered the swim party when it sounded like Malcolm was doing belly flops in the pool.

"Oh, no," Clive Devon said. "My wife's extremely allergic to animals of all kinds."

Breda turned to Lynn and said, "Anything else?"

Lynn said, "Not unless you can think of something, Mister Devon."

"Well," Clive Devon said, dropping his eyes diffidently, "I'd just like to offer an opinion. I wonder if there could be some mistake. He just couldn't be violent. He talked a lot about the desert. He had a *very* gentle way about him."

-19-

I was more than frustrating, this place. He was driving up the steep narrow road to the highest residential area in Palm Springs, but when he got halfway up the grade, he saw a kiosk with a guard inside. He stopped at the kiosk and the uniformed security officer came out immediately with a clipboard in his hand, accompanied by a guard dog.

"I am sorry," the fugitive said. "I am not allowed to pass?"

"This is a private road from here on up," the security officer said. "Is a resident expecting you?"

"No," he said to the security officer. "I am a tourist. No problem. Sorry. Thank you."

When he was driving back down from Southridge, he was dejected. He couldn't fathom how these people lived. Private streets with guards and dogs? Perhaps that's how they had to live in a country like this. He'd read a story that very day about a serial murderer in Rochester, New York, who'd been sentenced to 250 years in prison for the murder of eleven women. What made it even more horrible was that the man was on parole at the time of the murders from *another* pair of murders fifteen years earlier. He'd strangled two children. The fugitive kept asking himself: What kind of country *paroles* a man who has strangled two children?

While he waited at the foot of Southridge for an opening in the traffic on Highway 111, he saw in his mirror a gardener's truck coming down behind him. He got out of his car, rather certain that the gardener would be a Mexican, and he was.

The fugitive waved at the gardener and when the man pulled over, the fugitive said, in the macho slang of his country, "*¿Qué pasa, 'mano?*" What's happening, bro?

In Spanish, the fugitive also said, "I just arrived from Tecate, and I was trying to visit an old family friend who lives up there on that hill, but the guard won't let me through. My friend went away and forgot to leave my name."

The gardener also spoke the earthy slang of his country. He said, "Oh, no, *'mano*, they won't let you in unless your friend says to let you pass. Fuck no. No chance."

"The problem is, he's gone for the entire day. Do you happen to work for him? John Lugo?"

"No," the gardener said. "My job is up the left side near the top. Do you know that Bob Hope lives up there?"

"Yes, I've heard that," the fugitive said. "There can't be more than one *pocho* up there. Are you sure you don't know him? Or perhaps one of his servants?" Then the fugitive smiled and said, "I imagine that a rich *pocho* gets his grass cut by *real* Mexicans, true, *'mano?*"

The gardener laughed at that, and said, "Very fucking true." Then he said, "I think the man who has that big pink house with the tile roof might be your friend. I've seen an old man come and go with his driver. Yes, he's probably the one. There's a very big party going to happen there. Many people in vans have been coming all day." Then the gardener took a close look at the fugitive, and said, "Man, you have very rich family friends."

The fugitive laughed and said, "But I'm poor. Tell me, are the party arrangers still there now?"

"For certain," the gardener said. "I tell you, it's a big fucking party. You'll see them come down soon and then you'll see others go up."

"Well, I'll just have to wait until my family friend comes home," the fugitive said, waving goodbye. "Thanks."

Patience, they had a lot of that in his country. He could wait a long time, but he didn't have to. In twenty minutes a red van drove down the steep road. There was writing on the side that said HENRY'S GOURMET CATERING.

The fugitive followed the van to an address on East Palm Canyon Drive, near Smoke Tree Village. From there, the fugitive could look up and see not only Bob Hope's giant house, but the home of John Lugo as well. It was sprawling but undistinguished new construction, one of the tens of thousands of California homes that realtors lump together under the generic heading: Mediterranean. It had to be John Lugo's home, it was the only one painted orchid-pink.

The caterer was working late on Friday because of that big party up on Southridge. There were three young Mexicans running out the front door with folding chairs and cases of wine, and the fugitive saw a tall blond gringo with hair like a woman who seemed to be in charge of the Mexicans.

The young Mexican who had driven the van was talking to the gringo when the fugitive entered. He said, "Not enough wine. Henry say I tell you."

The tall blond gringo was wearing a purple T-shirt with the caterer's gold logo on the front. He said, "Goddamnit, why doesn't Henry make up his mind about how much wine I'm supposed to order? I can't make another trip to the store now!"

The young Mexican driver just showed him an embarrassed smile.

The tall blond tossed his writing pad on the counter and said, "Okay, I'll make another run, but I wish he'd make up his mind!"

The fugitive approached him, saying, "Good day, sir. I am thinking perhaps you could use some help? I have had seven years of experience at a catering company, both in Tijuana and San Diego. I need a job very much."

But the tall blond was beside himself with the stresses of the moment. He said, "Look, come back Monday. I'll let you put in an application then, but I got a big party tomorrow and I don't have time right now."

Before he could dash out to the van, the fugitive said, "Sir, I would be glad to help you at the party. I would work for minimum salary just for the experience with your company. And to show to you that I am a good worker."

"Sorry, buddy," the blond gringo said. "We can't hire somebody we haven't trained. Not for a party like the one we got tomorrow. Come back Monday." Then he was off and running to the catering van.

The fugitive started out to his car, but as soon as the blond gringo had driven off, he went back in and approached the young Mexican who'd driven the van down from Southridge.

The fugitive said, in Spanish, "You're working at a big party tomorrow, your boss told me."

"Very big," the kid said. "Three hundred people, at least." Then he grinned proudly and said, "Famous golfers and perhaps even movie stars!"

The fugitive looked at the cartons being stacked for loading: tablecloths, napkins, flatware. Each box was marked by a felt pen: *Lugo*.

"I wish I could get a job here," the fugitive said. "I have to make some money quick in order to go back to San Felipe and see my sick mother."

"That's a pity," the kid said. "I heard you ask Phil. He's a bastard. If Henry was here he might hire you."

"Do they provide you with clothes to wear at parties?" the fugitive asked. "Or would I have to buy my own?"

"They buy one shirt and one pair of trousers for you," the kid said. "We must provide our own shoes. If we don't have black leather shoes, they'll buy them, but we must pay them back from our first paycheck."

"Where do you buy your clothes?"

"I found a good sale at May Company," the kid said.

"What would I need to buy?"

"A white dress shirt with long sleeves, a black vest, a black bow tie, and black trousers. That's all," the kid said.

"And black shoes."

"Yes," the kid chuckled, looking at the fugitive's white Palm Springs tasseled shoes. "Those won't do."

"I could go to a department store this evening and buy what I need," the fugitive said. "Or even tomorrow morning. If I did that do you think Henry might hire me?"

"Henry would never let you work at this party unless you were properly trained by him."

"How many of you will be working tomorrow?" the fugitive asked.

"At least twenty serving people, not counting bartenders. And not counting those in the kitchen doing food preparation. The boss wants a fresh drink in everyone's hands at all times, that's what Henry says."

"I wish I could have gotten to work at this party," the fugitive said. "But maybe I'm lucky not to start with such a hard one. You'll work long hours, no?"

"Oh, yes," the kid said. "The serving people must be there at two o'clock. They expect the first guests to arrive at about five or six. We'll stay till two o'clock in the morning, perhaps. Twelve hours work."

"Well, I guess I'll come back on Monday," the fugitive said. "Thanks."

"Talk to Henry, not Phil," the kid said. "He's a nice man. Phil's a bastard."

"Are most of your workers Mexican?" the fugitive asked.

"Of course!" the kid said, laughing. "If the immigration rounded up all the undocumented workers around here, Palm Springs would shut down completely."

The moment she made a turn from Highway 111 into Windy Point, a gust of sand peppered the windshield.

"Just a balmy breeze, by Windy Point standards," Lynn said as the visibility from the headlight beams dropped to ten feet.

They followed Jack Graves' little street to the end, where it petered out onto the open desert. The wind now turned from gusting blasts to a steady blow, humming down through the mountain pass.

When they got out of Breda's Z they were actually blown backwards a step or two. Lynn thought he saw a silhouette floating along the desert floor beyond the cactus garden, a ragged specter propelled by the wind through the darkness.

"Jack!" he called, but only the banshee howl of wind answered him, forcing him to turn his back.

He and Breda stumbled toward the front door, and Lynn knocked, waited a few seconds, then opened it.

When they got inside, Breda said, "Good Lord!" Then she said, "What about my *car*? It'll be sandblasted!"

"It might settle down as fast as it started up," Lynn said, unconvincingly.

While Breda was shaking sand from her hair the front door opened and Jack Graves limped in from outside, wiping his eyes on the sleeve of his jacket, his black hair blown across his long sorrowful face. He brushed some sand from his coat and said, "Around these parts, we call this a gentle zephyr."

Lynn saw an angry blackening bruise on the gaunt cheekbone of Jack Graves. "What happened to your face?"

"Oh, nothing," Jack Graves said. "A stupid little accident, that's all."

"What kinda accident?" Lynn asked suspiciously.

"Stumbled and fell in the ravine when I was out walking this afternoon. Clumsy."

"Well then, why the hell were you back out there tonight? In a windstorm?"

"Listening for the coyotes," Jack Graves said, "but I guess they have more sense than to leave their dens when there's wind."

"More sense than some people," Lynn said. "Did you go to a doctor?"

"About this little bruise?" Jack Graves said, touching it gingerly.

"You're limping," Lynn said.

"Twisted my ankle when I fell, but I'm fine. No problem at all."

"I oughtta call Mister Goodwrench," Lynn said, with a glance at Breda. "Maybe get the nuts and bolts tightened up in your head." Then he massaged his aching knee and said, "And to put a little oil in my joints. I'm leaking."

Jack Graves said, "Anyway, shall we get down to business? First, tell me, what about the man Clive Devon picked up in Painted Canyon?"

"I'm convinced he doesn't know a thing about that guy," Breda said. "The smuggler sold him a bill of goods that his car had broken down, and Devon simply gave him a ride."

"Do you agree with Breda, Lynn?" Jack Graves asked.

"Yeah," Lynn said. "Clive Devon's about as sinister as a blueberry muffin. There's no connection."

"I had to be sure," Jack Graves said. "That was also my impression after meeting him."

"How'd *you* meet him?" Breda wanted to know.

"We had supper together in a joint up in Desert Hot Springs, the Snakeweed Bar and Grill. He doesn't hang around the same kinda places his wife does. But he's had money a lot longer, all his life in fact. Did you know he's never had a job? Never."

"Did *he* tell you that?" Breda asked.

Jack Graves shook his head and said, "None of this is a secret. I met a good friend of his, the man who took the semen sample, in fact."

"You even know his doctor?"

"First a little history," Jack Graves said. "Our Clive Devon's been in frail health since he was a kid. He's never been in the service, never went away from home, raised by a doting mother. He's a very insecure shy guy, but the kind you like immediately. Half the customers in the Snakeweed know the answer to your mystery. It's *only* a secret from Rhonda."

Breda was sitting with her legs crossed. Her left foot bounced impatiently, but she wasn't about to rush him. She realized you shouldn't force a methodical man like Jack Graves.

"Oh!" Jack Graves said suddenly, "Can I get you some coffee? Or a beer? Or . . ."

"Not for me," Lynn said.

"No, thanks," Breda said.

"Okay, where was I?"

"Everybody in the Snakeweed likes him," Lynn said.

"They sure do," Jack Graves said. "Anyway, Clive Devon never married till he met Rhonda. He was a middle-aged mother's boy. She was a real estate agent from Pasadena who sold his family home there when his mother died. That was when he decided to move out here to the desert. Clive and Rhonda started seeing each other. She was rebounding from a couple bad marriages. They finally got hitched."

279

"She didn't like the desert, I take it," Breda said.

"Hated it," Jack Graves said. "Eventually he also bought a house in Brentwood, close enough to Rodeo Drive for her to find fulfillment. And that's the way their marriage has gone. He goes to the Brentwood house for a short visit every blue moon. She comes here every other weekend for a couple days. They both manage investments from either end. She's a part-time real estate agent for a Beverly Hills broker, though she certainly doesn't need the money."

"That's a marriage?" Breda remarked.

"It suits them," Jack Graves said.

"What's *he* get out of it?" Lynn wanted to know. "Somebody to grow old with?" To Lynn, that wasn't something to sneeze at.

"He's growing old now," Jack Graves said. "According to his friend, Doc Morton, he loves Rhonda Devon in his own way. And Doc Morton thinks it's the same with her. He's probably the nicest guy she's ever met, and of course he'll give her anything she wants."

"Weird!" Breda said. "*Rich* people."

"Doc sees Clive Devon quite a lot, but only when Rhonda's in L.A."

Finally Breda could no longer contain herself. "I'm dying to hear, Jack. What's it about? Is it about the maid's daughter, or what?"

"It's about the inability to let go," Jack Graves said.

"Let go of what?" Breda asked.

"Unconditional love," Jack Graves said. "It's a very simple case, so simple we made it complicated."

"The sperm," Lynn said. "What's it about?"

"Clive Devon can't let go," Jack Graves said. "See, Malcolm's got an enlarged heart, and Malcolm's the best friend he's got. The best friend he's ever had. He thinks he can clone his dog."

"Malcolm's *his* dog?" Breda exclaimed. "The sperm belongs to a *dog?*"

"Malcolm's been his dog since Clive found him starving out on the desert five years ago."

Lynn said, "Five years?"

Jack Graves smiled. "Five years. Yet Rhonda Devon doesn't even know Malcolm exists. Doc says Malcolm could die any time, but Clive simply *cannot* accommodate that idea. So he's determined to replicate Malcolm."

"Replicate a dog?"

"There's no such thing as a proper animal sperm bank," Jack Graves explained. "People don't store animal sperm for long periods of time, so at Clive's request, Doc took the sample, froze it, and sent it by special courier to a real sperm bank in Beverly Hills, marked as a human being's sperm, of course. It's stored there under the name of Malcolm Devonson, bearing Clive Devon's social security number. You see, this sperm sample's worth a million bucks or more. To Clive Devon."

"But how can his wife not know anything?"

"That's the way they live, according to Doc Morton. She's highly allergic, or *thinks* she is. And she starts fussing every time she gets within ten feet of an animal. So, before she arrives at the desert house, Malcolm goes to stay with Esther, the maid's daughter down in Indio. That's why Clive's always out hiking when his wife's here in residence. He's with Malcolm. And when she goes back to L.A. Malcolm lives with him and sleeps on his bed. Blanca Soltero does a major housecleaning the day before Rhonda arrives."

Breda couldn't get over it. "And they've been living like this for five years?"

"Yeah."

"*Rich* people!" was all she could say.

"How long do they think the dog's got?" Lynn asked.

"Not long, but Doc doesn't know for sure. He's been given

281

the job of contacting every vet in the desert to try to find a suitable bitch—a big brown dog that's maybe part shepherd, part mastiff, part retriever. A dog with the dozens of magnificent wonderful irreplaceable characteristics that Clive Devon sees in Malcolm. They haven't found her yet. Every time Doc finds one, Clive thinks she's not quite right. They'll keep at it even after Malcolm's gone. Clive's determined to clone that dog."

"A poor little rich guy," Breda said. "Scouring the desert for a mongrel bitch. Pathetic!"

"I been doing that for years," Lynn said, but Breda let it pass.

"It's sort of a sad joke around the Snakeweed," Jack Graves said. "People smile and shake their heads, especially about the sperm bank."

"You can't produce identical DNA," Breda said. "The guy's crazy. So's the vet."

"The vet's an old friend. Sometimes you do crazy things for a friend," Jack Graves said. "He knows Clive'll fall in love with whatever pup he eventually ends up with."

"*No* more domestic cases," Breda said. "I gotta find some nice clean insurance work involving a lotta filthy lawyers. These domestic cases're too complicated for me."

"Well, there it is," Jack Graves said. "What're you gonna do with it?"

"I guess I'll just sit Rhonda Devon down and tell her she's a distant second in her husband's life, and she oughtta buy a year's supply of antihistamine in order to live with dog dander."

Jack Graves looked very serious then. He said, "I wish you wouldn't."

"What? Not tell her? She's my client. She's paying me. Us."

"You don't owe me anything," Jack Graves said. "I wasn't gonna take your money no matter what. Look, Clive's a sixty-three-year-old man who finds it real hard to get close to people. He has a certain kind of relationship with her. They respect each other's private ways. Don't humiliate him."

Breda said, "Jack, I've got a big fee coming in this case, if I get results! She'll be happy to learn she doesn't have a rival. At least not the kind she *thinks* she has."

"From what Doc told me about her, it wouldn't work," Jack Graves said. "If she even thought there'd been a dog in her house she'd have an asthma attack. Don't expect her to understand all this."

"Her understand all this? I don't understand all this!" Breda said.

"Please don't humiliate him, Breda," was all Jack Graves could say.

Breda looked at Lynn for support. He looked from her to Jack Graves.

Then she said, "Am I the crazy one here? What am I supposed to say to Rhonda Devon?"

"I've been thinking about that," Jack Graves said. "You could tell her you got to someone at his urologist's office who admitted that they botched up the handling of specimens. That his routine biopsy went to the fertility clinic and sperm samples went to the lab to be biopsied. And that the billing went to the wrong parties for a few months until it got all straightened out. You and Rhonda Devon could have a good laugh about your little secret. I promise you, she'll be so relieved, she won't question it very closely. She'll *want* to believe it so she can stop worrying about it."

"How about the young woman with the dog?"

"Tell Mrs. Devon the truth, most of it. She's Blanca's daughter. He offered to take Esther and her dog on an outing in Painted Canyon. That's all there was to that."

Breda said, "Give a false story to a client and take her money? I could lose my license! I could be sued! Successfully!"

"Then don't take the money," Lynn said. "If anybody ever found out you gave her a phony story, the refusal of payment would mitigate the thing. It would show you got a good heart, even if *that's* a little hard for some people to buy."

"You didn't say whether you're willing to give up your piece of it," Breda said to Lynn. "Or did I miss that?"

"Yeah, I guess I'm willing," Lynn said with a sigh. "I got too many worries as it is: tax shelters, capital gains, high yield bonds. Me 'n Sinèad O'Connor, we're sick a materialism anyway."

Everybody sat quietly for a while, then Lynn saw Breda get that little smirk of hers all frozen into place. And she said, "Am I the crazy one here? Somebody tell me."

The last thing Jack Graves said to her was: "Unconditional love. If you were about to lose it, wouldn't *you* get crazy notions? Haven't lots of people prayed, wished and fantasized about the dead coming back? Even in another body? I've read where that fantasy's fairly common in parents who lose children. It's not so hard to understand, is it? He can't accommodate the idea right now, the idea that Malcolm will be gone forever. That Malcolm won't *ever* come back to him."

The ride to Lynn's house was very quiet. He was the first to speak.

"Tomorrow I'd like you to help us," he said. "I think you owe us that. We're in this thing real deep now. I can't ask Jack to help us. It could get a little chancy, and Jack, he's not well."

She only said, "Okay."

After a few minutes, she said, "Isn't there something you can do to persuade Jack to . . . see somebody? A doctor?"

"I don't know him well enough," Lynn said. "I knew him from before, and I worked on his defense, but we never got to be close friends. After he shot the kid he became a recluse. Anyway, I don't know how to deal with something like he's got to deal with. Do you?"

"No," she said. "I never *have* known. Maybe he'd come to dinner sometime."

"You can try. I've invited him a dozen times, but he always has an excuse."

"Maybe after this case is over I'll give it a try."

Lynn said, "Breda, I'd like you to arrange with Nelson to meet at the Bob Hope Classic tomorrow morning. I'd like you to keep an eye on Nelson while *he* keeps an eye on John Lugo."

"Why on Nelson?"

"If Nelson spots our guy, or someone who's very likely our guy, I wanna be sure that the first deputy sheriff you see steps in and takes over. There'll be plenty a deputies working at that tournament. I want Nelson to back off and let *them* confront the guy. He's their problem anyway."

"You gonna adopt Nelson, or what?"

"He's a squirrel, definitely hazardous to his own health and safety. But he's a nice kid."

"Yeah, I know," she said. "And so's Clive Devon. A nice *kid*. I'm surrounded by males that can't grow up."

"People're always looking for immortality," Lynn said. "That's all Clive Devon's doing. And it's not even for himself."

They were silent again, both of them thinking about the money they were giving up. Her soft-hits radio station was getting on his nerves. He said, "Mind if I change stations?"

"Help yourself," she said.

He switched to the country station and of course they were still monitoring his every move. It was a Chet Atkins number: "Poor Boy Blues."

Breda didn't say anything at all till she dropped off Lynn at home. Then she sighed and said, "Okay, I'll baby-sit Nelson. I'll buy him a book in case the stakeout gets boring. And some crayons to color in it."

-20-

Lynn hadn't touched *any* gun since he'd been on medical leave. And he hadn't touched his off-duty gun in several years. He hoped the ammo still worked when he hitched the .38 two-inch Colt to his belt. He'd put on so much weight that even with his green flowered aloha shirt hanging outside, the slight bulge was noticeable.

He had no intention of confronting Francisco V. Ibañez; the gun was only in case Ibañez spotted him first. The gun was a last resort.

Lynn was surprised at how nervous he was that Saturday morning. He'd nicked himself twice while shaving. There was nothing in the house to eat, but he didn't care, his stomach was too fluttery anyway. He figured there was just about enough gas in the Rambler to get down to the hotel and back. He got a shudder when he realized that he might not *need* gas to get back!

Lynn arrived at the resort hotel just before 8:00 A.M. He went straight to the house phone and called the room of Francisco Ibañez. Still no answer, so he went to one of the public phones and called reception.

With a fair-to-middling Spanish accent, Lynn said, "Hello? This is Francisco Ibañez. I am on the way back to the hotel and will be there in twenty minutes. I would like a continental breakfast waiting in my room upon my arrival. And please have someone bring my clubhouse badge to the room. It is there at reception in an envelope. Do you have all that?"

The young man said, "Mister . . . Ibañez? Wait. A badge, you say?"

"Young man, it's there at reception! A badge for the golf tournament. Please, I am in a hurry. Do I have to repeat myself?"

"No, no, sir. I have it," the young man said.

After Lynn hung up he strolled back past reception pretending to be reading a paper. He overheard the kid say to the young woman assisting him, "Tell Tony to run this envelope up to room five-twenty-nine. These foreigners get *bossy* when they have a few bucks!"

Lynn spent the remainder of that morning on the fifth floor, on the wing across from room 529. That was a very long time to be leaning with his elbows on a railing, looking down at that humongous lobby. A couple of times he almost got vertigo.

"This ain't as exciting as the Indio Date Festival," Nelson said to Breda, after stepping off the shuttle bus and getting jostled into the grounds of Indian Wells Country Club by swarms of golf fans. "I went to the Date Festival last year. Ever been to it?"

Breda bought two tickets from a tournament volunteer, and then said, "No, maybe I'll go this year."

She was wearing a pink knit shirt, white walking shorts,

white Reeboks. It was already 75 degrees in Indian Wells and climbing to an expected 85 degrees Fahrenheit. Her pink visor and sunglasses, along with her athletic figure, made her look like a pro herself, Nelson thought. One of the mature tour professionals, of course.

"At the Date Festival you see mimes and magicians and guys on stilts roaming all around the midway," Nelson said. "And there's ostrich races and camel races. They tell me sometimes a camel or ostrich gets loose and the cops have to help chase them. I don't think I'd want an overtime job like that. The deputies working here at the golf tournament also get good O.T. pay."

"You'd rather work for free," Breda said, "which is what you're doing at this moment, and what you've been doing all week, you and Lynn."

"Funny," Nelson said, showing his rabbit grin, "I guess you're right. But I'll get my reward."

"In the next world?"

"Yeah, my *next* world's gonna be at Palm Springs P.D. after I catch the bad guy. I'll be the number-one draft choice in this whole valley. Everybody's gonna want me!"

Nelson had told Breda he'd worn his "golfiest" outfit, a striped knit shirt, Levi Dockers and Nike Airs, the latter so as not to scrunch up the turf with his high-heeled boots. Breda studied the little cop for a minute. Lynn was right in wanting her to watch over him. But they couldn't *all* be little boys, could they? Only every one she'd ever met in nearly forty-three years on this earth!

They found John Lugo's name on the pairing sheet along with two other amateurs and the professional who made up the foursome. The pro was some guy named Jim that Nelson had never heard of. He was disappointed it wasn't somebody like Arnold Palmer, who had a huge gallery following him.

"Ever been to one a these things?" he asked Breda as they wandered behind the crowds along the roped-off fairways.

"Just the Dinah Shore tournament," she said, looking at the scheduled tee times. "I think we might catch up with Lugo on number seventeen. He started on number ten."

"I wonder if we shoulda got here earlier? What if the guy had went for him right away on his very first hole?"

"Assassins need bigger crowds."

"Yeah, I suppose so," Nelson said. "Well, he's gonna get that, all right."

The unseasonable hot spell they'd been having all week brought out lots of extra golf fans. They were pouring in, and thousands would be on hand at day's end. Even on the opposite side of the clubhouse they could hear a noisy gallery at number one tee cheering on a couple of amateurs who'd tried in vain to drive it past Bing-Phil Lake, named for Crosby, and for Phil Harris, who still lived in the valley with his wife, former movie star Alice Faye.

Indian Wells was a tight golf course but in a beautiful setting coved next to the hills. The course was landscaped with pines, pepper and olive trees, some eucalyptus, and palms palms palms. There were white and yellow pyramid tents set up all around the clubhouse with booths for refreshments and mementos.

When they got to the side of the clubhouse Nelson heard someone say, "That poor fella's going snorkeling, wait and see!"

There was a puddle, which in the desert they call a lake, guarding the sixteenth green. Nelson heard the moan of the crowd and then a plunk! He watched the guy who'd predicted the disaster show everyone one of those ain't-it-a-shame Jimmy Carter grins, the kind where you just wanted to tear his lips off.

"I oughtta take up golf if I'm gonna make a successful life for myself in this valley," Nelson said.

"Wouldn't burn up enough of your nervous energy. I think you should consider marathon running. By the way, I don't see any sign of a gun. You *must* be carrying."

"You don't wanna know where it is," he said. "That's why I'm wearin these pants. They're a little baggy in the crotch."

"Try not to sit down," Breda said. "If you do, I sure hope you don't have a premature discharge of the uncommon variety."

The seventeenth was a 398-yard par four, with a dogleg left. Just about all the holes at Indian Wells had narrow fairways, and the amateurs they'd seen so far were usually on the wrong one. Standing between the sixteenth green and seventeenth tee gave them a lot to look at, including the clubhouse veranda, which was mobbed.

Breda, who was taller than Nelson, stood on her tiptoes to see over the gallery. She said, "I think his foursome's on the tee at sixteen. I'd sure like to see Johnny Mathis or John Denver come through."

"I'm waitin for Glen Campbell," Nelson said. "I'm bettin he *does* wear cowboy golf boots."

Fifteen minutes later, John Lugo was beside his golf cart on the sixteenth fairway waiting for the foursome in front to clear the green. There was no doubt which of the golfers was John Lugo. The other three looked, in various ways, about as Mexican as Tip O'Neill, former Speaker of the House, who for once wasn't playing.

John Lugo didn't look sixty-seven years old, and would've looked even younger if he hadn't dyed his hair and mustache black, an idea that had backfired. He was thick through the chest and shoulders but was two inches shorter than Nelson Hareem. Lugo wore a lavender Ben Hogan golf cap, a gray sweater-vest already damp with perspiration, a gray golf shirt and lavender plus fours. He carried the maximum handicap of eighteen, and was a *very* macho hacker.

When he flailed away at his second shot with a five-iron, it cost him a trip to the sand, and made all the sadists in the gallery titter, and say things like, "That swing reminds me of *yours*, Norman!"

"We oughtta find an opportunity to ask Lugo a few questions," Nelson said to Breda.

"About what? I'm sure he and his lawyer had a heart-to-heart. If there was any light to be shed the lawyer would've called us."

"Maybe Leo Grishman forgot to mention the Canary Islands thing. Remember, Lugo had a limited partner in Puerto Rico who came from the Canary Islands, just like Francisco V. Ibañez."

"Maybe after it's over, we can introduce ourselves."

"I hope Lynn's okay workin all alone," Nelson said, at about the time John Lugo put the gallery into hysterics by shoveling a skip-load of sand onto the sixteenth green, leaving the ball behind in the bunker.

"I suppose you want me to run down to the hotel and watch over *him*?"

"I kinda worry maybe he'll try to take Ibañez by himself. He's emotionally involved, what with the guy puttin him in the coffin."

"Do you *all* take something like a Masonic secret oath, or what?" Breda asked.

"Who?"

"Men," she said. "You men. Clive Devon's worried about the smuggler because he's a very gentle man. Jack Graves, he's worried about Clive Devon, who's a frail and timid man. Lynn, he's worried about you, and you're worried about him, and nobody in this entire world's worrying about me!"

"Don't you know why, Breda?" Nelson Hareem asked, just as John Lugo got out of the trap but sent the ball in the general direction of Arizona, to the delight of a gallery loaded with rack-and-thumbscrew types.

She showed him her defensive grin and said, "Can you tell me, Nelson?"

"Sure," he said. "It's because you're so capable. You're such an independent person, nobody has to worry about people like you. The rest of us, we all need somethin. We're all more . . ."

"If you say *vulnerable*, I'll rap you in the mouth," Breda warned.

"Okay, I won't."

"Let's start scanning this crowd for a dark bald husky guy about forty years old who's as capable and independent as me," Breda suggested. "Instead of having the guy arrested, I oughtta marry him."

At 11:10 A.M. Lynn was craving a cup of coffee, and decided to go downstairs to get one. He stopped by room 529 and listened at the door just in case Francisco Ibañez had come back in the four minutes it took him to run to the john an hour earlier, but he needn't have worried.

He was getting into the elevator at the same moment the other elevator arrived at the fifth floor. As Lynn's door slid shut he heard a woman giggle. A man with a heavy Spanish accent said, "You weel love the view from my room, Jennie." Only he said *Yennie*.

Lynn mashed the open button, but too late! Then he punched the button for the fourth floor, and when the elevator stopped he ran out, down the hallway to the interior stairs, then back up to the fifth floor three steps at a time. He crept along the empty hallway with his hand under his aloha shirt, resting on the butt of the Colt.

Lynn listened at the door but could hear only more female giggling. He thought of all the sensible things he could do. Instead, he took an impulsive course of action. He knocked, and said, "Room service."

The door was opened by a woman already partly undressed. Lynn hadn't planned on her opening it, and since he didn't look like room service he simply shoved the door open and stepped inside with his hand under the shirt.

"Sweetie!" the woman yelled.

Francisco Ibañez ran from the bathroom wearing only his shirt, shoes, and a semierection. He wasn't bald, he wasn't dark, and he wasn't husky. But he *was* terrified.

Lynn looked from Ibañez to the woman, who had hooker written all over her.

He said, "I'm with hotel security and we were told there was a prostitute and a john using this room. My mistake. Sorry." Nobody spoke when Lynn closed the door, saying, "Enjoy the continental breakfast, compliments of the house."

Five minutes later he was in his Rambler on the way to the golf tournament, where he hoped to find Nelson, Breda and John Lugo, all in one piece.

Before Lynn arrived at Indian Wells Country Club, all hell broke loose. It happened after Breda went to a refreshment stand to buy a couple of soft drinks, and a hot dog for Nelson. She thought she could leave him alone while the Lugo foursome teed off on number seventeen.

Breda was carrying the refreshments in a cardboard tray when she heard the gallery over on the eighteenth green start to scream. She thought somebody must've eagled the hole. But what they were screaming at were not the exploits of a finishing foursome, but the exploits of Nelson Hareem.

Nelson had been getting hot and tired and cranky. The gun strapped to his thigh was chafing his crotch, so he surreptitiously reached inside his trousers to move it around. He was only the second most miserable guy in the vicinity, the first being John Lugo, who'd double-bogeyed three in a row. Lugo had been swinging wilder and harder on each shot. He'd taken off his sweater-vest, and his shirt was hanging out. He'd chewed his cigar stub to shreds. He hadn't had a par since number eleven.

The man didn't arouse Nelson's curiosity until he moved

through the gallery in the general direction of John Lugo's party at the seventeenth tee. It was the way he bumped his way through, not like a golf fan at all, more like a Los Angeles Raider fan. He was middle-aged, burly, dark, and wore a red golf cap. It was a Bob Hope Chrysler Classic cap that he'd obviously just bought.

Nelson took a hard look at him, and yes, he *could* be Mexican, but somehow with that Semitic curve to his nose he looked more like the photos of Nelson's grandfather. He looked more like an Arab!

Nelson got even closer and watched the guy bump into yet another fan in the gallery. The guy smiled and said, "Excuse me." He didn't seem to have an accent, but the little cop couldn't hear him very well.

Nelson looked around for one of the uniformed deputies or a security officer, but there was none in sight. And Nelson wanted to be more sure. Nelson wanted to make the guy talk, so he shouldered his way through the gallery, managing to get right in the guy's face, and said, "Pardon me, sir, but . . ."

Just then the holster he'd moved around on his thigh broke loose and slid down his leg, thudding against the ground. In plain view, right in front of his suspect.

The guy looked down at the holstered gun, then at Nelson. Then he turned and burrowed through the gallery, knocking people helter-skelter, and in a few seconds he was racing behind the clubhouse, then clattering up the yellow metal stairway to a catwalk leading from the clubhouse to the man-made rock promontory overlooking the eighteenth green!

Nelson jammed his gun in the pocket of his baggy pants and went pounding after him, but when he got to the top of the catwalk he couldn't see the guy anywhere. He was *gone*! Nelson was frantic until he looked on the other side of the leader board and spotted the guy scrambling down the rocks, along the eighteenth green, under the TV cameras, in plain sight of the viewing stands and the Fuji blimp overhead, as well as a whole lot of people in the tented VIP seats.

And Nelson Hareem had to put on his game face and *go!* He sprinted after the guy, in a zig and zag, juke and jibe, and a plunge through startled tournament marshals in white hats and striped shirts, as well as shocked contestants finishing at number eighteen!

And then he hurtled straight down the cart path under the stands, past three security officers (Canadian pensioners who came down every year for this event), darting out toward the throngs gathered at number-one tee.

But he wasn't gaining on the guy. That old bastard was leaving him in the dust!

He bumped, jostled, whirled through a kaleidoscope of golf shirts, dazed hordes gawking at Fuzzy's sweet cut shot, or Curtis's knockdown wedge or Payne's bold putt. Nobody paid any attention to Nelson Hareem's desperate pursuit! Nelson was spouting adrenaline, and with blistered lungs he plunged headlong after his man and nobody gave a shit! Somebody actually tried to *stop* him, to ask if Desi Drive was named after Lucy's husband!

They ran, mouths agape, back into the mountain cove of number-three fairway, where at last Nelson's man showed some fatigue. He leaped into a pearl-gray Rolls-Royce golf cart belonging to a pair of amateurs who were looking for an OB ball on the hillside. Next thing the amateurs knew, their golf cart was plunging down the fairway away from the green!

One of those seigneurs of Corporate America ran after it for thirty yards, when all the veal chops, pasta and bread sticks caught up with him. Then he stood holding his chest and screamed, "That's a genuine crocodile golf bag I won at the Bing Crosby clambake, you thieving fuckhead!"

But he was shocked into silence when a *second* golf cart, belonging to his playing partners, got stolen by a *second* thief, who went flying after the first! The second thief was a little redhead with a demented expression, who yelled at everyone in his path: "Playing through! Playing through!"

The cart chase was on! Nelson's guy went screaming across the wash by number eight and across the fairway, almost getting smacked by a whistling wood shot hit by a CEO from New York who made five million a year in bonuses that gave him only moderate pleasure, but was in heaven because he'd just hit a 250-yard drive, thereby justifying the ten grand all this had cost him.

But as the CEO drove his cart toward that thing of beauty, a golf cart buzzed across the fairway, mashing his all-world tee shot into the ground! And causing him to cry in horror: "Official! Get me a ruling, goddamnit! Official!"

The chase ended on number nine where a foursome was on the fairway playing in. Nelson's man appeared to be banking on a disappearance among the masses around the clubhouse. He scattered the mud hens in the lake as he sped by, but he didn't scatter the intrepid gallery. He couldn't straighten out at the last minute, and drove the cart into the same lake that had punished a duck-hook three minutes earlier. His was the *second* car in the lake, the first being a white Chrysler on a display platform.

The guy got out limping and dripping, and with his head down, plowed into a fan from Billings, Montana, provoking a beer-bath and a popcorn blizzard. But then he was pounced on by Nelson Hareem, who'd daringly maneuvered his golf cart alongside the runner and leaped, like a cowboy bulldogging a steer.

When deputies and security people and tournament marshals finally got to the scene of the crash-and-splash, there were fifty golf fans encircling the antagonists and enjoying the battle. Nelson had the guy in a choke-hold and was scissoring the guy's ample waist with his stubby legs. The chokee's hat had fallen off and Nelson was delighted to see that the guy was balding!

Nelson had a mouse under his eye and his shirt was almost torn from his body. The pocket of his trousers was ripped, but he still had his gun and his pluck.

Nelson looked up at a uniformed sheriff's deputy who'd just arrived and was trying to figure out who the hell was the good guy, or if there was one. "This is the guy you been lookin for!" Nelson cried, meaning the airport fugitive.

But to Nelson's great surprise the suspect croaked, in un-accented American English, "Get this red-headed kangaroo off me! I'm not gonna give ya no trouble!"

The deputy dragged the suspect to his feet, patted him down, and found three wallets inside his Jockey shorts, all of them belonging to sadistic golf fans who'd been enjoying John Lugo's misery.

Nelson was exhausted and confused and decided not to tell them much at all, except his name, and that he was an off-duty policeman.

The deputy handcuffed the pickpocket and said to Nelson, "We'll take your statement as quick as we can and let you get back to the tournament. That was a great piece of work. This guy musta been going through that crowd like dysentery."

As a second deputy helped Nelson to his feet, a uniformed Palm Springs policeman ran up. He was Bob Hope's driver and bodyguard for the day.

The Palm Springs cop said, "Kinda ruined your tournament, didn't it?"

"Gotta be a cop twenny-four hours a day, I guess," Nelson mumbled.

"We need more guys like you on *our* department," the Palm Springs cop said. "What's your name, Officer? Maybe you'd like to meet Mister Hope? If I know him, he'll say something like, 'That pickpocket ended up with a *real* bad lie!' "

It was reported on the news that one of the contestants and witnesses, former astronaut Alan Shepard, was asked if he'd ever seen a more remarkable sight in all his golfing experience.

He said, "Not since I hit that golf shot on the moon."

When he awoke on Saturday morning he had actually thought of attending Mass, but then it seemed a sacrilegious thing to do on the day that he was to carry out his mission. He thought a long time about it. Would God have more pity on him or less if he went to Mass? Would God even look with favor on a prayer for protection, or be angry that he'd offered it, under these circumstances?

Finally, he'd decided *not* to attend Mass. He had dressed, shaved and gone downstairs to the hotel's breakfast room for coffee. He bought the *Los Angeles Times*, a huge newspaper by his standards, and began searching for stories about U.S. crimes in order to reassure himself that what he was going to do was correct, that they would have been laughed at if they'd taken their scanty information to the U.S. authorities and said: "Here, solve the murder of a good policeman, our friend Javier Rosas. And more importantly, provide his family and friends with *retribution*." That this was their only chance for justice in a country that releases men on parole after they mangle or murder children.

The police in his country knew how to deal with men like that. In his country they could even prosecute one of their own citizens for committing a crime in the United States, but how many gringo criminals had *ever* been extradited to Mexico for trial? And yet everyone knew that it was common for U.S. lawmen to ask favors of the *judiciales*, who would often arrest a wanted Mexican and deliver him to the U.S. authorities at the international border. Of course, the gringos could never return such a favor because their laws wouldn't permit it, because they were morally *superior*.

Yet the fugitive couldn't place all of the blame on the gringos. No, it was nearly as much the fault of the corruption within their own system, especially within the Federal Judicial Police of Mexico.

He was proud to be with the *Judicial del Estado*, the State Judicial Police. He had been a policeman for eighteen years, but he would be ashamed to be with the federals. The federals had no intention of helping the state police. On the contrary, it was apparent that they'd inform on them if they could. Anything to protect their *mordida*. The bite. The graft on which they survived, all of them, even the state police, even himself.

Gringo police would never understand. They didn't have to buy their own weapons and ammunition, pay for their own car radios, and repair their police cars out of their own pockets if they wanted to do the job properly. They didn't have to buy and develop their own film of a crime scene, and compensate laboratory people from their own pockets just to get them to respond to a crime-scene investigation. And they didn't have to pay their own typists! The gringos could get in their big new American police cars and do what they had to do without worrying about whether one or two vouchers a month would provide enough gasoline.

Oh yes, they could ridicule the police of Mexico, because they didn't have to live on the equivalent of $550 a month, and support children in a place where food was more expensive than in the States. Where everything except housing was more expensive than in the States, in an economy that had been in recession for years. Easy for them to think of him and his comrades as bandits with badges because they took money sometimes, money they used to do their jobs and to feed their children.

The fugitive had his new blue leather bag with him at all times. The weapons were in it, an untraceable 9-mm Beretta that had been stolen in the north, but ended up south in Mexico, the thief having been killed by state police in a failed holdup. The knife was there too, a killing knife. Swiss- or perhaps German-made, it was supposedly a favorite of foreign military personnel involved in clandestine activity. The fugitive couldn't imagine using that horrible instrument to stab or hack at the flesh of a human being, but they had insisted that he have it. One of his comrades had also wanted him to take an AR-15 with its thirty-round magazine they called *cuerno de chivo*, horn of a goat. He had told his friend that the suggestion was ridiculous. If he couldn't do the job with reasonable weaponry it couldn't be done at all.

He liked to think that he had been sent because he was such a dogged manhunter, a policeman who never gave up, but of course one of the main reasons was that he had a natural talent for language and spoke English better than just about anyone in his sector, *primer sector*, based in Mexicali.

There wasn't nearly as much U.S currency in the bag as when he'd arrived, that was for sure. It was mostly *very* dirty money, confiscated from drug dealers and car thieves. Some of it was a bit cleaner, having come from U.S. insurance companies. The state police would receive a "reward" from the insurance companies for getting the cars back in proper condition, about $500 per car. Yes, that money was a *bit* cleaner. The money had been pooled and entrusted to him to use because his comrades wanted to get justice for Javier Rosas, who'd been a good policeman, as good as any, and a good man.

The fugitive remembered the time he'd worked on a case with Javier Rosas in the *segundo sector* of Tijuana. They had arrested a team of American bandits who'd tried to rob a diamond merchant from Tijuana, shooting one bandit, capturing the other two. When Javier Rosas made the bandits pose, holding their weapons for photographers, the U.S. police had ridiculed him for it. The fugitive had tried to explain to Javier Rosas that the gringos did not understand their ways, and that he should try not to feel insulted. Now, after reading news accounts about people who were paroled after strangling children, free to murder again and again, he thought that perhaps they never would understand each other, the people of the neighboring countries.

But then, the state police couldn't even trust their own federals. An informant had told them that the drug runners who'd murdered Javier Rosas had made a point of stealing for the federals their favorite make of car, a Chevrolet Suburban with four-wheel drive, to be offered as *mordida*. The smugglers always dropped off at least one car for the federals whenever they made a big cocaine run from Mexicali to Los Angeles.

The fugitive asked himself what the gringos would do if it had been one of *their* men who'd been brutally murdered? They'd shown what they'd do after a DEA agent was kidnapped in 1985 by a gang of Guadalajara drug dealers and mercilessly tortured for days, his cries and screams recorded on tape by the criminals. That tape was found and later played before a U.S. jury hearing evidence against a Mexican doctor who'd allegedly participated in the torture.

What the DEA had done was to have that physician abducted by federal judicial police and brought across the border, where he'd been arrested by the U.S. officers. What would've happened if the Mexican police had abducted a U.S. citizen and brought him to Mexico for trial? Probably another Mexican War, only this time they'd take everything south to Mexico City to claim as their fifty-second state. That's what the fugitive thought, and why he had no other choice in the present matter.

Javier Rosas had never cared *who* was supplying cars or money to the federals. Javier Rosas was an honest man who'd wanted to be a policeman all his life, but had been one for only six years when he was murdered. Once, the fugitive and Javier had spoken of a confrontation in Tijuana, when the federal and municipal police had almost gotten in a gun battle with each other after the municipal police surrounded federal police headquarters during a dispute. Javier Rosas said the federals could never be trusted. He had no use for them and was positive they were protecting the cocaine runners he was after.

Ten kilos of cocaine from Peru were to be delivered to L.A. from Mexicali. The informant of Javier Rosas knew very little about a person in Palm Springs who was acting as middleman in the transaction. Ten kilos were significant enough for the informant to go to the home of Javier Rosas and get him out of bed to say that perhaps he knew where the cocaine was.

Unfortunately, Javier Rosas couldn't reach his comrades that night and had decided to investigate the matter himself to see if the information had substance. The informant told him there were only two couriers, but when Javier Rosas broke into their hotel room and confronted them at gunpoint he'd discovered that there was a *third*, standing behind him with a gun.

The other state police later learned all of this from that third courier after they'd caught the drug runners while they were queued up at the border waiting to cross. The first two were killed outright when the state police rushed the car. The third died later of "heart failure" during interrogation.

The fugitive had always hated that part of interrogation—the Pepsi challenge—the carbonated beverage shot up the nose until the suspect thinks his brain is exploding. But the murderer of Javier Rosas got more, he got the wires applied to his genitals. The point was, they all knew that in the end, he was no longer capable of telling lies.

About all he could say was that a phone call to an unknown number in Palm Springs was made from a pay phone by one of his dead companions. And that the man on the line told them in *pocho* Spanish how to handle the unexpected dilemma they were then facing: a state judicial police officer, handcuffed, a gag in his mouth, completely at their mercy.

The unnamed Palm Springs middleman told the drug-runner to pick up the cocaine as planned and proceed across the border in the car as planned. And the Palm Springs middleman also said that they'd have to kill Javier Rosas to guarantee their chances.

He'd made an ugly joke about it, a joke which became the only clue to his identity. The joke had to do with a tombstone and orchids.

–21–

The Furnace Room was getting pretty good play that Saturday afternoon. The Bob Hope Classic had been on TV, so the boozers had had an excuse to get bombed early under the pretext of watching a major sporting event.

Long before the TV coverage had ended, all of the male pensioners had about used up every hilarious golfing witticism ever uttered ("A short drive'll do just great, if you can keep your putter straight") on every female younger than the Tabasco sauce in their refrigerators.

By 4:00 P.M., Lynn, Breda and Nelson were occupying Lynn's favorite table beside the defunct fireplace, and the old babe at the next table was trying to sound like Dinah Shore, warbling "Something to Remember You By."

Nelson was wearing an oversized white cotton tennis sweater loaned to him by Lynn after a quick stop at the mansion for repairs. He had a Band-Aid over his eye where Breda had done some nursing, but he was still pumped, with every reason to believe that his heroics would get him an audience with the Palm Springs chief of police, according to Bob Hope's cop-driver.

Lynn held up three fingers to Wilfred Plimsoll, who poured another round. Then Lynn said, "Do I have the I.Q. of a rodeo clown, or what? All our work's been more irrelevant than an Emmy award and Baghdad Betty. More irrelevant than the eggbeater and Jimmy Carter."

Then everyone tried to top the others by coming up with examples of useless irrelevancy. It ended when Nelson cited the Secret Service contingent assigned to guard local resident Gerald Ford. *Nobody* could top that one.

"At least it looks like Nelson's gonna be rewarded," Breda said, "for doing what's always got him fired in the past. Beating the hell outta the wrong guy."

"I can't wait for my folks to see my picture with Bob Hope," Nelson said. "That reporter promised he'd send me an eight-by-ten!"

Lynn just couldn't get over it. He said, "Do you realize we haven't the faintest idea who the real guy is and what he wants with John Lugo? Not even a miniclue!"

"I still wanna get him," Nelson said, flush with the thrill of victory. "Maybe he'll make his move at the party tonight. There'll be hundreds a people there."

"We'll catch that guy when California condor eggs go for two bucks a dozen at your supermarket," Lynn said.

"I think we should go to Lugo's party anyways," Nelson said. "His lawyer said we only gotta mention our names to the guy at the shuttle bus."

"Where's the bus leave from?" Breda asked Nelson.

"Smoke Tree shoppin center. Because a the tombstone deal, Lugo hired a couple uniformed security people to check invitations at the bus."

"I wouldn't mind just being at a party like that," Breda said.

That, of course, got Lynn interested. "Well, I guess we *might* give our case one last shot," he said. "Nelson can do his thing tonight, maybe pounce on every guy that's bald. He'd probably end up with a couple a jewel thieves and Sean Connery."

"Everybody starts arrivin right after dark, so we can relax and have another drink if ya want," Nelson suggested.

"Drinks'll be free up there," Breda observed. "Now that I have an early morning appointment with Rhonda Devon to tell her that a silly little mixup at a lab caused her problems, and she doesn't owe me another dollar, I can't pay for your drinks anymore."

"Oh, lemme buy a round," Nelson said.

"No more for me, Nelson," said Lynn "but since you insist, well, okay."

When Nelson ran to the bar to get the round of drinks Lynn said to Breda, "He makes me know my age. When I'm around him I feel as up-to-the-minute as polyester. I got my forty-fifth coming up in a couple weeks!"

"You'll understand if I don't come to the party," Breda said. "I've already attended one of your *parties*."

"It ain't easy," Lynn said gravely, "being our age and looking down the tunnel. Is it? I'm so old I can remember when Jack Nicklaus was fat."

"You don't have to worry about it. The way you booze it up, you'll never get much older."

After Nelson returned with the drinks, he hoisted a beer and said, "To success! He ain't got away from us yet!"

Lynn said, "If we don't find the guy tonight, let's start looking for Amelia Earhart. It'd be a lot easier."

He'd paid his bill and checked out of the hotel, never to return. He was going to succeed or fail *this* night. He'd never have a better opportunity, with three hundred people and dozens of servers moving about in that big pink house high on the hill.

He'd always imagined it would have to be done in a parking lot somewhere, perhaps after he'd followed his man to a supermarket, or to a cinema, or to a restaurant. That was before he saw the private street with a guard and a dog. And a millionaire's house high on a cliff, near other protected privileged people. No, this party, this night—he'd never get a better chance.

There were three options: He could appear at the catering company and hope that both gringo bosses were at the Lugo house. Then he could try to bluff one of the Mexicans into driving him up there in a van. After all, he was properly dressed, in his new white shirt, bow tie, black vest, black trousers, and black leather shoes. They'd have no reason to doubt him if he said that Henry or Phil had hired him. But when he got up there the Mexican driver might mention the new employee to Henry or Phil. It might cause some concern, for there were bound to be very important people at this party, and people were still talking about terrorists. No, he was afraid of that option.

A second possibility would be to show up at the shuttle bus and try to convince the bus driver that he'd missed his ride up to the party with the other servers. But they'd probably have a portable telephone to call the house for verification. He didn't like that option either.

He made up his mind while sitting in his Buick across the highway from Southridge. He saw that not all of the guests were using the shuttle bus from Smoke Tree. Some partygoers were driving up the hill and giving their cars to the valet parking people, who would shuttle them back down. He watched this process for thirty-five minutes before making his decision. Even if it didn't work he could always fall back on one of the more risky options.

The fugitive left the Buick across Highway 111 at Desert Lakes Drive, where it was close enough for an escape, but not so close that the police would think it suspicious. He had every reason to hope that after he completed his mission, the resulting confusion would allow him to get down that hill and past the guard in the kiosk, whose job it was to stop people going in, not going out.

If need be, he'd *run* down that hill to his car, where he would then be only a few minutes from Gene Autry Trail, which led to Highway 10, which in turn led to Mexico. To *home*.

He felt an empty shiver in his bowels then, and a chill in his spine. His heart had been beating steadily faster for the past three hours. There was a swelling in his throat as if from overwhelming grief. It happened whenever he thought that he could actually be home with his family, this very night! Or *never* again.

He was carrying his new leather bag and looked every bit like one of Henry's catering employees as he stood by Highway 111 at the foot of Southridge, waiting for the cars containing special partygoers, mostly older ones, who required valet parking.

A car driven by one man turned off the highway from the direction of Indian Wells, but the fugitive turned his back on the headlight beams. *One* man? He couldn't be sure the man was a party guest. Then a white Cadillac with three men in colorful golf shirts made a turn, and the fugitive took a chance.

He pretended to be walking hurriedly up the steep street, but waved shyly when the headlights illuminated him. He offered them his most servile smile.

The Cadillac stopped and the electric window on the passenger side slid down. A man with a red face, a bulbous nose and a big cigar said, "What's up, *amigo*?"

The fugitive used a heavier accent than he really had, and said, "I am sorry, sir. Can you help me? I am to be working at Meester Lugo's party, and my car, it break down and . . ."

The back door swung open, and an old man in the back seat said, "Hop in, kiddo. We'll get you up there before your boss even knows you're late."

It worked! The driver said to the guard at the kiosk, "Harry Milford. Going to the Lugo party."

The guard hardly glanced at the clipboard as he waved them through.

When they arrived at the big pink house, there were at least fifty people—some in golf clothing, some in evening wear—milling around in the street, waiting their turn to get through the entry doors, which were wide open but jammed with the busload that had arrived a few minutes earlier.

Perspiring valet parkers were running every which way, and one of them, a girl in a blue T-shirt and shorts, opened the door for Harry Milford, who said, "Take good care of it, honey. It's momma's car."

"Sure will, sir!" she said.

"Thank you, berry much," the fugitive said to Harry Milford, who winked and said, "If your boss gives you a bad time, tell him to see me."

"Yes sir, thank you sir," the fugitive said, as obsequiously as he thought prudent.

Instead of trying to battle through the entry doors, he walked across the grass, around the house to the rear. The patio was composed of lighted flagstone terraces. There was a black-bottom pool, a spa and a fountain spewing water ten feet into the air. There was a putting green with a view as spectacular as any in California. The entire city of Palm Springs was laid out 1000 feet below, with an unobstructed view of Mount San Jacinto and Mount San Gorgonio, each of them two miles high and snow-capped, even during this blistering heat wave.

The naked display of opulence froze him for a moment, but then he gathered himself for what he had to do. He saw four Mexicans serving cocktails to the guests on his side of the patio where there were two bars set up, each with two bartenders. He didn't see the tall blond catering boss, nor the young Mexican driver, both of whom could recognize him. As long as he saw neither he felt he had a chance. The other catering people might think he was John Lugo's house servant.

The patio was only dimly lit; people's faces weren't easy

to recognize as they moved about on those terraces. The leather bag was a problem. He spotted a huge planter by a brick wall that divided this property from the neighbor. He crossed a lawn and dropped the bag behind an enormous clump of palm and banana trees, and as soon as his hands stopped shaking, he walked down to the first level of flagstone patio.

He was startled when a mariachi band struck up what had become the California mariachi signature: "La Bamba." The musicians were out of sight on the next level of garden and terraces below, near a lighted, stair-stepped koi pool. The guitars and trumpets of Mexico! It seemed like another omen, but for good or bad, he couldn't say.

The fugitive picked up three empty cocktail glasses in each hand and walked briskly, as though he knew where he was going. When he reached the far side of the house, he peered through the windows, seeing an open door leading from the dining room into the kitchen area. The tall blond gringo was working at a chopping block. The fugitive would not be spending much time around *this* side of the house.

Still carrying the empty glasses, he followed along the lighted flagstone path leading down to the second terrace. This one had railings protecting the guests from tumbling down the mountainside after too many drinks. Here, all of the upper patio furniture had been stacked to allow room for the mobs above. But even on this level there was a bar set up, right next to the six-piece mariachi band, now playing a passable version of an old song his mother liked, "El Reloj." It was easy to see that an escape down the sheer hillside would be impossible.

The fugitive had picked up a few more glasses when, suddenly, an exquisite woman in a pumpkin-colored tuxedo jacket, matching walking shorts, and a coconut-brown silk tank top, said to him, "I'll have another margarita, please. And ask Mister Lugo to please come down and see Maggie and George. Can you remember those names?"

"Yes, *señora*," he said, and bowed slightly, wondering if a bow was going too far.

When he got to the upper deck, he entered the main part of the house, where the humidity from over a hundred human bodies fresh from a golf tournament was palpable. The din inside was drowning out the piano player who was trying to sing requests at the other end of the living room.

There were people chattering, laughing, drinking, crushed together all the way from the wide-open sliding doors at back, through to the marble foyer in front. And clutches of people sat on every step of an open, carpeted spiral staircase leading up to the second floor of the split-level house.

Even if he'd known what John Lugo looked like and where he was standing, he wondered if he could have gotten close enough to give him the message from Maggie and George.

They got separated at the shuttle bus. There was space for only one, so Lynn said to Breda, "You go on ahead. We'll catch the next one."

When she was gone, Lynn looked up at the black desert sky and said to Nelson, "I hope this heat doesn't mean we're gonna have an early summer."

"Might not matter so much for me this year," Nelson said. "if I'm workin Palm Springs P.D. where there's some shade!"

"Either way I'm gonna buy you a little umbrella to wear with a headband," Lynn said. "Something to remember me by."

"I hope I'm gonna see you and Breda once in a while," Nelson said, as the second shuttle bus rumbled toward them across the parking lot.

"Me and Breda? Together?"

"Well, sure," Nelson said. "The way I see it, you got life-threatenin feelings for her."

"You figure I'm in love with Breda, huh? Clive Devon, he's

in love with Malcolm. Malcolm's probably in love with some Airedale. Nobody's lucky in love, not in this freaking town."

There were about thirty passengers on their shuttle. When they got up to the top of Southridge, Lynn estimated that another thirty were still out in the street, trying to squeeze through the gates onto the property.

"I don't know if I can handle this mob scene," Lynn said. "Maybe I oughtta take the next shuttle back down."

"We don't wanna leave Breda here not knowin anyone," Nelson said. "Follow me."

Nelson did what the fugitive had done. Instead of trying to squeeze and wriggle through the masses entering the foyer, he led Lynn around the side lawn toward the rear of the property, where they could breathe. Actually, he was just following the sound of mariachis playing "Guantanamera."

After that number started, about six couples started doing their ludicrous version of Mexican folk dancing on the flagstone patio, and fifty others started clapping and whistling. Lynn stood up on a planter trying to find a bar. He saw two bartenders pouring margaritas as fast as the pitchers could be delivered from the service area which was near the kitchen.

"Somebody's gonna be in the pool in half an hour or less," Nelson predicted.

Lynn pointed to one of the dancers, a bosomy babe with legs longer than his regrets, and said, "I hope it's her. We'll have a wet T-shirt contest."

Several guys stepped aside for Breda when she tried to squeeze into the house. In fact, two of them offered her their drinks, in that it was getting impossible for the servers to keep up with the orders.

Breda declined politely, and slid past the piano player, who had resorted to shouting Gershwin tunes that nobody could hear.

Breda perched herself on the spiral staircase and spotted John Lugo, still in his golf togs, surrounded by people in the marble foyer. His head was bobbing and he was kissing women on the cheek and shaking hands with men, trying to urge everyone toward the terraces out back. Breda saw a handsome younger man with a streak of white in his black wavy ponytail push his way through to John Lugo and whisper something in his ear.

Then a gorgeous young woman in a striped, cotton-knit sweater with a flashy tennis-racquet applique and white stirrup pants that only looked good on models cupped her hands over her mouth and started yelling, "Outside on the patio, everybody! FOOD!"

And enough people heard her that the masses started ebbing and flowing in that general direction, allowing enough cross-ventilation to cool down Breda, who felt like she'd been in a sauna with half of Brazil.

The fugitive had finally gotten himself into the middle of the new arrivals in the foyer. And though he was jostled, and nudged, and bumped, and almost lost his props—the empty cocktail glasses—he managed to move right behind the man who was greeting guests and getting all the attention.

He heard a new arrival say "John! Great party!"

Still he wanted to be sure, so he waited. A big man, wearing the ugliest neon-yellow trousers he'd ever seen, said to him, "Man, don't stand around! Get us three margaritas! It's an emergency!"

The fugitive bowed slightly and said, "Yes, señor, right away." But he lingered, even with the man glaring at him impatiently, until he heard a woman say what he wanted to hear.

The woman said, "Sheila, this is John Lugo, our host!"

Then the fugitive left, but he knew he couldn't come back to the foyer until the man in the ugly trousers was gone or unless he had the margaritas. He went to one of the bars where waiters, rather than guests, were picking up their orders. Then he got an idea and thought, Why not? So he turned and walked, not along the lighted path jammed with people, but across the grass, dangerously close to the kitchen window where he'd seen the tall blond gringo from the catering company.

One of the bartenders, incessantly blending margaritas in that area, was a Mexican. He approached that man and said, *"Tres margaritas, por favor."*

The guy just nodded, stopping for a moment to mop his brow with a white towel.

The fugitive said, in Spanish, "What a party, *'mano.*"

The bartender nodded again, and the fugitive said, "Mister Lugo needs Mister Sierra. Do you know him?"

The bartender said, in Spanish, "Man, I don't know nobody! I just took this job because my friend got sick. And if I'd known it was this hard I'd have demanded an extra two bucks an hour!"

The fugitive thanked him when he got the three margaritas, and risked an approach to the kitchen window. There were five Mexicans in serving whites, working furiously in the kitchen. The window was wide open so the fugitive put his face to the screen and yelled, in Spanish, "Tell Señor Sierra that Señor Lugo wishes to see him at once."

Then the fugitive returned to the foyer. When he got there the man in the neon-yellow trousers was gone, as were most of the other guests, who were queuing up outside at the four buffet tables.

John Lugo was finally getting free of the arriving throngs, and was only surrounded by a dozen people when Breda saw that the handsome guy with the white streak in his hair had returned. He whispered something into the ear of John Lugo, who shook his head and shrugged. Then the handsome guy walked away, as John Lugo kissed yet another beautiful woman, urging all to go outside and dine.

The fugitive had been watching John Lugo and the other

man. Then he saw an attractive woman in a pink shirt and white shorts sitting alone on the step. He walked over to her and said, "Margarita, *señora*?"

And Breda Burrows said, "Sure. Thanks."

The fugitive had started outside when he saw him—and almost dropped the remaining two margaritas. The policeman from the mortuary!

The fugitive spun around and mounted the stairs two at a time, nearly jarring Breda's drink out of her grasp. A blob of cold sticky ice splashed on her bare thigh and she was scooping it up and licking it off her fingers when Lynn and Nelson approached.

Lynn looked from her thigh to her mouth as Breda licked, and their eyes met. Hers said: Don't even *think* it!

"I say, old thing, must you sneer so?" Lynn said to her.

"Did you say hello to Lugo yet?" Nelson asked.

"He's too busy," Breda said. "Why would I want to meet him anyway?"

"You're in business in this town. Might not be a bad idea," Nelson said. "Even if we can't figure out why somebody's lookin for him."

"I might try later," Breda said. "Want something to eat? They just started serving."

"I want a drink," Lynn said.

"That's outside too," said Breda. "The waiter that gave me this one just ran upstairs with two more. Maybe you can find him."

"I think I'll find a tall cool Scotch," Lynn said. "I'll bet Lugo's Scotch beats the hell out of Wilfred's."

When they got outside, with the lights of Palm Springs spread out below them, Nelson gazed dreamily and said, "I wonder what he'd say now?"

"Who?" Breda wanted to know.

"The Indian that looked at the first white land developer and said, 'What, a golf course in the *desert*?'"

-22-

He had not been this frightened in his life! His jaw was trembling, and he couldn't keep the drinks from sloshing over the rims of the cocktail glasses.

Every room in the house was thrown wide open for guests to wander as they chose. There were valuable pre-Columbian pieces on display in the upper hallway, and the fugitive pretended to be looking at them as guests strolled past, meandering from room to room.

As soon as he heard the last of them go back downstairs, he entered a guest bedroom, put down the drinks, and pulled up his trouser legs, removing his weapons from where they were taped to his calves. The tape stripped the hairs from his legs but he didn't even feel it.

If only his hands would stop trembling! He didn't usually tremble, even in dangerous police situations, but this was different. He wasn't a policeman here. That man downstairs was a policeman. And who knows how many others were in this house!

He put his weapons under a satin cushion on a bay window bench. Without his weapons he didn't know if he felt more safe or more threatened. He crept along the hallway to the top of the stairway and looked down. The policeman with curly hair was gone. There was no one on the staircase now. He started back to the bedroom, but changed his mind. Better this way if his idea worked. *If.*

The fugitive hurried downstairs and took a bold gamble. He stopped the first Mexican waiter he saw, and said, in Spanish, "Tell Señor Sierra to come upstairs. There's a small problem."

"Señor Sierra?" the waiter said.

"Yes, Señor Sierra!" he said. "He works for Señor Lugo. Find him, and ask him to come upstairs. There's a lady who has had too much to drink."

The waiter nodded and hurried toward the kitchen, while the fugitive went back upstairs and waited.

Lynn, Breda and Nelson were by then about midway through the queue of people on the dimly lit patio. The mariachis were playing "La Paloma."

"Hope there's gonna be something left," Nelson said.

"I wouldn't worry about that," Breda said. "Whatever else John Lugo is, he does nothing on the cheap."

Lynn spotted Bino Sierra talking to one of the bartenders at the service bar by the kitchen. A Mexican waiter ran up to Sierra and said something. Then the waiter followed Sierra across the flagstone patio and into the house.

"That's Lugo's man," Lynn said to Breda.

"The guy with the white streak in his ponytail?"

"Uh huh."

"Good looking guy," she said. "Striking hair."

"Sure," Lynn said, "if you like a tango dancer with hair like a skunk. I saw better ponytails in *Gidget Goes Hawaiian*."

"I guess I like clean-shaven, *slim* guys," Breda said, with a glance at Lynn's stomach. "Wonder if they've got any pork left?"

His heart sank. He hadn't planned on the waiter coming back with Sierra! Couldn't *anything* go his way? The fugitive quickly picked up the two margaritas. He didn't know whether to speak English or Spanish. Sierra was a coconut, brown on the outside, white on the inside. He'd speak English to this coconut. He hated to hear their *pocho* Spanish.

The fugitive said to him. "Sir, I am sorry. The lady is gone."

"What're you *doing* up here?" Bino Sierra was furious. "I told Henry I didn't want *any* drinks served upstairs!"

The waiter who'd delivered the message didn't want any part of the ass-chewing and got out. And somehow it all fell into place. The fugitive now knew it was going to work, against all odds.

The fugitive studied that haughty lineless handsome face, and said, "I am sorry, sir, but the lady told me I had to bring them. She was in there." He pointed to the guest dressing room and bath. "Could she still be there?"

Bino Sierra turned his back and stalked across the bedroom to the dressing area. The fugitive closed and locked the bedroom door. When Bino Sierra came back out, the fugitive was bending over the love-seat bench, framed by one of the most spectacular views in all of California, the nighttime lights and silhouetted mountains of Palm Springs.

"What the fuck're you *doing* over there?" Bino Sierra asked, and then he saw what.

The fugitive pointed the Beretta with his left hand, holding his right hand down behind his leg. He said in English, "If you cry out, if you try to run, I will shoot you. Come *here*."

317

Bino Sierra automatically raised his hands to shoulder height and said, "Hey, man, what the fuck? WHAT THE FUCK?"

"Keep your voice quiet," the fugitive said, "and sit down over here. Just sit down and look from the window at the vista."

He stepped back to allow Bino Sierra to pass, noting the inky-blue silk shirt, like a *guayabera* shirt with epaulets, but finer than any *guayabera* the fugitive had ever seen. And Sierra wore perfectly tailored gray trousers, with a knife crease, perhaps linen trousers. But the shoes were ugly white Palm Springs shoes like the ones he'd bought for himself.

"Are *you* the guy?" Bino Sierra asked, his hand nervously touching his hair where the white slashed through.

"Don't touch your white stripe," the fugitive said. "Don't touch anything. Keep your hands away from your body, and look out at your city."

"Are you the guy that wrecked the mortuary?" Bino Sierra asked. "What's it about? The tombstone for Lugo's mother? What the fuck's it all about, man?"

"You are the one who arranged for ten kilos of cocaine to go to Los Angeles on day thirteen of last September," the fugitive said.

"I don't know what you're talking about!" Bino Sierra said.

"All three of your couriers were killed by Mexican police, and you never got delivery. One of them identified you."

"Man, you're crazy! You trying to say somebody gave you my *name*?"

The fugitive thought he was standing a little too close to the back of Bino Sierra's head, so he retreated a step. There, that was better.

"No, he did not know your name. You received a telephone call. The man told you of an unexpected problem. A Mexican policeman had interrupted their plans. You told them what to do with that policeman. Strangling is a cruel way to die."

"Just a minute!" Bino Sierra said.

And now the fugitive could see that the back of the man's shirt was already showing wet. That lovely silk would be slimy against his body, the fugitive thought.

Bino Sierra said, "If these guys got killed by the cops, who mentioned me?"

"One of them died later, during interrogation. He did *not* lie. He *could* not."

"Who are you?" Bino Sierra demanded. "Are *you* a cop? Are you DEA? If you are, whaddaya want me to say? I'll say it. I'll say anything! *Arrest* me!"

"I am not a DEA agent," the fugitive said. "I am a citizen of Mexico."

"Well, whaddaya *want* from me?"

"Javier Rosas was a good policeman and a good man," the fugitive said.

"Wait . . . a . . . fucking minute!" Bino Sierra said, and the fugitive could see rivulets running from the black hair at the nape of his neck. "You can't tell me that somebody claims Bino Sierra arranged a drug shipment and ordered some Mexican cop to be killed!"

"The man who spoke to you on the phone told us what you said on that night, September thirteen. You said, 'I just ordered a tombstone carved with orchids for an old dead woman. I can order another one for the cop. What is his favorite flower?' You see, it meant nothing to you, that little joke. You have forgotten it. Or perhaps you were enjoying too much of your own cocaine when you said it? Cocaine makes a man forget, sometimes."

Bino Sierra's voice was trembling when he said, "This is a *mistake!*"

"It is all we had," the fugitive said. "Tombstone and orchids. But in Mexico we don't expect much. We learn to work with very little in so many ways."

319

Bino Sierra sounded like he might cry when he said, "Maybe it was my boss! Maybe John Lugo talked to the guy! He didn't make all his money with vending machines!"

"He would not refer to his mother as an old dead woman. Also, the document from the tombstone company showed that the stone was ordered by Lieberman Brothers Mortuary, but payment was guaranteed by Mister Sierra, personal secretary to Mister Lugo. A note on the-invoice said, 'Mister S. wants two orchids, one on each side of name.' "

"Look, man, you ain't being rational here. Siddown and let's *talk*!"

"You see, sir, if only the invoice had shown your address I would not have gone to the mortuary at all. And if not for the mortuary problem, I would not need to be here so soon, because I would not be so afraid of the policeman with curly hair."

"*What* policeman with curly hair? Man, you're fucking crazy! You want money? I'll give you more money than you ever seen!"

"I have no wish to torment you, Mister Sierra," the fugitive said. "But I had to be more than sure about you. And now I *am*."

The Beretta moved toward the left side of the head of Bino Sierra, who turned ever so slightly to watch the steel muzzle.

And as he did the fugitive's right hand shot up and cut his throat.

It was a sawing slicing slash, first left, then right. Coming back it scraped on gristle, but the fugitive pulled and ripped with all his strength.

The fugitive dashed to the door then, shoving the bloody knife and gun inside his belt under his vest. As he opened the door he heard a sound, like radio static underwater. He turned and saw Bino Sierra with *two* gaping mouths, one above the other. Coming for *him*!

The fugitive ran in panic but stumbled and fell down in

the hallway. Bino Sierra kept lunging past, to the landing, tumbling down the staircase, rolling to the bottom. There was blood smeared along the wall and carpet and it looked like a hog had been slaughtered on his chest. And yet Bino Sierra got up and *ran*, his hands paddling like a man treading water, *thinking* he was screaming and breathing, but doing neither. Outside, he plunged into the black-bottom swimming pool, and against that lighted black bottom, his blood swirled up black. And with one last incredible effort, he pulled himself onto the pool steps, onto his back, half in and half out of the water. While people screamed.

Breda had her plate heaped with roast pork, and had said to Nelson, "The hell with the calories," when the screaming started. Then, *riot.*

Plates were flying, glass was breaking as warming platters crashed to the flagstone. One of the buffet tables was overturned by the panicking hordes. Some ran toward the body, then realized what they were doing and scurried away from it, crashing into others. Yelps of pain joined screams of panic.

Nelson plowed his way through, followed by Breda. They stopped at the pool, at the body of Bino Sierra, still oozing, staring up at one of the most beautiful skies in the world. Every star in the dipper was glittering.

The fugitive ran through the entry doors, colliding with the people running inside, almost getting knocked off his feet. Even valet parking attendants, along with the hired security people, stormed through the house toward the rear patio, toward the screams. The fugitive finally got outside and ran across the lawn to the banana trees. He plunged into them, groping for the bag, cutting his hand slightly with the bloody knife when he jammed it inside. Then with the Beretta still tucked inside his waistband he started to dash toward the street. Until he spotted the policeman with curly hair.

As soon as the screaming had started, Lynn dropped his drink and headed, not with Nelson and Breda *toward* the screams, but around the kitchen, across the lawn, straight toward the front of the house, to the only plausible escape route. He passed a clump of banana trees, then stopped in the shadow of the trees to watch who might be rushing outside to the street.

Lynn thought he was still too close to the light from the entry doors, and retreated even farther into the darkness. With his right hand on the Colt under his shirt, he backed up toward the banana trees, failing to see an elongated shadow move. It wasn't dark enough so he kept backing up.

Until a voice said: "No."

That was all the voice said. Then Lynn felt the steel muzzle press against his neck, and a strong hand gripped his own, the hand he had under his shirt.

The fugitive kept the pressure on both places, but it was the pressure against his neck that Lynn felt. Lynn relaxed his right hand and felt the fugitive slide the Colt from his holster. The gun flashed across the sconce lights and clattered into the banana leaves.

Then Lynn was forcibly moved by the fugitive, who slid the steel muzzle down into the center of Lynn's back and propelled him forward holding onto the collar of his aloha shirt.

The fugitive never said another word, and Lynn waited for a crash, for his head to explode. He knew he'd never hear the shot. The house was a crescendo of sounds, shouts and screams. The building was swelling and heaving, ready to burst like the belly of a dead horse. When it did it would cascade out of the entry doors, a writhing swarm in full panic. *No one would hear the shot!*

He waited forever, perhaps ten seconds. Then he turned slowly to look death in the face. He was alone.

An elderly couple who'd found the party far too tiring were at the door of their Lincoln when the screaming began. They'd started toward the patio along with everybody else, but changed their minds, realizing that whatever it was, it couldn't be good. They were trying to get into their car when the fugitive grabbed the valet parking girl and tossed her into the street. Then he shoved the man out of the way, and both old people, worrying more about hips than Lincolns, cried out in terror and scuttled away from the car thief.

By the time Lynn found his gun and ran out to the front street there was nothing to do but watch helplessly as the tail-lights disappeared. The guard in the kiosk, even if he'd *known* what had happened, wouldn't have left his little room when that Lincoln roared past.

The fugitive pounded the steering wheel in frustration when he got stopped by traffic at Highway 111. Saturday evening traffic was horrendous because of the Bob Hope tournament and the unseasonably hot weather.

He kept expecting headlights behind him. He knew he should've shot the policeman with curly hair in order to guarantee his escape. But he could not bring himself to shoot a policeman. When he found a break in the traffic flow he stomped on it, crossing the highway faster than he wished. What if he was stopped for a traffic citation? he thought. After *all* this!

His Buick was where he'd left it. He parked the Lincoln behind it, and when he got out he removed his black vest and wiped the steering wheel and anything else he might have touched. Then he realized that he had no fingerprints on file in this country. What was he doing? Just the reflex action of a policeman, he thought. No matter what he had done, he was still a policeman.

Leo Grishman was the first person at the party to grasp how to handle the horrifying event. He located his very shaken client and led him into the study, off the master bedroom suite on the lower floor. He looked in vain for Lynn, but gathered Nelson and Breda and brought them into the study too.

"Okay, *now* we know," the lawyer said to them all. "Bino was free-lancing. Once a druggie always a druggie. I *told* you not to hire him, John!"

"I trusted him. He was like a nephew." John Lugo was built like a block of concrete but had a flutey voice.

"Well, you shouldn't have. He was free-lancing with drug dealers." The lawyer pointed to Breda and Nelson and said, "These people're the ones I told you about. It's apparent that one of Bino's drug-dealing associates knew something about your mother's funeral, but nothing else about him. And that's the information they used to find him. There's nothing anybody can do about it now, John. Bino burned some dealers and they made him pay for it tonight. Period."

"What should we tell the cops?" John Lugo wanted to know.

"What *can* you tell them?"

"Nothing. I don't *know* anything," John Lugo said. "Except that Bino was free-lancing. I got nothing to do with drugs, and never have. This is what happens, you get involved with drugs. Crap like *this*!"

The door opened and Lynn Cutter walked in. He looked different somehow, but Nelson couldn't decide why. He remained somber and silent when Leo Grishman said to John Lugo, "This is the police officer that almost got the guy at the mortuary."

Leo Grishman turned to Lynn, and said, "Do you have *any* idea who the guy was or how to find him?"

"Not a clue," Lynn said gravely. "He had to've been a drug smuggler who came to pay a debt."

"Then why do you wanna stick around and muddy up the water?" Leo Grishman said. "There's no need to talk about your part in the mortuary business. Let's leave Mrs. Lugo's funeral *out* of all this, why don't we? What good would it do? Let the dead bury the dead, as they say."

Lynn turned to Breda and Nelson and said, "Let's go to The Furnace Room. I never did get that Scotch."

"Anything I can *ever* do for you!" John Lugo said to them as they were leaving.

They found themselves among a crush of people scrambling down the steep street after the shuttles were overrun. Three Palm Springs police units were trying to get through, but the road was jammed with pedestrians.

Nelson said to Breda, "Do you think that tan Palm Springs uniform'll look good on me?"

Lynn said to both of them: "Why? Why didn't he shoot me? Why didn't he cut *my* throat?"

The fugitive set the cruise control at fifty-five miles per hour during the drive out Highway 10. Thirty minutes later he was back on Highway 111, but at a very different part of the valley highway. He was heading southeast, past the Salton Sea, past the place where he'd slept in a stolen car hidden by a stand of tamarisk trees. It seemed like a month ago. He thought about those poor *campesinos* who'd taken the stolen car, those poor little boys. He found a good place to stop and bury the gun, the knife, the bag. It wasn't the first time that the desert had concealed bloody deeds. After that was done and he was back on the road, he finally stopped trembling.

He didn't want to think about it anymore until he got home. Then he could talk it over with his wife, his comrades, his priest. Instead he thought about what was in the trunk of the car, where the blood-stained bag had been. There was a Ninja Turtle Party Van in there for his youngest. The van had wheels like little pizzas. His baby wanted one desperately. They still called him a baby, but he was five years old. And there was a small computer for his daughter. It had cost $400, but all that dirty money needed a clean use. And there was a wristwatch for his older son, a Japanese watch, stainless steel, with a diving bezel.

Finally, there was a green leather jacket and matching skirt he'd found in the Palm Springs department store where he'd bought his waiter's clothes. It was double breasted with gold buttons, and the skirt was very slim. He'd measured the size against a salesgirl who was short and slender like his wife, whose favorite color was green. It had cost $500, but he didn't care. She'd never get a present like that again, not in her lifetime.

His comrades wouldn't be getting back much of the money that they'd taken from drug smugglers and U.S. insurance companies, but that was all right. He was sure that the family of Javier Rosas would say it was all right.

When they'd finally hiked to the Smoke Tree parking lot Lynn said, "My knees're begging for a drink."

"I don't need a drink," Breda said, heading toward her Z.

Nelson thought it was a good time to saunter to his Wrangler and give Lynn and Breda some space to say whatever it was they had to say to each other. The little cop plugged in a cassette and listened to country blues, and watched to see if their silhouettes got closer or stayed apart.

"I thought we could just . . . celebrate the end of our partnership," Lynn said to Breda as she stood by her car, keys in hand.

"I've enjoyed it, most of the time," she said.

"Ain't you ever gonna forget about that night?"

"It's forgotten."

"We work pretty well together, don't we? I mean, we solved your case and almost got the bald guy. I'm a pretty decent detective, right?"

"Yes you are," she said.

"I was thinking, after I get my pension maybe I could help you out once in a while when your work gets backed up."

"I don't think so, Lynn."

"You said you need somebody!"

"I do."

"Is it my personality? I mean, am I *that* hard to take?"

"Actually, you're funny and smart. You're even kinda nice to be with, sometimes."

"So why do I get the feeling this is goodbye? Why can't we go have a drink and talk it over?"

"I don't *need* a drink."

"So have a diet Coke!"

"Why don't you have one for me," Breda said. "And one for yourself. It's none of my business but a guy like you doesn't have to end up in The Furnace Room. Or like Jack Graves."

Breda unlocked the Z, but before she could get in, Lynn said, "Is that it? Are we finished? As a team, I mean?"

Breda nodded and opened the car door. But she impulsively turned and said, "I never did tell you: You got pretty nice buns."

Then she tried to grin, jumped into the Z, fired it up and drove into the night.

Nelson sat for a long time, watching Lynn's motionless silhouette. It looked so lonely under the velvet desert sky.

When the fugitive was twenty minutes from Calexico he looked at his watch and realized that his wife and eldest son might still be awake. After all, it was Saturday night and they had good TV programs to watch. He got unbearably excited. Suddenly, his throat swelled and tears started spilling.

He controlled himself when he approached the frontier, until he was waved across the international border. But when he arrived at his little street in Mexicali he began to sob and couldn't stop.

He pulled over until he was once again in control. He managed it by thinking of what the baby would say tomorrow when he saw his Ninja Turtles.

EPILOGUE

Jack Graves was pleased to have helped Lynn and Breda with the Clive Devon affair. It felt good to do a job of investigation once again; even if it hadn't been real police work it had the taste of investigation. He'd hoped that it might make him want more of it, but it hadn't.

He wasn't feeling well at all. He was having trouble with a fluttering heart and migraines. The only time he felt all right lately was when he went hiking out on the desert, like Clive Devon. And he'd suffered another accident, this one involving a nasty burn. He'd put his arm in the gas flame when he reached across the range top to fry bacon. By the time he'd thrust his arm under water, it was blistered and throbbing. The pain was excruciating. The coyotes came that night, but still he couldn't sleep with so much pain.

Jack Graves had decided to go hiking the very next morning. He wore a sweater because the hot spell had broken, and he wore his floppy hat, but he didn't bother smearing sunscreen on his face. And he didn't bother with a lunch, or even a canteen of water.

Jack Graves decided on a particular hike he hadn't made since the drought began five years earlier. He knew it would be a shame to see Upper Palm Canyon Falls when there was so little water, but for some reason he had to see it again. There simply was no more beautiful place for him. It was the kind of place that made him wish he could stay there for the rest of his life.

He parked his car by the Indian trading post. There were quite a few other cars there but nobody was going to hike up to the falls. He told the Indian woman in the trading post where he was going and she cautioned him to be careful.

When he got to the base of the trickling falls he tried to see it, not as bleak as it was, but as it used to be before the drought. He saw white water that wasn't there, splashing down between serpentine chutes carved by the ages through gray crystalline granite. The fan palms were clumped together, tall, leaning toward the water as though for a drink, when there wasn't much for them.

It was nearly a perpendicular climb to the top, and though it was early morning, Jack Graves began sweating freely and wondered why he hadn't brought his canteen. He knew there was something wrong with that.

When he got near to the top of the falls, he looked straight up and saw a solitary falcon, like a tiny kite in the towering desert sky. He tilted his head back to watch that falcon floating on the brooding wind while shredded clouds shattered the light on glittering granite below.

Then, a hush. Silence. The wind . . . sighed.

Almost one year to the day that Lynn Cutter had blown out his one good knee chasing after the Mayor of Palm Springs during his historic meeting with President Bush and Prime Minister Kaifu, Lynn's first pension check arrived. Moreover, he'd been able to arrange the temporary house-sitting job at Tamarisk Country Club. The owner of the house had decided to spend the spring in Hawaii, now that Maui had such terrific golf courses. It seemed that Lynn's luck might be making a turn for the better.

That was the day he got the phone call from Officer Nelson Hareem, the newest rookie member of the Palm Springs Police Department. Nelson called to tell him that Jack Graves had had a terrible accident while hiking in the Indian canyons. When he hadn't returned to his car the Indians had searched and found his body at the base of Upper Palm Canyon Falls, lying all alone on the rocks.

Nelson tried to reassure Lynn that Jack Graves couldn't have suffered much, falling from that height, and Lynn said no, Jack Graves couldn't have suffered much.

When he hung up the phone he couldn't stop thinking about Jack Graves, alone in that little mobile home. Alone on the granite rocks in the lonely canyon. Alone.

Lynn Cutter began to assess his options in life.

After the funeral, where he saw Breda only briefly, Lynn decided to conduct an experiment: He wanted to survive a month without taking a drink, just to prove that he could. On the sixth day of sobriety, an amazing incredible miraculous thing happened: He woke up to find he had an erection! Just like when he was a young sober man!

During his twenty-ninth day of sobriety, after his fifteenth AA meeting, he used up his first pension check at a bike shop. Three hours later, on a Saturday afternoon, the doorbell rang at Breda's house in Cathedral City. She went to the door and peeked out, but no one was there. Then she went to the window and saw him in the driveway, sitting on his tangerine bike.

When she opened the door, he gave her a self-conscious, silly smile. He was wearing a red and white biking helmet, a red shirt, and black biking pants with a Day-Glo yellow stripe. He was on a bike that she knew must have cost $500, quite an investment for him. He was dripping, having ridden all the way from Tamarisk Country Club, nothing but a sprint for her, but a killer ride for him.

"Whaddaya think?" he asked.

"That's a pretty decent bike," she said.

"Yeah, the doc says it won't hurt my knees if I don't ride up mountains. The only thing I changed is, I got rid a that razor blade they call a seat and put on a cushier seat for more ample bottoms."

"It's really a nice bike," she said.

"Notice anything about me?"

"Yeah," she said. "You got skinny legs."

"Anything else?"

"You still got a lotta blubber around the middle."

"I'll soon be lean and whippetlike," he said. "Haven't had a drink in twenty-nine days, eighteen hours and fifteen minutes. Notice anything else different?"

"You got rid of your mustache."

"Yeah!" he said. "Whaddaya think?"

"You don't remind me *quite* so much of Saddam Hussein," she said.

"See how sweet you can be when you wanna?"

"What's it feel like?" she asked. "Quitting drinking?"

"It's easy. You just gotta find substitute activities to occupy your mind. Me, I been eating live lizards. Don't worry, not the endangered fringe-toed lizards, just your average backyard dirt-bag lizards. Got any lizards under your house? Wanna go for a bike ride?"

"I don't think so," she said. "I rode this morning."

"I rode all the way over here," he said. "And I'm still full a juice."

"Thanks anyway," she said.

"It's your *age*," he said sympathetically. "You can't exercise in the morning and the afternoon. And it's your body chemistry. Something about women, I don't know what. You people can't take too much. I understand."

Then he saw it. That mean little killer grin of hers. She said, "Yeah? Give me *five* minutes."

"Sure," he said, "I'll listen to music."

He took a transistor radio out of his seat pack, tied it to the handlebars with a little bungee cord, and tuned to the country station.

She came out of the house carrying her lightweight custom speedster, wearing her black Coolmax shirt and Lycra pants. Her lustrous earth-brown hair billowed from under the black and white helmet. Jesus, she looked buff in black!

"You gonna listen to a radio while you ride?"

"Sure," he said. "I'm one a those people can do two things at once. Sometimes I even clip my toenails when I'm watching the news."

"We'll take it easy," she said. "Maybe go up to Dinah Shore, out to Bob Hope, back on Gerald Ford. And all the way to Frank Sinatra if you're up to it."

"Make it easy on yourself," he said, to make it more fun for her when she started ratcheting up to his pain threshold.

When they got out of the traffic and onto Dinah Shore Drive, he wondered if something spooky would happen on the country scene. It did. Don Williams started singing to him.

> *I wanna hear your heartbeat,*
> *In the darkness,*
> *Ev-er-ry night,*
> *Of my life.*

He was so fatigued just from the ride to her house that he was puffing and blowing. He rode two bike lengths behind, at what was for her a slow cruising speed. Then when the traffic thinned out he panted up beside her, trying to breathe through his nose to keep his tongue from lolling, and turned up the volume so she could hear.

> *I wanna hear your heartbeat,*
> *In the darkness,*
> *Ev-er-ry night,*
> *Of my life.*

"Oh, man!" he cried.

Breda looked over and said, "What's wrong?"

"This guy that's singing?" Lynn said. "He's at least our age. And he's got our number!"

> *I wanna hear your heartbeat,*
> *In the darkness*
> *Next to miiiiiine.*

"Night after night," Lynn said. "Alone like Jack Graves."

"Huh?"

"As alone as . . . as a fugitive," Lynn said.

"What're you *talking* about?" She pulled closer to the sandy shoulder as a Sun Bus whizzed by, blowing Lynn's bike in her direction.

"I'll tell you something!" Lynn shouted, dropping back just a few yards, while she kept her face forward.

Beyond her the desert sky was showing streamers of cherry red across a glaze of twilight blue. He smelled sage. The desert was performing right on cue.

"You'll tell me *what*?" She was irritated because he was blabbing about some cowboy when she was supposed to be enjoying a ride.

He said, "I'll tell you that fifty percent of a salary, *tax free*, and forty percent of another salary based on a salary that was more than the first salary, equals one hundred percent of either salary, no matter how you wanna look at it."

"What in the *hell* are you jabbering about?" She downshifted the bike, sat upright and rode no hands, looking at him.

"Just that you could probably rent out one a your bedrooms with that extra bath, and get quite a good piece a change. Which wouldn't hurt, what with a kid in college and all."

"Have you totally lost your mind? Maybe you *oughtta* start drinking again!"

"Not me. I don't like those parties where I'm the only guest to RSVP my own invitation. I'm gonna stick to diet Coke and reptiles. Anyway, whaddaya think?"

"Are you saying you wanna live in *my* house?"

That caused him to drop farther back because he didn't want to look her in the eye. "Only in one bedroom and one bathroom. I wouldn't use the rest a the house till you get more mellow, say in ten years or so. Whyn't you think about it? We could start out this new relationship by exchanging Polaroids in our bike suits. I'll attach yours to my fridge with this souvenir palm tree magnet I got. Soon as I can afford a fridge. Better yet, I could pay you an exorbitant percentage a my pension check and use *your* fridge to store a couple oranges in so I don't get scurvy, okay?"

Breda rolled her eyes, mumbled something, and started pumping. But she hadn't said no!

He watched her ripple inside those black Lycra pants while he pedaled to keep up. It was hard to yell things. His voice was pretty shaky, but he hollered, "We have a lot in common. We're both very enthusiastic about pain, as long as it's *mine*. We could take turns beating me up. In fact, I'm suffering so much at this very moment, I sense that we're both supremely happy!"

She shot him that mean little grin one more time, like he *might* be right, for once.

He sensed he was getting to her with all those money bribes. Lynn put his head down and pumped for all he was worth. He kept thinking about heartbeats in the darkness, and the terrible absence of same. When he saw it!

"OHMYGOD!" he cried.

"What is it now?"

"I can't tell you yet. Maybe someday!"

I wanna hear your heartbeat,
In the darkness
Next to miiiiiine.

Maybe there *was* a kind of destiny at work. It couldn't be a coincidence, not after all he'd been through. Her bike shorts had crept up. There it was: inescapable, undeniable, inevitable. *Another* one of those goddamn bittersweet chocolate freckles. It was *just* behind her left thigh!